HE HATE ME

SENCHA SKEETE

Copyright © 2024 Sencha Skeete
All rights reserved.
ISBN: 9798323290833

TABLE OF CONTENTS

Content Warning	8
Prologue	9
Chapter 1	22
Chapter 2	43
Chapter 3	60
Chapter 4	79
Chapter 5	97
Chapter 6	113
Chapter 7	128
Chapter 8	149
Chapter 9	156
Chapter 10	177
Chapter 11	188
Chapter 12	202
Chapter 13	219
Chapter 14	228
Chapter 15	244
Chapter 16	253
Chapter 17	265

Chapter 18	280
Chapter 19	295
Chapter 20	305
Chapter 21	318
Chapter 22	329
Chapter 23	341
Chapter 24	356
Chapter 25	370
Chapter 26	391
Chapter 27	412
Chapter 28	438
Chapter 29	458
Chapter 30	480
Epilogue	495
ABOUT THE AUTHOR	499

Content Warning: This book is intended for adult readers eighteen (18) and older. It contains content that may be disturbing to some readers including, non/dubious consent, sexual abuse, graphic descriptions of sex and violence, BDSM, drug use, incarceration, and bullying. A full list of content warnings can be found on the author's website.

Prologue

Brandon

I GLIDE FROM THE SMALL STAND OF TREES AND STROLL across the sun-warmed grass towards the nearest park bench. Children scream across the field in the playground. The sound makes me uncomfortable, but since most of my customers are middle and high school kids, I need to be close to the skatepark. I'm not much of a skateboarder, but I have one with me to give me cover. It's been a successful day. It isn't close to dark yet, and I'm nearly out of weed. I nod in acknowledgment at a kid I know, but these aren't my friends. Where I live, the sidewalks are uneven, and weeds
 grow through the cracks. Everything here is new and shiny, courtesy of gentrification. Merrill used to be part of Old Town, but now it's become its own little enclave

with better schools and nicer facilities. And bored teens with money.

I thrust my hands into the pockets of my new coat and stretch out my legs. It's the first one I've bought in a long time, and it allows me to blend in a little better in spite of my worn jeans and knock off sneakers. A kid around thirteen catches my eye, holding my gaze a bit too long. I'm about to give him the subtle nod that will let him know I'm open for business when I spot a police car rolling slowly by. Every instinct screams that I should look at them, but I keep my eyes lowered. I don't know if they were looking in my direction, but I'm going to assume they spotted me.

I stand up and walk casually around the skate park, pausing for a few seconds to watch a boy complete a trick, to the delight of his friends. When I hit the sidewalk, I turn in the opposite direction from where the car went. I live in the other direction, in a house converted into small apartments long ago. Long enough that our kitchen has real linoleum floors, and the radiator looks like it's out of an old movie.

Just when I'm starting to think I'm in the clear, I hear the screech of tires. A quick glance over my shoulder shows two black and whites pulling up on me. I don't think. Pure instinct has me racing along the sidewalk, jumping down the steps onto the path that runs along the duck pond. Cold, moist air hits my face, and I hear the calls of birds sharp enough to

HE HATE ME

pierce through the deafening sound of my heart, pounding in my ears, feeling like it's trying to burst out of my chest. I'm fast from playing soccer and I know I can beat a few out of shape cops wearing body armor.

"Stop running," one of the cops yells, but I'm almost to the fence. I just need to climb the hedge and jump the chain-link fence. From there I have five or six options to evade them. I'm already planning ahead, deciding to slip down the embankment and hide under the foliage, to turn my coat inside out and pull the hood up. I leap for the fence and hook my finger through a diamond made of wire. I'm sixteen, athletic but weigh next to nothing. I have no trouble hoisting myself up and over, but then disaster strikes. My coat catches on the top of the fence and it's all over.

* * *

I sit at a metal table in the visitor's room of the juvenile detention facility where I'm being held. It could have been much worse. With no priors and a great deal of groveling, I'll only be serving a few months. That doesn't erase the shame I feel sitting across from my mother, taking in the new lines around her eyes and mouth. She's a gentle woman, my mother, pale skinned and dark-haired like me, and not in the best of health. The money I was bringing in was supposed to make our lives easier, but I've only added to her stress.

"You look good, Brandon," she says, resting her work-roughened palm on my larger hands. When did I get so much bigger than her. "You're doing your exercises?"

SENCHA SKEETE

"Not much else to do in here," I tell her. We have "jail school" of course, and I have chores like laundry or kitchen duty (basically microwaving pre-packed food and tossing paper plates). The rest of my time I exercise. Lifting has allowed me to add some weight and there are enough guys in here that play soccer than I'm able to do a semblance of training. I have fantasies of playing professionally, but if I'm honest I just need something to focus on.

"We've got a new maid at work," she tells me. "She's from…" She pauses, trying to remember, then sucks her teeth. "She's not American. She's nice, though." Her hands tremble and she tries to hide it, tucking them under the table. She's getting worse, but she hates when I fuss over her, so I pretend not to notice.

"What's her name?"

"Maria, maybe."

We talk for a while about what's been happening in her life and I manage to come up with a funny story about one of the kids in my room. I share with three other guys—two black, one white. They're all right. The white kid is a thief, one of the black kids is a drug dealer like me and the other kid won't say what he's in for. I see him sometimes, staring off into space, clenching and relaxing his fists and I have my suspicions. I understand what he's doing because I do it too, imagining what I would do to the people I don't like if I could get away with it.

After the visit I'm strip searched and returned to my pod. There's not much to do except sit in my bunk and read a book I borrowed from the library. It's some bullshit self-help book someone told me would help me deal with being locked up better. It doesn't. Whoever wrote it has never had to deal with any actual problems. My boss doesn't see my potential. My diet's not working. Cry me a river.

"Keane," one of the guards says, glaring at me, "what you doing in here? It's yard time."

"I had a visitor, Sir. Collins brought me back here."

"Like I give a crap. Move your ass."

I close my book and bite my tongue. I hate a lot about this shit hole, but one of my least favorite things is having to call these assholes "sir" and "ma'am." It's fucking demeaning. I see the lust in women's eyes, I hear the jokes the men make, and I've seen the contraband they bring in for the right price. These people are no better than us, no more moral and certainly not deserving of more respect. What separates us from them is a conviction. I imagine punching him in his smug face, feeling the crunch of bone and watching his expression change from smug to surprised to pained. The fantasy warms me as I make my way outside.

The yard is crowded like it always is, boys as young as ten playing with their friends. I keep my eye on the teens. I'm not as skinny as when I got here, but I'm still a beanpole, a fact that some see as provocative weakness. My roommates nod from their separate corners, but most eyes are hostile or indifferent. I ignore a high energy basketball game and head straight for the outdoor calisthenics area. I jump to grasp the pull-up bar and adjust my grip before starting a set. It's a cold day and the wind cuts through my uniform, but between my activity and the bright sun I'm comfortable enough.

SENCHA SKEETE

I drop down, deciding to stop before my arms feel like noodles. I've never been the most outgoing person and juvie is not the place to turn into a social butterfly. I've gotten to know my roommates, but I don't give a fuck about anybody else and I'm not going to waste my yard time making small talk. I go over to the incline and hook my feet under the metal bar to do inverse sit-ups. One sit up, and then I have the upside-down view of two pairs of legs, their prison issue white sneakers placed in a wide stance. Tipping my head further back, I recognize them. Tweedle Dee and Tweedle Dumber, a pair of thugs who like to pick on the weaker kids and have made the mistake of thinking I'm one.

Dumber kicks sand in my face and I only have enough time to close my eyes. The cold, damp grit stings my skin and a rage like I haven't felt since I learned that my dad was living in another state with a new family explodes through me. I leap to my feet, my skin feeling like a sausage casing, too tight and stiff. Starting out from upside down leaves me at a disadvantage, though. I'm barely upright before Dumber's Neanderthal fist collides with my abdomen, knocking the breath out of me. I double over, only for Dee's knee to contact my chin. I taste blood, only later realizing how lucky I was not to have my tongue between my teeth. My head spins and Dumber's foot comes down on my kidney. I brace for more, but a familiar voice says something I can't decipher through the buzzing in my head. There's the crunch of feet and when I'm able to lift my head I see my roommate Theo "Felonious" Bridges standing over me. He offers me a hand up, but I shake my head struggling to my feet on my own.

"You gotta watch your back, man," he says, not a trace of sympathy in his expression. "They coulda fucked you up good before the guards got here."

Felonious is alone right now, but everybody knows he's backed by every guy in here who's part of his street gang. I have no one, and I'm not naive enough to think my roommates are going to come to my rescue whenever I need them. They have their own problems, their own loyalties.

"You either gotta crew up or make a statement," he continues. "Those assholes are just the beginning if some of them hard niggas taste blood."

In the water, he means. Like sharks.

"I don't want to be in here longer than I need to be," I tell him, spitting some of the blood pooling in my mouth onto the ochre sand. "I'll figure something out."

We dap and head our separate ways. I spend the rest of my yard time standing by the fence pretending my kidney isn't throbbing.

For the next few days, I sense Tweedle Dee and Tweedle Dumber watching me, and I make sure to stay within sight of the guards at all times. Not that they can prevent a beat down, but they can break it up lot faster if they can see me.

On Thursday Dumber finds me as I'm heading home from laundry duty. I can see on his face that he thinks he's got me. There are no guards nearby and he outweighs me by about twenty pounds, but he doesn't have his buddy to help him this time. He comes at me, and I go low, returning the punch to the gut he gave me a few days ago. He doubles over and I'm looking down at his head. My fist hammers into his ear, then into his cheek three or four times. I'm so fast and so hard before he can mount a defense, he's too disoriented to tell up from down. I should stop now—he's no longer a threat—but I love hearing his grunts of pain, seeing his skin split under my fist and blood gush from his nose. I don't know why I find this so satisfying, but every time my fist makes contact, I feel a surge of power, like I'm plugging into a source. He flails at me impotently while I break his nose and crack his ribs. I kick his chest, hearing the crack and the wheezing of his breath, and stomp on his fingers. He brings up his arms to protect his head and I coldly consider whether I should break his arm. His fear and pain are like food, and I feel like I've been starving my whole life. My mind comes up with a hundred gruesome ways I could feed myself on turning him into a corpse. But then he curls into a ball, and I see him for what he is, just another kid far from home and anyone who loves him. I'm angry at him but burning rage that fuels this beating isn't caused by him. He's not the right target.

I wipe my bloody fists on his uniform and check mine for spatter. There's some, but not enough to draw attention.

"Don't fuck with me again, okay." I say it in a low voice, almost soothingly. "And don't forget what happens to snitches."

He doesn't respond or even look at me. He just lies there moaning, his arms clenched tight. I leave him and walk back to my room. No one else is there and I wash my hands, enjoying the cold water for a change. My hands are a bit beat up, but not in terrible shape. I pick up the stupid self-help book and lie down to read, but the words on the page swim like they're underwater.

I can't stop thinking about Dumber, the way his eyes and nostrils flared when he realized that the tables had turned. The memory of his mangled face makes me smile. I turn the experience over in my mind. What made it so pleasurable? Was it winning, the sheer violence of the act, or something else. I'd loved seeing him bleed, but it was the whines of pain and submission that I had enjoyed the most, the way he'd collapsed from a brazen bully into a voiceless, weeping child.

Is it normal to feel this way? Even in this place of anger and violence, I don't think it is. Is there something wrong with me? I imagine giving into these urges and recoil. I see myself standing in the place of my bullies, targeting the weak to make myself feel stronger, and I reject it immediately. I don't want to be that type of person. I have enough self-awareness to understand that becoming the abuser isn't progress. It won't fix what's wrong in my life, it won't get me out of juvie any faster, and it might just turn me into the kind of man who spends most of his life in prison. Even if I didn't respect myself too much to go down that path, I can't do that to my mother. I see the hurt in her eyes from knowing that I was dealing pot. I can't imagine how it would wound her if I let myself become a bad man.

But maybe deep down that's what I am. There is something gleefully malevolent inside me. Reliving my recent act of violence, I feel good in a way that's almost sexual. If I told my counselor about this, she'd probably add violent psycho to my file. I need to keep this to myself, maintain control, be smart.

I stop pretending to read and rest the book on my chest. Felonious comes in and we exchange a look. Someone must have found Dumber; he knows what I did, and there's now a trace of wariness that wasn't there before. I close my eyes, not wanting to confront that look or the distance his awareness of my violence has put between us. Images flicker beneath my lids of Dumber's face. I can hear the popping sound his fingers made when I stomped on them.

"What're you smiling about?" my roommate Cody asks, coming into the room.

"Nothing," I grunt, rolling over. "I just had a good workout."

Chapter 1

Two Years Later

Deja

"You're hot!" Mackenzie yells out the open window as we whip past three shirtless white skateboarders standing on the curb. One of them raises his arms in a vee and yells something back, but it's blown away in the wind. Mackenzie's nearly black hair is pulled back in a ponytail, her pale skin pinkening despite the heavy application of sunscreen. It's a goddamn beautiful summer day, the afternoon sun streaming in through the moon roof of Mackenzie's five-year-old Lexus as we cruise through the perfectly manicured lawns and sprawling homes of my neighborhood. Stone walls and wrought-iron gates conceal the luxury cars of my neighbors.

We're driving a bit too fast, and Doja Cat is blasting at full volume. The breeze lifts my braids, whipping them around my head. I have my feet up on the dash, my dark chocolate legs sporting a light layer of salt from dried sweat.

"Can you close the windows?" I yell over the noise, and she rolls her eyes subtly before doing as I ask. To compensate for the closed windows, she flips on the air conditioning. We're on our way back from cheerleading, not wearing much, but still a bit overheated. Cheer camp is going hard this year. Coach made us run suicides till we saw stars. But the sweat and tears will be worth it when we step onto the field this Fall.

"I cannot wait to wash this grime off from practice," I say, leaning back against the plush leather seat.

"Me either," Mackenzie says, grimacing. I think she's sore. I certainly am, and Kenzie always struggles a bit more than I do. I was hurting during practice, but I didn't let it show. I was recently made captain of the squad, so I feel like I have to set an example for the younger girls. "Wanna hang out later?"

"I don't know."

"It's just a kick back. Last minute."

"Who's gonna be there?"

"The girls. Possibly Aaron and a few of his friends."

"Aaron, the college guy?" Mackenzie nods. She met him at a party a couple of weeks ago, but they haven't had a chance to hang out yet.

"Where is this party?"

HE HATE ME

"At his friend's house. Please come!"

"The girls didn't agree to come yet, did they?"

"No."

Mackenzie's love life is in my hands, but I'm not sure I want to go to party at a college guy's house. What if the little kick back turns out to be a rager. It's one thing to get drunk around other high school kids, but a bunch of older guys I don't know sounds a little sketchy. Where I go, the girls go. If I pass on this, Mackenzie will either have to go alone or not at all.

"I wish I could," I tell her. "Practice is kicking my ass. I just don't think I have the energy, especially since we have to do it again tomorrow. You wanna bring him on Saturday? Probably be fun for his friends, too."

Most Saturdays during the summer, I have a few people over to swim and lounge by our backyard pool. It's usually just some girls from the squad and maybe a guy they're dating. My mom keeps us supplied with lemonade and sliced fruit and monitors us from inside the house. Usually, I find that habit of hers irritating, but with strange guys about it would be reassuring.

"I don't know if he's gonna—who is that?"

Turning into my driveway we spot a boy carrying a cardboard box. He's standing in my courtyard, sun glinting off his black hair, toned arms and chest revealed by the tank top he's wearing. He's got on basketball shorts that show off a pair of calves sculpted from marble. Honey-gold skin is stretched over taut muscle. He turns to look at us, crystal blue eyes locking with mine, and my breath catches. His face is as perfectly sculpted as his body—a sharp nose, high cheekbones, well-shaped lips. His eyes burn like a flame, for a second admiring, and then his expression hardens. He stalks up the stairs and into my house.

"What a snack," Mackenzie says, and I nearly agree until my mind connects the dots. I forgot today was the day.

"That 'snack' is Brandon," I tell her as we park.

"Brandon Brandon?"

"I think so, unless it's one of his friends helping him move."

I see my stepdad, Devin, exit the garage carrying another box. The garage is attached, but the way the house is laid out it's faster to go through the front door to get upstairs. I remember Brandon from grade school. His crow black hair and cerulean eyes are unforgettable. He looked at me with such hostility and I'm a little surprised. I haven't seen him since we were in grade school. My friends and I used to pick on him, but that was years ago.

"He's still a snack," Mackenzie says.

"If you like bad boys."

Mackenzie taking an interest in Brandon is not a positive development. I get why Kenzie is into him—he's hot, but I stay away from boys with a bad reputation. However, Mackenzie is all about the wrong decisions. She thinks assholes are sexy, even though they keep screwing her over. It's funny how fast she jumped from Aaron to my new house guest, though.

Brandon's story, from what I understand, is that his mother, Lindsey, can't take care of him anymore and Devin

HE HATE ME

signed some paper a long time ago saying if anything ever happened to her, he'd be Brandon's guardian. What happened to her? I get the impression it has more to do with Brandon getting into trouble than Lindsey's capabilities. Rumor is he got in serious trouble at his old school, though Devin insists it's because he got recruited to play soccer where I go. Who gets recruited to play senior year after being on a mediocre high school team?

I climb out of the car and Kenzie pops the trunk so I can get my gym bag out. "Wanna come inside?"

Mackenzie sighs in irritation. "I wish, but I have to meet my mom at the club."

"Okay," I say, stepping back to give the car room. "I'll see you in the morning."

"See you."

* * *

Brandon

I hear her soft, off-key singing voice before I see her coming up the stairs. Long, thin braids are pulled into a high ponytail above a stunning face: a high forehead, large brown eyes, high cheekbones, full lips and button nose covered in skin the color of dark chocolate. Not a blemish there, even though her white tank top is stained with sweat. Cheer shorts reveal a pair of the longest, sleekest legs I think I've ever seen. There's a gym bag over her slim shoulder and a half-smile on her expressive face.

I still can't believe this is Devin's stepdaughter. The last time I saw her before today she was practically a stick figure with an oversized head. I don't remember her having a cute face back then, maybe because I was eight and maybe because she used to steal my lunch and once threw my notebook in the mud just to be spiteful. Why is she smiling right now, looking as radiant as a fitness model returning from a spa trip. I fight the urge to turn my head as we pass each other so I can see if the back matches the front, but when she walks by my room a bit later, I get a good look at the round tits and perfectly shaped ass I tried not to see earlier.

The immediate hunger I feel for her is an unwelcome complication. She isn't just sexy, she's beautiful. She may still be the same mean girl she was in grade school, but the warm playful looks she's given me suggest something else. She walks past in the other direction, and I want to call her over, ask her how she's been, watch her expressions change, find out what her voice sounds like.

I give myself a shake. What's wrong with me. This is Deja Marcus we're talking about, not some stranger. I already know she's bad news. I can't forget who these people are, or I'll fail, and the stakes are too high for that. I'm not going to let some spoiled brat distract me from my goals.

* * *

Deja

"Is that everything?" Devin asks, setting down a box outside the formerly empty bedroom down the hall from mine. Brandon, a sullen expression on his face, nods. He looks like he just tasted something bitter. He sees me standing in the hallway and scans me up and down so coldly that my skin prickles. I don't take it personally. I couldn't care less what this guy thinks. Still, he's the one moving across town. I can get why he might feel a little off-balance. And I have to admit I'm kinda curious. I may not want to date bad boys, but I'm as fascinated by deviance as the next person.

"Hey," I say, after Devin has gone downstairs, "how's it going?"

He looks right at me, but instead of responding he walks into his new room and starts unpacking boxes. Rude!

"Do you need any help?" I ask, really extending an olive branch here. I'm not generally an altruistic person, but I try not to be a complete jerk.

"No." He turns and looks at me, appearing to focus on the long expanse of bare leg on display and then shaking his head slightly.

"What?"

"I said, no," he responds. "I'm not interested."

"That's not what I meant."

"Not used to guys ignoring your little Hooters Girl outfit?"

"This is not—" I look down at myself. I'm wearing a fitted white tank top and black gymnastics shorts because that's what was comfortable for cheer camp, not because I want guys looking at me, and for damn sure not this particular guy. Yes, the shorts fit like underwear, but it's not to attract male attention. And even if it was, what right or reason does he have to be mad about it.

"This is not for you." I gesture at my body.

"Good," he says.

SENCHA SKEETE

"I could show you around later," I offer, trying again to be friendly. We're going to be living together for the next year. I want to at least be cordial.

"I used to live here," he grinds out.

But that was ten years ago, I almost say. Brandon's mom used to be the live-in housekeeper here, but she got fired when he was ten. They had to move to a bad neighborhood. Two years ago, Devin married my mother, and I moved in here. The house isn't quite the same as when he left—Devin had it updated a few years ago. There's a new security system, the basement's been redone, and the pool area wasn't even here when Brandon moved out. Even though Devin and my mom only got married a couple of years ago, they've been friends and coworkers a lot longer than that.

"I'm just trying to be helpful," I say, tossing a braid over my shoulder. Brandon might have a point, actually. I'm not accustomed to guys ignoring me. I am literally the most popular girl at my school, just turned eighteen, a cheerleader, five foot seven inches tall, and a perfect size 6. My skin is a flawless dark chocolate, and my hair is always on point. I don't expect him to be drooling or anything, but who in their right mind is rude to a girl like me.

"Get the fuck out of my room," he says evenly. He locks eyes with me, blue boring into brown, and I get the message. He's not ready to be friendly. I roll my eyes and leave.

"Let me know if you change your mind," I toss over my shoulder. This is going to be a long school year if he keeps up that shitty attitude.

HE HATE ME

* * *

A week later, Brandon's attitude has not improved. I'm sitting at the dinner table across from him. He looks at me like I'm last week's garbage when he even bothers to acknowledge my presence. Devin asks a question and Brandon's face is so tight, parts of it look as white as paper. His teeth are gritted when he responds to my stepdad's perfectly reasonable query.

"No," he growls. "I didn't make the A squad. Marshall doesn't have as good a soccer team as Briarwood."

"I know," Devin says. He says I can call him dad, but I don't. I'd just feel weird doing it. I think of him as more of an uncle, honestly. He's a good guy, though. "But if you'd attended the intensive I paid for…"

"Honey," my mom says, as reasonable as she always is, "you know Brandon couldn't accept that. His mother needed him."

This is a big fat lie that I'm sure Brandon made up because he didn't want to accept more 'charity' from Devin.

"Is there still a chance you can get on the A squad?" Devin asks.

"Sure," Brandon says, testily. "I just have to hustle. Coach says I have potential. He wouldn't have recruited me otherwise."

Playing soccer for Briarwood is Brandon's best shot at earning a college scholarship. A lot more scouts see the Briarwood players than ever bother to make it down to Marshall.

"How about you, Deja?" Devin asks. "How's cheerleading practice?"

SENCHA SKEETE

"Great," I say. I always tell the parents that no matter the question and it's almost always true. The squad isn't nationally ranked like the soccer team, but we're pretty good, and I'm not relying on cheerleading to pay for college. That's what my straight A's are for. Can't say I don't enjoy the power that comes with being the most popular cheerleader, though. I grin across the table at Brandon, and I can see his jaw tic. How he must hate that I'm the popular one while he's still trying to figure out where he fits into the social hierarchy at Briarwood. He knew a lot of the kids when he was younger, but that was years ago.

There's a party in a couple of days and I wonder if I should tell him about it. It would help him a lot if he got to meet some of the cool kids before the year starts officially. I know Mackenzie has been asking about him. He'd probably fit in, provided he dropped some of the attitude. He's not a bad-looking kid. He has all the raw material for popularity, but his attitude is 100 disqualifying.

"How hard can that be?" Brandon interrupts my reverie. "It's just memorizing cheers and looking cute, right?"

"Have you been living under a rock?" I ask, despite my decision at the beginning of the meal not to engage him. "Cheerleading is a real sport. Like, turn on a TV or do a Google search. Who on earth still thinks cheerleading's not a real sport?"

"So I'm supposed to believe you're Simone Biles or something?" he sneers. "It's frickin' dinner. I can't believe you guys just let her be on her phone the whole time. Mom always makes me turn off my phone before I sit at the table."

I just glare at him and smile sweetly.

I text Mackenzie: Make sure no one tells Brandon about the party. He's a complete tool.

* * *

The party at Perry Asterburg's house is lit and I'm piled on an antique George III settee with a bunch of cheerleaders including my girls Mackenzie, Lorelei, and Shelby. Yeah, they are as white as they sound. My school is not that diverse and I'm currently the only Black girl on the cheer squad. There are a couple of Asian girls on the squad, Melodie and Lin, and one Latina, Cristabel, and I make sure to keep them close, in addition to being friends with the most popular white girls. Staying on top of the social heap is as much a game of strategy as it is dominance. I never let anyone step to me or throw shade without repercussions, but I put a lot more energy into cultivating relationships. I'm in everybody's messages with encouraging words, always checking in and being a shoulder to lean on, always "humble," and never mean unless the other person was publicly out of line first. Then I'm merciless. That way I've got a bunch of people defending me if anyone tries to talk shit behind my back and everybody has stories about how I dismantled this or that bitch for trying to mess with me. Yeah, it's work, but it's also fun.

Unfortunately, Mackenzie let slip about the party to Brandon a few days ago, so by the time I asked her to keep it quiet, it was already too late. Kenzie was one of Brandon's friends back when we were in grade school. I'm starting to think she might like him. When she spotted him at church, she went straight over and started chatting. He's a different person around her—smiling and saying non-offensive things. Right now, though, he's just standing in a corner nursing a beer. A few people have tried to talk to him, then looked kinda uncomfortable and backed away. Even Mackenzie could only endure like five minutes of conversation with him before coming to sit with us girls. I guess I didn't have to do anything to exclude him since he's making that happen all on his own.

"Giorgio's looking at you," Shel says in my ear, tipping her head towards the other side of the room where a bunch of sloppy idiots are playing beer pong on a $20K dining table. Giorgio is the new exchange student from Italy and he's got all the girls thirsty. He's cute—don't get me wrong. He's got the same coloring as Brandon, but he's more olive-skinned where Brandon is paler, and he's shorter and bulkier. I am not into Giorgio at all. Shel is, though. Why her crazy ass would want me paying attention to a guy she wants, well that's about not stepping on my toes just in case.

"I think he's looking at you," I say. "You look super cute tonight." She blushes and pushes a hank of pale blonde hair behind her ear. He's not looking at her. I stand out in this room like a sore thumb. There are other Black kids here, a handful anyway, and even some other girls, but I am the darkest and the hottest. People who are new to the social circle always stare at me, and a fair number of them do it the way Giorgio does, like he's contemplating a walk on the wild side. Like he honestly thinks I'm a piece of low hanging fruit on the vine just waiting to be plucked off. I want to roll my eyes, but you know how it is. Gotta not come off like a bitch even when you're being a bitch.

"He's coming over," Shelby says, breathlessly. Mackenzie and Lorelei break off their conversation about a new TV show to smile at the new arrival. He stops in front of us, his body language screaming confidence. He's wearing a Zegna white linen shirt and nice-fitting khaki slacks with leather sneakers that look like they might be Berluti or Dior. I'm not completely versed on boys' sneaker brands TBH.

"*Ciao, tesoros*," he says, using a phrase that has to be cheesy even in its native Italian, "can I borrow this beautiful *cioccolata* for a moment?"

His accent is lovely, and the other girls seem charmed, which makes it impossible for me to say no. Shel's looking at me like I just won the lottery. I excuse myself and follow him into the sunroom, which is less crowded.

"You would like a drink?" he asks, looking at my empty hand. "I make a very good negroni."

"A negroni?" I ask, searching his face to see if he's trying to provoke me, the way people will call out "reneger" when you're playing Euchre. Or deliberately pronounce the country "Niger" wrong.

"It's a very popular Italian cocktail," he says enthusiastically. "It's gin, vermouth, and Campari, but I make with sparkling wine also. It's very good. I saw the ingredients over here behind the bar. I think you will like it."

"Because I'm a negrona?" I ask lightly. He looks confused for a moment. Then he seems to get it.

SENCHA SKEETE

"No, no," he says. "There is no such word in Italian. The word for black in Italian is *nera*. I don't know why negroni is called this. The color is…you will see."

And I do, my little accusation making me nicer to him that I might have been otherwise. I definitely don't want him to go telling people I accused him of being racist. And maybe I need to turn my sensitivity down a notch, but after he called me "chocolate" can you blame me for being a little suspicious? The drink turns out to be a deep red that lightens to almost the color of grapefruit juice when the champagne is added. It tastes good, but I'm mindful that it has liquor in it, so I drink it slowly. We wander out onto the expansive back patio with our fancy grownup drinks and eventually down among the roses in the English garden. It's peaceful out here, warm, and with the almost overpowering smell of flowers. The noise of chatter and electronic music drifts out to us from the house.

"I heard you don't have a boyfriend," he says, looking not at me, but back at the people standing by water fountain bathed in the floodlights that we've deliberately left the range of.

Chapter 2

Deja

"I don't have a boyfriend," I agree, a smile in my voice.

"You are very beautiful," he says, turning his head a bit and scanning my figure. He communicates heat without coming off as sleazy, which I think takes practice. This guy is an F-boy if I ever met one. And trust me, even though I'm only eighteen, I've met my fair share. "How can you be alone?"

"Thanks," I say. "I'm not alone. I have lots of friends. I had a boyfriend, but he left for college a couple of weeks ago."

SENCHA SKEETE

"You must be heartbroken," Giorgio says.

"I miss him," I say. "I'm just kind of letting myself feel it, you know." We were 100% dating because he was one of the most popular guys at the school and I was a cheerleader. I had fun with him, but that was pretty much it.

"I completely understand," Giorgio says. "It's very hard to give up your first love, but you cannot spend your whole life pining for the past."

"I wouldn't dream of it," I say. "I'm just taking a little break before I get into another relationship."

"You don't think you should try to relax in the meantime?" he says. "Have some fun?"

I give him some blatant side eye, and he shrugs like he doesn't even mind the disapproving way I'm looking at him.

"Whoever told you I was single should have told you I only do relationships," I say tartly.

"We are much too young to take ourselves so seriously, no?"

"So you don't date?" I ask. "Just hook ups?"

"Why does everything need to have a label?" he says. "We are young. Our organism needs affection, closeness, no? Why worry about the name that we put on it? We are all too young to be tying ourselves down as if we are getting married."

I almost laugh out loud. I've come across this one before, but not usually from guys who look like Giorgio. Typically, the "free love" proponent has dreads, and whether he's Black or white, his reasons for wanting commitment free hookups is that it's more natural and…

HE HATE ME

"My spirit calls to yours, Bella," he says, touching my hand. There it is. Somehow hooking up with a guy without commitment is the "spiritual, enlightened" thing to do. I know some girls fall for this shit but come on! I bite down on my lower lip and squeeze my eyes shut. My shoulders are shaking, though and he snatches his hand away and huffs.

"You are laughing at me!" he says, and surprisingly his tone is amused.

"It is on the weaker side as lines go. Do you have any idea how many of the guys at this party alone have tried to get with me?"

He shakes his head, drains his Negroni, and tosses the plastic "glass" to the side. He points towards a marble statue, one of several spaced around the garden. Like the others, it is lit from below by inset lights.

"Do you know what she is?" he asks, grinning at me. It's hard not to be charmed.

I move closer, examining the white statue of a healthy-looking white woman with layers of fabric draped from her hips and held up by magic. She's otherwise naked.

"That's Venus," I say, not quite guessing. It's not the Venus de Milo or anything, but I think I recognize the way she's dressed.

"Yes!" he says. "The goddess of love—of erotic love."

"Is that so?" We move nearer to the statue, her preternaturally firm breasts looking close enough to touch. But they're not. They're way above our heads.

"The ancient," he says. "They would pray to her to aid in their seduction. To persuade the reluctant lover."

SENCHA SKEETE

"Anything's worth a shot, right?" I tease. "Who's that?" I point down the same row to a statue of another woman, this one wearing a breastplate and a helm. Unlike Venus, she looks like she could lift me above her head and toss me into the next county. She's muscular and mean, and yet still feminine.

"She is...Bellona? Yes, Bellona. The goddess of war and maybe, too, blood, desire for murdering? I believe."

This is decidedly less cheery.

"She has something, though, yes?" he says. "Presence, power?"

I drain my fancy drink and look up at her. Yes, she has something indeed.

* * *

When I go inside to grab a bottled water, Brandon stands in the shadows at the end of the hall, just past the sunroom door. If anything, it's creepier than when he was in the living room. His face is in shadow. Since I'm entering through the side door, I have to pass him to get to the water. His hand lashes out, capturing my wrist. In the low light, I don't know if he can see the confused expression on my face. His hand is cold, and I feel the impression of each finger on my skin.

"Moving fast, I see," he says. I have no idea what he's talking about. Lorelei walks past the door at the other end of the hallway, sparing us a mildly curious glance, but there's nothing odd about me talking to him.

"That Italian guy. He's most wanted, and you've got your claws in him already."

HE HATE ME

"Jealous?" I drawl, trying to free my wrist, but he doesn't let go.

"Never," he says, scanning my body almost the way Gio did. The effect this time is most definitely sleazy. I'm wearing a tube top and paper bag shorts; my outfit's not even that sexy. There's a strange sensation in my stomach. I can feel his eyes on my skin like a physical touch. His upper lip curls; no words, yet his disdain for me is clear.

"Let me go, Brandon," I say, tugging at my wrist again. "What is your problem?"

"And you going to pretend you don't know what you did to me in grade school? Remember the time you pushed me in the mud and ruined my clothes?"

"Are you seriously mad at me about stuff that happened when we were ten? It's time to move on, brah."

"You're going to be sorry you messed with me," he says. I yank my wrist out of his hand and put some space between us.

"You need a hobby, Brandon. I think the community college has a class in get the fuck over it and leave me alone."

I give him the finger as I back away and take another exit outside.

* * *

Our house is by far not the biggest or fanciest house in the neighborhood. For one, we only have five bedrooms, and the style is Mediterranean. There's probably not a single piece of furniture that costs over five grand and while I have an ensuite, my walk-in closet is minuscule by comparison with most of my friends. Do I sound like a spoiled bitch? I know I do, but this is just how it is. At least I'm more self-aware than my friends, most of whom think $1,000 sneakers and cashmere sweatpants are normal. For teenagers. My dad was a doctor, and I grew up here in Twin Oaks, but we were never that out of touch.

I really do like a lot of things about Devin's house. It has one of those entrances in the front with a dramatic double staircase above a marble entry. Everything looks whiter or shinier or grander than it needs to. It actually used to be more traditional, Devin had the place renovated a few years ago. The house I used to live in was a well-maintained mid-century modern, with no pretensions of grandeur. My dad wasn't as flashy of a person as Devin, though I think Devin wants people to think he isn't either.

I like coming into this house and feeling like I'm walking onto the set of a soap opera or a reality show. Either my mom or our twice weekly cleaner always makes sure there are fresh flowers on the entry table. There are these two padded chairs on either side of it that no one ever sits in and a giant skylight that faces the driveway. And yeah, I know that's kind of tacky, but I don't mind being tacky sometimes. Devin's mused on and off about buying the currently vacant ten-bedroom mansion up the street, but what do three people need with that much house, especially with me heading off to college next year.

My very favorite thing about the house, aside from the gourmet kitchen and my room, is the pool. It's an in-ground heated pool with a built-in water slide and hot tub. Because I

HE HATE ME

don't really like lying in the sun, I had my mom buy enough cantilevered umbrellas so I'm always in the shade no matter the time of day. I'm lounging next to the pool in a bikini the Friday after the party when Brandon comes out of the house, rips off his T-shirt and goes diving into the pool. It isn't exactly graceful, and water splashes on my legs. I don't know what his deal is, but I ignore him while he does laps.

I pick up my phone and text Gio. That is the nickname we've agreed on, since Giorgio is a bit of a mouthful. We're just friends right now. I let him know after the party that I like him, but I'm a long-term investment. He said to let him know when I'm ready to find a new boyfriend because maybe he wants to throw his hat in the ring, maybe he doesn't. I'm not taking him seriously, but so far he isn't being a jerk and he's following the rules by not hooking up with any of my friends.

ME: *The guy who's staying with us just splashed me*
GIO: *Playfully? What are you wearing?*
ME: *Carelessly. A bikini.*
GIO: *Send a pic.*

I snap a pic of the pool just as Brandon's head pops above the water. He's staring me down like we're about to jump into an MMA ring. I send the pic to Gio anyway.

GIO: *Not what I was expecting. Is that him?*
ME: *Yep.*
GIO: *Does he always look so angry?*
ME: *Pretty much.*
GIO: *Why?*
ME: *He didn't make the A squad for soccer.*

SENCHA SKEETE

Of course I know that's not it, but I'm not going to get into all the emotional BS with a guy I'm flirting with. Brandon's been galumphing around the house like a morose moose for the last week. I think he found out I didn't want him at that party, but he hasn't confronted me. It's more of stare down, lots of flared nostrils, and snide comments over dinner. This kid must think I've been living in a fairy castle all my life. I may be queen of the school now, but I wasn't always. Kids have been mean to me since I was the only dark-skinned first grader in my class. I didn't know the words "suck my dick," back then, but I found my own six-year-old way of saying it. Brandon simply does not know who he's trying to fuck with.

I text back and forth with Gio for a while and then I go check the hot tub. I really need a soak. Cheerleading practice, after taking it a bit easier over the summer, has been brutal. I need to lose about ten pounds by the first game, which is only a couple of weeks away, so I'm living off whey powder and pulverized vegetables. Lean protein and steamed carrots at dinner are the closest thing I get to a treat right now. Put that together with an aggressive training regimen and I'm both sore and exhausted.

The water is perfect, and I climb into the hot tub and set the jets. This is just what I need. I can feel some of the ache easing right away. I sink lower and let my head fall back against the edge of the tub. Where did I put my sunglasses? Usually, I do this after evening practice, but we had an afternoon practice today so it's still sun out instead of being

HE HATE ME

dark like I'm used to. I close my eyes and try to ignore how bright it still is. Slow breath in. Slow breath out.

"Get out of the fucking hot tub," Brandon growls from much too close. I open my eyes and he's standing right above me, looming really. He's got the same pissed expression he's worn for the past two weeks.

"Keep dreaming," I respond. This guy has got to be nuts. His lips thin and he looks ready to spit. I'm cracking up on the inside. What a douche.

"This is my time, Deja," he says stabbing his index finger towards the floor. "I always use the hot tub around now. Get the fuck out and come back when it's your turn."

"Well, change with the times motherfucker," I respond. "I'm not going anywhere. Why don't you go hit Devin's gym some more? I'm sure you could use the extra conditioning."

His chest expands with rage, and I have to admit that dig was uncalled for. He is so cut it's ridiculous. Every muscle in his chest and abdomen is clearly visible under his lightly tanned skin. He must have 0% body fat, and if I'm not mistaken his chest is bigger than it was at the beginning of the summer. Just going off of looks he's been killing himself in the gym. I know how those training schedules work, the hours of precise exercises and drills, the careful diet, and the regular routines that keep it all together. Using the hot tub right now might not seem like a big deal, but I bet he can't stand any disruption to his usual routine. It must be driving him crazy. If only I cared.

His eyes narrow and I think I've won for a second, but I've underestimated him. Instead of stalking off like I expect, he climbs into the tub and sits next to me. Something about the way he moves has made me think of him as lanky, but with him right up next to me I realize he's actually pretty big. I'm not tiny, but he's got several inches on me and at least sixty pounds of muscle. I'm not going to say I'm intimidated, but I have to fight the urge to scoot away from him. He raises his arms and spreads them across the back of the seat. His right arm is resting behind my head and lying on the long braids I draped outside the water.

"Get off my hair, you jerk," I say, sitting up higher and twisting around to pull the waist-length braids out from under his biceps. Instead of letting up, he grabs a handful of my hair and yanks on it, forcing me closer to him until our thighs touch. He pulls downward, and my head tips back, our eyes locking in silent battle. His face is way too close to mine and a quick glance at my lips betrays him.

"Never gonna happen, tickle dick," I sneer. I try to pull back and not only does he tighten his grip on my hair, his other hand lands on the seat next to my hip, trapping me.

"You don't seem appropriately scared." He laughs. "Did Devin not tell you how I ended up here?"

"You're too stupid to get into college off your grades, so you're trying to get a soccer scholarship. Too bad B squad never gets recruited."

"I'm going to let you in on a little secret, Deja." I feel his warm breath on my ear. He toys with the tie on the side of my bikini. "Moving in with Devin was a condition of my release."

I try to stand up, but he still has a firm grip on my hair.

"So? Let me go!"

"Do you want to know what I was in for?"

"I don't—" My mouth is arid. I want desperately to know, but I need even more desperately to put some space between us.

"Keep prancing around here every day in that piece of floss you call a bathing suit, and you'll find out. You never get in the pool. Do you even know how to swim?"

I'm pissed, but trust I've been dealing with micro aggressions my whole life. I can handle that shit. I pretty much expected him to say something like that when I told him his dick was small. But what comes next is so across the line. His hand inches across the seat to press against the outside of my thigh. I can feel the fabric of his trunks against my other hip, though he only just brushing against me on that side.

"Do you know how many girls like you I've had over at Marshall," he says into ear. "Ready to drop to their knees as soon as they see my big white cock. You know your mom must have been under Devin's desk all day long to get him to marry her."

I feel a rush of heat through my body like being doused in fire. My mother raised me on her own after my dad died and never dated ever until Devin. He was our friend for years, always kind, always reliable, until my mom broke down and gave him a chance. Yes, they worked together, but it was nothing like Brandon was saying. It was one thing for this entitled piece of trash to insult me, but my mother?

I'm not even aware of pulling my fist back, but I definitely feel the jolt up my arm when my fist makes contact with his throat. I was aiming for his ugly face, but he moved at the last second and I hit his neck instead. He reels back, choking and clawing at himself. I stand up to rush him with more blows, but instead of looking scared, he looks smug. The need to wipe that look off his face is so intense I'm already closing the space between us when I see him angle himself to the right. He isn't trying to get away; he's trying to make sure the backyard security camera has an unobstructed view of me hitting him.

This fucking snake. This dirty lowlife cheat. I look into his face, and I can see the triumph lurking there, just under the surface. He scans my figure, his gaze so intense it's almost like he was brushing his fingers over me. I'd always been proud of my body—my firm breasts, my flat belly, and toned legs, but he made me feel ashamed of being so bare in front of him. There is a combination of desire and contempt in that look, and they are equally unwanted. What right does he have to make me feel like this in my own backyard. I'm not sure how yet, but I'm going to make him pay for the things he's said and the way he's made me feel.

"Fuck you!" I say, climbing out of the hot tub. He spreads his arms and legs like he's claiming the whole thing for himself, and I turn my back to him, going to grab my phone and towel. He doesn't know it yet, but he's going to regret this.

Chapter 3

Brandon

IT'S ONLY 7:00 A.M., BUT ALREADY GETTING HOT. I STRETCH my arms and legs, then cue up my workout playlist. I could run on the treadmill in the air-conditioned home gym, of course, but every second I'm in that house I feel like I'm suffocating. If I had a better choice I wouldn't be here. At least when I run the trails I get to be by myself, away from Devin, his airhead wife, and her annoying daughter.

Neither of the women seem to know the real Devin. They seem to think his nice guy facade is the real man. I see him watching me sometimes, probably trying to figure out

SENCHA SKEETE

how much I remember from living with him when my mother was his housekeeper. Much more than I let on, for sure. Does he think I'll tell his wife about the debauchery of his single days, the things I saw that no kid should see? The first time I saw a naked stranger passed out in the living room I thought she was a mannequin, but when I touched her, she was warm. Devin laughed, throwing her unconscious body over his shoulder and taking her upstairs to his room. After I told my mother, she arranged for me to be out of the house or in our room on weekends. But I was a kid, so of course I snuck out whenever I could, and what I saw is still seared in my brain.

When the Briarwood principal and coach requested that I live with Devin, he said it was his godly duty to take me in. You would hardly imagine this was the same man who did all those sketchy things. He technically didn't have to accept me since I was about to turn eighteen, but he agreed to have the guardianship extended until I finish high school. He's soaked up the praise for his generosity. I know he's given at least one speech at one of those businessman clubs about how he rescued a juvenile delinquent from a life of despair because he had me sitting in the room like a prop.

But the first time he and I were alone he promised to "destroy" me if I sold drugs again because if I embarrassed him, I'd regret it for the rest of my life. At least he has his priorities straight, am I right?

A combination of fast-paced rock and aggressive hip-hop drives me forward, the uneven ground forcing me to focus on placing my feet as I run. The burn of exertion gradually transforms into the ecstasy and clarity of mind that only comes from a challenging workout. I feel the pressure lift away, my focus narrowing to the sensation of my feet on the path, the rush of air over my sweat-damp skin, and rhythm of my controlled breathing. My mind shifts though images of the last few weeks—my mother's face the last time I saw her, Devin sitting at his desk in his study droning on about his expectations, Deja standing by the pool in a yellow bikini that barely covers anything.

Shit! I don't want to think about her, but my mind keeps circling back. Those long, lean legs that terminate in her lush, heart-shaped ass. Her flawless, smooth brown skin. Shouldn't your bullies grow up to be trolls with a moustache and unibrow? Mine turned into a baddie so hot it's all I can do not to drool. Those dark eyes, at once innocent and knowing. From minute to minute I think she's a virgin or a vixen— either the least or the most experienced girl in our senior class. I imagine her on her knees, those soft, full lips opening to accept my cock, hearing her gag as I force myself deep inside.

Damnit. Now I'm getting hard. Thank god my running shorts have a compression liner, but there is no comfortable way to run with an erection. I try to think of something unsexy. Oatmeal. The smell of the locker room after soccer practice. Taking a math test.

Arriving at the chalk-marked tree does the trick. I'm limp as a noodle again as I dig through the leaves and dirt until I find the small metal case about the size of a cigarette lighter, but a little longer. It makes barely a lump in my pocket. I continue down the track, the brief pause making the next few hundred steps torture. It takes almost until I return to the back gate for my muscles to relax again.

When I enter the house, I'm also dripping with sweat. As much as I'd like to take a shower, I need to lift weights while my muscles are still warmed up. I hope all this effort is worth it. Coach will put me on A squad soon, and I have to be able to keep up with the other guys or people will suspect I don't belong there. But working out is more than just for soccer. It's the best method I've found for keeping my mind off the things I don't want to think about.

Of course, when I step inside the gym, who do I see running on the treadmill but Deja, dressed in a sports bra and yet another pair of tiny shorts. The movement of her ass is hypnotic. My cock jerks against the stiff liner and she spots me in the mirror just as I wince. A frown flits across her face, but then she makes her expression blank. She knows what she's doing, dressing like that, even though she pretends not to. It would serve her right if I accepted the invitation and took what she was offering. I'm bigger and stronger and have a lot fewer scruples. What could she do?

We ignore each other for the next twenty minutes while I do my sets until she finally stops the treadmill and leaves. I know she's avoiding me because she usually lifts as well, but not today. I'm just about done, too, but I get a sick pleasure in knowing I messed up her workout.

She's generally impervious to my digs, so I get extra enjoyment when I'm able to get under her skin. That day in the hot tub was glorious. I got so close to getting her in big trouble. Maybe if she wasn't such a stuck-up bitch it would be different, but people like her need to be put in their place. I imagine winding her long braids around my hand and forcing her down unto her knees and... damn it! Again? I'm going to have to jerk off in the shower.

* * *

Deja

Here I am again, sitting across the table from last week's trash. Same old soccer jersey, same resentful attitude, but this time there's that smug triumph underneath it all. He thinks he's winning now. I shouldn't let it, but it gets under my skin. He may think of me as the interloper here, but I'm not. He is the one who doesn't belong and it's not like it was my decision that kept him away from this house or out of Briarwood. That was all him and his mom.

"Did you pick up your schedule yet, Deja?" my mom asks, twirling pasta around her fork. I could be mad that she gets to eat carbs and I don't, but honestly I think it was really sweet of her to make one dinner for her and Devin and another for us athlete kids. Mine is chicken breast and steamed broccoli. Brandon is pushing his salad around his plate. I guess he doesn't like broccoli.

"Of course, Mom," I reply. "I'm almost done getting my planner ready."

Brandon gives me a weird look across the table. Apparently, detailed daily outlining isn't part of his way of life. No wonder he's on the B team. I have every minute of my day pre-allocated before the week starts. I leave a little flexibility in there for socializing, but if I don't know what I'm doing Sunday at 10:00 pm by Monday at 6:00 a.m. then something is wrong.

"Do you have a planner, Brandon?" my mom asks.

"Uh, yeah," Brandon says, but not in a convincing way. I know he's flying by the seat of his pants and thinks he's on top of things. Loser.

"Do you want me to give you some tips?" my mom asks. I don't know why she's trying to ingratiate herself. "I'm a whiz at coordinating."

"Cause you were a secretary?" Brandon asks with exaggerated sweetness.

"I've never...," my mom starts to say, looking a little confused. I don't think she's really, though. I think she just likes to give everybody the benefit of the doubt. Too much of the benefit of the doubt.

"Tanisha's the controller at my company," Devin breaks in. "She's a CPA. You know that."

Brandon shrugs. "Sure, Devin."

"There's nothing wrong with being a secretary," my mom says. "The work they do is important too." It sounds like a condescending borderline douchey thing to say, but I know my mom really means it.

"What does your mom do, Brandon?" I ask, stabbing a piece of chicken. I enjoy the way his jaw tightens before he answers.

"She works for the county," he says stiffly.

"Part time, right?"

HE HATE ME

He doesn't answer and we both know why. His mother is a high school dropout who's spent most of her life cleaning other people's toilets. Honest work, but I'm just trying to warn Brandon off of throwing stones while his mother's been living in a glass house for the last twenty years. Not trying to be mean, but my mom was left high and dry when my dad died and if she could work her way up, then I don't see why Brandon's mom can't do it too.

"Sir," Brandon says, "I was wondering if I could borrow your car tonight."

"What do you need it for?" Devin asks, slipping into his "Boss of You" persona.

"I'm meeting one of my friends at the movie theater," Brandon says. "Then we were going to go to hang out at the arcade."

The arcade, my ass. More like smoking weed in the field behind the mall. Not sure who he would be doing it with, though. I haven't heard of him hanging out with anyone.

"Is this with a girl?" Devin asks. Super awkward now. "Or a boy. Either is fine."

"It's not a date," Brandon says, quickly. "Just hanging out with a couple buddies from the team."

"Bom chicka bom bom," I sing, earning a disapproving look from my mom. Brandon gives me a 'what the fuck look,' but he also colors a little. No, it doesn't really make sense to imply he's having sex with his guy friends but if it embarrasses him, I'm doing it.

"Do we know these boys?" Devin asks.

Brandon shrugs. "I don't think so. They were recruited from other districts like I was."

"I'm really not comfortable—"

"Why don't you take him, Deja," my mom interrupts Devin. "You're going to the movies tonight, aren't you?"

"Uh," I say, caught off guard. Usually I'd have a lie at the ready, but I've been talking about going to see this new movie for weeks and was even griping about how I couldn't see it on opening night because one of my friends was grounded and we'd all promised to go see it together. I should also explain that Devin's car is a two-year-old Mercedes E class that he still caresses with his fingertips every time he walks past it. There is zero chance of him lending it to Brandon, or anyone else for that matter.

"What time does your movie start?" I ask, trying to think on my feet.

"We hadn't picked one yet," Brandon says. I try giving him the 'work with me' eyes, but it's a no go. "I think that would be a great idea."

"You can give him a ride home after, can't you?" my mother presses on. "You girls weren't planning to go anywhere else."

"We were actually going over to Lorelei's house after," I improvise. She lives in the opposite direction from us, so it is definitely out of my way to bring him home.

"You could take Brandon and his friends with you," my mother suggests.

"So have boys over?"

HE HATE ME

"Her parents are going to be home, aren't they?" Devin asks, that much too sharp brain of his picking up on my careless mistake.

"Yeah, of course," I say. We aren't going to Lorelei's house precisely BECAUSE her parents are going to be home. We are going to the field behind the mall.

"Just make sure you guys are home by midnight," my mom says, cheerfully. "It will be good for you to spend some time together. You two snipe at each other too much."

Brandon and I exchange a look across the table and for once we are on entirely the same page. We don't like each other, and we don't WANT to like each other. What we both wish is that the other would disappear and never come back.

* * *

Brandon is as rude in my car as he is everywhere else. He rolls down the window, lowers the seat way back, and tries to change the radio station. My car is not that new or that nice because I bought it with my own money that I saved up over two summers. Or two-thirds was my money and the other third Devin and my mom gave me. Devin was very adamant about getting it checked by a mechanic and all that before I bought it. He paid for that, too.

I mean, I really love Devin. You might be like, 'why didn't he just buy you a car?' but that would never be him. He believes learning how to get things for yourself is worth way more than you getting things the easy way. And it's not like my car isn't cute. I stay pretty low-key with it though, because most of the other girls drive nicer cars. Melodie Yang drives a

SENCHA SKEETE

Range Rover. A sixteen-year-old in a Range Rover is not something I can compete with but thank goodness she's kinda awkward and still has braces on. By the time she realizes the power she could have over these materialistic bitches, I'll be in college.

"Where you meeting your friends?" I ask Brandon, deciding to keep it somewhat professional.

"At the mall," he says like I'm stupid.

"I'll drop you off outside the theater," I say, smacking my gum.

"Where are you going to be?" he asks. "Mommy and Daddy are going to be so disappointed to hear you've been lying to them."

"I'm meeting the girls in the parking lot, asshole," I respond.

"You must think I'm stupid if you think I'm buying that," he says.

I ignore him and pull up to the mall entrance closest to the theater. I stop the car and Brandon just sits there at first, his head cocked to one side. I wonder what's going on in his head. Most likely he's just trying to be as difficult as possible.

"Get out of the car, loser," I say, getting tired of it. My phone vibrates with a text coming in. I have nothing to prove to him, but I don't try to hide the screen, which reads:

MACKENZIE: Get over here. Movie starts in 15 and we still need to get snacks.

"Brandon," a male voice calls from the direction of the mall. I look over and two guys are approaching the car. I guess these are Brandon's friends, and they are not what I expected. They are both fine—I mean F.I.N.E—brothers. One of them is chocolate and about Brandon's height. He's got thick dreadlocks tied back from his gorgeous face. I'd say his eyes are his best feature. They're big and brown and he has thick lashes to match. The other guy is a little shorter, but still taller than me. He's just slightly thicker than his friends and a mellow caramel color. He's got a tight fade and waves on top. He's wearing a diamond stud in one ear too. He unleashes a sexy smile on me that goes with his look like butter goes with dinner rolls.

Brandon gets out of the car, and they dap. I should peel out of there and tell Brandon "bye sucker" with the squeal of my tires, but instead I get out and stand by the car, twirling one of my braids. I'm not exactly serving looks over here, but the little ruched-bodice strapless minidress I'm wearing is cute.

"Hi," Chocolate Prince says to me. Then to Brandon, "This your girlfriend?"

"Oh, hell nah," Brandon says. "I don't date evil." His friends grin in unison, giving his shade no never mind.

"What's your name, beautiful?" Caramel King asks. His voice is deep and manly. I almost forget Brandon is there until he steps between us.

"Aren't we late?" he asks, impatiently.

"Come on, man," CK says, grinning. "Don't be that guy."

"Let's go," Brandon yells waving his arms towards the mall entrance, though he says it in a joking tone. He doesn't wait for the guys to agree, but lopes away on his long legs.

SENCHA SKEETE

"See you later, Goddess," CP says and then he winks. Those are the two best looking guys I've seen since I ended things with my ex. Either of them would be a perfect way to spend my senior year, but unfortunately, hotness isn't high on my list of criteria for a new boyfriend. Popularity is what matters. It's one of the reasons that even though I like Gio, I'm still just texting with him. I need a guy who's on my level socially.

* * *

Three hours later, I am sitting on the hood of my girl's car in the field behind the mall. It's around 11:00 and I am under the influence. Oh, God. Sometimes I feel like the car is falling away from under me and the stars, all twenty gazillion of them, are rushing towards me like a massive meteor shower. Then it all flips and it's like I'm flying up and up into the black sky. You might think this would freak me out, but I love rollercoasters and though this is the first time I've tried these pot candies that Lorelei got from her cousin, I am not unhappy. Kristie is saying something to me, and I have no idea what. It takes me five minutes to figure out she's asking me if I want to go hang out by the soccer fields where a bunch of guys are goofing around. Some of them are from our school and some are from "other schools," which, if you know these kids, means they're not as rich and therefore have an aura of danger and the forbidden.

I get there and I don't even have to ask before someone gives me a drink and a folding chair to sit on. There's a little contest going on between the boys and girls. Some of the guys have the look of basketball players, others are thick like they play football. Most of them are white, but there is a smattering of everything here. I feel like there's a huge crowd of kids, but as I mentioned, I am high, and so I don't really have the clearest mind right now. The sound of hip-hop breaks through the fog in my brain and the disparate pieces of input organize themselves into something that actually makes sense. The kids are taking turns dancing, first a boy and then a girl. The boys are breakdancing, and my girls are coming with all kinds of moves, but mostly hip-hop. I know it's a lame teen movie cliche, but what really are a bunch of suburban teenagers going to do behind a mall other than drink, smoke weed, and act the fool.

"You alright?" CK asks me after I do a couple flips and throw myself down at the side of the soccer pitch. He's lying next to me on his side, his eyes, going again and again to my bare legs.

"I'm good," I say. "What's your name?"

"Carmello," he says, tickling the inside of my elbow with a blade of grass.

"You lying," I say. "Caramel Carmello?"

"You not trusting, girl," he says. "You as high as a kite!"

"And you smell like weed," I observe, laughing. Soon we're both laughing, staring up at the sky and howling like we're watching the funniest movie in history.

He abruptly sits up and presses something into my hand.

"Call me," he says, winking. Then he stands up. I sit up too, not sure why he's leaving all of a sudden and then I see Brandon, looking at me and shaking his head.

"We have to go," he says. "I don't want to miss curfew."

"Your friend is cute," I say in a stage whisper as we walk back to my car.

"Stay away from my friends," Brandon says, shaking his head.

"Your other friend is cute, too. And I'm single."

"You cannot date my friends, Deja. Nope."

"Selfish."

Chapter 4

Deja

I'M SITTING IN MY CAR, KIND OF IN AND OUT OF IT AS Brandon drives me home. I'm still high, but the intensity is coming down I think, and I'm just sober enough to realize that I've fucked up big time. Brandon hasn't said anything since we got into the car, and he insisted on driving. The radio is off, making the silence that much more deafening. I turn my head a bit to the side, and I can see that his face is not angry at all. No, he looks pleased, the smug look from earlier in the day even more deeply etched into his features.

"You're gonna rat on me," I say as we turn into our subdivision. It's just before midnight on a Friday night, but most of the interior lights are off. I know my parents are already in bed. They don't wait up for me anymore, just check the logs to see what time I entered the code into the security system. Add the external security cameras, and there is no way of fooling them about when I got home.

"What would be the fun in that?" Brandon says, smiling thinly.

I am not fooled. It's only been hours since Brandon cornered me in the hot tub and called me a hood rat. He's openly hostile towards me in front of my parents. There is no way he'll waste this opportunity.

"We can work something out," I suggest. "You know I'm the most popular girl in school. I can make sure you get invited to every party that matters this year."

"I'm focused on soccer, " Brandon says, smugly, "but thanks anyway."

"All my friends are super cute and most of them are cheerleaders—"

"Are you trying to pimp your friends out right now?" he asks, pulling onto our street. "I mean you all dress like hoes, but I didn't realize it was that serious."

"Fuck you," I say, sounding more exhausted than angry. I want to crawl in bed right now and wrap myself around the oversized teddy bear my ex gave me.

"Okay," he says, as we pull up into the circular driveway in front of the house. "I won't tell 'em anything. But that means you owe me a favor."

"What kind of favor?" I ask warily.

"Whatever I want," he says, laughing.

"I'm not fucking you." I roll my eyes, reaching for the door. When I climb out of the car, the cobblestones are whirling under my feet. I lean against the car, wanting to do nothing more than slide down the side of it and lie on my back. I've heard before that edibles can hit you hard, but this is ridiculous. It was one piece of candy! Brandon walks around the car and wraps his arm around my waist, half-dragging me over to the stone bench next to the entry. We sit down, my head on his shoulder, and the only thing keeping me upright is his arm around my middle.

"I know this is hard for you to believe, princess," he says, "but not every guy who meets you wants to bone you, and not every teenaged guy's life revolves around getting sex. I can get sex whenever I want. I don't need to blackmail girls or get pathetic queen bees to set me up."

"You called me princess," I say, inanely. "That feels like progress."

"I don't even have to turn you in at this point," he says, stroking my back. "I could just go inside and leave you out here, then sit back tomorrow morning and watch you try to explain why you were lying on the bench for an hour past curfew."

"I'll be soberer soon," I say, pouting.

"No, you won't," he says. "I don't know what the hell you took, but if I scooted over two inches, you would fall on your face."

You might be thinking I was weighing pros and cons at that moment, but honestly all I was thinking was that I was cold, and the bench was hard, and I wanted to be in my soft bed under a blanket. I just wanted to go inside, and the challenge of standing up and walking there seemed insurmountable.

"Okay," I say, nuzzling my head against his neck, my eyes tightly shut against the spins. "Take me inside and I'll owe you one favor of your choice."

"You're going to hate yourself tomorrow, you know that?" he says, chuckling.

"I hate myself now," I respond.

* * *

Brandon

Deja wears a loopy smile as I guide her up the steps and into the house. I feel a weird twist of something in my gut. Tonight is the first time I've seen her happy. That carefree smile while she danced in the field is so different from the practiced expressions she usually wears. She's a cute girl, but when she smiled like that, she was downright beautiful. It's making me weak. I should be setting her up to get caught. I haven't forgotten how mean she was to me when we were kids. Instead, I'm helping her evade the parents.

I scoop her warm body into my arms and carry her upstairs. She's not heavy, but she's more solid than I'd realized. I don't know why I'm surprised. I make fun of cheerleading to piss her off, but I know it's a real sport; of course she's fit as hell, not just skinny.

HE HATE ME

I set her down on the edge of her bed and she raises her arms like a toddler. Is she asking me to take her dress off? Fuck me!

"Get on the bed, Deja," I tell her, titillated and annoyed that I'm titillated.

With some coaxing she awkwardly climbs onto the bed, flopping face down on top of the comforter. Almost unbidden, my phone is in my hand and I'm taking a picture of her prone body. The flash is blindingly bright. How would this look if one of her parents came along right now. Me up-skirting a zonked-out Deja.

I should leave right now, I think as I lock the bedroom door. I flick on the bedside lamp so I can see better. Her skimpy dress rides up her hips, exposing the luscious curve of her ass and sending a surge of primal lust through my body.

I give myself a shake. I need to stop obsessing over this girl and pay attention to what's important. This is a rare opportunity to access Deja's room. The chances of finding what I need here are low, but I've been advised to search thoroughly and I'm not having much luck elsewhere in the house. In her bathroom, I search under the sink and tap the walls and floor, listening for signs of something behind the wall. Every inch of the bathroom is pristine. There are no uneven spots, no variations in paint color or wall depth. The mirror is definitely just a piece of glass glued to the wall.

I try her closet next with similar results, though it takes longer because of all the shelving and cubbies, the clothes and shoes blocking access to the walls and floor. There's even a rug in there. Who has a rug in their closet?

SENCHA SKEETE

Back in her bedroom, my eyes keep straying to her nearly naked body laying across the bed. At some point she flipped over onto her back and her dress slipped down. I can see her two perfect tits pointing skyward. Yeah, I know teenage girls have nice tits in general, but hers are next level, so round and firm, and yet soft looking, and her nipples look super inviting. I'm not a tit man. I'm not an ass man either, or even really a chick man. I'm straight, but usually I can take or leave most girls. But Deja has gotten under my skin without even trying. I can only imagine how horrified she'd be if she knew how hard she made me every time she pouted in annoyance.

I check the walls and confirm there's nothing behind them. I look under the bed, but as I expected, there's nothing there. I run through a list of places I haven't checked yet—the parents' room, Devin's study, the part of the basement sealed behind a locked door—basically all the places I'm most likely to find what I'm looking for. Also, the places I'd have no plausible reason to be. I may have to measure interior spaces and compare them to exterior dimensions to see if there is a hidden room or crawlspace. Fuck me.

I need to turn the bedside lamp before I leave, and that's all I'm planning to do, except for taking one last look at her, maybe snapping one quick image to use for...persuasion? I may need someone to help me access those hard places after all. I'm not a pervert. Not just a pervert at least.

But when I look at her my breath catches in my throat. She's not asleep like I thought. She's rubbing her tits and watching me. She bites her bottom lip in a deliberately provocative move. What's happening right now? Deja hates me. Is this a trick? Is she going to yell rape if I go near her? She pinches her nipples and I feel an answering pulse in my cock, the blood rushing from my head and leaving me unable to think straight.

My mind fills with images I've only half let myself imagine, doing things I shouldn't be thinking about a girl I hate. Now I'm sitting on the edge of the bed, trying to ignore my incessantly throbbing dick, but it is shamelessly running the show. I put my hand on her calf, feeling the softness of warm skin over taut muscle. Emboldened, by her soft grunt, I slide my hand upwards, relishing the sensation of her body under my fingertips. I reach the top of her thigh, and she makes a soft sound of approval. Her skirt rises even higher, giving me a clear view of her white boy shorts, stretched tight over her pussy. My eyes lock onto the shadow of her lips through the thin cotton fabric, and I can feel any self-control I might have had slipping away. She meets my gaze with half-closed eyes, offering no resistance.

My phone clicks softly as I prop it up on the bedside table, its red recording light blinking. I haven't decided how far I want to go tonight, seeing her discomfort in that bunched-up dress gives me the justification I want to take her dress off. I grip the ruched fabric of her bodice and slowly pull it down to her waist. Up close her tits are gorgeous, just the right size for her slender frame, round and firm with a honey brown shade that sets them apart from the rest of her body. I wonder if the skin covered by her bikini bottoms is the same color. Her nipples are dark and protruding, larger than I expected. I bet they're sensitive. I can imagine how they'll feel under my tongue, growing swollen and stiff. I can already feel the heat radiating from between her legs. I need to explore more of her tight body and see just how wet she gets with a little foreplay.

I ease the dress down, and she raises her hips to help me get it off. I toss it towards her clothing hamper, but it slides off and lands on the floor. My heart hammers in my chest as I look down at her nearly naked body. I'm only inches away from all the parts I want to touch.

I kick my shoes off and climb onto the bed, making sure to lie so that she is in clear view of the camera. I lay my hand on the silky skin of her abdomen and place my head next to her ear. Her smell invades my brain, a hint of coconut oil with a top note of vanilla.

"How are you feeling, baby?"

"Good," she says softly.

"You like when I touch you?"

"Yeah."

My right hand covers her breast, gently pushing hers out of the way. I feel the heat of her body against my palm as I squeeze and mold her supple flesh. Her tits are firm and resilient, and her skin is like silk. I lightly trace her areola, and she arches her back, trying to get more contact.

"How about when I touch your tits? Does that feel good?"

"No," she says, sulkily.

"Why don't you like it?"

"You don't touch my nipples."

"You want me to touch your nipples?"

She nods.

"Can I pinch them? Tell me out loud."

"Yes, you can pinch them."

"How about if I suck them, is that ok?"

"Um hmm."

How can I deny a pretty girl when she asks so nicely? I take her nipple between my lips, sucking firmly, then lashing it with my tongue. My teeth graze her swollen peaks and love the little moans she makes while I play with her tits. I bite down hard on them, drawing out moans of pleasure and pain. I'm being a little rough, and in response she's threaded her hand through my hair to encourage me. It's surprising and such a turn on that she likes what I like. I wasn't expecting that. My cock feels like it's going to break my zipper.

I have enough recorded now that I could stop if blackmail was my only purpose, but I don't want to stop. Let's not pretend I'm better than I am. A good guy wouldn't be working for the guy I'm working for. A good guy wouldn't take advantage of her like this. She's giving me come hither looks, and stroking my chest, but I'd have to be an idiot not to realize her change in behavior is probably because she's zonked. I've already crossed the line by touching her tits, so why pretend stopping here will make a difference? I mean I'm not going to fuck her, but in for penny in for a pound.

"Lift your hips up, honey," I tell her.

She does it, and it's as easy as pie to take her white panties off. I push her legs wide open, her flexibility allowing them to easily fall to the side. She lies there, helplessly exposed, her thighs splayed in an almost unnatural angle. I

65

pick up the phone and her bedside lamp so I can get a clear shot of her naked body, and especially her little pussy.

"Can you straighten your legs?" I ask her. "Like you're doing the splits."

She's such a good girl when she's high. I need to buy a case of those candies. She giggles and spreads her legs in a perfect center split. Her outer lips separate, exposing her coral pink core. I adjust my dick, trying to find a position that works, but there's no way to make that hungry monster fit comfortably in my pants, so I take them off. The front of my briefs protrudes like a freaking circus tent.

I pull her to the edge of the bed and prop the phone against a pillow, pointing at her face. The important thing is to capture her reaction. I kneel next to the bed and gently separate her labia with my thumbs. She has a neat patch of pubes on her mound and a line of fine, soft hair on the inner edges her labia. Everything else is shaved for swimwear.

"What are you doing?" she asks, drowsily.

"I'm gonna lick you out." I say.

"Mmm. Jayden did that one time."

"Who's Jayden?"

"My ex."

"Did you like it?"

"It was okay."

"I think I can do better than okay."

"Jayden's hot, though."

"Hotter than me?"

"I don't know. You're hot, too."

HE HATE ME

"Thank you for saying that. Keep your legs open, honey."

"I am!" She's not. Her legs are drifting lower, but at my urging she does the splits again, grumbling inaudibly. Then clearly, "What's the fucking hold up? Do it already."

"You want my tongue in your pussy, Little Thorn?"

"I'm not little. I'm eighteen."

"Well, I turned eighteen first, so I can call you little."

"Will you just put your tongue in already?"

I smile, thinking about what this will sound like on playback. Deja Marcus begging me to eat her out, not even challenging me when I call her a thorn in my side.

Her pussy smells like heaven, but the opening looks barely big enough to fit my finger. Well, we're going to find out, aren't we. I dive right in, plunging my wide tongue into her narrow passage, feeling her walls clench around me in resistance. I stiffen my tongue and stab deeper, wiggling it around inside her. She tastes delicious. Not like candy or fruit or any of that bullshit. She tastes like pussy—clean, fresh, aroused pussy. She moans and circles her hips subtly.

I give her whole pussy a lusty lick. I do it again, flattening my tongue over her clit. Her ass clenches as I home in on the sensitive nub, tracing its sides and sucking on it with just enough pressure to make her hips jerk. She's glistening with a combination of my spit and her juices, and there is a lot of juice.

I push my index finger inside her, just to my first knuckle. She's so hot and tight it feels like she's sucking me in. I want to do so many things right now. Her clit is begging to be licked, her hot, tight, wet pussy needs a good fingering, my cock is throbbing like it's about to explode and her nipples are begging to be kissed. So are her lips. They are full and soft. Her head is thrown to the side, her lips parted as she pants for air. Shit, I haven't even kissed her mouth yet, but I'm eating her pussy.

I'm going to claim those lips, though. If not tonight, then very soon. I don't know what I was thinking when I started this, but now I want everything. I want to come in and on every part of her body. I want to taste her lips and her belly button and her ass. I want to feel her come on my cock and make her drink my come. I want to make her do every nasty, fucked up thing I've ever imagined. She doesn't like me grabbing her hair? She's going to have to get used to it.

"Am I better than Jayden?" I ask, pumping my finger into her pretty pussy.

"Yes," she gasps, rocking her hips in time with my thrusts.

"Do you like me now?"

"No! You're an asshole."

I smirk as I struggle to work a second finger inside her tight opening. She makes a sound that's halfway between pleasure and distress.

"I'm going to make you come. Do you think you can be quiet?"

She shakes her head, grinding her pussy on my fingers. She loosens up just a hair and I'm able to get two fingers in to the second joint. It's ridiculous. Her pussy is drooling, but nearly impossible to get inside. Either she's a virgin or her ex had a micro-penis.

With a firm grasp, I pull one of her nipples sharply away from her body. She lets out a soft mewl of pleasure and begins to play with her other breast. My hand moves experimentally, twisting and tugging at her sensitive nipple, eliciting even more moans from her. Encouraged by her response, I jam my fingers into her wetness, and she shudders. That response is everything I've ever dreamed of. My roughness giving her pleasure is like fuel on the fire of my lust. I've always held back when I've been with girls my age, avoiding the things I most want to do because of how it makes them flinch and cry. What if I don't have to do that with her? We've barely scratched the surface, but just the possibility makes my balls throb.

I have to get her off before I embarrass myself and come all over the floor. My mouth latches onto her clit, sucking and licking as my fingers hammer into her. Her legs close around my head, muffling the sound of her cries. She digs her hands into my hair, nails scoring my scalp as she grinds her pussy into my face. I suck even harder. Her heels dig into my back and her back arches as she comes shuddering like a leaf. I ease up, but I continue licking her gently until she pushes me away, her cheeks wet.

She gives me a sleepy smile before closing her eyes. She's drifting off, satisfied, but I'm still hard as a rock. That's not a problem. I almost stop the recording, but then I have another idea. With one hand I pick up the phone and aim it at her body. The other frees my dick and strokes it from root to tip.

SENCHA SKEETE

It only takes a few pumps of my dick to get me to the edge. The first shot of hot come hits her in the middle of her chest, oozing down towards her collarbone. The next splashes onto her breast, dripping off of her pretty nipple like donut glaze. Then I aim for her stomach, coating it with my essence before finally reaching the thatch of hair at the top of her mound.

"Fuck," I moan as the last spurt lands on her thigh. My legs feel like jelly. I want to sink down next to her and pass out too, but I can't do that, can I?

I pan the camera one last time over her come splattered body, then turn it off. The sight is both erotic and satisfying, like a stamp of ownership, however temporary. She may not know it, but as far as I'm concerned, she's now mine. I think I'll take my time in claiming her fully, though; savor the experience.

I go to her ensuite and soak a washcloth in warm water. I meticulously wipe down every inch of her so well you'd never know how thoroughly I despoiled her if I didn't have the photographic evidence. I poke through her drawers and find an oversized T-shirt I've seen her wear before as pajamas. The whole time, she's as floppy as a sex doll. I've got to find out what that stuff was she took so I can avoid it like the plague. I could do anything I wanted to her right now—it's sick.

Once I've tucked her in, I turn out the lamp.

"Sweet dreams, princess," I whisper before slipping out the door.

Chapter 5

Deja

NOT TO WAX TOO PHILOSOPHICAL HERE, BUT THERE ARE times when we think we know what we've gotten ourselves into and we are not even on the same planet. First off, I think I know what regret is when I wake up the next morning in just a T-shirt with no underwear and no idea how I got out of my clothes, and no memory of anything that happened after we sat on the bench outside. I'm even a little buoyant because not only do I not feel any ill-effects from the pot, my body is incredibly relaxed. I feel like I've had the best sleep of my life.

SENCHA SKEETE

But then, after I put some clothes on, I discover a text on my phone from Brandon. It has a caption "More where this came from," and a picture of me lying face down on my bed with a hint of ass showing under my dress. So obviously he's not happy just extracting a future favor from me, he intends to give me a hard time about it too.

I go for my usual Sunday morning run and get back to find my parents eating cereal and Brandon in the kitchen making a smoothie. I have to wait for my turn, so I'm just standing around waiting for him to finish because I don't want to get sweat on the dining chairs. He smirks at me, and I discreetly give him the finger, which only seems to amuse him more.

"It's already 9:15, Deja," my mom says. "You should take a shower now if you don't want to be late for church."

It's fine. I don't get my usual protein shake before church. I make do with a banana. It's no big deal. I'm not as anal as Brandon about my schedule being disrupted. I swear I'm not. I'm just irritable because instead of sitting with my parents where he sat the last few weeks, he's put himself in the same pew as me and my friends. Even more annoying, Mackenzie is actually talking to him, even though she knows how I feel about him. I've told her that he just got out of juvie, but that only made him more attractive to her. I shoot him a dirty look that I don't try to hide from the girls, but a few seconds later my phone vibrates and when I sneak a look it's a picture of us sitting on the bench last night. We look very cozy and my heart thunders at the thought of anyone seeing us like that. I can't even come up with a plausible excuse for why I would be all over him, not even one that would fly with people who know how fucked up I was. I close the text, but not before Shelby gets a quick look at it.

"Is that you and Gio?" she whispers. She's trying to sound like she doesn't care, but I can see the hurt in her eyes. We haven't talked about it, and she knows Gio and I are talking, but I think she's still holding out hope he'll notice her. I think quickly. If I say it's Gio, Shelby's feelings will be hurt. But if I don't say it's Gio, then I'll have to explain who I'm in the picture with. Before I can think of an answer, the pastor tells everyone to stand and by the time we're done singing that hymn, Shelby's not focused on the picture anymore.

After service we congregate in the fellowship hall. Shelby has to go get her little brother from childcare, and I see that Mackenzie and Brandon are STILL talking. What the hell? I step right into the middle of that and say,

"Can you go check if they have any hot chocolate, Kenz? I gotta talk to Brandon about something."

She looks at me in confusion, but none of these girls are going to gainsay me without good cause.

"You need to stay away from my friends," I hiss in a low voice. He smirks at me, his blue eyes twinkling in amusement.

"Or what?" he asks. "Mackenzie and I have a lot of catching up to do. I just found out she's a math tutor. Did you know that?"

"What do you mean 'catching up?'"

"Kenz and I were best buds back in pre-school. I'd say small world, but this is where I grew up, isn't it. This is the church where I learned to say the Lord's Prayer. My mom used to be in the choir."

"Well, it's my church now," I say, "and she's my friend."

He doesn't respond. He's wearing a dress shirt, dark slacks, and a tie and honestly, he looks like he belongs here. There's an air of teenage recklessness about him, but also a kind of confidence like he knows this place. He could be any of the boys here, and it hits me even harder when he gives a slight upward nod to one of the guys, I know who doesn't go to our school. In five or ten years, he'll look like any of the young dads I see leading their toddlers out of the nursery. But I won't look like these pink floral-dress-wearing young wives no matter what I do, because I'm the wrong color and I have the wrong face. I want to scream sometimes because it's not fair. I have to work so hard for it and he just slides in effortlessly.

"Can you introduce me to your friend," Reverend Billingsly says over my left shoulder and the world rights itself. He's the main pastor of the church and he just got back from a mission trip, so he hasn't been here since Brandon started living with us. It's my turn to smirk. Brandon might as well be a stranger to the pastor of "his church."

"Hi, Reverend," I say, graciously. "This is Brandon. He's going to be staying with us this school year."

"Welcome, Brandon," the pastor says. Brandon makes the right noises, but I can see the tightness around his eyes. He's embarrassed for some reason, and later I find out it's because Rev. Billingsly knew him when he was little and doesn't remember him. It's a big church, so I can't blame the pastor, but I'm reminded again that I'm the one everyone knows and loves, and Brandon is just some guy in a tie.

* * *

Later, when we're back home, Brandon finds me when I'm cleaning the downstairs bathroom because, yes, I have chores, and sticks his head in. I'm in the middle of wiping down the mirror and the room reeks of vinegar. He's wearing shorts and a sleeveless tank top and there are smears of dirt on his legs and arms, so I figure Devin had him doing yard work.

"I need to make something clear to you," he says, folding his arms.

"What?" I ask, sighing.

"You're going to need to stop being a bitch to me."

"I'm not the one being an asshole here," I counter, shocked at his gall. "You threatened me, if I recall, over fucking hot tub time. You touched my hair!"

"You all don't like that, do you?" he says, mockingly.

"You mean girls?" I practically yell. "No, girls do not like it when you grab them by the hair." Yeah, I know that's not what he meant, but regardless there isn't a woman on earth who wants some rando yanking her by the hair.

"Oh, I don't know about that," he drawls. The insinuation is unmistakable, but he knows damn well it can't be that between us. The suggestion is gross, at best, because of the things he said to me yesterday. You may have heard that women like assholes, but not all women, and certainly not me. Calling me a hood rat is not the way to my heart.

"Why are you here, Brandon?" I ask, cutting to the chase.

"I'm planning to call Mackenzie this week and I'm just telling you don't get in the way. And you know damn well what kind of 'or else' I'm talking about. My camera roll is full of shit you don't want popping up on IG or TikTok."

"You know what? Go ahead and show people those pictures. I don't think anyone who's seen us together would believe that we're anything but enemies."

"Okay," he says, amusement tinging his voice. "But I'll let you pick which one."

I swallow hard, feeling a knot form in my stomach as the glee on his face sends a shiver of unease up my spine. Me falling asleep on his shoulder or a shot of my butt that doesn't show my face shouldn't inspire this kind of reaction.

With a triumphant smirk, he pulls out his phone and holds it in front of me. My brain stutters for a minute, not believing what I'm seeing. The screen shows me lying on my back in my darkened bedroom, naked except for my panties. My face is hidden by shadows, but you can tell it's me. The sense of violation is profound and the blood drains from my face as I realize what he has is much more damaging than I'd originally thought. I hadn't been sure whether he undressed me last night or if I undressed myself, but even though he's been such a dick, I didn't think he'd go this far.

"One slip of my finger…"

"You realize I'm not eighteen yet, right? Those pictures are illegal. Do you want to go to jail?"

He smirks, crowding me against the wall. I hate how vulnerable his size makes me feel.

"You're eighteen," he says confidently.

"What makes you think that?"

He leans in closer, his hot breath tickling my ear as he whispers, "You told me last night."

"What?" I search my memory, trying to recall when I might have told him how old I am. Could he have overheard me talking to someone about it? But no matter how hard I try, I don't remember my age coming up in conversation. I'm hoping if he thinks I'm underage he'll delete the pictures just to avoid getting in more trouble. Maybe he's bluffing about knowing my age just like I'm bluffing about being underage.

"We had a really good time in your room last night," he says with a grin. My mind whirls with confusion. What could he possibly be talking about? We sat on the bench, and I rested my head on his shoulder...but then everything goes blank. He could be talking about anything. All I know for certain is that between standing up from the bench and waking up this morning, every article of clothing came off my body. In the picture he showed me I'm lying on the bed in just my panties. But here's the thing - when I woke up this morning, I was wearing a sleep shirt. How did I end up wearing only a shirt after getting into bed in nothing but underwear? Did I wake up at some point and put pajamas on? I can't tell from the picture if I was awake or passed out when it was taken. I don't want to believe he's depraved enough to take the underwear off an unconscious girl. But meeting his gaze, I can't rule it out.

"You're just lying," I decide. I cross my arms below my breasts and give him a challenging look. "I can't see how one person spying on the other equals both of them having a good time."

"That's not what happened," he says, with a self-satisfied smile, "but don't worry about that. What you need to know is that last night changed the equation for me and you. You're mine now."

My blood runs cold at his words. "What the fuck does that mean? Just because you have blackmail material doesn't mean you can just bully me."

"No," he says, his expression suddenly serious, "that's exactly what it means. Whatever I say goes, or these pics start popping up online."

There's something lurking behind his eyes, a dark emptiness that chills me. Before I can fully process it, it's gone, replaced by a sneer. Anger boils inside of me.

"How long do you think it would take before your cool friends dropped you?"

I try to brush off his words, telling myself they wouldn't do that. But deep down, I know popularity is fickle and as much as everyone claims to be sex-positive these days, it's as easy as blinking to be labeled a slut and tumble down the social ladder.

"Poor Little Thorn," he taunts, cupping my cheek and stroking it with his thumb. He's close enough I catch the earthy scent of sweat and grass. I feel a tingle on my skin where he touches me, but quickly flinch away and step towards the door, putting much-needed space between us. "I'm not—"

"Brandon, I need you," Devin yells from the direction of the foyer.

"Just a sec," he calls back. He passes within inches of me on his way to the door, purposefully invading my personal space.

"Tomorrow at lunch, meet me in the library and I'll tell you what you're going to do."

"I can't do that. I eat lunch with the cheerleaders."

"I'll be waiting." He saunters out the door like he has the world on a string. I want to hurl obscenities after him, but I can hear Devin talking to him. The back door opens and closes, and I don't hear them anymore.

My hands tremble as I grip the edge of the bathroom sink. I stare at my reflection in the mirror, hardly recognizing the fear in my own eyes. How did things spiral so far out of control? I knew Brandon was trouble, but I never imagined there was a true monster lurking beneath his handsome facade.

I feel sick as I replay his threats in my mind. He plans to blackmail me with those awful photos, to control me and isolate me from my friends. If he exposes me, everything I've worked for could come crashing down—my social status, my cheerleading, even my college prospects. I can't let him destroy my life like that. But refusing him could lead to the same outcome. I'm trapped. And for what? Some perverted power trip just because he's holding a grudge from grade school?

SENCHA SKEETE

Panic rises in my chest, making it hard to breathe. I try taking slow, deep breaths to calm myself. Think, Deja, think. There has to be a way out of this. I just need to outmaneuver him somehow.

I'll go to the library at lunch tomorrow like he wants. I'll act like I'm too scared to resist him. Get him to lower his guard. Then I'll snatch his phone and delete those pictures once and for all. Or maybe I'll threaten to tell Devin about his little blackmail scheme. Considering Brandon's already been in trouble with the law, I'm pretty sure Devin will believe me. Although, if I do that, I risk Devin and my mom seeing the pictures, and without knowing all of what happened last night that could be dangerous. Plus, wouldn't I have to explain that an edible I suspect contained more than just weed is the reason this happened?

Argh! I hate that kid so much!

* * *

Brandon

My phone vibrates in my hand. A text notification pops up obscuring the zoomed in image of Deja's bare tits.
MACKENZIE: *Church was nice today! How're you liking Briarwood*

I dismiss the message and start pumping my fist again. In another few seconds, there's a second notification:
MACKENZIE: *BTW, you looked really good today at church.* ☐ *Did you enjoy the service?*

I sigh, cover my crotch with the nearest piece of clothing, and type out a response.

HE HATE ME

ME: *Thanks! Yeah, it was cool. Your school has a different vibe than my old one, though. Feeling a bit stressed with these classes.*

MACKENZIE: *Totally get that! I was not ready when I started there. It's so much harder than public school. But I'll help if I can... and maybe give you a little distraction.*

ME: *He-he. Does it get better?*

MACKENZIE: *So much better.*

Is she talking about school or something else? I almost hope this is about school, because it's kind of weird flirting with Mackenzie right in the middle of jerking off to another girl. My erection's softened a bit, but I'm still horny as fuck. I fully intend to finish as soon as we end this conversation.

Should I tell her I want a distraction? How likely is Mackenzie to send me a picture of her tits? Unlikely, but that's the only kind of distraction I'm in the mood for right now.

ME: *I don't know. Calculus is rotting my brain. I'm not feeling a lot of hope about that improving.*

MACKENZIE: *No worries! I can help you with calculus. I'd love to tutor you.*

ME: *You don't have to do that.*

MACKENZIE: *I want to. Unless you don't want to hang out with me.*

ME: *Of course I want to hang out with you.*

MACKENZIE: *Great. Call me tomorrow, okay?*

ME: *Sure thing.*

I wait a minute to see if she'll send another text and when I'm sure she won't I navigate back to Deja. I queue up the video to the point where I propped the phone on the pillow. I can see her face, her shoulder, and one of her breasts.

SENCHA SKEETE

I wrap my hand around my throbbing dick and stroke from root to tip. The faint glow of my phone screen casts a blue hue over my skin. My fist moves rhythmically, my pulse quickening as I watch her face reflect the pleasure I was giving her.

I can see everything I missed while my head was between her legs. She bites her bottom lip, her face twisted with pleasure. My hand enters the frame as I pull her nipple, causing it to stretch and strain against my touch. I hadn't realized at the time, but a steady stream of encouragement is flowing from her lips.

As we both build towards climax, she turns her head and looks directly into the camera. She makes the ahegao face—crossing her eyes and sticking out her tongue. Then she winks, her tongue still extended. In that moment, I lose all control is as I imagine wrapping her braids around my fist and forcing her to her knees. I see those large dark eyes gazing up at me pleadingly, her pink tongue still stretched out like a welcome mat.

I stroke myself harder and faster, my cock throbbing with the memory of her laughter, that soft hazy look she wore last night lying in the grass. I imagine her on her knees, begging for me, licking her full lips. She cups her breasts, pinching her hard nipples between her fingers. On the screen, her body convulses in ecstasy, and her face contorts in sheer joy. I groan gutturally, and come with her, maneuvering my discarded t-shirt over my dick just in time to prevent my semen from painting the ceiling.

HE HATE ME

I toss the T-shirt in the dirty clothes and pull on some clean underwear. Next time I watch the video, I think I'll put it on my computer monitor so I have both hands free. I've jerked off three times today, and I can't remember being this horny since the days when I first hit puberty and I was little more than an erection with a pair of legs attached.

I like sex, but I'm not obsessed with it. I have plenty of more serious things to worry about than where to put my dick. But now that I've tasted Deja, it's like something woke up inside me. Maybe I'm just excited at the possibility that I've found someone who can give me what I need. Of course, I don't know if that's true yet, but I have a plan. That little wink gives me hope that inside that vapid self-righteous shell is a woman who can handle all of me.

But not yet, obviously. It's going to take time and coaxing to get her there. In the meantime, Mackenzie is giving me eager vibes. I suspect she's ready to go. And won't it piss Deja off something fierce to see me with her friend and not be able to do anything about it. There's nothing like jealousy to bring out the worst in a woman, and since Deja's worst is what I want, I think this will work out just fine.

Chapter 6

Deja

I DON'T SLEEP VERY WELL ON SUNDAY NIGHT, MY MIND going over and over the things that Brandon said to me. When I'm not trying to infer what happened the night before, I ponder what Brandon wants from me. The obvious answer is sex. I haven't missed the intense way he looks at me, nor the frequent glances at my tits and ass. But that seems too straightforward. After all, he's asked me to keep out of his way so he can pursue Mackenzie, so why come after me? Could he be that insatiable? I'm pretty sure he hasn't hooked up with anyone since he moved in, unless he wasn't really with his mom the two Saturdays he went home. But even then, twice in two months isn't a lot of sex. I'm just not able to find a conclusion logical enough to calm my uncertainty, and that anxiety keeps me up late into the night.

I'm finally able to fall asleep around 2:00 am. When my alarm goes off at 5:30, the last thing I want to do is get out of bed, but I drag myself through my usual run, then waste twenty minutes figuring out what to wear. No skirts, no low-cut tops, no button downs. Nothing that could be interpreted as easy-access, basically. I settle on jeans and a T-shirt that I got at church camp a couple years ago. It's so cringe, but if anyone asks, I'll say it's ironic and if I know people they'll pretend to get it even if they don't. Of course, the real reason is to make Brandon think of church and hopefully feel too guilty to ask for anything too outrageous.

By the time I get downstairs, Brandon has already left. One of his friends from soccer gives him a ride to school every day because they have the same practice schedule. I've only seen the car, not who drives it, but I wonder if it's one of the guys from Saturday night. Carmello was cute, and I found his number on the floor mat when I was cleaning out my car yesterday.

The more I think about it, the more I like the idea of texting him. Brandon's messing with Mackenzie and forcing me to butt out, well turnabout is fair play. See how he likes me talking to one of his friends. I find the piece of paper in the cupholder when I get in my car to drive to school and stick it in the pocket of my backpack.

SENCHA SKEETE

* * *

I spot Mackenzie, Lorelei, and Shelby hanging around my locker when I get to school. Mackenzie is cute in a short denim skirt and cowboy boots. Her red, off the shoulder top sets off her dark hair perfectly. She put a little extra effort in today, and I wonder if it's for Brandon's benefit. I want to ask, but that feels like it could be opening a can of worms. Lorelei and Shelby are wearing everyday uniform of most girls on our team—yoga pants and a hoodie. Sometimes we mix it up with jeans or sweatpants, but we don't usually dress up like Mean Girls or anything. Looking like we're trying wouldn't be cool. This is the Midwest; people don't wear flashy jewelry or runway fashions. Well, except for the uber-richies like Rourke van der Hoff and his friends, who weren't born around here. They dress like they think we're in New York or Monaco or something. For those of us from here, it's all about quality brands and understated style. My three friends are deep in conversation but stop to give me quick hugs as I walk up.

Hey girlie, love the shirt!" Mackenzie says with more than a trace of sarcasm.

I point at the tacky, bedazzled cross on the front of it with both index fingers, and give them a little curtsy. "You know me, just keeping it holy."

The three of them laugh.

"What's the tea, ladies?" I ask, twirling the combination on my lock.

"Just talking about who's taking who to homecoming," Shelby says. "I can't believe it's only two weeks away!"

"Ugh, don't remind me," I groan. I've been nominated to homecoming court, but I really haven't had time to campaign. I was supposed to be going over the flyer designs with Mom last night and planning the treat table, but I was so distracted, I forgot. "I still don't have a date."

"Really?" Lorelei looks surprised. "Throw a rock and you'll hit a guy who wants to go with you."

"But do I want to go with him?"

We're interrupted by Gio sauntering up to our group. He leans casually against the locker next to mine and gives us that crooked smile that makes all the girls swoon.

"*Bongiorno bellezze*," he says smoothly. "I see the stars have come to Earth."

Mackenzie and Shelby giggle while Lorelei tosses her hair over her shoulder flirtatiously. I resist the urge to roll my eyes again.

"Hey, Gio," I say. "What's up?"

"I am drawn to all this beauty; I could not resist to say hello." His smile encompasses all of us, but he leans against my locker in a way that forces me to angle my body towards him.

"Deja, *bellissima*" he says, lowering his voice as if sharing a secret, "you glow like the sun today."

His eyes travel down my figure, and I fold my arms over my chest, silently laughing. I'm dressed like an awkward twelve-year-old and even with make up on I look tired AF. Mackenzie and the other girls are watching eagerly, waiting to see how I'll respond.

"Thanks, Gio, but we both know you say that to all the girls," I reply dryly.

He grins, and it's like we're sharing a private joke; he knows he's a flirt, and he knows I know he's a flirt. "Not all the girls, and I mean it most with you."

I can't help smiling at his cheesy response. He reaches out and brushes a braid back from my face. His fingers linger for a moment against my cheek. I'm actually disappointed that I feel nothing. Brandon makes me tingle; Gio's touch leaves me cold.

He winks before pushing off from the lockers. "See you soon, Deja."

"When are you going to put him out of his misery?" Mackenzie asks, her eyes on his departing figure.

"Gio flirts with anything that moves. You know that."

"Yeah, but he seems extra thirsty today. I think he wants to ask you to homecoming."

I scoff. Last week I'd have been pleased, maybe even excited to hear that, but today I have other concerns. I'm on tenterhooks about what Brandon will ask me to do, and the anxiety is taking up too much space in my mind and body to leave room for much else.

I close my locker, and as the first bell rings we head to our first-period class. It's English, and I'm looking forward to it because my teacher, Mr. Lewis, is one of the few here who isn't just going through the motions. It's an excellent school, but most of the teachers lost their enthusiasm for kids before I was even born.

HE HATE ME

* * *

I float through most of the morning in a daze. After fourth period I reluctantly walk back to my locker, barely paying attention to the people around me. There's a sinking feeling in my stomach that I hate. When I get to my locker to stash my books, I look at my phone like I always do. I think I'm stalling a bit as well. We're not supposed to have phones at school, though most people keep them on them anyway and try to be discreet. I got detention freshman year and my phone confiscated, so I'm not going to risk it. I can wait a few hours to see social media updates, and if it's something really important my parents will call the office.

I do always take a quick look before lunch, though, just in case one of my friends texted me. That's what I'm focused on when Shelby pops up next to me, her pale blonde ponytail swinging.

"I heard they have chicken fingers today," she says, cheerfully. "I know we're not supposed to eat fried food, but they're so good."

"Oh," I say, looking up from the screen. "I have to skip lunch today. I have a thing in the library."

"A thing?"

"Like a project."

"But you have to come. What if somebody was going to ask you to homecoming?"

"They can ask me tomorrow." Shelby is so cute. She's not dumb—hardly anybody at this school is—but she's really naive. Everything is simple and uncomplicated to her.

SENCHA SKEETE

"Okay, well," she says, backing away in the direction of the cafeteria. "I hope you don't miss out." She does a little wiggle with her neck and shoulders that makes me laugh. She gives me a wave and hops away towards Lorelei, who is waiting at the end of the hall. I turn my attention back to the phone. There's a text from Brandon (filed under AH) telling me to meet him in the classics section.

If you went to a regular high school, this probably sounds weird to you, but Briarwood has the kind of huge two-story library you'd usually see on a college campus. Our library is a neoclassical monument to learning (I'm quoting the brochure here) constructed of Indiana limestone and white marble. The facade features columns and friezes that conjure the symmetry and grace of ancient Greek and Roman public buildings, yada, yada.

Here's the takeaway—it's huge and there are a lot of little nooks and crannies where you can have a private conversation. The classical section is right next to a set of private study rooms, so maybe that's where we're meeting? I'm not necessarily looking forward to being alone with Brandon, but at least if we're in one of those rooms we won't be overheard. It would be beyond mortifying for anyone to find out that he had something over me, even if they didn't actually know what.

It takes five minutes just to get to the library building. I push through the heavy wooden doors, pause for a moment, still overwhelmed after three years by the grandeur of this space. The ceilings soar thirty feet to a glass domed roof. Sunlight streams in, giving the room a bright, airy feel. The

HE HATE ME

foyer alone is about 1000 square feet and around it, wooden shelves extend in both directions. Large oak tables lie in rows from front to back of the room, stopping in front of a grand staircase leading to the second floor. Just inside the entrance is the check-in desk, where one of the librarians sits, sharp eyes focused on her computer screen. She glances up at me and I hand her my school ID, which she quickly scans. My tennis shoes make the occasional squeak against the polished marble floors, earning me curious glances from a few of the kids at the tables. I jog up the stairs to the second floor, aware that I only have forty-five minutes total for lunch, and I've already burned through ten.

I spot Brandon at the end of a long row of shelves, holding a hardbound book. His expression is serious. What is he reading? I doubt he knows Greek or Latin. Those aren't exactly at the top of the list of subjects to include in a public-school curriculum, especially not at a school like Marshall.

He places the book on a library cart as I approach, looking entirely too pleased with himself.

"I wasn't sure you were coming," he says, unlocking one of the study rooms with his student ID. You have to reserve them in advance, and I guess he was lucky enough to find one available this morning. He's wearing all black—a plain t-shirt, worn-looking canvas pants and work boots. I wonder if the all-black clothing is a deliberate choice to intimidate me.

"Wouldn't miss it," I say scanning the room.

There's a square table and four chairs. There's nothing else in the room except a small built-in bookshelf. It's very quiet—probably soundproofed—and fairly private. There's a decent-sized glass window in the door, but no one can overhear what you're saying. His backpack is lying on the table.

He plops down in one of the chairs and motions for me to sit. From the bag, he pulls a thick sheaf of papers inside a glossy pocket folder. He pushes it across the table at me.

"What's this?"

"That's homework and class projects for the rest of the semester. Due dates, book lists, handouts, everything's in there."

"You've lost your mind."

"Be glad that's only the stuff we're assigned ahead of time. I could be giving you the day-to-day homework, too."

"Won't they notice there's two sets of handwriting?"

"No. You're going to get everything to me at least a day early so I can copy it. Or if you're smart, you'll type up anything that can be typed up and email it to me."

He's grinning, but I'm not remotely amused.

"I can't. I have too much to do already."

"I'm sure you can find time."

"When? I have school, cheer, club commitments, chores. I'm sure you've seen my planner. There is literally no time."

"Club commitments?" He scoffs. "I'm sure you can drop some of that."

"I can't," I insist. "Everything I'm doing is to get into the college I want to go to. I picked every one of those things for a reason. I can't drop out of anything."

You're going to think I'm silly when I tell you I was panicking, but I've had my eye on a particular university for the last five years. I got into Briarwood to boost my chances of going there. I can't throw away five years of effort just because Brandon is too lazy to do his own school work.

"I can't," I say.

"And yet you have time to go to parties?"

"I need a social life. I can't just work, work, work all the time. I'd lose my mind."

"That's too bad, because you have to give me something, Deja, and the list of things with equal value is very short."

He stands up and comes around the table, sitting on the edge of it next to me. He's so close I can feel the heat coming off him and his masculine scent envelopes me. I don't want to be aware of him like this, but I can't help it. His muscular thigh is inches from my hand and there's a noticeable bulge at his crotch. I can't tell if he's turned on or just larger than average, and I'm embarrassed that I even noticed that.

He slips his hand into the collar of my shirt and pulls out the cross pendant I always wear. The feel of his skin against mine is electric. My instinct is to pull away, but his other hand is on my shoulder, practically pinning me to my seat.

"What do you want?" I ask through gritted teeth.

"You."

"What?!"

"I want you to do whatever I want whenever I want. You can take the place of all the fun I won't be having because of this workload."

"Yeah, of course. Wasn't it like two days ago you said you didn't need to blackmail girls to get sex, but here we are."

SENCHA SKEETE

"Why do you think I'm talking about sex?" He lets go of the pendant and dragging his finger along the neckline of my t-shirt. I'm finding it harder to breathe, tingles skittering across my skin from where he's touching me. There's no reason his touch should make me feel anything, but the tingle is migrating across my chest and lower until I want to squirm in my seat. The hand that was holding my shoulder cups the back of my neck, his fingertips slipping between my braids to pet my scalp. With his other hand, he tips my chin up. His eyes are darker than I've ever seen them.

"Then what are you talking about?" I hate the soft, raspy sound of my voice.

"TBD." He stands up and stuffs the folder into his backpack. "But since you're not helping me with this, I'm going to take Mackenzie up on her generous offer of free tutoring. Don't make it a thing."

"Fine."

"Also, do you know when the next parental date night is?"

"I think it's Friday. Why?"

"I'll need you to help with something while they're out."

"There's a football game on Friday."

"I'll meet you after the game."

"I made plans with the girls for after."

"Cancel them."

"I—"

He pats the backpack and shrugs.

"One or the other, Deja."

I nod reluctantly, though I'm determined to find a way out of this. I expected him to have his phone on him, to taunt me with the pictures giving me a chance to snatch it. Now I don't know what my next move will be. I could bide my time and hope he'll eventually leave it unattended. I'll have to watch him closely, figure out his lock screen password before I do, though. I didn't even consider how I'd get access to the pictures if I snatched the phone. My plan was pretty cringe. Snatch a phone from a guy a head taller and sixty pounds heavier? Waiting and looking for the right opportunity is a much better strategy. In the meantime, I'll have to play along and let him think I've given up resisting him.

"Fine. I'll meet you after the game."

He swings his backpack over his shoulder and turns towards the door. It's a trick, I realize, as soon as I stand up and he turns around, now only inches from me. He cups my face, rubbing his thumb across my cheekbone. I can't read his expression, but his focus is on my face, like he's searching for something. What does he want?

"You can relax. This has nothing to do with sex."

"I don't know if I believe you."

His thumb traces the outline of my lips, calling him a liar. I have no control over my body's response. My nipples tighten, and a quick glance confirms they are poking through the thin fabric of my bra and t-shirt. My eyes draw his and he grins, that smug look that I want to slap off his face.

He leans down to my ear and whispers, "We are gonna fuck. But only after you beg me for it."

SENCHA SKEETE

"I will never…" But I don't finish the statement because he opens the door, and I don't want to risk someone overhearing me. He exits the room, leaving me all kinds of fucked up inside. What the hell is going on? Why did my own body betray me? I want to deny it, but I can't any longer. I'm attracted to Brandon in a way I'm not attracted to Gio, or even my ex-boyfriend, Jayden. It makes no sense. Brandon doesn't even like me. Maybe he wants me, but even that isn't for sure. He may just be messing with me for his own amusement. He does seem like exactly the kind of person who would do that.

With a sigh I start walking back to the main building. If I hustle, I might just have enough time to buy a sandwich and a sports drink from the vending machine before the end of lunch.

Chapter 7

Deja

THE NEXT DAY, MACKENZIE STARTS TUTORING BRANDON and it's super uncomfortable hearing her voice drift down the hallway from his room. She's using her breathless, flirty voice a lot, which is really annoying. When she drops by my room on the way out, though, I say nothing negative about it, just gossip about homecoming and a few other things. She lets slip that Brandon is way behind the rest of his class. Of course, no one suggests it's cause white boys just aren't any good at math, but I need to be less bitter. Hate the game, not the player. Well, I hate this player, but for entirely different reasons.

SENCHA SKEETE

Our schedules keep us apart for the rest of the week. I'm at cheerleading practice or some other extra-curricular and he's got soccer. I'm busy trying to keep up with everything, so I don't have a lot of free time to be worried about what Devin's ward is getting up to.

Maybe that's not quite accurate, though, because I've started texting Carmello, initially to spite Brandon, but I'm finding that I really like him. He's so damn cute and he sends me pics of him with no shirt on that would have any girl drooling. He's really cut, kinda like Brandon, but unlike Brandon he's not a complete asshole. He's got that kinda thick muscle, where Brandon is a little leaner. He's funny, too. He's already tried to edge things towards sexting, but I've been holding off, not only because it's kinda soon, but because I'm still flirting with Gio. I'm feeling a little guilty, because I know I won't make Mello my boyfriend. If things were different, I'd probably let Shelby have a go at Gio and see if Carmello wants to start dating me.

I can't get Shelby's sad little face out of my mind. Every party we've been to she doesn't tear her eyes away from Gio whenever he comes into the room, and when he and I are talking she looks like she wants to die. So yeah, Gio is one of the most popular boys in school and he is openly and undeniably interested in me, but Shelby has been my friend since first grade when I was the only Black kid in the class and some of the other kids weren't sure about me. She is sweet and kind and she hasn't had a boyfriend yet. I feel like even if Gio doesn't want her and she doesn't say anything directly, I'd be a bad friend to get more serious with him.

HE HATE ME

I get a text from Carmello on Thursday,

MELLO: Wanna hang out this weekend?

I'm about to text him back that I'm busy, when I hear Mackenzie's fake laugh. I know that laugh. It's the one she uses to make boys think she thinks they're hilarious. Why shouldn't I hang out with Mello? I don't have to make him my boyfriend, but wouldn't it be nice to see the look on Brandon's face when he sees Mello and me together?

ME: I'm going to a party at Brayden J's house on Saturday. Wanna come?

MELLO: Sure. Where's he live.

I text him the details and smile smugly. See how Brandon likes the shoe on the other foot.

* * *

The game on Friday night is a disappointment as usual. We did well last year mostly due to Jayden, who was a pretty good quarterback. With him gone, the team is back to their usual mess. We lose 19-0. The guest team is exuberant and obnoxious as they steam out of the game. Briarwood fans gather their blankets and empty soda cups and leave more slowly, the mood subdued. I don't make it out to the parking lot until about twenty minutes after the game.

I'm tired and lugging my gym bag. I tell the girls I can't join them for burgers after the game like I usually do. Lorelei gives me a weird look. It's the second time in a week I'm bowing out of activities I usually take the lead in, and I wonder what she's thinking. I don't really have much time to ponder it before I get to my car to find Brandon waiting for me. He's bent over his phone, his backpack over one shoulder and his hip propped against the side of my car. He looks around when the car beeps before he spots me and smiles in a way that heats my skin.

I say nothing to him as I stash my bag in the trunk and walk around to the driver's side door. Lorelei's Jeep pulls up with Mackenzie hanging out the passenger window.

"Hey guys," she yells, "Brandon, you wanna come get burgers with us?"

Did she just invite him alone? I mean I know I just told them I can't make it, but I'm kind of annoyed that they just went, okay, fine, but let's ask Brandon to come without her. Before I can say anything, though, Brandon responds.

"We can't," he says. "Her parents are making us come home."

I don't know why, but I like that he said "we."

"Why?" Mackenzie asks.

"I don't know." He shrugs. His facial expression is kind of cold, and I can see it bothers Mackenzie. She shrugs, too, pursing her lips, then says something to Lorelei I can't hear. She tells us bye and they leave. We get in the car, still having said nothing to each other.

Brandon rests his hand on my bare leg, just below the hem of my tech skirt.

"Relax," he says, giving it a light squeeze. "Nothing bad is happening tonight, okay."

Before I can tell him to take his hands off me, he's already putting on his seatbelt and adjusting the seat for his overly long legs. I guess he thought touching me on the leg

HE HATE ME

would be calming, but it's the opposite. The low-grade anxiety I've been carrying around all day just ramped up higher.

"If you want me to not worry," I tell him, reversing out of the space, "touching me on the thigh without asking is probably not the right way to go about it."

"Okay," he says, sounding amused. "Should I add that to the list of things not to do until you beg me?"

"Yes." My voice is firm, but now he's grinning as he reaches for the radio.

"Nah," he says, casually. "I think I'll just do that whenever I feel like."

"You're a pig!"

He laughs, turning up the volume. It's a hip hop station and I try to ignore him, letting the beat and flow relax me.

"I'm hungry," I say as we approach a strip with a bunch of fast-food restaurants. The light from the street lamps flickers through the windows—light, dark, light, dark. "Can we hit the drive through?"

"I'm not really in the mood," he says. "I can make you something when we get home."

"You cook?"

"Of course. You don't?"

"I do, a little, but I'm a girl."

"I don't think it's a boy-girl thing," he says. "At some point we're all going to be living on our own and we should know how to take care of ourselves."

"Did your Mommy teach you that?"

"She did. Taught me how to cook, clean, the works. I do most of the cooking at home, actually. She…ah… Anyway, I don't mind making you something. What are you in the mood for?"

"Burgers," I say, because that's what I always have on Friday nights. It's a special treat for me because I have to watch my diet all the time.

"I'm sure I can do better than that."

"Okay," I don't see the point of arguing about it.

We pull into the driveway a few minutes later, the house dark. Brandon gets out and helps me with my bag before we head inside.

"I'll be right back," I tell him, running upstairs, leaving him alone in the kitchen. Feeling a little grimy, I take a very quick shower, slather on some lotion, and get dressed in an oversized tee and an old pair of leggings.

In fifteen minutes, I'm back downstairs. Brandon is chopping something on the counter. He sniffs in my direction and smiles.

"Vanilla," he says.

"You're making something with vanilla?"

"No." He chuckles. "You wanna get some plates out? It's almost ready."

"That fast?"

"It's a simple dish."

There's a sizzle as he tosses whatever he was chopping into a pan. The smell of garlic fills the kitchen. I place the plates on the kitchen island and get cutlery out of the drawers. The sizzling intensifies again, and I peek over to see that he's added halved grape tomatoes to the pan.

"You want something to drink?"

HE HATE ME

"Got beer?" he asks, as if Devin and Tanisha Thompson wouldn't tan our hides for drinking their beer.

"I've got sparkling water."

"That's fine."

A few minutes later I'm presented with a plate of pasta. It smells amazing and I'm totally impressed. He even serves it with a sprig of fresh basil on top. He sets his plate next to mine and sets down some extra grated Parmesan.

"This is good," I tell him after taking a bite. It's bowtie pasta with a bunch of chopped vegetables. The pasta is perfectly cooked, and the flavor is amazing. "You really know what you're doing."

"I told you," he says, grinning.

I'm still really curious about what he wants from me tonight, but I decide to just wait for him to tell me when he's ready. I am really hungry, and I give the food all my attention. It's quiet in the kitchen except for the hum of the refrigerator and the clink of silverware on porcelain. I glance over at him sitting next to me. He's wearing a faraway expression, focused on a spot high on the opposite wall. He takes a bite and chews, his firm jaw tightening. I notice his hands, large and long-fingered with blunt-cut nails. I suppose he feels my eyes on him because he turns his head, meeting my eyes frankly.

"What's your favorite color?" he asks.

"Why do you want to know?" I'm mystified by this question. What's his angle.

"It's just a basic getting to know you question."

"What if I don't want you to get to know me?"

103

"Do you need to make everything a fight? It's a pretty innocuous question. What's your favorite color?"

"Bite me!"

"Happily. But I thought you might like just telling me something about you instead of me putting my mouth on you."

Fucker.

"Yellow."

"No, it isn't."

"How do you know?"

"Cause you don't have a single yellow item in your room. You hate yellow."

Observant.

"So why ask me? You probably already know."

He sighs. "Just tell me."

"Purple. I know, it's cheesy, but I like purple."

"What shade?"

"Brandon!"

"Come on..."

"It's a bluish purple, but with some shimmer. Like this."

I pull out my phone and show him a picture of a piece of fabric I've been considering for my prom dress. A smile plays across his lips.

"Mine is forest green," he says, and starts clearing the table. I put my hand over my glass to let him know I want to keep it.

"I didn't ask," I tell him.

"You don't have to ask," he says. "I don't mind telling you."

HE HATE ME

"Let me help you clean up," I say, sliding off my stool.

"That's not necessary."

"So you can say I wasn't raised right? Uh unh."

I wash the dishes and he dries, making quick work of the task. It's only a couple of plates, a cutting board, two pans, and miscellaneous kitchen tools. He goes into the family room when we're done, and I follow him after I've wiped down the counters. Is it time, then, for whatever mysterious task he wants me to do?

"I've got a couple questions for you," he says.

"Okay…"

"Do you know if there are any old pictures or mementos, stuff like that in the house?"

"Why?" That's not a suspicious request at all. Is he planning to steal something, I wonder. I mean I don't have any idea why he was in juvie. He kind of hinted it was for SA, which I find totally believable, but then again, he might have been trying to intimidate me. And I have to believe that my mom and Devin wouldn't knowingly let a rapist move in with us.

"When my mom got fired it was really sudden. She had been feeling sick and she wasn't really paying attention to whether she got everything."

"Why doesn't she ask Devin for them?"

"She didn't exactly say she wants them back, but I know she does. Sometimes she'll talk about some photo albums she lost or some of my baby stuff—like I had this engraved rattle. I thought it would be nice to find that stuff and surprise her for Christmas. I've kind of put her through a lot this year."

105

SENCHA SKEETE

I look at Brandon in surprise. This sounds so thoughtful. Almost too thoughtful.

"I'm supposed to believe you're blackmailing me to help you find a present for your mom?"

"I'm not trying to say I'm a nice guy, Deja, but she's my mom. She's all I have."

"What happened to your dad?"

"He left when I was two. He got remarried and has a new family in Missouri. He just hung us out to dry, and then started over fresh like nothing happened. I've seen him once in the last ten years."

"Wow! That sucks."

"I figured you would understand. Your dad—"

"My dad is dead, Brandon," I reply. "At least your dad is still alive."

I see his shock, like he didn't know about my dad, but it's quickly replaced by an anger I just can't understand.

"If you won't help me," Brandon says, glaring at me, "then we're back to you completing my assignments."

"I can't—"

"So option three, then." He pulls his phone out and opens the media app. I stifle the impulse to snatch the phone, only too aware of the size difference between us. He sits too close to me, putting his arm around my shoulder and positioning the phone so we can both see it. On the screen I'm lying on my back topless and he's next to me on his side facing the camera. I think it's a still until he touches the screen, and it starts playing.

In the video, his hand lightly caresses my bare tummy.

HE HATE ME

"How are you feeling, baby?" he asks.

My response is too low to hear, but I can see him smile at whatever I've said.

"You like when I touch you?"

"Yeah." My voice is clear this time. It's so much worse than I thought. I suspected he had pictures of me passed out on my bed, maybe even ones where I was totally nude, but not this, not a video that makes me look like a willing participant.

"Stop it!" I hiss, reaching for the phone. He pins me to his side with his free arm as the video keeps playing. In the video he's touching my breasts and I'm letting him. Worse, I hear myself asking him to touch me more intimately, to use his mouth on me. I lash out with my fist, hitting his arm hard enough that the phone flies across the floor, ending up under the coffee table. He grabs both my arms, holding me there and I have to listen to my own voice encouraging him.

"Stay here!" he says, and I nod. He retrieves the phone and stops the video. When he sits down again, he's a few feet from me. My hands are shaking. I feel so violated.

"How could you?!"

He ignores the question, all trace of softness having left his expression. I guess the guy who wanted to know my favorite color has left the premises.

"So, like I said, pictures, mementos." His voice is maddeningly calm.

"In the basement."

"I've checked the basement."

SENCHA SKEETE

"The unfinished part of the basement. They keep the door locked. There's a bunch of boxes. I know my mom stashed some of our papers and pictures down there, so that would be a place to check."

"Where's the key?"

"It's in the junk drawer." I go over and retrieve it, handing it over reluctantly. I'm not worried about what might be down there, I just feel defeated. My social life will be destroyed if that video gets out. There is no way for a high school girl to weather a sex tape; we always get blamed and labelled sluts, even if it just shows us doing the same thing every other girl is doing.

"How much more video is there?" I hate how small my voice sounds.

"There's more," he says, "but as long as you're doing what I ask, you don't need to worry about it."

"I want to see it."

"I don't think that's a good idea."

"I have a right to see it!"

"I think it would upset you and you're already upset. Maybe another time, okay. Can you show me the boxes? I may need some help finding the right box."

I nod reluctantly.

We spend the next hour in the basement, separating the boxes into different piles. Based on how dusty the area is, I'm guessing no one ever comes down here. I don't know why Brandon doesn't want our parents to know he's looking for something, but suspicious as I am, I have to go along with him. There are a lot of boxes, but we make significant progress before he calls a halt. I kind of regret showering, because I'm now covered with dirt all over again. We both shower and change and are back downstairs watching a movie from opposite sides of the sectional when my mom and Devin get home. They barely spare us a glance as they grab bottled waters and make their giggly way up to bed. I follow them up within minutes. I can't stand to spend even five more minutes with Brandon.

* * *

Brayden is a football player, and his party is pretty chill, just a few people hanging out including most of the football team and all the cheerleaders. So not that small, honestly, but still relatively chill. I'm sitting with Gio and Shelby, when Carmello and CP, whose name I now know is Devonte, walk in. Carmello's looking fly as fuck, fresh fade, dripping outfit, a tattoo I haven't seen before peeking out the cuff of his shirt when he takes his jacket off. He smiles at me and for a moment I forget where I am till Gio says,

"Who's that?"

I startle and immediately feel ashamed.

"They're Brandon's friends from the soccer team," I explain. "I'm going to say hi."

I don't wait for him to respond before I go over and greet them. I give each of them a quick hug. I feel pretty bad because I completely forgot I invited Mello and have been flirting with Gio all night, mostly to distract myself from all the Brandon drama. I lock my arms through theirs and take them over to meet the host.

SENCHA SKEETE

"Hey Brayden," I explain, "this is Mello and Devonte."

"Von," Devonte corrects me.

"Von. They play soccer."

"Wow, that's cool," Brayden says. "You guys must be really good. Do you know Carter?"

"Sophomore? Yeah, he's fast."

"He's my brother. I don't think he's here, though. Probably somewhere in the woods with his dopey friends."

"You're fast, too," Von says, "I was at the game last night."

"Fast doesn't mean much if your quarterback can't throw for shit." Said quarterback is playing beer pong only a few yards away. "I wanted to play soccer, but I just wasn't good enough."

"I get it," Mello said, "I gotta tell you, it wasn't easy getting on that team." They start talking about local youth clubs and competitions and I'm rapidly losing interest.

"You guys want a beer?" I ask them. "I'll go grab you a couple."

"You don't have to do that."

"It's fine. I need one too. I'll be right back."

As I walk by, I see Mackenzie and Brandon on a loveseat all cozied up. I feel a pang of jealousy. He puts his hand on her shoulder and whispers something in her ear, and she giggles. I don't even know why I want to smash her face in so badly. It's not like I want Brandon for myself. But what he was doing with me on that video a week ago, I think it's not cool that he's all over Kenzie like that. It's gross.

HE HATE ME

In the kitchen there's a tub with ice and lite beers. I stoop to get us each one and when I turn around Gio has slipped into the room. This is one of those older houses with the kitchen closed off from the rest of the house, and we're alone in the fairly small room. He steps closer, and I don't move. I'm standing there, near the back door, holding two freezing cans in my hands and something about the way he's looking at my face holds me firmly in place. Gio's been saying that he likes me, but the heat in his expression makes it real. His dark eyes are filled with intensity. He takes one more step and then his lips are on mine, cool and soft. Why kiss me now? We've been hanging out at parties like this before, but this is the first time he's made such a bold move. I pull away instinctively, not sure why I do it. Don't I like Gio? Shouldn't I be enjoying this?

The beer cans slip from my fingers and bang loudly on the tile floor. His eyes search for the cans, and as he bends to pick up the dropped beer, I see that Brandon and Mackenzie are standing in the doorway. Mackenzie winks at me, but Brandon's expression is stony.

"…beers," Mello says, appearing behind them in the doorway. His eyes go from me to Gio and there's a flicker of something that makes my stomach drop, because I do like Mello, but the slight shake of his head tells me that I might have blown it. I don't even understand what I'm feeling. My body is hot with embarrassment, and there's something like loss from what I'm seeing on Mello's face. Which boy do I want? And why do I feel like it may be neither. Do I like the way jealousy made Gio more forward or is it weird that he didn't even try to kiss me until he thought another guy was in the picture? And what about Mello seemingly giving up without a fight (if I'm not just reading too much into a flinch). Doesn't he like me enough to fight for me?

I don't know what I want, and my mind is still whirling while I get Mello and Von drinks, and we all head out onto the back deck at Mackenzie's suggestion. Gio puts his arms around my waist and asks the soccer players about themselves. His questions are general and focused on the sport itself, but his attention is locked on Carmello. I let my mind drift, enjoying the way the cold air feels against my heated skin.

"You're on," Brandon says, smirking, bringing my attention back to the conversation.

"What?" I blurt, forgetting myself for a moment.

"Me and Von vs you and Carmello," Gio says, clasping hands with Brandon in that macho way that guys like to do. It's a quick dap and then they all pile down the deck stairs onto the cold, nearly icy grass of Brayden's back yard.

"Are you guys kidding?" I say. "You don't even have cleats."

"We got everything we need, babe," Gio says, laughing. "I got mine in my trunk. You guys got yours?"

"Hell yeah, we do," Mello says.

"This is stupid," I say to Mackenzie as the boys set up folding nets and shit in the backyard. People start filtering outside onto the deck. I wrap my arms around myself. The cold isn't as soothing anymore.

"It's Gio's fault," Mackenzie says, as if the fact that he and I are talking somehow makes me responsible for his

HE HATE ME

decisions. "He was saying how Americans can't play 'football' and Italians are the greatest. You know Brandon wasn't going to take that sitting down."

Brandon. But this isn't about Brandon at all. This is Gio's roundabout way of starting a fight with Carmello, which is stupid since he doesn't even know for sure there's anything between me and him. Gio has been a bit of a Lothario so far, but I wouldn't have pegged him for a hothead.

They start playing and right away I can tell that this isn't Gio's first rodeo. He's not as tall as the other guys, but he's fast and agile. In the backyard floodlights I can see Von kind of hanging back and watching his teammate. The first couple of times Gio tries to pass to him he's a little slow, but it doesn't take them long to find a rhythm. Brandon and Mello don't even look at each other, but their big bodies dominate the pitch. It's not that they're slow, but their energy is all efficiency and patience. They break up a long pass and nearly score before Gio races like a speed demon to stop them with a wild kick that sends the ball smashing into the side of the house. The loud slap makes me jump, but they all laugh and bump into each other like oversized toddlers.

They go back and forth for a little bit, Brandon and Mello clearly dominating, and finally kicking the ball into one of the little nets. I see Gio spit on the grass and wipe sweat from his forehead and then his eyes lock with Mello's. I can't say what passes between them, but it's not good. Gio rolls his shoulders and pulls his long-sleeved t-shirt off, leaving his surprisingly toned torso bare to the mid-40s air. Mello follows suit, those acres of amazing skin and rippling muscles sheeted with sweat. Brandon and Von exchange a confused look and then Brandon shakes his head, locking eyes with me. Whatever happens now, he's going to blame me.

Chapter 8

Deja

MORE THAN ANYTHING AT THIS MOMENT I WANT TO TURN ON my heel and run. Straight through the house, out the front door, and into my car. Forget that I'm Shelby's ride. Forget that these are my friends. Just turn away from whatever is about to happen in my name and drive away as fast as I can. Instead, I fold my arms and cock my head nonchalantly, looking for all the world like I don't particularly care about what's happening in front of me.

Brandon's lips tighten and he drops back into a defensive position. Gio whispers something to Devonte and they slap hands. The next few skirmishes are quick. Gio pushes forward towards the other goal, almost like he's playing 1:2. Von gets into position for a pass a couple of times, but Gio ignores him, losing possession twice to Brandon. The lack of teamwork makes them easy to dominate, and it should reassure me, but I just can't shake the feeling that something is going to happen that I won't like very much. Finally, Gio acknowledges Von, passing the ball forward to him. He dribbles, eyes focused on Brandon's approach. His foot snaps and the ball sails across the yard to Gio, whose body seems to float upwards, his feet off the ground as he heads the ball towards the goal. It's a crazy move with the little practice goals they're using, but the ball drops like it's being drawn forward by a magnet. Brandon throws himself sideways, trying desperately to intercept, but it's too late. The score is tied.

Shelby shoots me a nervous look. There is a smattering of applause and I think this is where most people were expecting this impromptu backyard soccer match to wrap up, but the four guys don't look like they're ready to quit. Mello flexes his muscular shoulders and spits on the grass. Mello and Gio stare at each other intensely, eyes narrowed, and jaws clenched. I've heard that some women are flattered by having men fight over them, but I'm telling you this is not it. Take away Brandon's annoying ass and I'd still be unhappy about this. It's a fine line between people seeing you as a hot girl that guys want and seeing you as a duplicitous bitch who leads them on. I close my eyes and take a deep breath, wanting to shut out the whole situation.

HE HATE ME

There's a collective inhalation and I refocus on the guys. I missed whatever caused the group to react, but now Mello has the ball and is spinning around, his long arms swinging outwards from his body. He kicks the ball down the grass and chases after it, no one in position to stop him from scoring. Just as he closes with the ball, Gio slides in at an angle, clipping Mello at the ankle and entirely missing the ball. I'm not an expert on the rules of the game but based on everyone's reaction that is not an okay thing to do. Mello's legs fly out from under him, his body flipping up into the air. He lands awkwardly on his right side, and Gio turns the ball around going for the other team's goal.

Only no one is paying any attention to Gio anymore. Brandon and Von are rushing to check on Mello, whose face is twisted in agony. I'm down the stairs too, before I can really think about it. I get there just as a couple of other guys from the soccer team do. Brandon shoots me a hard look as I crouch next to his friend. Mello is sitting up, but his ankle does not look right. His breaths are coming fast and sharp.

"What do we do?" someone asks, above my head.

"Is it bad?" another voice says.

All I can think is that Mello is hurt, and that it's my fault. I didn't tell Gio to do any of this or even give him a solid reason to think that there was something between Mello and me, but if I wasn't talking to both of them Mello wouldn't be lying on the ground right now with an injury that's probably going to keep him from playing the rest of the semester, if not longer.

Just like that I lose it. I'm on my feet and in Gio's face forgetting for the first time in a long time that everyone is watching me. I jab him in the chest with my forefinger and he jerks backwards, a confused look on his face.

"What the fuck is wrong with you?" I yell, shoving him hard. "Are you crazy?"

"It was an accident," Gio says, his fingers half curled. No palms up, nothing soft there—he's angry.

"I don't believe you," I scream, shoving him hard again. He takes a half step back, but not as much as I'd like. I want him on his ass, but he's too strong and too mad.

"Fuck you!" I grind out and stalk off towards the stairs. I should stay with Mello and make sure he's okay, but I'm so angry I'm afraid of what I'll do. I can hear the crowd murmuring behind me, and someone calls my name, but I don't stop till I'm locked in the downstairs half bathroom. The last person who used the toilet didn't flush it, and the hand towel is pooled on the floor below the loop where it's supposed to hang. I'm breathing fast in and out and the assault of unpleasant odors is immediate.

There's no bathtub to curl up in, no calming scent of ocean breezes or fresh linen, just a huge mirror above the sink reflecting my dark eyes and pinched lips back at me. Out of nowhere comes a memory of my father yelling at my mother, "Your problem is that you don't know what you want," and my mother replying, "No, David. The problem is that you won't accept it."

I shake my head, feeling disoriented. Where had this come from and what did it mean? The voices were angry and there was fear attached to that memory. Had my parents fought? From my mother's description of him, even from the way other folks who knew him had talked about him, my dad had been near perfect. All my memories of him are pleasant. He taught me to ride a bike and helped me with my homework. He had a deep rumbly voice and I liked to press my ear to his chest and feel what he was saying.

"Are you in there?" Shelby's tentative voice drifts under the door. It's followed by an equally repressed knock. I sigh and crack the door open so she can slip through. The smile she gives me is a little sad, but sympathetic.

"Are you okay?" she asks, resting her hand lightly on my biceps. I nod and fight the urge the pull away. It's not that I want to reject her affection, I'm just feeling raw.

"Is Mello okay?" She frowns. "Brandon's friend," I clarify.

"I don't know," she replies. Her nose wrinkles and she glances at the toilet. I shrug and flush it. The smell of strong pee begins to dissipate. "I think they decided to take him to the ER. Brandon and the other Black guy already left."

"That fast?"

"You've been in here for nearly fifteen minutes."

I frown. That doesn't sound right? "I must be..." I stop myself from finishing the sentence. Why give voice to the idea that I might be mentally unstable. I rub my eyes tiredly.

"I'm just tired." I AM tired, drained actually.

"What was all that about?" she asks, eyes rising to meet mine. This is pretty bold for Shelby, but I let her have it.

"What do you mean?"

"Those two guys were…they were like fighting or something. And then you got mad at Gio. Are you dating both of them?"

"Wow!" I say, letting my eyes bug out. I push my way out of the bathroom to see that a lot of people have left, but there are still plenty of bystanders. "You really think I would lead two guys on like that?"

Shelby flushes, her pale complexion doing nothing to hide the rush of blood to her face. It's not a pretty blush. She's splotchy and red. "No," she sputters. "I mean—"

"Whatever, Shel. No way I'm screwing around like that; you know that." I turn around to see that Gio is standing down the hallway, right between me and the room where we stashed our coats. His face is stony. I look right at him when I continue. "I just think that my friends should be mature enough not to act like children and hurt others when they get up in their feelings. Especially when we're just friends."

Not breaking eye contact until I pass him, I walk straight ahead to grab my coat and leave.

Chapter 9

Deja

BY THE TIME I GET HOME AFTER DROPPING SHELBY OFF IT'S close to midnight. Brandon is standing in front of the house, tucked into the blind spot where the doorbell and courtyard cameras don't quite cross. Clever, I think grudgingly, because he hasn't lived in the house that long but already knows its secrets. His eyes meet mine, dark and hot. I feel like they could burn through me. My usual armor is thin, like a sheet of rice paper, offering me no protection. I don't want to talk to him.

As I walk towards the door, I pretend not to see him, but he snags my arm and pulls me into the shadows with him. I glare right back at him, all my frustration and hurt coiled to strike out.

"Let me go," I hiss, trying to pull my arm away, "we're going to miss curfew." He doesn't let go; he turns me around, pushing me further into the corner.

"Why don't you ever fucking listen," he says quietly. It's not a question. It's a reprimand.

"Maybe I'm not hearing anything worth listening to."

"How can you be so stupid?" He looms over me, much too close, and I can smell his body, turning ripe with sweat and musk from the earlier exercise. I shouldn't like it, but I do.

"What do you want?" I ask, my voice full of hostility.

"How about for you to act right," he says.

"I didn't do anything wrong," I insist. "Mello getting hurt was fucked up, but it had nothing to do with me."

"You're the one who invited Mello, correct? He came to that party to see you."

"So what? It's not any of your business, anyway." He shakes his head and fists his right hand. His bicep bulges. I can't help my reaction: I retreat, coming up against the brick wall behind me. You'd think I waved a red flag in front of him. He advances until our stomachs nearly touch. His arm is laid against the wall next to my head, fist still clenched. It takes effort not to turn my head and look at it. There's an ache behind my ears that I recognize as the sudden rush of blood to my head.

"Leave my friends alone," he says, menacingly.

"I am not doing anything to your friends."

HE HATE ME

"So you haven't been texting Mello?"

"I can text who I want. Since when is texting people a crime?"

"Do you get off on guys fighting over you?" he asks. The suggestion is offensive, but I won't let him know that I'm bothered by it.

"Oh, yeah," I say. "That's me. Big, bad woman making them do whatever I want. I'm so good I turn men's brains off."

"Shut up," he says. It's not the cleverest retort and I roll my eyes.

"Make me," I taunt.

He presses closer, our bodies flush now, and his free hand comes up and wraps around my throat. He's not squeezing or even holding me tightly, but my heart begins to hammer in my chest. My eyes are level with his neck, and with him this close I can't see his face. I tip my head back and our eyes lock. The intensity there scares me, and I don't have time to react before his lips come down on mine, my gasp of surprise letting his tongue in.

I try to turn my head, but he won't let me. His lips are soft, his breath clean, and the heavy press of his body against mine feels right.

"Stop," I say, moaning into his mouth.

He pulls away but doesn't let go of my throat. His eyes are wild. "I don't know what to do with you. I warn you, you know exactly what the consequences are, but you don't listen. If you're not going to follow the rules, then why am I holding back?"

"Holding back from what?" I ask, though a part of me already knows.

"This," he says, and he dips his head to kiss me again. His tongue invades my mouth with a desperation that shocks me. All week I've felt like Brandon was toying with me, like a cat tormenting a mouse, but this is pure hunger. The wall bites into my back as Brandon presses me against it, his hips grinding into mine, my soft body molding to his hardness. The kiss is deep and messy, our tongues dueling in a dance that makes my insides melt like butter on a griddle. He tastes like beer and smells like sweat and grass and male arousal. My knees feel weak. His hand on my throat loosens just enough to slide around my neck, pulling me up onto my toes. The arm goes around my waist, hoisting me up so our bodies align, chest to chest and hip to hip. The bulge I feel pressing into me cannot be real. No one's penis can be that long or that thick.

"You guys coming inside?" Devin's voice breaks through the haze of desire; he's poking his head through the front door. Brandon steps into the light, giving me a moment to gather myself.

"Yeah," he says, shoving his hands into his pockets.

"Aren't you cold?" Devin chuckles.

"We had kind of a weird night," I say, stepping out of the shadows. "One of our friends got hurt."

Devin's steps outside, his face showing concern. "What happened?"

"He and another guy were playing soccer in the backyard and he…they…"

"Carmello broke his ankle," Brandon says flatly.

"It's broken?" I ask, dismayed.

"Yeah," Brandon says. "Pretty sure."

I say nothing else. Devin must see that I'm uncomfortable, because he gestures for me to go inside. I hear the door close behind me and a part of me wants to look back, to see if Brandon's face reflects any of the confusing emotions churning inside me, but I don't.

I go to my room and shut the door, leaning back against it as my mind races. Why did Brandon kiss me like that? I'm not totally surprised that he kissed me—he's been subtly threatening to all week. But I wasn't expecting that out-of-control need, the hunger I sensed in his touch.

Is he just messing with me? Trying to throw me off balance? Or could he actually have feelings for me? I think back to the desperation I felt in that kiss, the raw need pulsing through his body. It didn't feel like a game or manipulation. But with Brandon, it would be foolish to let down my guard.

I touch my fingers to my lips, still tingling from the pressure of his mouth. My heart is pounding as I remember the way he pressed me against the wall, his muscular frame pinning me in place. I've never been kissed or touched like that before. A part of me was terrified, but another part felt thrilled by his dominance.

But he's blackmailing me and he's talking to Mackenzie. Two very solid reasons this can't happen between us. And yet it's happening. I close my eyes, and I can see the hunger in his eyes as he broke away from the kiss. Hear his ragged breathing in my ear. Feel the heat of his body molded against mine.

My phone vibrates with an incoming text. I frown, wondering who would text me so late at night. The text is from Brandon, and it reads, "You will receive discipline." What the heck does that mean? My brain is confused enough with the kiss we just shared. I send back a text with multiple question marks, but he doesn't reply right away, and I'm tired. I climb into bed and let sleep take me.

* * *

I wake up a few hours later, disoriented by the darkness, wondering where I am. My bedroom is pitch-black, but it doesn't feel right. The mattress is too firm, and there are unfamiliar smells in the air—new carpet and the overwhelming sweetness of a plugin air freshener. Panic sets in as I realize I'm not in my room anymore; I'm in the basement guest room. My hands are bound behind my back with something soft like a scarf or a T-shirt, and duct tape covers my mouth.

Brandon looms over me, holding a dim flashlight, his features half hidden by shadows. The bedside lamp flickers on and I'm blinded for a moment by the sudden influx of light. Brandon sets the flashlight down and sits next to me on the bed, his friendly smile belying the situation we're in. I try to scream, but the tape over my mouth is very effective. Barely a squeak gets out.

HE HATE ME

"Shh," he says, stroking my thigh the way you'd pet a cat. "Don't be scared. I'm not going to hurt you. Well, I'm not going to hurt you, hurt you."

He must see the way my eyes bug out at the words, but he doesn't react to that. He leans closer, sniffing my hair.

"Mmm, coconut," he says, then burying his face in my neck, "and vanilla. I love the way you smell. So edible." There's a sharp sting as he nips at my collarbone with his teeth. My heart is pounding so loudly I can hardly hear my own thoughts, much less focus on what he's saying. I guess he's monologuing now, like a true villain. He frowns at me, cocking his head to the side. He stops talking, and strokes my face gently, breathing slowly and deeply until I find myself matching him. My heart slows down, much of the tension easing from my chest and limbs.

"Are you hearing me now?"

I nod watching him warily.

"You need to know you're safe with me, Deja. Everything that's happening right now is for you, to help you. Do you understand?

I shake my head, no. He sounds like a lunatic who's trying to gaslight me.

"I set clear boundaries for you, correct? I told you to stay away from my friends. I told you to do what I ask you to, but instead you're defiant. Mello is hurt because of your desire to what? Feed your ego?"

I shake my head vigorously. He holds me by the neck with one hand and uses the other to peel off the tape. It stings a little, but not as much as I expected. There's a warning squeeze, reminding me that he's got his hand on my throat and can cut off my air supply if I decide to scream.

"Why did you do it?"

"I forgot I'd invited him," I say hoarsely.

"How did you get his number?"

"He gave it to me last Saturday."

"And when did you call him?"

"I texted him on Tuesday."

"And you knew I didn't want you to."

"I guess. I kind of remember you saying something, but I was high. How is that fair, though? You're dating my friend, so why can't I date yours?"

"What do you expect me to do when you defy me, Deja? I'm betting you don't want me to post your sex tape online, so we've got to find some other way to maintain discipline, don't we?"

"I won't do it again," I say hastily. The word "discipline" sounds ominous enough without me being tied up.

"I'm giving you a choice. Discipline or humiliation."

"When you say humiliation…?" I swallow roughly, acutely aware of his hand on my neck.

"I release the video." An unacceptable option.

"And discipline?"

"Whatever I decide. That's the point I've been trying to drive home all week. What I want in exchange for keeping the video secure is your obedience. Your complete obedience." I bristle at the word. I hate the idea of just doing whatever I'm told. Not even my mother has ever gotten my complete obedience.

HE HATE ME

"What if I do all your assignments? I'll make time, I swear."

"It's too late for that. Twice I gave you the opportunity and you turned me down. Now choose: discipline or humiliation?"

I imagine a college admissions office getting their hands on that recording. Or a potential employer five or fifteen years from now. It would forever hang over my head. It's not even a choice.

"Discipline."

"I'm so happy to hear that," he says. He strokes my shoulder gently. He stares at my lips for a second like he's going to kiss me, but then seems to change his mind. He reaches over to the bedside table, and I wrench my head around to see him picking up a roll of tape. "I know this isn't that comfortable, but you might have a hard time staying quiet and we definitely don't want to be overheard. Press your lips together; not too hard. Just relax."

He cuts a piece of tape off with a small pair of scissors and tapes my mouth again.

"Can you breathe okay?" I nod. Adrenaline is pumping through my body at this point. Why does he think I'll have a hard time staying quiet? Just because I agreed to this (was coerced into it) doesn't mean I'm not scared out of my gourd. Brandon seriously frightens me. He acts cool and removed most of the time, but I know there's a core of barely contained rage underneath. Even Mackenzie has sensed it, though she finds it sexy. I don't know how you confuse scary and sexy.

SENCHA SKEETE

"I'm going to take your pajama bottoms off now. If this becomes too much, or you want me to stop all together, just kick your feet and I'll stop."

I kick my feet immediately and he laughs, his smile almost indulgent.

"I meant I'll stop and give you a breather. You need to take your punishment like a good girl, okay?"

I nod. My heart is thudding in my chest. Too late to back out now. Brandon reaches down and hooks his thumbs inside the elastic waistband of my pajama pants. He slides them down my legs, then over my feet. I'm left in nothing but a camisole and underwear.

"I'm going to spank you over your panties," he says, "as a warmup."

My forehead crinkles at his words. Spank me as a warmup? A warmup to what? He doesn't appear to notice my reaction.

He flips me over so that I'm facedown across his lap and positions my arms so they're resting above my buttocks. The cool air hits my bare skin and goosebumps rise across it. His hand rests lightly on my ass through my underwear, and it feels like a branding iron even before he starts spanking me.

Smack! The first slap falls, harder than I expect. My eyes squeeze shut, and a muffled scream escapes through the tape. Brandon's other hand immediately soothes the sting away with his palm.

"Breathe through it, Deja. Breathe," he coaches. I take a shaky breath and exhale, trying to focus on anything but the pain throbbing across my bottom.

Smack! Smack! "You know why you're here, right?" he asks, punctuating each word with a spank. "No? I'll remind you." *Smack! Smack!* "You were disobedient." *Smack! Smack!* "You were selfish and careless, and that got Mello hurt."

The room starts to spin just a little bit, but I keep my legs spread apart and my ass in the air for him as he hits me over and over again. Tears leak out from behind my closed eyelids and drip onto the comforter below.

"I said breathe!" Brandon growls, sounding angrier than before. I gasp for air, sucking it in through my nose and willing myself not to cry too much. He may have control, but that doesn't mean I have to let him see me weak. *Smack! Smack! Smack!* "And when I'm done, you'll thank me for this."

I glare at him through my tears. If looks could kill, he'd be reduced to ashes on the floor. He gives me a final sec to regain my composure before continuing. "You ready for the real punishment, princess?"

I shake my head violently, but he doesn't stop. He wedges his fingers into the elastic of my panties and pulls them down to my knees. Cool air envelops my heated cheeks, and I can feel him staring at me, probably enjoying my humiliation. Vulnerability has never been my strong suit, but here I am, nearly naked in front of the guy I love to hate most. Well, maybe love isn't exactly right... Lust? Hate lust? Whatever it is, it's twisted and wrong and I'm starting to like it way too much.

SENCHA SKEETE

His hand slowly extends towards the bedside table, his fingers gracefully wrapping around a familiar object. My heart races as I see that he's holding a wooden spoon, its smooth handle and round bowl gleaming in the low light of the room. Dread settles in my stomach as I know what this means—more pain.

He takes his time positioning me just how he wants me on his lap again. "This is where you stay until I tell you otherwise," he says, running the cool wood along my now bare bottom.

Thwack! The first swat would have shifted me off his lap all together if it weren't for Brandon's grip on my wrists. *Thwack!* The second one stings just as bad, if not worse. *Thwack! Thwack! Thwack!* I try to twist out of his hold, but his grip only tightens.

"Stay still," he growls in my ear, before delivering another series of spanks. Tears stream down my cheeks faster now, mingling with sweat. *Thwack! Thwack! Thwack!* The spoon lands on my cheeks again and again, creating a rhythm that would be almost hypnotic if it didn't hurt so damn much.

The pain starts to build, my nerve endings on fire as he methodically covers every inch of my behind with hard, stinging swats. My ass clenches and unclenches involuntarily, and that's when I feel it—an ache between my thighs that catches me off guard.

As much as I don't want to admit it, humiliation aside, it feels... good. God, I hate him! *Thwack!* I flinch at the sting that shoots through me.

HE HATE ME

"You like that?" Brandon pauses, his breath hot against my ear. I shake my head, feeling his hand firm at my waist, but he doesn't believe me. He chuckles darkly before continuing his assault on my bottom.

Thwack! Thwack! Thwack! The pain is unbearable, but with each swat, the ache between my legs intensifies. I can't believe I'm aroused by this. *Thwack! Thwack!* The spoon bites into my tender skin, but it's no match for the fire between my legs.

"I knew it," Brandon says smugly, delivering one last hard smack before tossing the spoon aside. "You're just like me." I can't deny it anymore—I'm hot, needy and soaked between my legs.

Brandon's breathing is labored as he lifts me onto my feet and presses himself against my me from behind, his arousal evident. He grinds against me, his cock hard and throbbing against my ass. His hand glides down my side, gently caressing the same cheek he just spanked seconds ago. The pain has been joined with an insatiable need for him—a need that trumps all logic. He whispers in my ear, "Can I kiss you?"

Under the thrall of this unfamiliar passion, I nod. He pulls off the tape and traces my lips with his thumb. Brandon's lips are fierce and hungry when they meet mine. His tongue teases mine, devouring me like a starving man.

His hands roam, fondling my breasts through my thin camisole. He pinches my nipples, causing me to moan into his mouth, and the sting shoots straight to my core. This shouldn't turn me on, but it does. It feels so damn good. His fingers slip under my shirt, finding my naked breast while his other hand cups my ass, squeezing the punished cheeks.

The pain and pleasure meld together into a sensation that ignites my body even as it shuts off my brain. I can't get enough of him—his taste, his touch. I have never in my life given in to my id like this, and it's glorious. Our tongues twine together as he deepens the kiss, probing and exploring every inch of my mouth.

He spins me around and guides me to the bed, sitting me down, my hands still bound behind my back. His fingers deftly loosen my bonds, but instead of setting me free, he coaxes me up onto the bed and secures my wrists to the headboard. My arms are stretched above my head, my breasts thrust skyward.

His hands explore my body, squeezing my breasts and pinching my nipples, sending a jolt of pleasure straight to my core. I'm reduced to a puddle of desire in his arms. He kneads my breasts roughly, and the sensation is almost too much to bear.

"Stop," I beg, but it comes out as a whimper. He only laughs and continues to fondle me. The pain and pleasure are a heady mixture, leaving me reeling and dizzy with lust.

Brandon leans in, his breath hot against my ear. "I've always wanted to do this." His voice is a growl, and it sends shivers down my spine. Before I can protest, his lips are on my breast, sucking and biting through the fabric. He bites down harder, the sting turning into a delicious ache that shoots straight between my legs. The sensation is indescribable—exquisite agony.

"You like that, don't you?" he asks, his tone smug as he looks up at me. His eyes are dark with lust, and I can't find the words to respond. All I can manage is a whimper of agreement.

He returns to my other breast, lavishing attention on it as well. His teeth graze against the sensitive skin causing a well of desire to pool between my legs. My hips buck up, seeking more contact with him. He chuckles darkly before moving his mouth higher, trailing passionate kisses over my neck.

"Brandon," I gasp as his fingers trace the neckline of my camisole. He pauses, his gaze locked with mine, waiting for me to stop him—but I don't know if I want him to anymore. Lust owns me now, and logic is far from my mind as he slowly slides the camisole down so that it frames my breasts like two dainty teacups on a shelf.

Brandon's heated gaze drinks me in. He takes one pebbled nub between his lips, sucking gently at first, then increasing the force until I'm moaning his name. His other hand explores my body, leaving a trail of fire in its wake. Each touch sends me closer to the edge, but I'm still achingly aware of my virginity.

He looks up at me again, pools of lust swirling in his eyes.

"Tell me to stop," he commands, his tone so neutral I can't tell what he wants. I take my best guess.

"S-Stop," I manage to gasp out, and excitement flares in his eyes. With deliberate slowness he plumps my breast with his hand and captures the sensitive peak in his mouth. He sucks harder and harder until I can't help writhing against him in agony and ecstasy, struggling to stifle the cries that would bring our parents down on our heads.

A light dawns: he asked me to tell him to stop just so he could walk right through my no. And I love it. Instead of being angry I'm more turned on than ever. What's wrong with me? If any of my friends told me they were acting like this, I'd think she was brainwashed. But the body doesn't lie. My pussy is practically drooling. Thankfully, I'm too turned on to be embarrassed by how wet I am.

Brandon continues his ministrations, alternating between sucking and biting my nipples while his fingers roam lower, teasing my slick skin. I arch my hips in response, desperate for more contact. His hand slips between my legs, caressing my swollen folds, but with a growl of frustration, Brandon stops short of where I need him most.

The sudden absence of his touch is almost painful. "Tease," I pant. I spread my legs wider, raising my hips in a shamelessly attempt to rub myself against him. He doesn't tear his eyes off me as he removes his shirt and pajama pants. He's wearing dark boxer briefs through which I can see the outline of his erection. It's scary big. I can't imagine that thing fitting inside anyone, but the shape of it still intrigues me.

Tentatively, then with more confidence, his finger breaches my core, my slick arousal easing its entrance into my tight passage.

"Is that okay?" he asks, slowly pumping it in and out.

"It's good," I tell him, gasping. He goes a bit faster, his thumb making occasional contact with my clit on the upstroke. I push my hips forward to meet his fingers. Our tongues wrestle, wet and hungry. The burn of a second finger inside me is less urgent than the fire in my veins, the need to be closer to him, to consume him and have him consume me. I rock my hips, encouraging him to plunge deeper and faster inside me.

His erection is hot against my hip. He's thrusting against me, his hips stabbing in a rhythm that nearly matches that of his fingers.

"This feels amazing, Little Thorn," he whispers hotly into my ear, "You feel so good, so tight, so wet." Each word seems to excite him more. His fingers burrow deeper into my channel. I let myself imagine what it would be like, his thick, heavy shaft stretching out my little pussy. I'm going out of my mind with arousal and I'm honestly not sure how much longer I can hold out. I know it's the worst idea in the world, but if he wanted to have sex with me right now, I'm not sure I could say no to him. Yet the notion fills me with fear rather than anticipation. Just two of his fingers are stretching me as much as I can take, and his cock is so much bigger. It would rip me in two.

He palms my sore ass, his touch rough and jerky, the grips me behind the knees, using one hand to force my knees towards my chest.

"Squeeze your legs together."

"What?" I'm confused, and his two middle fingers probing my pussy don't help.

"Knees together," he says, even as his large fingers hook inside me reaching something that feels incredible. When I don't move, he pushes my legs together and rubs his hand over my slippery sex. His wet fingers land on either side of my clit, giving it a gentle pinch. My hips move of their own accord, rubbing the sensitive little bud against his hand.

He pulls his boxers down, and a moment later his cock pushes between my legs, the shaft compressed by my legs and the underside running along the furrow of my cunt. The head bumps into my clit, producing the hottest sensation I've felt in my life. He pulls back and thrusts again, groaning while he mashes my clit. I grind my hips, working my smooth thighs and wet slit against his shaft. We're so close to fucking and yet we're not and it's still incredible. He tells me how good my body feels and how much he likes the way I move, how wet I am, and the sounds of pleasure I'm making. He swirls his fingers over my clit and my orgasm hits me like a tsunami. I'm bucking and shaking under the weight of his body, crying out and he's thrusting, using my thighs, my lubrication, my pussy lips to get himself off. A groan rumbles through his chest and spurt after spurt of hot come coats my pelvis. His hand goes back to my clit and uses the slippery ejaculate as lubrication to force another orgasm out of me. It's painful and mind-melting. Tomorrow, I'll worry about that much come on and near my pussy, but tonight I'm reeling with pleasure and so drained I fall asleep in the wet spot.

Chapter 10

Deja

"Deja!" my mom yells and I jerk awake. I panic for a second before I realize I'm back in my room, in my own bed. I'm under the covers dressed in my pajama bottoms and a faded gray tee instead of the camisole I wore last night. The surest sign that last night wasn't a dream, however, is the soreness in my nipples and ass.

"You're still in bed?" I mother asks, coming into my room. "It's after 9:00. Hurry up. We leave in twenty minutes."

I'm tempted to tell her I'm sick, but after what happened last night with Gio and Mello, I feel like I need to show up to church just so no one thinks I'm hiding out of guilt.

SENCHA SKEETE

Brandon is back to his usual self. You would have no idea by looking at him that anything had happened between us last night. He's sitting in my pew, flirting with Mackenzie. He gives me this half-smirk when she's not looking, and I feel a horrible sensation of insecurity in my gut. How should I interpret the way he's teasing Mackenzie? He didn't make any promises to me last night, but he was so passionate. My whole body feels hot when I think about it. It had started out as blackmail, but by the end I'd completely given in to him. I had acted like a slut, so it shouldn't surprise me he's moving on. Guys only like a challenge, after all.

After the service, Mackenzie and I go freshen up in the bathroom. She looks really pretty in a navy skirt and blue and white striped sweater. Her makeup is on point too, and she's got on two-inch heels. I want to ask, "Why are you trying so hard?" but I know why.

"Are you and Brandon talking?" I ask her while we check our hair in the mirrors.

"Yeah," she says, smiling. I give her a fake smile in return, but she knows me too well. "What? Why are you making that face?"

"No reason," I say, innocently. I pull out my lip gloss to redo my lips even though they look fine and we're about to have snacks anyway.

She grabs me by the shoulders and turns me to face her. "What. Is it?"

"It's nothing," I insist. "You guys aren't even really dating, right?"

HE HATE ME

"Whoa, whoa, whoa," she says. "You don't even like Brandon and you're covering for him? That's some bullshit."

"I'm not covering for him."

"Then what is it?"

I sigh. I need to get my shit together. "I think you should talk to Brandon, okay."

"What do you know? Does he have a girlfriend?"

"No," I say too quickly. "I mean, I don't think so."

"So what is it, then?" she presses. "You saw something, or you heard something. What was it?"

"This is none of my business," I say, turning towards the door. She grabs my arm again, holding me in place.

"I thought I was your friend," she says, hitting me where it hurts. This is so fucking messy. How did I get myself into this situation? If I'd just remembered to dis-invite Mello from the party, the last fifteen hours would have been a whole lot simpler. No injury, no spanking, no almost having sex with a guy I hate.

"I am your friend," I say. "And as your friend I'm telling you to talk to Brandon."

I leave the bathroom before she can stop me again and find my mom and Devin. I notice when Mackenzie makes a beeline for Brandon, but I turn my back on that because I don't want her to wave me over or for Brandon to give me the stink eye.

It occurs to me I may have made a mistake. What if Brandon decides I did something wrong again? My ass barely survived the last spanking. I can't handle another one any time soon.

141

SENCHA SKEETE

* * *

The rest of the day I'm on tenterhooks. I'm sure Mackenzie told Brandon something. She texts me after church to thank me for giving her the heads up, so I guess the talk didn't go that well for Brandon. Between my Sunday chores, I text Gio to see how he's doing. His responses are all one or two words. He is clearly mad at me, probably because I yelled at him in front of all our friends. I can understand why he's upset. Mello sends me a three-part text telling me the details of his injury and how he's doing.

The entire afternoon is spent on chores, and I don't really see Brandon since he's raking and bagging leaves and I'm cleaning the bathrooms and dusting. We sit across from each other at dinner, chewing quietly through bland chicken breast and underdressed salad while my parents talk. He doesn't so much as glance at me till the meal is nearly over, but when he speaks, I am shocked.

"Deja's going to start tutoring me," he says, looking only at Devin. "Kenzie can't anymore, so she volunteered."

"That's really nice of you," my mom says, smiling. She sounds both surprised and happy, probably because she thinks this means we're getting along better.

"I…" I trail off. Brandon is giving me a hard look, as if daring me to contradict him.

"Why can't Mackenzie tutor you anymore?" Devin asks, clocking the tension between us.

"She's getting overwhelmed with all her commitments," Brandon says. "And since Deja lives here, we figured it would be easier."

What do I say? I am up to my neck in commitments too, but I can tell from Brandon's expression that if I call him a liar, I'm going to regret it later.

"We don't want Deja to be overwhelmed either," Devin says, training narrowed eyes on Brandon. I'll give the kid credit. He doesn't even flinch.

"It's not too much, is it Deja?" The smile is syrupy sweet. Devin's eyes narrow even more, but I'm pretty cornered.

"I'll have to look at my schedule," I say lamely. I need to know Brandon's plans before I can push back.

"Let me know ASAP," Devin says. "I can always pay for a tutor if necessary."

"That's a great—," I start to say, but Brandon is speaking too.

"I don't know—." We both stop talking. Brandon is first to recover. "We'll work it out and let you know tomorrow." I nod, tension stiffening my shoulders. What does Brandon want, anyway? It's better for him to have a real tutor; he and I are in the same year. Why does he even want me? It's probably just some game to torture me.

The chicken breast is dry, but I choke it down anyway.

* * *

I've just finished putting my pajamas on when Brandon knocks on my bedroom door. He comes in and locks it behind him. I move to open it again, but he rests his forefinger on his lips to let me know he did it so we won't be overheard. I motion for him to sit in my desk chair.

"I don't want to tutor you," I tell him bluntly. His eyes flick up and down my flannel covered body, expression flat.

"I ended things with Mackenzie," he says by way of an explanation.

"What was there to end?"

"Not much. But she came over in a lather, asking me to define the relationship, so I defined it out of existence. Did you have anything to do with that."

"Not really." I try to defend myself. "I just asked her if you guys were talking. It's not like she was your girlfriend."

"Then why did she tell me you said I was seeing someone else?"

I cross my arms under my breasts. Am I feeling a niggle of guilt?

"I didn't say anything remotely like that; she just read a novel into my facial expression. I didn't mean to break you up."

"You didn't," he says, mildly. "I like someone else."

I feel my face heat.

"She got pissed, though, when I told her I just want to be friends and said she wouldn't tutor me anymore. I really do need your help with that."

He phrases it like a request, but I know it's not a request. I'm lucky he didn't punish me for talking to Mackenzie out of turn. I'm not going to risk another spanking.

HE HATE ME

"Of course," I say, swallowing bile. "We just have to work out a time. My schedule is pretty tight."

He grins, and I guess the words "pretty tight" have made him think of something else entirely.

"Come here," he says, "and turn around."

Reluctantly I walk over to him, turning to face away from him when I'm about three feet away. I hear the wheels of the desk chair scrape across the floor, then feel Brandon's hands on my waistband.

"What are you doing?eighteen

He pulls my pants and underwear to my knees, leaving my bare ass in his face. He asks me to bend forward a little and cups my bottom in his large hands. His palms are pleasantly cool on my tender skin. His fingers press into my flesh, just enough to make me flinch.

"How does it feel?" he asks.

"Sore," I tell him, "especially when you squeeze it."

He loosens his grip and smooths his hands over my butt.

"On a scale of 1-10, how much does it hurt?"

"Three, maybe?"

"You had no trouble sitting? You seemed okay at church and tonight at dinner."

"I'm just used to being sore, from cheer. Trust me when I say I'm still feeling it." I've learned to put pain out of mind when I have to, to just push it to the side and focus on the right now. On the minute I'm currently in.

Brandon lightly strokes the outside of my thigh. "You're beautiful," he says. I feel his warm breath on the small of my back, then soft press of his lips just above my buttocks. I freeze, afraid to move. I'm really conflicted. Last night, in the heat of the moment I gave in to my sexual desires, but the unequal power dynamic that I forgot about when my quim was doing the thinking for me is impossible to ignore. How can anything intimate between me and Brandon be positive when it's built on coercion?

I feel something cool land on the top of my right butt cheek. Gently, Brandon spreads it with his fingers, till all the areas he spanked are covered. He repeats the action on the other side.

"What is that?"

"It's healing ointment. It's supposed to soothe the skin and help you heal faster."

"Thanks."

"It just needs a minute to absorb. You can just stand there—I don't mind the view."

"You're a bit of a pervert, aren't you Brandon."

"You don't know the half."

"I know you like spanking."

"Spanking, discipline, sure, but what I really like is inflicting a little pain. When I take your virginity, it's going to be exquisite."

Forgetting that he can see my face reflected in the vanity mirror, I do nothing to hide my horror. Brandon steps closer, brushing my braids over my shoulder. He rearranges them, admiring my reflection in the mirror. His middle finger pushes between my butt cheeks, teasing my other virgin hole.

"Judgement from the girl who creamed when I spanked her and practically purred when I tortured her nipples? A little hypocritical there, Deja."

"I didn't do those things."

"I was there, remember. Not only do you like receiving what I like to give, you turned into a pool of goo when you asked me to stop, and I didn't. We're a match on multiple dimensions. You just have to relax and listen to your body."

"I would prefer to use my brain, thank you very much."

"It's not the easiest thing to accept your own deviance. It took me a long time to understand and embrace my kinks. I can be patient, Deja."

"Can I pull my pants up now?"

"Sure." Instead of letting me, though, he reaches down and pulls them up for me. He turns me around and hands me a bottle that reads, "Aftercare Skin Lotion."

"You can put this on morning and night for the next few days. It will soothe the skin and speed up healing. I put some on your skin after our session, or you'd probably be in more pain right now."

It's on the tip of my tongue to thank him for that, but why should I. He'd orchestrated the whole thing. Why should I thank him for cleaning up a mess that he made? Taking care of me had been the least he could do.

"Okay," I say, "I have some reading to do, so..."

"Okay. I'll see you in the morning." He gives me a little wink, then unlocks the door and exits.

Chapter 11

Deja

Monday morning, I wake up at 6:00 a.m. I usually get my day started with a run on the treadmill, but my ass is still feeling pretty sore. I wash my face and give the scrubbed clean surface an honest appraisal. There are slight bags under my eyes from a restless night. I spread some of the ointment on my butt and let it soak in while I do my makeup.

Staring at my reflection under the harsh, white light from the bulbs above the mirror, I wonder what Brandon sees when he looks at me. He called me beautiful last night, but he was probably just referring to my butt, which is 100 the best-

HE HATE ME

looking ass I've ever seen, if I do say so myself. As for my face I'm cute, but I don't know about beautiful.

After getting dressed, I go downstairs and sit at the breakfast bar to eat my egg whites and oatmeal. Brandon sits across from me. His gaze flicks down to my chest and lingers for a moment. My sore nipples perk up for him. I stare him down, and he shrugs, a hint of the smirk playing across his lips. He's so annoying.

"Mom," I say. "I'm going to Ms. Khadijah this weekend to get my braids touched up. Want me to see if Tina has an opening?" Tina does my mom's perm and cut. She works in the same salon as Khadijah.

"Sure," she replies absentmindedly, her attention focused on something on her iPad as she picks at her cut-up fruit. "Could you give Brandon a ride to school?"

"Um—"

"Mello can't drive," Brandon says, ruefully. It's my fault is what he's saying without saying, and this is not an argument I want to have in front of my mom. So I paint on my best fake smile.

"Not a problem. Meet me in 20 minutes."

* * *

"So, you're going to have to drive me to school for the next few weeks," Brandon yells, his head down as he fiddles with his phone. The open passenger window lets in a blast of cold air, making it difficult to hear anything over the loud wind. I keep my eyes focused on the road, determined not to let him see how much he bothers me.

SENCHA SKEETE

"Fine," I reply, raising my voice.

"What? I can't hear you," he shouts.

"Then close the window," I snap.

"What?"

I use the button on the driver's side door to raise the window and engage the child lock to keep it shut. As we approach campus, traffic starts to thicken. I'll have to navigate through a sea of fancy cars during the drop-off rush to reach the student parking lot.

"I said, fine," I repeat.

Brandon lifts his head, still hunched in his seat. "I'm not annoying you, am I?"

"Never," I lie, earning a wan smile.

"Well, I'm not sorry," he retorts.

I shrug. "Why would you be sorry? Like I said, I'm not annoyed." He begins adjusting the seat controls, moving it back and forth.

"I thought you'd ask me how Mello's doing."

"I know how he's doing. He texted me yesterday."

"You're still texting him?" Brandon's attention is fully focused on me now, scowling as he sits up straighter.

"He texted me. I'd like to text him back so he knows I'm not ghosting him."

Brandon shakes his head. "I told you not to mess with my friends."

"He's my friend too. And I'm not messing with him. Come on, Brandon. He's hurt and I feel like I kinda owe him…something."

HE HATE ME

"Nuh uh. Cut it off, or I'm going to text him some of those pictures."

"Pretty sure those pictures would make his day."

"Even the ones where we're...cuddling?"

"Are you jealous right now? Is this because you think I like Mello?"

"Then why are you trying to talk to him?"

"Same reason anybody would want to talk to him right now. Because he's my friend and he got hurt. I feel like I've said that already."

A loud honk sounds behind us as the traffic light has turned green. I pull through the intersection. Taking a deep breath, I compose myself.

"My ass is still sore, Brandon. I am not trying to get another licking on top of it. I just feel like it would be super rude not to get back to him. That's all it is."

"As long as that's all it is," Brandon says, giving me a stern look. I keep my expression neutral, but inside I'm feeling a little something. Has Brandon been jealous this whole time? Could that be the real reason he spanked me, because he thought I was into another guy, or even two other guys? It's kind of a weird way to go about it, though. And yet I have to admit without that spanking I probably wouldn't have fooled around with him.

* * *

When I get to school, Mackenzie and Shel are waiting for me by my locker. Kenzie looks hot as shit in a crop top, Levi's

SENCHA SKEETE

501s and an oversized jacket. She's giving 90s and I'm here for it. One of the football players winks at her as he walks by.

"You recovered quickly," I tease, opening my locker.

"She's actually just making sure he knows what he's missing," Shel says. Like me, she's dressed jeans, a t-shirt, and a hoodie.

"Did I see you guys come in together?" Kenzie asks, her eyes focused on the entrance.

"I have to give him a ride to school from now on." My tone is bitter. "He was carpooling with the guy who got hurt on Saturday."

"That sucks." I shrug. "Hey, Deja," Shel says in the tone of someone pretending that their question is spontaneous when it's anything but, "Kenzie told me you saw Brandon kissing somebody."

"No, I didn't. I told her to talk to Brandon."

"But why, though? What made you think he was cheating?"

"Cheating is a strong word. You guys were only talking for two weeks max," I point out, pulling a book out of my locker. "It was just a vibe. And by the way, Kenz, why are you making Shelby ask the questions you want answers to?"

Mackenzie gives me a disgruntled look.

"I hate being cheated on," Mackenzie says, petulantly.

"What even happened on Sunday?"

"I told him you told me there was another girl and I deserved to know if there was. And he said that he had been talking to someone and he really liked her. So I said I didn't like the idea that he was talking to somebody else. And he said, okay then, we don't need to be talking anymore."

Ouch! Poor Kenzie.

"Seriously, though, Kenz, it's not that weird to be to talking to two people at the same time. I was—" I catch myself just as I realize what I was about to say. Shelby looks at me with wide eyes and Mackenzie is shaking her head. She stops walking, forcing us to stop too.

"I knew it!" she says. "You were talking to Gio and that black guy. That's why they were acting aggro."

"I don't know," I answer. "I probably shouldn't have invited Mello to the party knowing Gio might be there, but I never thought Gio would act like that. I don't even think he really likes me."

"Really?" The hopeful lilt in her voice just makes me sad. You are too good for that guy, I want to tell her.

"That guy's just a flirt," Mackenzie says dismissively. "But going back to Brandon I guess you're right. It was barely a thing. I wonder who it is, though. Probably some fugly soccer chick."

"Or a ghetto chick from his old high school," Shelby says, brightly. She has the decency to blush when I give her some side eye. I can't sometimes with these white girls. First calling Mello "that black guy," now this?

"Can we focus on English right now?" I say, allowing some of my irritation to slip into my voice. "I think we've already given Brandon way too much of our time."

"True," Kenzie says, walking into the classroom and finding her seat. I take mine next to her, with Shel on my

153

other side. All eyes are on us, the boys admiring, the girls jealous or wishing they were us. The sensation of being watched settles over me like a familiar blanket. I sit up straight, school my features into a half-smile, and wait for class to begin.

* * *

I get to the lunchroom a few minutes late that day because I stayed back to ask my chemistry teacher a question. Mackenzie, Shelby and Lorelei are already at our table. Gio is standing next to it and talking to them. I can't see Mackenzie or Shelby's expressions, but I catch Lorelei's subtle eye roll. I wonder if he's going to ask to eat lunch with us. They know not to say yes to anyone before I get there. I don't like to be mean, but I will be if I have to be. I guess he's not as pissed anymore if he wants to sit with us. I wish I could check my phone to see if he's texted me, but of course my phone in my locker, and I was in a rush since I was running late.

By the time I grab my lunch and saunter over to the table, Gio is nowhere in sight.

"So then she says, 'If you can't figure out how to calculate the density of a liquid, I'm not sure what you're doing in this class," Lorelei says, and the girls all laugh.

"Hey, girls," I greet them, setting my tray down and joining the conversation.

"Hey, Deja."

"What's the deal with you and Gio?" Lorelei asks, pushing a French fry around her plate. She loves fries, but she's paranoid about gaining weight. She usually gets them, eats two or three, and then gazes longingly at the rest for the remainder of the meal. I always think, "Why even tempt yourself?" but it works for her.

"What do you mean, what's up?" I sound nonchalant because I really am. I had my reasons for talking to Gio, but I'm much less bothered by his giving me the cold shoulder than I'd expected to be.

"He was just over here acting like he'd never heard of you."

"What'd he say?" I ask.

"We told him you were running late, and he was like, 'Whatever, that's not why I'm here.'" I chuckle.

"Then why…?"

"He asked me to Homecoming," Shelby says in a small voice. She's as pink as a rose petal.

"Interesting…" I say, taking a bite of my salad. I debate whether I want to point out that he could have asked her in private but chose to do it in front of everybody after making sure everybody knew he didn't give a fuck about me anymore. I'm worried that this isn't about Shelby at all, and she really likes him. She could get hurt here. But if I say this in front of everyone, it will make her look stupid if they start dating, so I hold my tongue. I'll give her that warning when we're alone and let her decide if she thinks it's worth the risk.

"It's fine if you want to go with him," I say, smiling. "We're not together."

"Did you guys break up?" Lorelei asks.

"We were never together." I chuckle good-naturedly. "If you like him, Shelby, I say go for it. He wasn't the right guy for me, but he's not an asshole. I'd say give him a shot."

"It's just a dance," Shelby says in her usual small voice. She's trying to play it off like this isn't a big deal to her, but the look I share with Mackenzie assures me that I'm not the only one who noticed her crush on him.

"Does everybody else have dates?" I ask, lightly.

"I'm going with Jackson, of course," Lorelei says. They've been boyfriend-girlfriend since sophomore year, so that's not a surprise.

"I was going with Brandon," Mackenzie says, tightly, "but, ah, I changed my mind."

"That fucker," Lorelei says. "I can't believe he was seeing another girl the whole time."

"Who are you going to Homecoming with, Deja?"

"Jayden," I say, smirking. I haven't asked him yet, but my ex-boyfriend's college is only two hours away and he's always down to do me a solid.

"That's awesome," Lorelei says. "How's he doing?"

"Good."

I glance at the wall clock and notice that we only have another ten minutes of lunch.

"Hey," I say, getting an idea. "Why don't we get our hair and makeup done at Melodie Yang's house like we did for prom?" Our school isn't that big, so we have a junior-senior prom. All my friends went during our junior year.

"You mean trick her into paying for it again?"

"Do you want to pay for it, Kenz?" I ask her.

HE HATE ME

"Melodie!" Mackenzie yells, waving at a nearby table. "Hey, girl. Can you come over? What are you doing after cheer practice?"

* * *

It's almost 8:00 pm and near the end of long day before I have time to call Carmello. He picks up on the second ring, but he doesn't sound exactly excited to hear from me.

"How are you feeling," I ask him.

"Better," he says. He sounds tired. "Wish I could get something stronger than Tylenol."

"Are you in a lot of pain?"

"Some. But I'll be fine," he assures me.

"When are you coming back to school?"

"As soon as I get my hard cast on. Probably by Thursday."

"That's good." The conversation isn't flowing very smoothly, and I struggle to find the right words.

"I'm sorry for what happened," I finally settle on.

"Huh. Why? You didn't tackle me."

"I know." There's a brief pause.

"What was the deal with that guy? I know he's not your boyfriend, or Brandon would have told me, but you guys looked pretty cozy when I got to the party."

"Not gon' lie, we were kinda talking." I hear the sigh through the phone.

"I thought we were talking," Mello says.

"We were," I admit.

"But you're going to keep talking to him?"

SENCHA SKEETE

"No," I insist. "I'm definitely not talking to him anymore." I consider for a moment whether to tell him about Gio asking Shelby to Homecoming, but it might sound like that's the reason I stopped talking to Gio.

"Cause he got all jealous?"

"Nah," I say. "Maybe. He was acting the fool on Saturday. That's a whole mess I don't need."

"I want to be happy about that, Deja," Mello says, "but I don't really like that you were talking to another guy and didn't tell me."

"Why would you think I wasn't?" I shot back. "We haven't even known each other for two weeks. Shit, you haven't even asked me on a date."

He doesn't answer for a minute, but what he says next isn't totally surprising to me.

"I been talking to this girl from my old school too," he admits, his voice filled with embarrassment. I could get mad about this, but like I said, we've never been on a date. TBH we barely know each other. At least he doesn't act holier than thou and pretend I was the only one keeping my options open.

"Do you like her?"

"I like both of you," he says. "You're really different from each other—"

"Don't tell me any details." To control the urge to bite my nails, I grab a marker and start doodling on a piece of paper. A densely petalled flower starts taking shape. "If you're trying to decide who you want to date, don't wait for me, okay? I'm not even sure I want a boyfriend. I have cheer, games most Friday nights, we're going to start preparing for competition pretty soon, and I'm taking two AP classes. It's just a lot. And I know Brandon is your friend, but he won't stop giving me a hard time."

"Yeah, he can be kind of lot sometimes."

"Right!"

"But he's a good guy, you know."

"I'll have to take your word for it. Also...I'm going to Homecoming with my ex. It's not a real date or anything. We're just friends. I just want you to know that I wasn't blowing smoke up your ass just now."

I wish I could see his face, to gauge his reaction. He's not saying anything back. I don't want him to think badly of me. I'm pretty sure I'm not going to date him, but he's a good guy. I genuinely don't want to hurt his feelings.

"I've gotta go," he says. "I have to turn in my homework before I go to bed." I assume he has to either email it or upload it to Blackboard.

"Okay. Talk to you soon."

"Talk to you soon."

I disconnect the call and lean back in my task chair, sliding my knees back and forth so the chair turns in a tight half circle then back. What a day.

I pull my chair up to the desk and open my AP Physics textbook. I mark the end of the chapter with a flag, pull out my notebook and pen, and start reading. Time to put the drama aside and get on what I've got to do. It's less than an hour before bedtime, so I'd better focus and get this shit done.

Chapter 12

Brandon

THE CAR DROPS ME OFF IN FRONT OF A NONDESCRIPT office building. At this point in the afternoon, the streets are almost deserted, office workers back inside the cloistered warmth of their cubicles. I use my keycard to access the elevator controls and press the button for the top floor. The guard behind the security desk gives me a curious look as the door closes. My guess is that not a lot of people that look like me visit this building, and when they do, it's never with the kind of pass I have.

HE HATE ME

The elevator opens on a glass reception desk staffed by a nice looking blonde close to my age. She's beautiful, with an athletic body and full pink lips, but she's also icy. Working for Anton, god only knows what that coldness means. She could have a dozen kills under her belt for all I know.

"May I help you?" she asks forcefully and there's no mistaking her accent as anything but Russian.

"I'm here to see Anton," I tell her.

"Name?"

"Vole." She doesn't react to the odd sounding name, but I imagine she probably encounters them several times a day.

"One moment, please."

She types something into her computer and then motions for me to go ahead. I hear the click of the glass door just before I push it open. Anton's `desk is straight ahead, at the back center of the floor taking up more room than seems reasonable even for the president and CEO of a multimillion-dollar organization. Corporation. I'm a legitimate businessman now, Anton told me, a statement about as believable as a shark claiming to be a goldfish.

As I approach his glass-walled office there's another click, unlocking the door ahead of me. He's sitting behind his desk, wearing a Brioni suit that doesn't hide the bulging muscle underneath. Anton looks like a man who's been in a lot of fights and won most of them. His hair is cropped short, his neck thick, his gray eyes cold. Maybe the girl at reception is his sister. They share the same snake-like quality.

"Sit," he says, pointing to a chair. Unlike the girl outside, Anton's accent is American, east coast maybe, though I'm only going off TV. I've never left the Midwest. I lower myself into the chair cautiously. Anton's driver showed up outside school unexpectedly to bring me here, and I'm sure it isn't to be told good news. "How are you, Brandon?"

"I'm good," I tell him, nervously. His unblinking eyes spark alarm in my lizard brain. I can't help it—it's instinctive.

"I've received your progress reports, but I was hoping you could talk me through them."

"Um, of course." I'm kind of confused because we have a standing meeting every two weeks to do exactly this, so I'm not sure why I'm at this impromptu meeting. I'm missing soccer practice to be here.

With the press of a button, a projector screen lowers from the ceiling to our left and we pivot to face it. With a few mouse clicks, Anton has a 3d model of the house projected onto the screen. The rooms are color coded blue for Devin and Tanisha and red for Deja. My room and the common areas are shaded yellow, with the frequently used rooms a brighter shade than the less frequented ones. Rooms I've cleared have a thick black border around them.

I clear my throat.

"Since we last met, I've had a chance to search two of the high-profile targets: the master bedroom and Devin's office. No one else was home when I did it, so I had time to be thorough."

"I'm guessing you didn't find what we're looking for?"

"No. There's a floor safe in the walk-in closet. The code was written on a card in a lingerie drawer. There wasn't anything significant inside—some jewelry, financial documents, birth certificates. I took pictures and forwarded them to you. There's also a small safe in the office, but I couldn't get that one open."

"So what you're telling me is that you found nothing?"

"I…yeah. But if I can get the office safe open there's a chance what we're looking for is in there."

I point to each room on the model as I count off. "I also hit the second-floor guest room, the linen closet, the back stairs, and the laundry room. There's still the maid's room next to the laundry. It's really unlikely that's the place, but we can't rule anything out."

"What about the attic?"

"I used the snake you gave me through the ceiling, and it looks like nothing but blown insulation. If you want to be sure, I can provide the domestic schedule. You can probably swap someone in for the pest control guy."

"That's not the worst idea, but I'd like to keep that in reserve till we've eliminated every other option. I don't want Devin to sniff anything that might spook him."

"I need some help with the safe in his office. I don't know how to open it."

"What kind of safe is it?"

"I'm not sure. There's a combination lock."

"Send me a picture and I'll arrange something. I'll let you know when it's in the pickup location."

Another trail run, then. At least it helps my stamina and balance.

"How are you adjusting to the new school?" he asks, leaning back in his chair.

163

SENCHA SKEETE

"Fine," I say. "Everything's great."

"Wonderful. Any new friends? A girlfriend?"

"Not really. I'm trying to stay focused on the job."

"Is that right? Then why did I have to scrub video of you carrying an unconscious girl through the foyer from the security system?" His stare is withering. I want to climb under a rock.

"I, uh, forgot there was a camera there."

"You cannot afford to forget things like that! You jeopardize everything for what? Some pussy? I can get you ten girls just like her. You do something that careless again, and the deal is off. You can move your mother to whatever nursing home Medicaid will pay for, you understand me?"

I nod, keeping my expression blank even as anger begins to simmer inside me. Of course Anton doesn't care about my mom. I'm just a tool he can use, a means to an end.

"You have been in that house now for nearly two months with nothing to show for it. Our deal is you find the item and I pay for your mother's medical care. Right now I'm the only one holding up my end."

But Anton's right. I've been living in Devin's house for weeks now and I'm no closer to finding the evidence he's been using to blackmail Anton. I don't know the details, but whatever it is it's bad enough to have Anton scared. Devin has promised that if he's not paid, or if any harm comes to him or his family, the evidence will zip its way to the police.

When Anton approached me months ago, I wasn't sure who he was. Online he's depicted as an entrepreneur, and you can find a few pictures of him attending events with model-

HE HATE ME

looking chicks on his arm. But I have enough experience with criminals to know when I'm dealing with one. The minute Anton walked into the meeting with my coach at my old soccer club, I knew he was some kind of reptile. He pitched the Briarwood scholarship and only when he had me alone later did he explain what he actually wanted me to do.

He was searching for any kind of leverage on Devin when he located an old guardianship agreement Devin signed when my mother worked for him. Seeing the unique opportunity I presented to get inside Devin's house, Anton arranged my scholarship to Briarwood and my spot on the soccer team, and now that my mom's in a facility where she's receiving proper care, he knows I'll do anything to keep her there.

"I'm trying," I say. "It's just...not as easy as I thought it would be. The house is enormous. There are so many places something could be hidden."

Anton leans forward, his eyes boring into me. "Then I suggest you search more thoroughly. Every inch of that house if you have to."

"I'll keep looking."

I still haven't thoroughly searched the basement. Too many boxes and pieces of junk piled up over the years. There's also the small wall safe in Devin's office that I haven't been able to get into. If what we're looking for is hidden anywhere in the house, those are the most likely spots.

I want to see Devin go down nearly as much as Anton does. He deserves to burn in hell. After he fired my mother without notice or explanation, I'm convinced he's the one who circulated rumors that she was a thief. My mother was blackballed from working in Twin Oaks, and since she was live-in, we instantly lost the roof over our heads. We'd lived in shelters and my mom's car for months. Eventually she found a decent job that allowed us to get an apartment, but we've been homeless more than once and it's been a struggle to stay above water. My mother's deteriorating health has only made it more challenging as time goes on. I'm also pissed at my dad for abandoning us, but he's not the one I have the opportunity to take down.

I also know that once I find the evidence Anton will likely find some other task for me and another. I feel his claws burying themselves in my skin and I'm filled with impotent rage. Reprimanded and controlled by this piece of shit, and there's nothing I can do about it. My state of mind edges towards despair when I think that I was likely destined to end up here. Between my mother's illness and my father's abandonment, this feels like fate.

"Thanks," I say through gritted teeth. "And I'll keep looking."

"See that you do," Anton says. "And try not to let your little head lead you astray again. I'm not going to be so understanding next time."

My blood boils at his condescending tone. As if he has any right to judge me, when he's the one holding my mom's safety over my head like a carrot on a stick. But I force myself to nod.

"Don't worry about me. I'll get it done."

"Good man," Anton says with an oily smile.

HE HATE ME

He dismisses me with a wave of his hand. As I make my way back to the street, I fantasize about putting my fist through his smug face. I need a drink or a spliff or something to calm me down. I feel like I could beat the shit out of the next person I see. My mind turns to Deja, and I imagine a more pleasurable way of working off my frustrations, wrapping my hands around her neck and fucking her till she bleeds. Goddammit, no! I have to get control of myself.

Hunching my shoulders, I prepare to trek to the nearest bus stop. I'll take the bus as close to Briarwood as I can get, then grab a ride share the rest of the way. That should give me some time to center myself before I pop off and do something I'll regret.

* * *

As I'm strolling down the sidewalk approaching the gates of Briarwood, a red Tesla Model S makes a Uey and drives next to me, matching my pace. I peer inside to see Rourke van der Hoff behind the wheel.

"You need a ride?" he calls out.

"Sure." I don't know Rourke well. He's a junior but one of the stars of the soccer team. He's as tall as I am, with dark blond hair cut long on the top and an unnerving pair of moss green eyes.

"I didn't see you at practice today," he says conversationally. I don't know how long Rourke has lived here, but he has a vaguely British accent, one that sounds upper class, and he dresses in expensive tracksuits and sportswear. And when I say expensive, I mean outfits that cost thousands of dollars. I've seen him get muddy in them, so I don't think he really cares about them. I guess that's what happens when daddy's money is unlimited.

"I had an appointment," I explain. Coach doesn't give a fuck because I'm on the team as a favor to Anton. Apparently, our Coach has a little gambling habit.

"You just made it onto A squad," he says, shaking his head. "I'd think you'd prioritize practice."

"Couldn't be avoided," I say, getting a little irritated, but trying to hide it. Just by sheer dint of dough, Rourke isn't someone you wanted to piss off.

"Why not?"

"It was a family thing," I say, sticking as close to the truth as was possible, which actually isn't very close at all.

"Speaking of family," he says, "I heard you were related to Deja Marcus."

"Not really. Her stepdad's my guardian."

"She's a very popular girl. Any chance you could…"

"Introduce you?"

"Well, of course we know each other. I just can't get her to come to any of my parties."

"You trying to impress people or something? I don't think you need to do that. I'm pretty sure people will come to your parties just because they're your parties."

"True, but she's not just popular, she's also hot as fuck. What's that look? You can't blame me. You live with her. When she's walking towards you it's that figure and those gravity defying tits and then when you walks past you it's that ass, those legs. You just want to bend her over and—"

"Can you not talk about her like that?" I ask, feeling a surge of the anger that's been simmering inside me since I left Anton's office.

"Uh! You're fucking her."

"I'm not fucking her. I just don't like hearing people…"

"You are most definitely fucking her. And I think that's good news for me. You can make her come to my next party."

"I have no control over Deja." That's just a lie, but I'm not sure how I feel about Rourke yet, and in any case, I don't think he wants a pissed off girl souring the mood.

"Just ask her. Do it after sex, they're more agreeable then."

"I'm not—"

"Give me your number. Let's hang some time. My dad's always in Europe, so any day, any time, any booze, any…treat, can be had at mine."

We share contacts and I point him to a corner where he can drop me off. I'm still a quarter of a mile from Devin's house, but I don't mind a short walk through the woods.

"I'll give you a call," I promise, hopping out of the car.

When I get home Deja and her parents are already home. I run upstairs to drop off my backpack in my room, it's time for dinner. I'm not really in the mood to sit at a table with Devin and his wife, but I don't want to start a whole thing by refusing to eat at the table. They are so annoyingly conventional. I'm convinced people like that are really screwed up or evil, that's why they try so hard to make everyone think they're normal.

Tonight's dinner is a little more creative than usual. We have turkey chili and sweet potatoes roasted and sprinkled with pumpkin spice. Dessert is Greek yogurt panna cotta.

"Enjoying the food?" Devin asks when he sees me wolfing down the food.

I nod, not wanting to talk with my mouth full. I wipe my lips with a napkin and say,

"This is delicious, Tanisha. Thank you." Her eyes bug out. I think this may be the first compliment I've ever paid her, but it's well-earned.

"It's been getting colder," she says. "Time to start bringing on the soup."

"Yeah!" Deja says. "Can you make butternut squash tomorrow?"

"Sure," Tanisha says. They start talking about recipes and side dishes and I tune them out. I hate Tanisha's voice. It always sounds forced and artificially high-pitched. Instead, I watch Deja's face. She's animated, and gesturing with her spoon, she smiles, her full lips separating to reveal even, white teeth. I'd love to see her look at me like that, with affection in her eyes instead of irritation. Especially if she was wearing something cute, like lingerie, or just the skirt of her cheer costume and she'd flip the skirt up and show me—

"Brandon," Devin is saying, "are you there?"

He asks me about soccer and offers a bunch of useless platitudes about hard work and consistency. I mention that I got a ride with Rourke and Deja makes a face.

"You don't like Rourke?" I ask.

"He's okay," she says. "He just parties a little too hard for my taste."

"What do you mean?" Tanisha asks.

"Binge drinking, basically. I've heard crazy stories, and he's still a junior."

I know that when she said "hard", she wasn't talking about alcohol. Two months at Briarwood and I already know Rourke loves his candy and is generous with it. His whole crew of too-rich boys in $100K cars live dangerously close to the edge.

After dinner, I hunker down in my room to do homework and study. I'd initially wanted Deja to take most of this work off me, but I'm glad she refused. While my mission at Briarwood is not to learn, I'd be an idiot to waste the opportunity. I wish I'd come here sooner; I'll never catch up with these kids academically, but I can still try to get closer to their level.

My phone buzzes with a text notification. It's Anton telling me to pick something up from the drop spot.

ME *I'll do it in the morning.*

ANTON: *Do it now. I need this done ASAP!*

Fuck me! It's 10:30 at night and I have to sneak out, make a three-mile round trip through the woods and sneak back in without being detected. I wait another half an hour until everyone's lights are off, then tiptoe downstairs.

ME: *Turn off the alarm and exterior camera.*

SENCHA SKEETE

If I didn't know Devin was blackmailing a criminal, I'd probably think his security set up was overkill, but as it is I totally get it. Anton responds after a few minutes.

ANTON: *Done*

I go out the kitchen door, past the trash cans, and through the narrow passage that leads to the alley gate. I'm cold and sweaty by the time I get to the marked tree, and I will tell you that is not a fun combination. I pull what looks like a pencil case out of the usual hiding place. Inside are several small devices.

ME: *Got it.*

ANTON: *Let me know when you get home. You need to install them tonight.*

Is this motherfucker kidding? I'm livid all over again. Why can't he just be patient and let me decide the safest time to do things. I could so easily get caught tonight but he's really insistent that I get the equipment in place before dawn. I hate being ordered around. I begin to fantasize about Deja, sitting on my lap, all sweet and naked. Then I'm doing things to her that make her writhe in agony. She begs me to stop and pleads for mercy. And she comes.

Chapter 13

Deja

THAT NIGHT I TOSS AND TURN. IT MAY NOT SEEM LIKE a big deal—me not having a boyfriend—but I feel a little uncomfortable. I watched the popular girls when I started high school. They were always athletic and always had a popular boyfriend. I've been cheering since middle school, so I knew that would be my sport, and I'm cute and fun enough that I've never had trouble finding a boyfriend.

Not that I couldn't find a boyfriend now. There are plenty of guys at Briarwood who would be happy to be my boyfriend. But I don't know how Brandon would react. What am I saying? He would react very badly. He hasn't come right out and said he doesn't want me to be with anyone else, but I haven't missed that possessive gleam in his eyes. He told me he owned me, and that I was his. Those don't sound like the statements of someone who would be okay with me dating other people.

I flip over onto my stomach and grab my phone off the bedside table. It's 11:34. No wonder my eyes are aching. I scroll through my social media feeds. Shelby's posted another cute meme about Fall that I think is a little cheesy, but I like it anyway. A couple of the younger cheerleaders have posted selfies of themselves sharing a sno-cone. In my texts, I see messages from Kenz and a few of the other girls. Nothing from Gio, though that's hardly surprising. I scroll through articles about fashion trends and celebrity gossip before I give up. I'm not feeling any sleepier than I did twenty minutes ago.

Getting out of bed, I slide my feet into my house slippers and trudge downstairs to get some hot tea. The house is eerily quiet. I turn on the lights in the kitchen and put on the kettle. From the back windows, I see the lawn and beyond it the shadowy trees of the park-like jogging trail behind the house. The neighborhood is dark, except for a few lights visible in the distance. Not a surprise. Everyone around here is tucked up in bed like I'm supposed to be. I wrap my arms around myself, wishing I'd grabbed a robe before I came down. The air holds a slight chill because the thermostat is set to 65 degrees at night. A whooshing sound comes from the kettle as the water heats up.

"You're up late."

HE HATE ME

I nearly jump out of my skin. Brandon is standing next to the outside door, which opens into a little enclosed area where we keep the trashcans. The gate at the end of it is locked and has a camera outside it, so he can't have gone any further than that without my parents knowing. What was he doing out there? He's not wearing a coat or sweatshirt, just a plain white tee and lightweight sweatpants. He glances over my outfit—the same as his, except that I'm wearing a camisole.

"Want some tea?" I ask, too tired to think of anything clever to say.

"Why not?" He opens the cupboard and grabs a pair of cups and a peppermint tea bag. "What kind do you want?"

"Chamomile."

He emits a low hum and brings the cups and tea bags over to where I'm standing. Now that he's closer to me I can smell the cold on his skin and the unmistakable traces of tobacco smoke.

"I can't believe you smoke," I say, not trying to hide my disapproval. Smoking is bad for anyone, but for an athlete it seems especially dumb.

"You smoke," he says, resting his hip against the kitchen counter. The slight bend brings his face almost level with mine.

"I don't."

"Weed…"

"No," I say. "You have never seen me smoke."

He edges closer, grasping one of the braids that has slipped loose from my silk scarf between his thumb and forefinger. I move to swat his hand away, but he's faster, dodging my blow with a chuckle.

"I get it," he says, opening the tea bags and dropping them into the cups. "You do drugs, you just don't smoke them."

I look towards the stairs, paranoid that one of my parents will overhear, even though logically I know they're probably fast asleep and Brandon spoke pretty softly.

"I take my sport seriously," I say, tartly. The pitch of the kettle is getting higher. I don't want to wait for it to start screaming. Just a few more seconds now.

"Your sport?" He laughs more loudly this time, the sound echoing in the quiet of the night. I shoot him a quelling look.

"Go ahead and wake Devin," I say.

The water is just about there, and I snatch it off the stove using an oven mitt. The water in the cups begins to change color as the tea steeps into it. Brandon's is a brighter green, while mine remains paler and slightly yellow. The smell is warming.

His body gets much too close to mine when he picks up his cup. He wraps his long fingers around it, the heat not seeming to bother him. I hold mine by the handle and sip. It's grassy and bland. The heat spreads through me, not quite overcoming the cold of the room. I stifle a yawn. We don't speak to each other, but I feel his eyes on me. His expression is inscrutable.

I look down at my cup to avoid looking at his face. In my head, I run through the things I have to do before homecoming. I'll need a dress, maybe shoes, and to get my nails done. I'll need to call Jayden. I think of anything I can to distract myself from how close Brandon is to me. My cup is still half-full, and I should stay here and finish it, but I feel trapped. Brandon takes the cup from me and places it on the kitchen island. The granite ledge presses into my back. His other hand, still warm from the tea, wraps around my waist. I want to say something cutting, remind him that I'm not a toy, that position of strength notwithstanding he can't just do whatever he wants to me, but I know it's a lie.

"Why do I want you?" he asks, searching my face. I should tell him it's because I'm that irresistible, that amazing, but I can't bring myself to say those words—the ones that would turn this into the fight it ought to be.

"You shouldn't," I respond softly.

"I shouldn't," he agrees, then his lips are on mine, hot and seeking. I want to hate it so much, as much as I hate him, but Lord knows I don't. His lips are soft and supple, his tongue agile. He tastes of peppermint and even the trace of bitterness from the tobacco doesn't turn me off. I want to open myself to him, wrap my arms and legs around him, and kiss him forever. He shudders, his free hand sliding into the braids at the back of my head. His nails press into my scalp.

"Fuck, Deja," he says. He bites down sharply on my earlobe. I moan, grasping a fistful of his t-shirt and trying to pull his body against mine, but he resists. I reach for his waistband with my other hand, and he stops me, holding my wrist against my hip. The bulge at his crotch is impossible to miss. Our harsh breathing fills the room.

"We can't," he says, roughly. He's holding our bodies apart, but his hand is still gripping my hair.

"Why not?" What am I saying? What is wrong with you, Deja?

He pushes me down until my butt makes contact with one of the counter stools and drags my hair, pulling my head back so my face points at the ceiling. His other hand grips my throat, holding my head in place. I can't move it. His lips crush mine until they're flat against my teeth. His tongue forces its way inside, licking and tasting me like I'm a dish laid out for him to sample. His tongue thrusts deep into my mouth almost like he's trying to choke me on it. It's overwhelming and dominating and my clit throbs in response. I press my hands to his chest, feeling the thick muscles of a body that could literally break me. I start sliding my hands lower and he pulls back, his eyes hooded. He squeezes my neck to remind me how easily he could cut off my breath and kisses my forehead gently.

"We need to stop," he says, his eyes as dark as I've ever seen them. "I don't have the self-control right now not to hurt you really badly. Physically hurt you.

I swallow, nodding. "Okay." I forgot for a moment what kind of creature I'm dealing with. I'm honestly surprised at his sudden attack of morality, but I'm grateful for it.

He loosens his grip and I breathe in deeply. My scalp stings but I don't massage it. Pride, or maybe I like the pain and the way it makes me feel alive. Brandon rubs his hand over his face, his features tense. He moves to the end of the kitchen island, putting some space between us.

HE HATE ME

"Do you know when their next date night is?"

"It'll be on the board," I tell him, "On the fridge." I point at the whiteboard calendar, each date labeled with my mother's neat handwriting. For both this and next Friday I see the name of a restaurant and a time.

"Two weeks in a row?"

"Next Friday is the homecoming game, so they're probably taking us to dinner. This week might be a date night. Or some business thing."

"Are you busy?"

"Kind of. I can't keep skipping out on social obligations. People are going to think something's wrong."

"That's okay," he says, still perusing the board. "I don't think I'll need you."

With a curt nod, he leaves the kitchen. I pick up my still warm cup of chamomile tea and drain it. My hands are shaking slightly as I set it in the sink. I melt into the nearest chair, trying to ignore the strange buzz in my limbs and the heaviness in my pelvis. I don't know how far I would have let things go, but it's scary that Brandon had to be the one to stop us from going further than we did.

He's dangerous, and actually not a very nice person. I chalk it up to the novelty of the sexual experience we had. My stupid libido wants more and isn't smart enough to tell the person it's attached to is not someone I should get close to. Stupid hormones.

Worst of all, I'm no closer to being sleepy than I was an hour ago. I close my eyes and an image of him forms in my mind's eye. At first, he looks like he did in the kitchen, then the image shifts and he's stripped bare like he was on Saturday night. In my fantasy Brandon proudly shows off his cock, taking the thick shaft in his hand. He grins at me and tells me I make him hard and that he wants to go down on me, although what he actually says is something about licking me. The image is vivid in my mind, and for a moment I feel a sense of deja vu, like this was something that actually happened. My hand, masquerading as his hand, slips into my underwear. His fingers circle my swollen clit and dip inside me.

Pleasure swells inside me, building and building until I peak. Only then, finally, am I able to sleep.

Chapter 14

Brandon

ONE OF THE CHALLENGES OF SEARCHING THE HOUSE IS that it's rarely empty. Deja's parents don't have a very active social life. Other than date nights they're usually home in the evenings. I have soccer practice four days a week, so I get home around the same time they do, or even later on days when I go visit my mom. A lot of areas of the house I can make up a plausible excuse to be in, but not Devin's office.

I'm left spinning my wheels for most of the week, so when Rourke invites me to grab dinner with him after practice I say yes. We end up at one of those casual dining places that serves healthy food. We make small talk about food and soccer while we wait. I'm wondering what's going on, because Rourke is not the kind of dude I'd expect to seek me out TBH. I'm one of the poorest guys at Briarwood and he is one of the richest. We dress and act nothing alike and we don't have the same kinds of friends. I keep to myself, speak as little as possible while he's loud and cocky and likes to flash his expensive toys. I can't decide if I like him or if he's annoying, but maybe it's both. No one's gone out of their way to befriend me like this since Mello did it when we were eleven.

Rourke starts talking about college scouts and how he thinks different guys on the team will fare. I think he's flattering me a bit when he says I have a good shot. I know he DGAF about college scholarships, so I figure he's talking about it because he thinks I'm interested and if I wasn't on a secret mission I would be. I probably should be. Once I find what I'm looking for at Devin's I should have a plan for my life, shouldn't I? That gets me thinking about getting into the safe again, and I'm only half paying attention while Rourke rambles on, hardly seeming to care that I only offer the occasional word of agreement.

Our plates arrive, piled high with grilled chicken, brown rice and steamed vegetables. We dig in, and the conversation shifts to practice and the set piece drills Coach has been having us run.

"I heard a rumor about you," Rourke says in an abrupt change of subject.

'What'd you hear?"

"That you have the hookup."

HE HATE ME

I'm taken completely off guard. I haven't dealt for a while. I didn't think anyone would know about it at Briarwood, but I guess it makes sense. I sold to a lot of kids back in the day.

"What are you looking for?"

"Candy." Cocaine. I've managed to stay away from the hard stuff so far. I can't believe a top-level athlete is using it.

"Is high school that boring?" I quip.

"Come on, man. Don't hold out on me."

"I don't have it."

"Can you get it?"

I'm about to answer when I hear someone saying Deja's name in a nearby booth, and then laughing. He's speaking in accented English and a quick check confirms it's Gio, sitting with a group of football players. He's not being discreet at all as he says that he dumped Deja for a hot blonde.

"That's not what I heard," one of the other guys says. "I heard you struck out."

"It is no matter what you heard," Gio says, clearly annoyed by being contradicted. "Friday night after your football game she spread her legs for me in the back of my car. La *puttana* she tell me I am so good." He wrinkles his nose and sniggers.

"She's not good, though. Somebody left the fish out in the sun too long."

The other boys laugh, though I can tell some of them aren't sure whether to believe him. How dare this piece of shit even say Deja's name. I heard about her calling him out at the party on Saturday night, so I know he's trying to save face, but he's not allowed to do it at Deja's expense. I take the reins off, letting my rage build as he keeps mouthing off. It feels good, like my super power getting activated, the energy spreading through my muscles.

"What are you smiling about?"

Gio gets up from the table and heads to the bathroom.

"I'll be right back,' I tell Rourke. My heart pounds with anticipation.

Gio is the only person in the bathroom when I get there. I pull out my knife and flick it open. I love this thing. It's an all-black spring-loaded tactical knife with a four-inch blade. It looks scary and it's sharp as fuck, too. Gio is whistling and doesn't notice me until he turns towards the sinks to wash his hands and spots me in the mirror. He jerks around in surprise.

"Oh, hello," he says. The corners of his mouth rise as he starts to smile, then fall when he sees the knife. His face pales as a grin spreads across my face. "What...what's up?"

"You're really stomping on my nerves, you know that."

"I'm sorry," he pleads. "I don't know what you want."

"First you mess with Mello—"

"That was an accident."

"And now you're talking shit about Deja?"

"I'm just joking around, man. It's just..." His words trail off when I press the tip of the knife to his side. It's sharp enough that it pierces his shirt and the top layer of skin. His eyes bug out in fear.

"You and I both know you didn't sleep with Deja."

He nods, his cheeks turning red in stark contrast to his clammy skin.

HE HATE ME

"If I ever hear a bad word about her out of your mouth, I'm going to demonstrate for you exactly how sharp my knife is? Capisce?"

"Yes, of course. I won't say anything about her again. I'm sorry."

"I do want you to say one thing, though?"

"What?"

"That you made the whole thing up because you're a pathetic loser she wouldn't spit on if you were on fire. Tell them the truth—that you blew it with her, and you were lying to compensate for how badly she humiliated you."

"I can't tell them that."

"Really?" I ask, running the knife up his ribcage. He tries to back up, but he's sandwiched against the sinks. He starts trembling, his breathing jerky and shallow. What a wuss.

"Okay," he says, "I'll tell them. I'll tell them I was lying. I swear. And I'll never say anything bad about her or even talk to her unless I have to."

"Good. Because if you don't, I'm going to make you regret it."

I fold and pocket my knife, a little disappointed at how easily he folded. But as long as I'm here…

I whip my arm back and punch him in the solar plexus as hard as I can. He doubles over, his hand on the sink the only thing holding him up. A hoarse groan issues from his lips, giving me at least a tiny bit of the thrill I was hoping for.

Unhurriedly, I return to the table to find Rourke on his phone. I sit down and sip the last of my iced tea through a straw. Rourke looks up as Gio stumbles by, clutching his stomach.

"Nice," he says. "Wanna bounce?"

I nod. I don't need to hear Gio fulfill his end of the bargain. If he doesn't, I'll have even more fun teaching him why he should have.

* * *

I get into Devin's office by the end of the week. With the device Anton gives me I'm able to open the office safe. There's a shocking amount of cash inside and stock certificates. That much bread is tempting, but I can't risk getting caught. Anton would fry me. I photograph everything. The most promising find is a little bag of metal keys. They look like the keys to lockboxes and at least one is a safe deposit box key with a leather tag that reads 0437. I lay them all out on a piece of paper and photograph them. It's pretty easy to get key copies made from pictures—there's even an app for it—but I figure I'll let Anton handle that.

Saturday, I have nothing to do. I can't search without drawing attention to myself and I'm not doing homework. Even Deja doesn't do homework on Saturdays. She has people over in the afternoon, as usual, watching a rom com on the TV in the family room and throwing popcorn everywhere. I try sitting with them but that lasts all of five minutes. Shelby keeps saying the most inane things possible and even though I know I need to keep my distance, the temptation to go over and kiss Deja till she passes out from lack of oxygen is fierce.

HE HATE ME

I figure I'll do a little extra credit. Not for school, for Anton. When I mentioned hanging out with Rourke, Anton asked me to get closer to him and his friend Javi. I figure now is as good a time as any to reach out. Deja may think she's the queen of Briarwood, and in a way, she is, but she can't touch the kings. These guys are the kind of rich Devin can only dream of. Rourke van der Hoff's dad is part of an old money banking family and Javier de la Garza's family was lucky enough to get out of Venezuela early and with most of their oil wealth intact. I know Javi is here because his mother's family is originally from around here, but why the son of a European banker is at some random midwestern high school, I don't know.

I invite Rourke and Javi to a pickup soccer game at the field near Devin's house. It's on the other side of the woods, part of a big public park. I invite a bunch of other guys too, including Von and Mello, even though I know Mello's not back on his feet, I want to include him. He's a good kid and I still feel guilty about him getting hurt. He's on the A squad with Rourke and Javi, and I don't think it hurts for him to hang around them.

I walk over to the field with all my gear in a duffle and get there around 3:00 pm. I'm still kinda pissed that Devin won't get me a car. He'd be paying with Anton's money, anyway, though of course he doesn't know I know that. Maybe I can just ask Anton directly, but I need to deliver for him first. There's probably enough money in the safe to buy a car. I walk past Javi's McLaren 720S Super Series and feel a pang of embarrassment. A part of me hates being around all these rich kids. They make me feel small, and with their years of private schooling, stupid too. But another part of me is enjoying casual access to expensive food and alcohol and fast cars.

The pickup game starts out pretty casual, just guys messing around and having fun. But once we actually start playing, the competition comes out. Rourke and Javi are crazy good, even better than they are at school games. I hold my own, but some of the other guys are struggling to keep up.

About halfway through, I see Mello sitting on the sidelines, looking frustrated. His ankle has a ways to go before it's healed, so he can't join in. I call a timeout and jog over to him.

"How's it going, man?" I ask.

He shrugs. "It sucks just watching."

I nod. "I know. But you'll be back out there soon."

We're quiet for a minute, both of us watching the other guys practice tricks and shots.

"So what's up with you and Deja, anyway?" Mello asks suddenly.

I tense up. My relationship with her isn't something I want to discuss. "What do you mean?"

"I see the way you look at each other. And how she pushes your buttons. There's something going on."

I force a laugh, going for casual. "Yeah, we don't really get along. She's just obsessed with being popular. It's annoying."

HE HATE ME

"What is all this, then?" Mello asks, gesturing with his hand. "We're hanging out with Rich Douchebags of Briarwood for shits and giggles?"

"I'm just trying to get to know the guys on the A squad. My new teammates."

"And here I was thinking us transfers were going to stick together." It wasn't said bitterly, but Mello's tone was dry. I felt a pang of guilt. I would have preferred to stick with Mello as well; we've known each other since middle school. But he had no idea about my relationship with Anton or my real reason for trying to get closer to these guys.

"I'm still your friend, man," I say. "But I'm probably the weakest guy out there. I need all the help I can get."

I can see that Mello doesn't buy my bullshit, but I can't let him know what's really going on.

"Come on, Keane," Rourke calls out, "let's go!"

We kick the ball back and forth. There's no real strategy to our game, just a bunch of guys messing around and trying to one-up each other. Rourke juggles the ball on his knees, showing off.

"Quit hot-dogging and pass the ball, Rourke!" Javi shouts.

Rourke smirks and lobs it over to Javi, who traps it neatly on his chest before dribbling it towards the goal. I run alongside trying to steal the ball, but Javi is too quick. He feints left, then fires the ball into the top corner of the goal.

"Yeah! Suck on that, Keane!" Javi gloats as we bump fists.

"Lucky shot," I say with a grin.

We play for another hour or so until the sunlight begins to fade. My limbs feel loose and warm, the thrill of movement keeping me energized. For a little while out here, running and yelling with my teammates, everything else faded away. I almost forgot why I'm there till the game wraps up and Rourke comes over, slapping me on the back. His blond hair is dark with sweat.

"This was a good idea, Keane," he says. "Sometimes I forget how much I love soccer until I get to play without Coach breathing down my neck."

"I know what you mean," I say. "It's a great way to blow off steam."

"Not the only way, though," Rourke says. "Wanna come hang out at my place. Or do you have to get foster daddy's permission?"

I don't correct him. I don't think there's that big of a difference between a foster parent and a guardian, not in practice. "It's cool as long as I'm home before curfew."

"You have a curfew?" He seems amused. "Aren't you a senior?"

"As long as you live under my roof…"

"I get it. Is that why it's so hard to get Deja over to my place."

I raise my hands in the universal gesture of, "I'm not touching that."

"Doesn't she like me?"

"You'll have to ask Deja that."

"Text her. See if she wants to come." Reluctantly, I do as he asks. The response comes back almost immediately.

HE HATE ME

Deja: Sorry. I have plans. Have fun.

He shrugs when he sees the response, apparently not surprised. I'm relieved, because if he was being friendly to me to get to Deja, I'd have been SOL. Instead, he has me climb into his Tesla and ride with him to his house. It only takes about fifteen minutes to get there. Most of the expensive houses in town are in this area, more spread out from each other than less expensive houses, but still a cluster.

Rourke's house, or should I say mansion, is one of the Big 4. These are the largest and most expensive estates within a 200-mile radius. All were built during the gilded age and would be tourist attractions, I'm sure, if the owners let the public get anywhere near them. The other three are owned by families that have been in the area for generations—basically the local high society. One of the men used to be mayor. How Rourke's dad came to own the place I have no idea, but he only lives there on paper.

Rourke points me to one of the many bathrooms for a quick shower, handing me an ugly as fuck Burberry tracksuit with the tags still on. I'm free balling, but there's no denying the thing is comfortable. I wander until I find Rourke on the third floor playing Xbox solo.

"Hungry?" he asks.

"I could eat." I shrug. "But what I really am is thirsty. I'd kill for a Gatorade right now."

He picks up what looks like a miniature TV remote and speaks into it, requesting drinks and a snack tray. While we wait, I grab my duffle and pull out the reason Rourke asked me over in the first place. I unroll my toiletry bag. Instead of lotions and aftershave the little pockets are stuffed with plants, pills, liquids, and powders. I pull out papers, weed, hash oil and a grinder and get to work. This lavish spread is a gift from Anton, or more like a starter kit. It wasn't my idea, but Anton's position is that when people feel good around you, they tend to like you, and drugs make people feel very good.

A black woman around my mother's age comes in carrying a tray. It's weird to get served Gatorade off a silver tray. She also leaves behind a charcuterie board with cured meat, cheese, fruit, bread and crackers. It's not an actual meal, but I'm glad to have it. I down the sports drink and finish rolling the joint. We smoke, then eat. Javi shows up, then Christian and a couple of sophomore girls I don't know. More people trickle in as the hours go by. Pretty soon I'm the candy man, distributing (selling) the shit Anton gave me. No charge for Rourke, of course.

Getting back into drug dealing might seem stupid, but guys like this have no interest in befriending NPCs like me unless we can benefit them in some way. Randomly handing out drugs would look suspicious but comping the host for access to his guests—that's believable.

Around 11:30, I bid the partiers goodbye and take a ride share back to Devin's. The house is dark, and I wonder if Deja's curled up in her bed or racing home to make curfew. I wish this was a world where I could go straight up to her room and climb in bed with her, tuck her head under my chin, and squeeze her tight. But instead I go to my room, discard the $1,000 track suit on the floor, and climb into bed.

Chapter 15

Deja

THE DAY OF THE HOMECOMING DANCE I HAVE TO SIT the ACT in the morning, but after that the day is free. I think I do well on the test, so I let myself relax and do nothing for a change—no training, no studying, minimal texting. I do some yoga, but more for the loose way it makes my muscles feel than as exercise. Brandon comes into the gym while I'm doing it and watches me while he lifts. I really can't miss the size of his erection, but he pretends it's not there, so I do, too.

"Hey," he says, when he's done, chugging from an oversized water bottle. I'm in corpse pose by this point, and he's standing above me, shiny with sweat. He smells like the outdoors, so I think he took another one of his trail runs in the woods. He crouches next to me. "So you're going to the dance with that Jayden guy?"

"Yeah."

"He's your ex, right?"

"Yes." I'm tempted to laugh. He needs to get to the point.

"So, uh, are you getting back together with him?"

"What's it to you?" I ask, propping myself up on one arm and facing him.

"You know exactly what it is. You're mine."

"Really? Cause last time we kissed you were too scared to take it home. Maybe Jayden can handle me a little better."

I'm goading him, but he surprises me by laughing.

"Yeah, no. I'm pretty sure he can't."

"How do you know that?"

Amusement lights up his blue-sky eyes and it seems like he's going to say something, but then he bites his lower lip. He chuckles.

"Because I can tell no one's ever made you come the way I do. You were so surprised the first time."

"And you're so full of yourself. Maybe I was faking it."

"You're going to be full of my cock if you don't control that saucy little tongue." He adjusts himself and I catch myself staring at his oversized bulge. I swear I can see his heavy balls with the way he's positioned less than two feet from my face.

I look up at his eyes and if I believed in telepathy, I'd say we were both imagining him leaping on top of me and shoving that fat cock into my mouth. I'm suddenly short of breath, and a bright red flush climbs from his chest up towards his eyebrows at breakneck speed.

He clears his throat and stands up, his gaze so hot I want to leap to my feet and rub myself against him like a cat.

"I, ah, better go before one of your parents comes by to…do something."

"Yeah," I agree, swallowing with difficulty. "And for the record, Jayden and I are just friends."

* * *

We avoid each other until it's 3:00 pm and Mackenzie picks me up for the drive to Melodie Yang's house. We spend the next few hours doing girl pampering shit. Shelby, Lorelei, Mackenzie, Melodie and I get our faces beat by a makeup artist Melodie's parents hired. Her house is bigger than mine. Like Perry she lives in a true mansion. They not only have six bedrooms and a three-car garage, but their yard is so huge you have to call it "the grounds." A lot of kids at Briarwood live in houses like this.

Melodie is a sweetheart—basically the opposite of a spoiled, rich brat. She's on the shorter side, a little round in an attractive way, and she's really kind. The makeup artist sets up in one of the ground-floor rooms and we take turns in her chair. I bring my own supplies since I know she isn't likely to have my shades and it turns out to be a good call. We gossip and joke around throughout the whole process.

Once we're ready, we get our phones out and snap a bunch of pictures for the 'Gram. I do the classic black girl pose—back to the camera, then twist and look over one shoulder. Do it right and all your assets get captured and flattered—face, hair, boobs, waist and ass. We start posting to our social media and the responses are pretty positive.

Melodie's parents are really the best. Sure, I know they're kind of showing off, but it's still nice that they take us all to dinner. The food is amazing, noticeably better than any Japanese food I've ever had. The rest of the girls look equally impressed.

We're among the first to arrive at the dance. Melodie's date is waiting by the door, holding a yellow corsage that matches his boutonniere. Melodie blushes pink, a huge grin on her face. Her cute but pimply date smiles back. Now that I'm getting a good look at him, he was in one of my AP classes. I see Melodie wave at someone behind me and I turn around to see Jayden walking up looking like a frickin model.

The last time I saw him he had cornrows, but he's changed his hair since then. He now has a frohawk with the dark-blond hair on the sides cut in a high fade. His long legs eat up the distance between us, that loose-limbed swagger that was always Jayden bringing to mind a jungle cat. He shoots a peace sign at Dr. Yang, and if I didn't know better, I'd say my friend's middle-aged mother preened.

Jayden's hands are empty, but he's not shy about pulling me into a hug.

"No corsage?" I tease.

"Aren't we past that?" he says cockily. His green eyes are bright in his golden-brown face. Jayden is light skin, but a shade darker than you'd expect with those eyes and that hair. He has the coloring of a blonde surfer at the end of summer.

HE HATE ME

"You're looking pretty fucking sexy," he says, licking his full lips suggestively. "Did you get hotter since the last time I saw you?"

"Absence makes the heart grow fonder, right?" I quip. He grins wolfishly, folding his hands over his crotch.

"Yeah, my heart."

He greets the rest of the girls and asks how they've been. We all used to hang out last year, so they know him well. I think he knows Melodie the least, but he talks to her too and coaxes her date into the conversation. The date's name is Henry and he's a junior. We decide to wait out front until everyone's dates arrive, but Gio takes forever to get there.

After half an hour, we've just about convinced Shelby to come inside with us when Gio shows up. He's wearing a white tuxedo jacket, black pants and a bowtie. He walks up to us from the direction of the student parking lot, a whole lot of swagger in his step until he sees my hand clutching Jayden's arm. He does an honest-to-god stutter step.

"That's him," I whisper to my date. Jayden wraps his arm around my waist possessively. I ease out of his arms, taking a more casual pose. I know he's doing it to annoy Gio, but if Brandon sees another guy touching me like that there'll be hell to pay.

"Hey, baby," Gio says to Shelby when he walks up, kissing her on the cheek. He opens up a clear plastic box and offers her a corsage. It's pale pink and white, and I have to admit he did good—it really suits Shelby. Shelby introduces Gio to Jayden and Henry. Gio tries a dap with Jayden, but Jayden just ignores it and asks me if I'm ready to go inside.

SENCHA SKEETE

"I've been ready," I say pointedly, looking at Gio. He gives me a sour look but doesn't respond.

Inside we all cluster together, except for Gio and Shelby, who run off to the dance floor. The place is filling up, with more and more kids still arriving. The dance is being held in the auditorium. There's a DJ on the right of the stage and two "thrones" side by side in the middle. The homecoming committee did well. The space is festooned with green and white balloons. There's a photo booth in one corner and a refreshments table that's passing out bottled water and popcorn. I clock the chaperones around the room, mostly chatting with each other or looking at their phones.

After getting a drink, I squeeze onto the dance floor with Jayden in tow, swaying my hips to the music. When I stop, he presses right up into my back, grinding against my butt. It draws no attention because that's pretty much what everyone else is doing. If prom has class, then Homecoming has ass. There isn't a girl in the place who's white enough not to twerk or do a hip roll. The heavy hip-hop beat of the music adds to the funky, heavy feel on the dance floor. The nearly overwhelming odor of Axe body spray, floral perfumes and sweat hangs over the crowd. I loop my arms loosely around Jayden's neck. He moves his hips against me, the very picture of a sexy young man.

As I watch his face, his eyes move over the crowd behind me. This was always the problem with Jayden. He's fun and cool, but he's never completely focused on you. I can't be sure he's checking out other girls without looking, but

HE HATE ME

based on experience, that's exactly what he's doing. Even when we were dating, he would do this.

But I really can't get mad this time. As he's checking out girls, I'm subtly searching the crowd for Brandon. I know he's here because he got the same curfew extension I did, and I know he has a date because I saw a corsage in the fridge this morning. I didn't want to be caught asking about him, but keeping my ears open I haven't heard who his date is. Probably a freshman or sophomore. Definitely not a cheerleader.

Why do I even care, though? Our chemistry is fire, but I don't see how we could work as a couple. I list in my head all the reasons why "us" is a bad idea: 1. He's an asshole. 2. He's blackmailing me. 3. He's probably a sexual sadist. 4. I don't even like him; we have nothing in common. 5. He looks at me like I'm raw meat and he's a wolf.

"Earth to Deja," Jayden says.

"What?"

"They're calling you up."

Homecoming court is being called up on stage. It's no surprise that Christian Dubrov and I are crowned King and Queen. They put on our sashes, and we sit on our thrones. A photographer flitters around taking pictures. The vice-principal, Mrs. Godwin, gives a little speech about each of us. She says I'm in the National Honor Society, captain of the cheerleading squad, a member of a bunch of clubs, etc. It makes me sound like some kind of super participator, which I guess I am. I smile and wave like a classy queen, then we sit

SENCHA SKEETE

on the thrones while she drones on about Homecoming and other school stuff.

Finally, Christian and I have to dance together. The song they pick is Thinking Out Loud by Ed Sheeran. By mutual unspoken agreement, Christian and I stand as far away from each other as it is possible to do while doing a slow dance. As soon as it's over, I find Jayden and drag him to get our pictures taken in front of the Homecoming backdrop. I get a few group shots with my girls, too. After that, there's no reason to stay at the dance, so I round up the crew and head to the coat check.

Chapter 16

Deja

MACKENZIE'S HOUSE IS SIMILAR TO MINE, BUT IT'S decorated in more of a country chic style. There are always flags hanging outside, and right now is no exception. Two big orange flags hang from wall-mounted poles. One reads, "It's Fall Y'all," and the other is a jumble of pumpkins, fall foliage, and fall fruit. Above the door, a banner reads: "Briarwood Academy Homecoming," and the year. There are Homecoming lawn signs as well. On either side of the front door, hay bales are stacked with pumpkins and gourds artfully arranged on top of or next to them. The largest is a bumpy green and white fairytale pumpkin that must have cost a fortune.

SENCHA SKEETE

We're the first to get to the party—me, Jayden, Mackenzie, and Tim. Tim's talking our ears off about yesterday's game and the upcoming football season. I don't know if I misjudged him, because I thought he was shy, but I guess football unlocks his chatter button. I'm not too surprised. Everybody goes a little nuts over high school football around here.

When we get inside Mackenzie tells us we can hang in the family room while she checks on something. I snap a couple shots of the snack table and post them to social media. Mrs. Taylor went all out as usual. There are giant bowls of popcorn and cheese balls, every kind of fresh fruit you can imagine cut into pretty shapes, cheese cubes and fancy cured meat, a veggie tray, and deviled eggs. There's a whole separate dessert table with bite-sized apple and pumpkin pies, mini cupcakes—half fall themed, the rest in Briarwood colors—, candy apples, caramel popcorn balls in foil cupcake liners and bowls of random candy. There's also an area with pop, sports drinks, and water bottles floating in tubs of ice.

"What's he doing here?" Lorelei asks and I look over at the door to see Brandon walking in with a cute redbone on his arm. She's petite and curvy with a halo of soft brown curls. I can't imagine a girl looking less like me and still being black. He smiles down at her, and I feel a pang in my gut. I'm sure she doesn't go to Briarwood, because I know all the black kids. Mello, Von and their dates enter right behind him.

"It's cool," Mackenzie says, huffily. "Deja's parents asked my parents. It would be kinda stupid for me to hold a grudge longer than the two of us were talking, anyway." I can't disagree with that, but I think her cavalier attitude has more to do with her liking Tim at the moment than any kind of magnanimity.

Von's date is a soccer girl I vaguely recognize. She's cleaned up very nicely for the occasion, her dirty blonde hair out of a ponytail for the first time I can ever remember. Mello's date looks like me on Miracle-Gro. Her boobs are a little bigger, her hips are a little wider, her skin is a little lighter, but just as smooth. Her sleek, permed hair reaches down past her shoulder blades. I guess Mello has a type, but then looking between Mello and Jayden someone might think the same of me. He's wearing a boot but doesn't seem otherwise bothered by his broken ankle.

Brandon makes a beeline for Mackenzie as soon as he spots her, and thanks her for inviting him. He introduces us to his friends and their dates, Finley and Alicia. Finally, he points to his date and says, "Last, and least, this is Lisa." She swats him on the arm and tries to elbow him in the ribs, but he just laughs. Mello wraps his arm around her head and gives her a noogie. My friends and I look on in confusion. Lisa retaliates by giving Mello's rock-hard abs a solid thump, but he doesn't even flinch.

"What the fuck?" I mouth to Brandon, and he mouths back, "She's his sister." I can kind of see the resemblance—they have the same coloring—though Mello is huge and Lisa's tiny.

Mackenzie clears her throat loudly, and says, "Feel free to grab some snacks and drinks. Let me or my mom know if you need anything."

SENCHA SKEETE

She leaves to perform some other hosting duties and Jayden introduces himself to the soccer players. Almost immediately they launch into a conversation about professional sports that I do not care in the least about. I excuse myself, but looking around Shelby is with Gio, Lorelei and Jackson are making googly eyes at each other, and Melodie and her date have joined a group of kids playing a board game.

I head outside to get some air. The crisp fall breeze hits my face as I step onto the deck. I lean against the railing and look up at the night sky. I'm mesmerized by the twinkling stars. For a moment, I let my mind to wander. It's calming, like relaxing a muscle.

The sound of laughter draws me back into the present. I look over and see a group gathered around the fire pit at the other end of the deck than runs along the back of the house. Brandon is among them, smiling and talking with his friends and Jayden. The firelight flickers across his face. I make my way over, stopping to grab a can of pop on the way.

"There she is," Jayden says, on my approach. "Do you want a s'more?"

"Of course!"

"I'll make it for you," Lisa volunteers. "You live with Branflake, right?"

"Yeah. My stepdad is his guardian," I respond. "You call him Branflake? I have to start doing that."

"It's cause he so stiff and boring. He not even Raisin Bran; he don't have enough flavor for that."

HE HATE ME

I remembered the sullen withdrawn Brandon who had moved in a few months ago. The most lively he ever was, was when he was sparring with me verbally. That changed at some point, though. I think it was around the time he brought me home high. Something that happened that night lit a spark in him that's been growing ever since. Brandon doesn't have flavor, he has fire, hot enough to burn any girl he gets close to. Looking at Lisa's grin, I don't think she's seen that side of him.

"Where do you go to school?" I ask her.

"Marshall," she says. She explains that she and Mello have known Brandon for years, since the boys started playing soccer together as pre-teens. They played in the free league sponsored by the city. Lisa, still in grade school, would tag along behind them.

"They was always tryna shake me loose, ya know, but I'm like a tick. You can't get rid a me." She laughs, and it's a charming, melodic sound. She has the kind of smile it's hard to resist and I find myself grinning at her.

"Do you play soccer, too?"

"Me? Nah. I'm not the sports type.

She hands me my s'more, gooey and warm, and asks who wants one next.

"I'll take one," Brandon says. He kneels next to the fire with her, and I watch them interact. She talks softly to him as she toasts the marshmallow, giggling at something he says. The gentleness in his expression is something I've never seen before, certainly not directed at me. She bumps her shoulder against him, her face flushed, and he pokes her in the ribs. Something ugly twists inside me.

I drop the uneaten portion of my s'more in the trash, suddenly finding it unappetizing. I go into the house through the nearest door, stepping into the kitchen. Mackenzie is leaning against the counter drinking a bottled water.

"Hey," I say, trying to read her mood. "You hiding out?"

"No, just taking a breather. There's so many people here. I guess I invited all of them, but it's kind of overwhelming having so many damn people in my house."

"I get it. That's why I haven't thrown a big party since sophomore year."

"That was so much fun, though. You have to do another one before we graduate."

"I don't know," I say. I'm not sure if I want to do that. The last party was so much work and I was running around the whole night trying to make sure no one stole or broke anything. But once I'm out of high school I'll never recapture this feeling of being with my friends. We'll scatter to who knows where after we graduate. "I'll think about it."

We go back into the living room. Mackenzie and I sit on the sofa and Tim joins us. We talk about professional football and TV. Lorelei and her boyfriend squeeze into a nearby chair, with her on his lap. I wrinkle my nose at the faint smell of marijuana. Some kid comes over and starts telling funny stories. He's lean, blonde, wearing a hemp necklace inside the collar of his dress shirt. We laugh and tease him a bit, but not in a mean way.

HE HATE ME

Eventually I relax enough to enjoy being with my friends. Kenzie puts on some music, and we start doing TikTok dances to everyone's amusement. Water comes on and we try to do Tyla's moves, but none of us is quite nailing it.

"I know dat one," a little voice calls out. Lisa hops in front of us and executes it perfectly. She has just the right kind of hips and butt for those moves, too, and pretty much all our dates are watching her jiggle. The longer the antics go on, the less amused I am, and I can see an answering annoyance in Mackenzie's eyes. I give her the signal and go into the kitchen to do my part. When I hear the music change to something mellow, I come back and stop next to Lisa.

"You want pop?"

"Sure," she says. I hand her the can and walk towards Jayden just in time to hear her squeal as the soda sprays all over the front of her dress.

"Oh, no," I say, turning around as if I'm surprised. "I'm so sorry. I don't know how that happened." She looks at me with suspicion for a second, but I don't think she knows what to believe. Kenzie rushes in and starts fussing over her. She's covered in sticky orange liquid and looks miserable. I watch as Kenzie pushes her up the stairs.

I turn back towards Jayden, and find Brandon standing an inch from my face, shaking his head.

"Picking on children, now?"

"She's not a child," I say, pushing past him.

"Did you mean to do that?" Jayden asks. I'm standing between the two of them, two giants, neither of whom look happy with me.

SENCHA SKEETE

"Of course not!" I'd been planning to talk to Jayden since he's my date and we've barely spent any time together, but I don't feel like being yelled at for a harmless prank. "Excuse me."

I exit the living room and take the hallway past the powder room, through the laundry room and out the exit to the side of the house where the porch wraps around. There's no one here, since it's kind of hidden, which is exactly why I chose it. There are few lights out here, and my arms and legs are freezing, but I spent entire days in this backyard with Mackenzie. There's an old treehouse out here we used to play Barbies in, and we'd hung a sign that said, "Girls Only" to keep Kenzie's brother out. I lean on the railing, trying to glimpse it among the dark tree branches. The door creaks open, and I turn to see Brandon stepping onto the deck. He shuts the door behind him and lets the screen door swing closed on its own.

"Running scared?" he teases.

"Just wanted some fresh air," I say, giving him my back. "What was that about?" I know he's talking about the prank.

"Nothing. Just being silly."

"You ruined her dress!"

"It'll wash out and I'm sure Kenzie's given her something else to wear."

"Yeah. She gave her culottes and a Raider's jersey."

"Warm," I say, deadpan.

"What's going on, Little Thorn?" he asks, coming closer.

"Nothing," I insist. "We're just petty bitches, okay. Her dancing was making us look stupid."

HE HATE ME

"Is it cause Jayden was staring at her ass?"

"Jayden?" I'd forgotten about him. Of course Jayden stared at her ass. Jayden stares at every ass.

"Is it because she's my date? Are you jealous because you think I'm interested in her?"

I can't speak past the lump in my throat. I feel so stupid. What has this boy done but hurt me, and instead of being happy he might be interested in someone else, I want to scratch her eyes out.

"She's pretty," I say, still not looking at him. I hear the creak of the deck and feel the heat of his body at my back. His arms come down on the outside of mine, caging me against the railing.

"Yes," he whispers in my ear. "She's pretty and soft. But you're beautiful."

Warm pleasure spreads in my belly at his words and I feel like a fool. His presses against my back, making me feel surrounded, protected.

"I need a woman who can bend without breaking, not some delicate flower that will rip the first time I touch her."

"So I'm not soft?"

"You are," he presses the softest kiss behind my ear, "but you're not fragile. I really believe you can handle me, Deja. She never could."

I want to ask him if that's the only reason he's into me. Is that the kind of girl he really wants, but he thinks he's too messed up for her? Oh, God. I don't want to be this person, looking for reasons to question my own value.

We stand like that for I don't know how long, just breathing together and listening to the laughter drifting over from the party. We freeze when we hear the door open behind us.

"Is that you, Brandon," Mackenzie asks. He doesn't move. If he does, she'll see me. "What you doing out here in the dark?"

"I have a little bit of a headache," he says. "The light hurts my eyes."

"I can get you a pill if you want. By the way, have you seen Deja? Jayden wants to leave soon."

"I haven't seen her for a while," he says. "Sorry."

"Is she still being a bitch to you?"

He laughs softly. "Why would that change?"

"You should give her a chance," Kenzie says. "She's usually so nice to everyone. Kill her with kindness and she'll come around."

"Maybe..." Brandon says, noncommittally.

The door closes and we're alone again.

I turn around in his arms. It's too dark to see his face, but he pulls me in for a lingering hug before letting me go.

"I'll slip through the railing and go around to the fire pit," I tell him.

"Sounds good. If I don't see you at home later, I'll see you in the morning, okay?"

I nod and slip away into the darkness.

Chapter 17

Deja

THE NEXT MORNING, BRANDON AND I STARE AT EACH other groggily over the breakfast bar. It's 8:00 a.m., and we're both still wearing our pajamas. My face burns from scrubbing off my makeup because I fell asleep with it on last night. I don't know what industrial-strength setting spray the makeup artist used, but I had a hell of a time getting the stuff off me. Brandon, for his part, is red-eyed and pale, his hair sticking up in all directions.

"You two don't look like you're up for church today," my mother says, sipping her green juice. Devin smiles knowingly, hugging her from behind. We regard them with matching expressions of "screw you." My head is pounding, and all I want to do is crawl back into bed.

SENCHA SKEETE

"I could use a few more hours," I say, propping my head on my hand. "Of sleep, I mean. Sleep."

Devin should be tired too, but he looks as fresh as a daisy. He was up when I got home at 2:00 a.m. and hung out with me and Jayden for half an hour before we all went to bed. Jayden's still asleep in the basement guest room, insulated from the noise of my parents stomping all over the second floor.

"How was the dance?" my mother asks.

"Good," I say, my head lowered over a cup of herbal tea. The warm steam is soothing to my oversensitive skin. "We had a lot of fun."

"And you, Brandon?"

"It was fine." His voice sounds gravelly.

"I didn't see you at the dance," I say, stifling a yawn. He got home a few minutes after me last night, mumbled something unintelligible at Devin, and went straight upstairs.

"I couldn't miss you, Homecoming Queen," he says, derisively. "Saw you bumping and grinding all over Jayden." I meet his eyes, and they're full of challenge. Why is he bringing this up now? If he wants to throw down, I'll throw down.

Forgetting that my parents are there, I sing back at him: "I don't see nothing wrong with a little bump and grind."

"You would quote a pedo," Brandon says, and my face goes hot.

"I'm not the one who took a child to homecoming," I shoot back.

He nods, conceding the hit. I'm not really mad, because I know this is all a performance so my parents don't suspect we

HE HATE ME

like each other. At least I think we like each other after the sweet things he said last night.

I catch Devin's expression, which is kind of suspicious. But suspicious of what? Hopefully, it's the bump and grind comment. My mother is doing that thing where she tries to have no expression. She always ends up looking constipated instead.

I fail to stifle a yawn. Brandon, who was looking at me, yawns too.

"Can I go back to bed?" he asks. "I'm just going to fall asleep in church if you make us go."

Devin accedes with a sharp nod. I slide off my stool and pick up my cup. I'm climbing the stairs before I realize I have company. My mother stops at the door to my bedroom, and I turn to see what she wants.

"Do we need to have a conversation?" she asks.

"About what?" She raises her eyebrows, and I get it. That kind of conversation. "No. Emphatically no."

The questioning look does not go away. She throws in the flat-lipped "don't bullshit me" expression, too.

"We've had the sex talk, Mom," I point out, wearily.

"This would be the safe sex talk," she says.

"They teach us sex ed at school, and I can always go on the internet." This does not seem to have mollified her. "If I have any questions or something changes, or I need something, I will ask you, okay? Brandon and I were just giving each other a hard time because we can't stand each other. All Jayden and I did last night was dance."

SENCHA SKEETE

This seems to do the job. She sniffs and gives me a little nod. Finally, I can go back to sleep.

* * *

I wiggle deeper into the cottony warmth of my bed. I'm halfway between sleep and wakefulness, the remnants of a dream still floating inside my brain. My speaker is on in the background playing *champagne problems* by Taylor Swift. It may be on repeat or perhaps my perception of time is distorted so that seconds stretch on forever. There's a velvety octopus's arm wrapped around my waist, hugging me tightly against the six-foot tall stuffed green dinosaur that I lost when I was five.

"Wake up, Little Thorn," the dinosaur whispers against the back of my head. I moan in denial. I don't want to wake up; I am feeling too content to wake up. The dinosaur rubs my tummy with a large paw. Don't dinosaurs have really tiny hands? Relatively small hands? These hands are warm, and shouldn't the body be softer?

"What is it?" I ask, only half awake. The dinosaur smells really good, like citrus and something herbal. His large hand moves up to lightly collar my throat and I jolt awake, my heart pounding. I don't have to turn my head to know who's in bed with me. There's only one person who would hold me like this.

"Brandon. What are you doing?"

"Just want to talk," he breathes into the nape of my neck. His breath is warm and mint scented. My skin heats. I'm starting to love the feel of his hand on my neck.

"You were being such a dick this morning."

"Don't want them to think we like each other, do we?"

"Do we like each other?" I tease.

He chuckles, honest to goodness. Can't remember hearing that sound before. Most of the time he's either grim or angry. It's a welcome change.

I sit upright, dislodging his hand, and make a dash towards the edge of the bed. He jumps for me. It's really awkward because we're both tangled in the covers, but I'm no match for him physically. He throws himself on top of me, heavy thighs weighing down my legs. I struggle, trying to throw him off, but I have no luck. The only effect is the shifting of our positions until I'm on my back and he's smiling down at me. He looks like a wolf who's cornered a lamb. Are you still prey if you want to be caught?

"Get off me, you jackass." He's got me pinned to the bed, his features sharp and feral. A thrill of delicious fear slides down my back. In that moment he has complete control. He could do anything he wants to me, and it should be terrifying, but I feel a pulse between my legs that's becoming all too familiar whenever he manhandles me. I push against him, and he flexes his muscles, showing his strength.

"Seriously," I hiss, "get off me. I don't want to get caught."

"Chill," he says. "I just want to talk."

"That makes even less sense with you on top of me."

His focus shifts to my lips, his eyes growing heavy-lidded. His head lowers, his mouth getting closer and closer to mine. I hold my breath, my lips parting in anticipation of his touch.

But then he laughs and levers himself up. The blue, agate marbles beneath his brows mock me. I regard him warily as I sit up, easing away from him. I don't get too far before he grabs my ankle.

I plop on my butt, now truly confused. What is he doing?

He's sitting cross-legged, holding me by the foot. We square off as much as you can square off in your pajamas among mounds of fluffy white bedding.

"I found something downstairs I want to show you."

He produces a messenger bag and pulls out a photo album. It smells a little musty, which isn't surprising if it's been in the basement for a while. It's wedding album with the words Lindsey and Sean on the front. Inside are photos of a white couple in their twenties. They both have dark hair—hers brown and his black like Brandon's. I can see both their features in Brandon. He's tall like his father and has the same general build, but the unblemished skin and striking features are all mom.

"They look so happy," I say, then I realize how that must sound since Brandon's dad left them.

"I think they were," Brandon says, "at least back then. I like to imagine this is the real them, loving each other. They had me out of love."

"Of course they did," I say because I know that's what he needs to hear. It must be a terrible feeling to wonder whether you were loved and wanted by both your parents.

"I don't remember them being together. I was so young when he left. But look how he's looking at her. It's like he thinks she hung the moon. I just don't understand what could have happened to make him leave."

"Whatever it was, it wasn't your fault." I squeeze his hand to comfort him, and he squeezes back.

"After my dad left, we moved in here."

"I didn't know that. How'd that happen?"

"My mom was working for Devin and when she couldn't afford to keep her place, he told her she could take the servant's quarters."

"That little room?"

"It was free, and housekeepers don't really get paid very much. Devin was actually cool. He taught me how to read, played ball with me. I don't mean he was like a surrogate dad or anything, but he paid more attention to me than my real dad."

"So what happened? You don't seem to like him now."

"He fired my mom, that's what happened. I woke up one morning and went into her room and she was slurring her words and stuff. I asked him to take her to the doctor and he said she'd be fine in a bit. And she was later in the day, but the problem kept coming back. She broke some household items, and he fired her. After ten years, she's out on her ass. We ended up in a homeless shelter."

I can't believe that's the whole story.

"But he did become your guardian, though. That has to count for something."

"That didn't mean he helped us out. If I wanted his help I'd have had to stay here without my mom. Fat chance."

SENCHA SKEETE

I feel like there's subtext here that I'm missing, especially since Brandon is now doing exactly what he said he wasn't going to do—living under Devin's roof without his mom. Big difference between eight and eighteen, but still, you'd think he wouldn't be so pissed off.

"What are you going to do with the album," I ask, changing the subject back.

"I figure I can get some pictures of her and her friends and put them in frames as gifts.

"I think she'll like that."

"Cool." He bites his lip.

That's all the warning I get before he's on top of me again. When I struggle, he grabs my wrists, holding them above my head in a tight grip. His face is inches from mine.

"Brandon, you're hurting me," I say, trying to pull away. But he's too strong, too determined. He leans in, his face inches from mine, his breath hot and heavy.

"But you like it when I hurt you, don't you," he says, and I have to look away, because he's right. I can feel the hard line of his body pressed against mine, his weight pressing me down into the bed, and it's delicious. He leans closer, his lips brushing against my ear. "You know what turns me on, Deja? The way your body tenses when you're afraid. Yes, that's it. Fight me."

My heart races as he trails kisses down my neck. I try to push him away, but it only makes him press harder against me. He's enjoying this, I realize with a weird feeling in my stomach. He's getting off on my fear and I'm getting off on his violence.

HE HATE ME

I feel his hand slip under my pajama top, his fingers tracing circles around my nipple. My back arches, seeking more of his touch.

"Brandon, stop," I say, my voice weak. "What if somebody catches us?"

As if I never spoke, his lips crash down on mine, sending shivers down my spine. He kisses me deeply, his hands tangling in my braids as he moves against me. He's dominating the kiss. His lips move against mine with a passion that shuts off my brain. My resistance melts away as Brandon deepens the kiss, his tongue exploring my mouth like it was made for him. My thoughts are all jumbled together, my heart thundering in my ears.

Suddenly, we are interrupted by a voice coming from the doorway. "Well, well, well…what do we have here?"

We both freeze as Jayden steps into the room. His gaze roams over our intertwined bodies before he smirks.

"I didn't know you two were so close!" he says, sardonically.

I push on Brandon's shoulders and this time he lets me up, pushing his hands through his hair.

"It's not what it looks like," I blurt, my voice high-pitched and shaky. Jayden's right eyebrow goes up as if to say, "Bullshit."

"I can see nothing's happening here," Jayden says, dryly. "Just like you weren't grinding on me last night."

I'm flushed with embarrassment. I dirty danced with Jayden last night, but it didn't mean anything. Bringing it up feels like shit stirring. It certainly didn't turn me on. Not like what Brandon and I were just doing.

"I wouldn't talk to Deja like that," Brandon says, his tone dark. He's staring at Jayden with an expression that's the polar opposite of Jayden's breezy smirk.

"Calm down, brah.," Jayden replies, "She wasn't even into it and now I get why."

"I don't know what you're talking about," I say, getting off the bed. Brandon stands up too, on the other side. We exchange a wary look. Brandon looks like he's ready to leap across the room and deck my ex-boyfriend.

I can see the anger rolling off Brandon while Jayden stands there coolly, like he isn't afraid of anything. I have no idea how a fight between these two would go down, but both of them are big, buff dudes. Jayden probably has an advantage as far as upper body strength, but Brandon is a rage monster.

"Calm down," Jayden says, chuckling. "I just came to get you for lunch. Your mom picked up soup and sandwiches."

Shit! Imagine if my mom or Devin had come to get us for lunch? I didn't realize it was so late; I thought Devin and my mom were still at church. I shudder at the thought of either of them walking in on me and Brandon kissing, and take a deep breath to steady my nerves. I can only imagine the look of shock and disappointment on my mom's face. I glance at Brandon, who is still standing awkwardly on the other side of the bed.

"Why don't you guys go ahead," I say. "I need to change." Brandon leaves the room with a tight nod in my direction. Jayden winks at me and closes the door on his way out.

Chapter 18

Deja

I'M CLIMBING INTO BED THAT NIGHT WHEN I HIT MY TOE against the messenger bag Brandon had earlier.
ME: *You forgot your bag in my room.*
BRANDON: *Look inside. I found a scrapbook with pictures of baby Deja.*

I see it, a photo album in pastel pink with my name bedazzled on the cover. I can't believe my mom ever did anything so cheesy.

I really was adorable as a baby. There are pictures of me fresh from the hospital swaddled in a white blanket with thin blue and pink stripes. Each two-page spread has picture of a different life stage. Newborn pics, pics of me before and after I learn to crawl, messy pics of me stuffing random mashed things into my mouth and so on. I especially love the ones where one of my parents is holding me. My mom's expression is soft, and any expression is loved on my father's face since I'll never see it in person again. Ten years after he got killed in a random mugging, I still miss him terribly. He was funny and so smart. He and my mom would fight sometimes, something she and Devin never do, and I remember no matter how angry he got, he never insulted my mom or called her names. I'm not going to say fighting with your husband is better than not fighting, but their relationship was so full of passion.

As the youngest pediatrician in his practice, my dad was on-call more often than anyone else. I remember him taking calls at all hours of the night and occasionally having to run out to deal with an emergency. I used to wait up for him as long as I could until my mom would make me go to bed. I'd try to stay awake even then, listening for his voice. Mom would scold me for it, but if I heard him, I'd get out of bed and run downstairs and get him to tuck me in.

Other memories rush back now. The feel of the dirt we tossed on top of his casket. The physical pain that came with lack of sleep because when I closed my eyes, I would picture my father being stabbed. The anger, boiling and bubbling like poison in a witch's cauldron, that spilled over onto the kid with the worn shoes and bad haircut. I pushed him into the mud and spread a rumor that he had lice and punched him in the kidneys once, then ran. Not long after that he switched schools, and I didn't see him again until he was standing on the steps of my house hauling moving boxes. Until he moved down the hall from me.

Everyone thinks I'm so nice, but Brandon knows the other side of me, the one that sensed his pain, saw the other kids pulling away and decided he was a safe target because no one would take his side. My dad had been a doctor and my mom drove a Lexus. Brandon's single mom got fired as a housekeeper and now cleaned our houses. I hurt him because I was hurting, but I also hurt him because I could. He knows me better than any of my friends do. He knows what I'm hiding behind my practiced smiles. He knows I'm not any nicer than he is, I just know how to make people like me.

There's a metal tin in the bag as well, kind of like a large pencil case with a hinged lid. There are sticker pictures on it, many of them rubbed off. My mom is in most of them, but there are a few cute cat stickers too. I guess my mom was into cats when she was my age. Inside are a few photos, my mom's college ring and a folded-up card stock invitation to a fraternity formal. I never heard of my dad being in a fraternity, so did my mom date someone else during college. One of the pictures is of my parents looking about my age in formalwear. My mom's dressed like she's going to prom in a poofy grape jelly colored dress. I stifle a giggle because she looks like a jar of Goober and my dad looks like a bar of Special Dark, complete with a red tie.

My parents met at a forensics competition when she was a freshman, and he was a sophomore. She was going to state university, and he was a student at a liberal arts college a few hours away. My mom told me about visiting Dad at his college

HE HATE ME

a lot that first year, then he transferred to her school and graduated from there. I'm curious what college he went to. The invitation doesn't have a name on it, but there's an address and a chapter name. I type the chapter name into my phone, and it says it's at McCrystal College. Why does that sound familiar?

* * *

"Does the name McCrystal College mean anything to you, mom?" I ask at breakfast the next morning.

"That's where Devin went to school," she says, rubbing the bridge of her nose.

I lower my head to hide my confusion. Did my mom go to a fraternity party with Devin? As far as I know they didn't meet until they started working together at the same company, the one they're still with. Could she have mixed his invitation up with her stuff? It seems pretty unlikely that a guy would even keep something like that. Is it possible my dad also went to that college?

"Where did dad go to undergrad the first two years?"

She freezes, her spoon halfway to her mouth, and says,

"Why are you asking?"

"I was wondering if I should apply for legacy admissions or something."

"I don't think that's a thing, honey." my mother says, "Your father graduated from state just like I did. In any case, your grades are excellent. I doubt you'll have any trouble getting into college."

"It can't hurt, though, right?"

"I thought you had your heart set on the University of Chicago?"

"I do, but I need safety schools. You told me it was a really good college, so I could definitely do worse."

"Why don't I look into it for you and let you know," she says.

"I can just add them to my list."

"Why waste time if they don't do legacy admissions? I'll ask my admin to look into it for you. She's great at research and you have so much to do already."

"Okay," I say reluctantly.

Brandon gives me a "what the fuck look," so I know it's not just me. That was weirdly evasive.

* * *

"What was that at breakfast," Brandon asks on the drive to school. He's looking relaxed today in a Special Interest t-shirt and a faded navy hoodie that almost matches his eyes. He needs a haircut, but I still want to grope him. Bad Deja!

"I looked inside that metal case in your bag last night."

"And?"

"There was a bunch of my mom's stuff inside including a fraternity formal invitation. It was for a frat at the college Devin went to."

"And?"

"They've both told me at different times, that they met at work. She introduced him at my dad's funeral as a friend from work. But there was a picture in there I'm pretty sure is of my parents at a McCrystal frat formal."

HE HATE ME

"Just because Devin and your dad went to the same college doesn't mean they knew each other or that Devin knew your mom."

"Sure," I say, "but then what was that crap with refusing to tell me my dad's undergrad? That's fishy, right?"

"It does sound like she's trying to hide something."

"They must have meet years before they told me they did. They lied about meeting at work. But why would they do that? It doesn't make sense."

Brandon gives me a sympathetic look. "Maybe there's an explanation. Your mom could come clean later. That invitation might not have anything to do with the picture." He doesn't sound like he believes what he's saying, but I appreciate that he's trying to make me feel better.

"Do you want to meet at lunch?" he asks. "I have a study room reserved."

"I can't." I do an exaggerated pout. "I have to have lunch with the girls. They want to rehash homecoming."

"So important!"

"They're my friends. I don't give you crap about hanging out with your friends."

"That's cause my friends are cool." God, he's so cute. Every time I see that smile, I just get gooey. I want to grin back at him just as hard.

I pull into my space in the student parking lot, and he grabs his backpack.

"I'll miss you," he says with a saucy wink, then he hops out of the car and strolls away towards the main building.

SENCHA SKEETE

* * *

That night Brandon texts me to meet him in the kitchen. He's sitting at the kitchen island staring intently at his phone. He's not using the phone; he just glances at the screen and then out the window, then back at his phone. His expression is intense, controlled. There's a tension in his body that makes me think of a cat, poised to strike, all potential energy.

"Hey," I say, walking over to grab the teakettle. This is the thing I do when I come down to the kitchen late at night—I make tea. It's almost instinctive. He looks at me without responding, then sticks his phone in his pants pocket. He walks over, hovering too close as I fill the kettle and then turn on a burner. His finger touches me under my chin, turning my head so I'll look right at him. He tilts his head one way, then the other as if he's examining me.

"Something on my face?" I ask, moving away from him and perching my butt on a barstool.

He shakes his head. "Let's go have a cigarette."

I know my brows are raised, but he knows I don't smoke. And the way he said it, like my compliance is without question. He has no reason to think I'd just do what he tells me. He's so different now than he was earlier in the day. This is the side of him I should hate, but I don't. He's got a violent energy around him that makes him feel dangerous. There's an answering buzz under my skin.

"No thanks," I say, rolling my eyes.

He shrugs, then grabs me by the arm and pulls me off the stool.

"What the—"

HE HATE ME

"Shh," he says. "One cigarette's not going to kill you. I don't want to be alone."

I see vulnerability in his eyes. Is it real or a ploy to get me to do what he wants? Am I being manipulated?

I don't know, but I find myself going along with him. Maybe there's a part of me that's curious about cigarettes. It's such a no-no among kids my age. It's seen as old-fashioned and stupid, and we're all aware of how it can hurt your athletic performance. I have wondered what attracts people to it. It stinks, it's bad for you, and it stains your teeth. It has to feel pretty good for people to do it at all. Stupid thinking, I know, but I'm eighteen, not twenty-eight—you can't expect maturity.

We go out to the little enclosed area where the trash cans are stored, and he hands me a cigarette. Thanks to the cold, I can't smell the garbage. I nervously hold the cigarette to my lips while he lights it, telling me to inhale. If you've never had a cigarette, well, don't. It tastes foul, and I'm coughing loudly enough I worry we'll wake my mom and Devin up. Once I've taken a few more drags and my eyes have stopped stinging, I do feel something. It's like a mild warm feeling, a slight zing of energy or something, but it's nothing to write home about. Brandon finishes his cigarette first, having taken deeper and more frequent drags than me, and I toss what's left of mine onto the pavement when he does. He smashes both with his feet, since I'm wearing my house slippers.

I turn to go back inside, but he takes hold of my forearm, his hand sliding down to cuff my wrist. He's breathing harder than he should be.

"I like when you do what I tell you," he says.

SENCHA SKEETE

Why does that statement make me feel good? I don't react when he herds me against the wall and starts kissing me. The taste of him is tobacco-heavy, his tongue probing my mouth like he's trying to search out its every secret. I'm dropped into a mishmash of conflicting emotions like someone plunging through ice into a murky lake. I'm shivering from cold? From want? From fear? I don't know, but my nipples are hard, and my heart is thundering in my ears.

Then a bit of my brain sparks on, and I question whether this is right. I've never been the girl that gets told what to do by some guy, and I'm definitely not easy prey. I don't know what's going on in Brandon's head, but I need some space to think. I push against him, and as usual, he's unyielding and ignores me. I turn my head to break the kiss.

"Stop, Brandon. I want you to stop."

"No, you don't," he says. He closes his hand around my neck—again!—and kisses me harder. This time I feel my lips pressing into my teeth. The kiss is brutal, and my adrenaline spikes, edgy excitement fighting arousal for dominance. He's going to take what he wants, and it's making me wet. Why am I so fucked up?

He breaks the kiss and licks my cheek like an animal. He wraps my braids around his fist and tugs my head back, baring my neck to his kisses. His mouth scalds my chilled skin. He nips on my ear firmly enough to cause pain and I stifle a yelp. He yanks my hair downwards harder until I'm forced to my knees.

HE HATE ME

I stare up at him, looking like a giant from this angle, his pale face glowing bright in contrast to the black of his hair and clothing. The damp concrete is cold under my knees and rough.

"Take me out," he says, releasing my hair, and I comply, unbuckling his belt with stiff fingers and easing his zipper down. I reach into the opening and fish him out, the engorged shaft resisting the motion. Seeing him up close for the first time I'm flummoxed. His size is unimaginable, so huge that I want to laugh hysterically at the thought of it fitting inside me, and it's still growing, getting stiffer. I take it in both hands, caressing the velvety soft skin with my curious fingers.

"Kiss it," he commands. His voice is steely, but his gentle touch on my face betrays affection.

I hesitate, unsure how to react to the contrast. I lean in tentatively, my tongue flicking out and lapping at him, tasting him. He's sweet, and clean, with undertones of sea salt body wash from a recent shower. It's not gross like I thought it might be. I think I like it. Brandon groans above me and pushes my head downwards, forcing me to take more of him into my mouth. I suck on the head, eyes watering, then back off for air before repeating.

He smells strong here—soap and musk and the all-consuming scent of arousal that fills my lungs, making me dizzy. I use both hands to stroke his shaft, working them in time with my lips, trying to please him. His cock is too big for my mouth, but I do my best, focusing on the tip. Brandon's grip in my hair tightens as he pushes himself further into my mouth, forcing me to take more of him, his hips rocking in a primal rhythm as he fucks my mouth. His breathing escalates, and he grunts and groans above me, the noises he makes only heightening my confusing arousal.

Suddenly, he grips the back of my head and forces himself so deep he hits the back of my throat. My gag reflex kicks in, and I start to cough, spitting out his cock and gasping for air.

"Breathe," he says, stroking the back of my head. I struggle to catch my breath, a brief coughing fit seizing my lungs. As soon as it's over, he tips my head back, examining my face.

"Open your mouth," he says. It's not phrased as a question, but somehow I know that if I wanted to stop, he'd be fine with that. I don't want to stop, though. "Stick out your tongue. As far as you can. Don't look away."

Eyes locked on mine, he lays the tip of his cock on my tongue. "Suck."

I close my lips around his glans and suck, using my tongue to tease the underside of his cock. He pulls me forward gently, just far enough to fill my mouth, but not enough to make me gag. My jaw aches from the strain. He fists his cock and pumps the shaft, like he's jacking off into my mouth.

"Eyes on me," he says, when they start drifting closed. It's intense feeling him in my mouth while we stare into each other's eyes. I can see his pupils dilate, the flaring of his nostrils as his breathing gets rougher. His fist speeds up, just missing my lips on each downstroke. I feel him swell in my mouth, taste his essence as he gets closer to orgasm. His jaw tenses and his erection jumps, blasting jets of seed into my mouth. I'm not prepared to swallow, but he holds me in place, filling my mouth until it spills down my chin and wets the front of my pajamas.

He lets me go and I spit, finding the taste unlike anything I've had before. It's salty, with notes of bleach, and I don't think it will ever be my favorite thing.

He helps me to my feet and kisses me on the cheek.

"Thank you. That was great."

"I didn't know what I was doing. I choked."

"You did good. It's so hot when you do what I ask and it felt amazing. I want to make you feel good, now."

"You don't have—"

"Can I touch you?" The polite request surprises me. He just forced me to my knees and commanded me to blow him, but now he's asking permission?

I nod, realizing I can't find my voice. His fingers find the waistband of my pajamas and slip inside. He swears softly when he feels how wet and swollen I am. In less than a minute I'm gasping for air, and riding Brandon's hand. He is not inexperienced, or if he is, he has an amazing natural talent for fingering. I bite down on his pec so I won't scream and when my legs give out, he holds me up and drives me to the edge of sanity.

* * *

The kettle is screaming when I stumble inside, and I can only count my lucky stars that neither of the parents came down to check. My pajama top is stained with his come and my bottoms and underwear are soaked with mine. My pussy is still so sensitive I can barely walk, but if I'd stayed outside any longer, I would have died by orgasm. Brandon's all put back together, smoking a cigarette with hands that smell like me. I turn off the stove and head upstairs. I'm pretty sure I'll have no trouble falling asleep now.

Chapter 19

Deja

I MEET BRANDON IN THE LIBRARY AT LUNCHTIME, SLIPPING into the study room around 11:35. He's got books spread out on the table and notebook, densely scrawled with his nearly illegible handwriting. I'm a bit surprised because I didn't think Brandon was taking school this seriously, but I guess I was wrong.

When I come in, he motions for me to sit in the chair nearest the door and repositions his chair to face mine.

"Let me guess," I say. "You have a new threat and/or demand."

"No," he says, vigorously shaking his head. "Nothing like that. I just thought we should talk."

"About what?"

"All the things that have been happening between us."

"This isn't a DTR is it? Cause I call situationship."

He frowns as if trying to figure out what I mean and then he smiles faintly.

"I think a situationship is like defining a relationship as undefined."

"Fair."

The brief smile disappears. Whatever he wants to talk about he's serious about it.

"We're not even at DTR yet, Deja. It's more basic than that. Do you feel like you consented to what we've done together."

I look around in confusion. "You cannot seriously be asking me that."

"I know I haven't always gotten your verbal consent—"

"My verbal consent? The first time we fooled around I was pretty much passed out on drugs."

"You weren't passed out. We had a whole conversation. You agreed to everything."

"I remember snatches of it, and I was into it at the time, but I was in no mental state to agree to anything, and you knew that."

His cheeks flush and I can see that I'm right. He knew he was taking advantage of me when he did it.

"And then," I press on, "you blackmailed me, which makes any kind of consent coerced at best."

"I never blackmailed you into doing anything sexual," he says, shifting uncomfortably in his seat. He initiated this conversation, but I can tell he isn't enjoying it.

"The spanking?"

"You agreed to it, and it wasn't sexual. At least that wasn't the purpose."

"Coerced agreement, Brandon. The other option was unthinkable. That was textbook blackmail. Plus, you want me to believe you didn't enjoy having me over your lap half naked?"

He swallows, unable to maintain eye contact.

"Yes, I liked it," he admits, "but after you went and caused that whole mess with Mello, I felt like things were getting out of control. If I didn't give you a consequence for disobeying me, then you'd just ignore me. I couldn't go as far as releasing the video; that would have ruined your life. But I had to set a boundary. I told myself spanking you was better than the alternative, and it would make you take me more seriously."

"What gives you the right to set boundaries for me?"

He looks embarrassed, cheeks reddening even more. He leans back, resting his palms on his thighs, looking intimidating even in this humbled pose.

"If I'm honest I was feeling guilty. After I went to my room, my brain wouldn't shut down. I just kept thinking that Mello might lose his chance at a college scholarship because I pushed you into a corner and you used him to get back at me. At two in the morning, it made sense to 'take you in hand.'

And maybe I was influenced by that kiss and rewatching the video of that night."

"The night I was high?"

"Yeah. I've watched it dozens of times, jerked off to it." He's staring at the floor, clearly uncomfortable revealing all this to me.

"You showed me the first part. What happened after that?"

"I went down on you, you made the *ahega*o face, you—"

"The what?"

"The anime orgasm face. With your tongue out."

I know what he's talking about. Pictures of Belle Delphine doing it were really popular at one point, I remember, and all the girls would do it in class when the teacher wasn't looking.

"So I had an orgasm?"

"Yes, but not then. You were enjoying the oral sex, then you turned your head, looked straight into the camera, and made that face. Then a couple minutes later you had an orgasm. I didn't see it until I watched the video because, well, my head was between your legs."

"Okay…"

"Then the last part is just me coming on you."

"On me?"

"On your torso, and that's the end of the video."

"Is that everything that happened?"

"Except for me cleaning you up and putting your pajamas on, yeah."

HE HATE ME

I stand up, unsettled by the revelation. I had wondered exactly what happened that night and learning that we had sex—oral sex is sex—is disturbing. Brandon and I still hated each other at that point. Knowing what happened makes me feel like an object, like my feelings and consent didn't matter to him.

"What are you hoping to get out of this conversation, Brandon?" I ask, crossing my arms under my breasts. I keep my eyes on a spot above his head, not wanting to look at his face.

"That night when I spanked you, you were scared and crying. I thought I'd blown up any chance I had with you. Then I realized you were as turned on as I was. And I don't think it's all that common that two people are both equally turned on by something like that. I caused you genuine pain and the more it hurt, the more turned on you were. I thought we connected. So I asked if I could kiss you, and you said yes. To me that was a turning point. The next day when you warned Mackenzie off, I figured if you didn't like me, you must at least feel possessive towards me.

"Last night was amazing. I just love how you resisted a bit, but then did exactly what I wanted. When you do that, it feels like a gift. Your obedience has value to me, Deja. I felt like a king, like chest thumping silverback gorilla kinda shit. But then after you went inside, I started to wonder if maybe you were going along with it because you were worried about me releasing the video. And that wasn't satisfying at all."

He looks at me, like he wants me to give him the answer the will put him back on top of the world. I don't know what to say.

"I swear I will never release the video, okay?"

"And you'll delete it?"

"Sure."

"Right now."

He sighs and pulls out his phone. He plays the start of the video so I can see that it's the right one and hits delete.

"Can I see that?"

He looks annoyed, but he gives it to me. There are a few other pictures from that night, including the ones he sent me before, and I delete those, too.

"Thank you," I tell him, handing the phone back. "You said you thought you blew your chance with me by spanking me. Does that mean you liked me already?"

"I don't know why," he chuckled. "You were so mean to me, but you were so clever with the insults. And you stood up to me despite being such an itty-bitty thing."

"I'm five-seven." He's amused at my response.

"So anyway, yeah, I liked you and after the night I made the video I needed you to be my girl, but everything was so fucked up."

"Why didn't you just ask me out?"

"Would you have said yes?"

I shake my head. I would have said no in the most humiliating way possible. And not just because he was being obnoxious, but also because I knew without asking my parents would never let us date while we were living in the same house together.

"I need to think, Brandon. I know what you want me to say, but I don't think I can say that right now with complete honesty."

As I could have predicted, he stands up and approaches me. Holding me loosely by the upper arm, he tries to pull me close. I turn my head to avoid his kiss and wrench myself out of his arms. His hurt expression doesn't sway me. Kiss him and I'm back in the fog of sexual desire. I need a clear head to figure out what I actually want, devoid of his influence.

"Are we still meeting tonight for tutoring?" he asks when I'm at the door to leave. I consider telling him no. Tutoring was something he blackmailed me into, and he did it after the night when he said that everything changed. But he wasn't going to pass that class without my help.

"Okay," I say. "But until I say otherwise, let's keep it professional. I'm your tutor and that's it."

* * *

That night he comes to my room for tutoring and acts perfectly. He's focused, doesn't try to touch me or stare, it's nice, but a little disappointing. I think I've gotten used to the way he looks at me like he wants me. If this is a ploy to make me choose him, it's kind of working. I didn't notice how good it is to feel desired by him.

"You know what I wanted to be when I grew up?" he asks out of the blue midway through the session.

"Thanos?" I ask, deadpan. He disappoints me by smiling in response.

"I wanted to be an astronaut."

"Don't think I'm that good of a math tutor."

"You're the best," he says. "I thought I would go to Mars and help terraform it."

"That's an awfully big word."

"What did you want to be?" he asks. I sigh. I'm starting to feel like a real jerk being rude to him when he's being so nice. Of course, he's only being nice to get in my pants, so there's that.

"I wanted to be a pop star."

"No kidding?"

"You don't think I can do it?"

"If it was just dancing, you'd hit it out of the park."

"But?"

"What do you want to be now?"

"Why are you sidestepping my question?"

"I don't want to be mean, but you can't sing. I can hear you sometimes when you're in the shower, and cats fighting in the back alley sound better than you."

I am a terrible singer, and I can vividly remember the afternoon when I was in my room singing along with and dancing to a Beyonce song in front of a mirror, and I caught my mother's pained expression as she walked by my door. It was then that something clicked in my brain, and I could actually hear myself for the first time. It was crushing. I think I might even have been too sad to eat dinner that night. Hearing it now, I feel a twinge of that pain, but it's a fact I

HE HATE ME

faced years ago. At least he isn't lying to me. That's a point in his favor.

"I want to either get an MBA and work for a Fortune 500 company, or I want to become a math professor."

"A professor? That won't be easy."

"You know that saying, 'Shoot for the moon, even if you miss, you'll hit the stars?' I figure if I don't get to be a professor, I can still probably teach high school math or go into accounting or something."

"Very sensible."

"What about you? What did you land on?"

"I don't really know. It's kind of hard to think long term."

"You're in your senior year of high school. All anyone is thinking about is the future and what they're going to do with their lives."

"Not me," he says, flippantly. "Just taking it one math test at a time. By the way, do we still have time to do a practice test?"

"Not a full one." We go back to the work, but the tension between us has eased a bit. It's almost like I'm talking to a friend and not whatever complicated thing Brandon and I are to each other.

Chapter 20

Brandon

I HEAR THE SOFT PATTER OF FEET AND FEEL THE MATTRESS dip slightly. I must have been asleep, because I didn't hear my bedroom door open. I don't need to open my eyes to know who it is. I can smell her, coconut oil and vanilla blended with the natural scent of her skin. My heart swells. Deja is in my bed of her own free will.

"Are you awake?" she whispers.

"Yeah," I reply. She gets under the covers and scoots closer to me. Her knee jabs into my thigh and she makes a little sound of dismay as she pulls back. I don't let her. I put my arm around her waist and haul her against my body. She giggles softly, apparently not minding my boldness.

"I couldn't sleep," she says. "I went downstairs to make tea, but then I…"

She doesn't continue and I'm not sure what she was going to say. My ability to speculate ends when her hand cups my cock through my pajama pants. Her touch is curious and exploratory. She traces the shape of my stiffening shaft and takes hold of my balls, squeezing gently.

"Harder," I whisper, and she listens, giving my balls a firm tug.

I grunt and roll onto my side to face her. In the moonlight spilling through my window, I can see her eyes glinting. They're wide with desire, uncertainty, and something else. Fear? No time for that now. I want her, and judging by the way she's touching me, she wants this too.

Slowly, I lift up her camisole, revealing perfect, round breasts that are the color of mocha. Her nipples are prominent and stiff, too tempting to resist. I cup her breasts in my hands and tease her nipples with my thumbs before lowering my head to take one into my mouth.

"Oh, God," Deja moans softly, arching her back. I tease her with my tongue and teeth until she's writhing under me. Her hand goes underneath the waistband of my pants, wrapping around my bare cock. She strokes up and down, her soft hand cool on my heated skin.

I trail my mouth down her stomach, biting and sucking, leaving hickeys in my wake. Her hands comb through my hair, her breathing audible in the quiet room. I hook my thumbs into the waistband of her shorts and panties and pull both down, baring her pussy to me. In the dim light I can't see her well, but her scent is intoxicating, musky with arousal.

I slide my thumb along her folds and find them swollen and slick. I lower my head and give her little clit a kiss, stroking it with my tongue and exploring her wet groove. She's hot and slick, juicy and delicious like a goddamn peach. I slide a finger inside her. She's wet enough that there's almost no resistance. I add another finger, preparing her for what's to come. Once she adjusts, I add a third finger, pumping them in and out of her soft, slick cunt. She's humping my face, her hand covering her mouth to stifle her sounds of pleasure. I want to make her scream, and since I can't, I'm going to make her fall apart.

My tongue returns to her sex, zeroing in on her sensitive bud while my fingers continue to pump and twist, stretching her out. I've already decided. I can't wait any longer. I feel her body tense, even her glutes tightening as her thighs tremble. I don't slow down, driving her closer and closer to ecstasy. I hear a muffled gasp and then she shudders, once, twice, three times, with each practically crushing my head between her legs. I gentle my touch, planting a final kiss on her pussy before easing away just long enough to strip off my clothes.

"Brandon," she pants, her tone plaintive. I've never had a woman look at me like this, like she's starving for every inch of me. It's like she's devouring me with her eyes, making me the center of her world. I can't get enough of it; nothing else matters when she looks at me like this. All I want is to drown

HE HATE ME

in that intensity, to lose myself in her dark eyes, again and again.

"I'm right here," I tell her, settling between her thighs. I lay myself flush on top of her, the head of my cock nudging her soft folds. She feels warm and open, eager to welcome me in. But I know it's her first time and even though she doesn't have a hymen I am bigger than average, a bit longer and much thicker than most guys.

I line up and nudge the head of my cock against her entrance. She tenses, so I stop. "You ready, Little Thorn? I'm going to break in that little pussy for you." She stifles an incredulous laugh, for the moment focused on my audacity and not what I'm about to do. I ease inside her slowly, first an inch, then two, then three. Her eyes squeeze shut, a tear sliding down her cheek like a sparkling gem. Her nails dig into my back, her tiny sounds of distress urging me to drive deeper into her slick, tight heat. It feels so good being inside her that I almost can't believe I've waited this long. I fight against my kink, the primal desire to plunge into her with one brutal stroke and deliver the kind of pain that will fuel my own pleasure. But this is her first time, and as much as I want to hurt her, I also don't want to hurt her. My heart desires to give her exactly the pain she wants, and no more. So I hold still, the forbearance torture, while I let her adjust to me. Eventually her breathing evens out and her eyes open.

"Fuck me, please," she says sweetly.

Jerking her hips, she seats me fully inside her. Deja's warmth envelopes me like a second skin, silky wetness gripping my cock like a glove. I can't remember ever feeling so close to another person. It terrifies me, but I push the thought aside for later. Right now I just want to feel her, to lose myself inside her.

"Fuck, Deja," I moan, unable to hold back any longer as I thrust deeper. Deeper still, until our hips slap together with a wet smacking sound that seems to echo off the four walls of my bedroom. Her nails score my back as she greedily begs for more. She's as into this as I am, which arouses me further.

We fuck so hard the bed creaks and the headboard slaps against the wall in an almost musical rhythm. The only sounds in the room are our ragged breathing and muffled grunts of pleasure as our bodies move together. My balls tighten; I can't hold back any longer. I drive deep inside her one last time, then explode, erupting my seed deep inside her tight, wet heat. Her pussy contracts around me, milking every last drop from my balls. She screams, her body arching upward as she comes, her short nails digging into my back. I collapse on top of her, our breaths ragged and uneven. Slowly, our breathing returns to normal and I roll off her, pulling her into my arms.

"This was so stupid," she says, sending a chill through my heart. I move so that I can read her expression. Does she regret what we just did? Is she still upset about the things I did before?

"They could have heard everything," she continues. "We were so loud."

"Thank God," I blurt out.

"What?"

"I thought you were saying us having sex was stupid. You're not sorry, are you?"

HE HATE ME

"No," she says. "That was so much better than I imagined."

"So you're forgiven me?"

"No," she says. "I don't know. I think I just really like sex. I was lying in my bed, and I couldn't stop thinking about how you made me come on your fingers. I've, um, touched myself to the memory of it a few times. Tonight I just couldn't take it anymore. I couldn't help myself."

"So I'm not special," I say. I keep my tone light, not wanting her to know how much what she's saying hurts me.

"Am I?" she asks. Her voice betrays vulnerability, despite her attempt to sound flippant.

"I already told you that you're mine, Deja," I say. "You're fucking perfect for me."

"It feels different when you touch me," she confesses, "more intense. Sexier. I don't think anyone else could make me feel the things you do."

She gives me a shy look and an almost embarrassed smile. "That means you have to give it to me when I want it. You have to be my boy toy."

"Really?" I wiggle my eyebrows, grinning. "That sounds sexy as hell. But you know I was trying not to hurt you tonight, right?" I press down on her bottom lip and push my thumb into her mouth. "I'm not going to go so easy on you next time."

Her eyes light up, excitement animating her features. She sucks on my thumb then bites it, nodding, letting me know that she understands exactly what I mean.

SENCHA SKEETE

I pull her close for a deep kiss, savoring her warmth and the heady taste of her. We kiss for what feels like forever until our lips are swollen and I feel myself getting hard again. If this was any other time, I'd flip her over, and take her again, but she just lost her virginity and I know she must be sore. Reluctantly I let her go.

"You'd better go back to your room," I say. "I wish we could sleep next to each other, but…"

"You're right," she says, stroking the side of my face. She adjusts her top and we dig around till she finds her underwear and shorts. I get dressed too, my mind already spinning ahead to when I can have her next. She unlocks the door and peeps out, checking that the hallway is empty before blowing me a kiss and slipping away.

* * *

Deja

I want to skip down the stairs the next morning. I mean the heart is certainly willing. I'm discovering that an orgasm—specifically one induced by Brandon—is the key to a great night's sleep. I didn't fall asleep until 3:00 am last night and yet I feel like a million bucks.

But you know, the flesh is weak. I didn't want to let Brandon know because what we did last night was very wanted and intensely pleasurable, but it also hurt like a motherfucker, and I'm really sore both around my labia and deeper inside where his giant cock stretched me the fuck out. I feel it with every movement I make. My labia feel abraded

HE HATE ME

and there's a sensation like the shadow of him is still inside me, feeling both sore and deeply erotic. Every step I take I feel him, and I remember our intense coupling and I want it again. My panties are slick by the time I make it down to breakfast.

As soon as I sit at the breakfast bar Brandon excuses himself saying he'll meet me by the car in a bit. I shrug and dig into my usual health-conscious breakfast, enjoying the special treat of chicken sausage links. My mother appears slightly nervous as she sits across from me, stirring honey into a small container of plain Greek yogurt.

"How are you this morning, Deja?" she asks. I wonder where Devin is. They've been joined at the hip lately, so it's rare not to have him with us at a meal.

"Great." Her yogurt looks yummy, but she's just playing with it. I wonder if I can wheedle it out of her.

"I got the info back from my assistant about your dad's college. It's bad news I'm afraid. They ran out of funds a few years ago. They're not accredited anymore. It's so sad; they'd been around for over a century."

"What college?" I ask.

"St. Joseph's College."

"Thanks, Mom. That's kind of disappointing, but I'm sure I can find someplace else."

My appetite has suddenly deserted me. My Spidey senses are tingling like crazy. First my mom wants to confirm they do legacy admissions and now they mysteriously went out of business. I'm smelling bullshit. I choke down the rest of my food and excuse myself.

SENCHA SKEETE

* * *

As soon as we get on the road, Brandon reaches over and takes my hand. His fingers are cold, but I like it. It's welcome distraction from the thoughts swirling around in my head.

"How are you feeling?" he asks, stroking my knuckles. "Regretting it yet?"

"Oh, ye of little faith," I respond. "No, I don't regret it. It was awesome."

"You seem kinda, I don't know, off?"

"Not because of last night. Why'd you rush away from breakfast like that? You're not regretting it are you?"

"Of course I do. I just hate when beautiful girls give me their virginity." He's being facetious, of course, but I play along.

"How many girls are we talking about here?"

"Just one. But she has the beauty and sass of ten grown women." He turns his palms up like he's cupping my ass when he says the word sass. If I wasn't driving, I'd smack him on the arm. The thought makes me smile because I realize I feel comfortable enough to do something like that without worrying that he'll take it the wrong way.

"Seriously, though?"

"I could never regret last night. I've been imagining being with you since the minute you walked past my room in those little cheerleading shorts while I was unpacking my stuff. I could not believe the scrawny little kid from grade school had turned into such a goddess. I tried to resist my feelings, but...I couldn't. I can't. "

"I wasn't scrawny."

"We were both scrawny," he insists. "Do you remember hitting me with a softball in third grade?"

"What? No."

"Oh, yeah. I made a rude comment about Shelby while I was walking past you guys at PE, and you 'accidentally' drilled me in the ass. I thought my butt was broken and when I told my mom she laughed at me so hard. Women are cruel."

"This from the guy who spanks us."

"It's been a while," he says, raising an eyebrow. He's subtly asking, and I wiggle in my seat, imaging how good it would feel to have him spank then fuck me. Less than six hours since losing my virginity and I'm already lusting for more. I'm turning into a regular old sex fiend.

"But still…breakfast?"

"Oh, yeah. I didn't think I could hide the way I was feeling from your mom. When I saw you walking into the room I wanted to grin like the Joker."

"I know," I say. "I probably would have been cheesing just as hard. We took a big risk last night doing it in your room. I don't know what I was thinking. Where are we going to do it next time? I don't think we can hide the sound of a spanking."

"I have an idea where we can go."

"Where?"

"I need to check with someone first, then let you know."

"Why do you always have to be so mysterious? And speaking of mysteries, Mom told me this morning that my dad went to St. Joseph's College."

SENCHA SKEETE

"Where is that?"

"I don't know."

"Why don't we meet in the study room. I'll bring my laptop and we can look it up."

"That's a good plan." I pull into my parking space and turn off the car. I want to lean over and kiss him, and I see him start to move, then pull himself back. It sucks that we have to hide how we feel about each other. I want to run to my friends and tell them all about my first time, but I can't say peep because of the drama with Mackenzie. We also have to think about my parents finding out, since information always seems to make its way to the last person you want to know.

"See you at lunch," he says, getting out of the car.

"See you," I wave goodbye, then grab my stuff and follow him inside.

Chapter 21

Deja

WHEN I GET TO MY LOCKER, SHELBY IS WAITING FOR ME, looking really nervous.

"Hey," I say, cheerily, not exactly oblivious to her mood, but too hyped to mirror it. Usually, Shelby's the kind of person who would put aside her concerns to ask me what's making me happy, but this morning she's too preoccupied. She tugs at my sleeve and asks in a low voice, "Did you get my text?"

I shake my head. Based on her tortured facial expression, I surmise that she wants me to look at it now. I didn't even think to check my messages this morning like I usually do. I honestly didn't care what was going on with other people.

I see it:

SHELBY: *Can you go to PP with me after school?*

"What happened?" I ask her, growing concerned.

"I have an appointment," she whispers, "but I got scared to go by myself. Can you please?"

"What's the appointment for? Did something bad happen?"

"No," she says, her voice barely audible "I just need to get checked and start birth control."

I feel a little queasy. Until that moment I hadn't even thought about birth control. The last thing Brandon and I need is to get pregnant. Can you imagine me explaining to my parents that the "troubled kid" they let move in with us got me pregnant?

"How did you make the appointment?" I ask.

"Online. Why?"

"I need to make one, too. What time is yours?"

She tells me the location and time and I navigate to the website on my phone. The bell rings and she heads off to class, thanking me one more time. There are way too many screens, but finally I get to the page where I can choose a slot.

"Ms. Marcus," a stern voice says, "please proceed to class." It's one of the vice-principals, a woman in her fifties who always gives me the impression of being someone who would have fit in back in the days when teachers used to hit kids. I conceal my phone behind my books and close my locker, giving her an apologetic smile. She nods, satisfied, as I rush down the hall towards my next class. Once I'm sure she can't see me, I pause long enough to confirm the appointment. I feel a slight sense of relief, but I'll be much better once I've been to the clinic.

* * *

I race over to the library as soon as the bell rings and start running up the stairs before my body reminds me to take it easy. It's already a lot better than it was this morning, though. I get to the last study room at the end of the Classics row and Brandon opens the door like he was standing right there watching for me.

As soon as I'm inside he traps me against the wall and kisses me like we've been apart for a century. I melt into Brandon's kiss, momentarily forgetting everything else. His hands slide down my sides and grip my hips, pressing me harder against the wall. A familiar heat pools in my core as his tongue explores my mouth. Our breaths mingle, hot and urgent, my heart pounding with excitement. His erection is thick against my hip. I feel an answering pulse between my legs. He captures my wrists, holding them at my sides while he kisses my neck and grinds into me.

"I want you so much," he whispers, his voice raspy. "This is insane."

I look at his flushed face, and I can only agree with him. Sex has changed things between us, made it more intense and our desire for each other more difficult to resist. It's hard to remember that we're basically in a public place with a viewing window, when all I want to do is feel him inside me again. I tug on my wrists, and he lets me go, raking his hand through his hair and pacing to the far wall and back. I sit at the table, and after a moment, so does he. He licks his lips, adjusting himself under the table. His laptop is open on the table, a detail I hadn't noticed until now.

"I'll meet you at your car as soon as school is out," he says, his knee bouncing.

"I can't. I have to go to the clinic."

"No!"

"We didn't use protection last night." I voice is colored with chagrin.

Brandon buries his face in his hands and groans. "How could I forget about that? I have condoms like three feet from where we had sex. I'm sorry. I don't know where my brain was."

"Why do you have condoms?" I cross my arms below my breasts.

"Because I figured, or more like I hoped we'd have sex soon. I wanted to be prepared."

"So it's not because there's, like…" I can't finish the sentence. Why would I expect him to not have sex with other people? We've never had that conversation and he's made me no promises. He's a horny teenager and an athlete, not to mention hot. Those blue eyes alone are panty melters, and that's before you take in his lips and that sinful black hair. There are probably a dozen girls in his phone he can call for sex whenever he wants.

"There's no one else," he says, "not since the first time I touched you."

HE HATE ME

"What about Mackenzie?"

"That was me being a dick. I needed a tutor, and I knew you told her to stay away from me. I wanted to make you mad. But nothing ever happened between us. We never even kissed."

"For real?"

"For real. And can you call me after you're done at the clinic? Let me know how it went?"

"I can text," I offer. I don't know if Shelby and I will be carpooling, and I don't want him to know that she's going with me. It's a pretty private thing, and Shelby and Brandon aren't friends. "So just for the record, can we agree no other people."

"No other people," he confirmed. "We are officially exclusive."

"Cool." I glance at my watch and note that we've used up a lot of our time without talking about what we're supposed to be talking about.

"Can I borrow your laptop?" I ask, and he nods.

I position the screen so that we can both see it. A search for St. Joseph's College brings up an institution in Indiana. Like my mom said, it's no longer accredited, but I know immediately that she's lying about my dad going there.

"My dad didn't go here," I tell Brandon. "She lied."

"How…?"

"She and my dad used to visit each other regularly when they were in college. She told me she practically lived in his dorm room on weekends. But this place is what? Six, eight hours from where she went to school. That doesn't make any sense."

Brandon leans in, scanning the St. Joseph's College website. "Yeah, you're right. That doesn't add up at all. Could she have mixed up the names or the locations?"

"I don't see how? She spent a ton of time there. There's no way she'd get the name wrong, and she drove there all the time." I gesture at the screen. "This place is in a whole different state. But this is all guesswork. I can't confront her if I'm not sure."

"Why don't we just call McCrystal and ask if he went there?"

"Will they just tell me?"

"It can't hurt to ask."

I speak to a very nice older woman in the registrar's office. It doesn't take long to confirm my dad went to McCrystal for a period that coincides with Devin's sophomore and junior years.

* * *

It's dark when I get home after getting an IUD inserted and driving Shelby home. I don't pry, but she's already had sex with Gio, and my sense is that he's pressuring her to let him stop using condoms. I want to ask her more questions, because I'm concerned by how fast they're moving. My gut says Shelby is going to end up regretting giving her virginity to Gio. But I keep my mouth shut because Shelby isn't prying into who I'm having sex with, and I appreciate that.

HE HATE ME

My steps are heavy as I enter the house. My backpack feels like its weight has doubled and my uterus is cramping. Everything from my bellybutton down hurts. They said I might have discomfort for the next day or two, but this is much worse than I expected. At least it's dampened my libido, because if I was as horny now as I was this morning, I'd be pissed at not getting to spend the afternoon with Brandon. I'm also exhausted. I think the lack of sleep last night is catching up with me.

I shuffle over to the sofa in the family room and flop on my back, dropping my bookbag on the floor. It's been a long time since I've so completely ignored my planner. I'm supposed to be working on a paper and doing something else, though I can't remember what. The sound of pans banging in the kitchen stops and my mother's face appears over the back of the sofa.

"Are you okay, honey?"

"I have a headache and my stomach hurts."

"I was expecting you home over an hour ago."

I sigh. "I had to help Shelby with something. I lost track of time."

"Well, dinner will be ready in a few minutes."

"I'm not really hungry. I'm just going to lie here, okay."

"Okay." She sounds uncertain, but I hear her steps as she retreats, and my eyes drift closed.

SENCHA SKEETE

* * *

Many hours later, I wake up in the darkened family room. Someone, probably my mom, repositioned me and got me a pillow and a blanket. I feel slightly better, but I could still use a painkiller. I'm not sure what time it is, but from what I can see all the lights are off, so probably close to midnight.

I get up and climb the stairs slowly. In addition to the cramping I feel wetness. I hope nothing leaked through. I go straight through to the bathroom without turning on the lights in my bedroom, pop some pills and take a warm shower. I feel a lot better once I'm clean, diapered and pajamaed. Yes, I call pads diapers because they feel like what I imagine a diaper feels like. I usually wear tampons, but the clinic said I have to wait 24 hours to use one.

Now that I'm feeling a bit more human, I need to catch up on my task list. I'm grateful to see my backpack is on my desk. I pull out my planner and start organizing but feel a pang of hunger. I haven't had anything to eat since lunch. I should go see what we have for leftovers.

When I leave my room, I notice light leaking under the door of Devin's office. I wasn't expecting anybody to be up, but I should say hi. We need to talk about my college applications, anyway. I wonder what he's doing up so late. The doors to the master suite are closed, so my mom's already asleep.

"Hey," I say, poking my head in with a smile. Brandon, behind the desk, nearly jumps out of his seat. I'm momentarily confused.

"What are you doing in here?"

HE HATE ME

Chapter 22

Brandon

My heart feels like it's going to explode from my chest. The expression "almost had a heart attack"? I never got how visceral that was until now. My sternum aches. If I had to pick someone to find me in here, it's Deja, but that doesn't mean this is a good thing. I see her confused frown and know I'd better come up with some kind of explanation and fast.

I discreetly tap my phone screen to end my call with Anton and slip my Bluetooth earpiece into my pocket.

"How are you feeling?" I ask, moving over to pull her into the room, and closing the door. In the process I notice the towel I was supposed to lay in front of the door to block

HE HATE ME

light draped over an armchair. I could kick myself, but there's not time for that now.

"Still not great," she says. She texted me "*Got an IUD,*" after the clinic visit and the next time I saw her, she was passed out on the sofa. I made some joke about her being drunk to cover up for staring at her so much. I wanted to take care of her, but my crass joke got her mom to get her bedding and make her more comfortable. She looked so adorable curled up on her side, her head lying on her folded hands.

"How not great?"

"Pain, mostly. They said there'd be momentary discomfort. They didn't tell me it would be like the worst period cramps I ever had and that it would last for hours."

She pouts and I pull her into my arms, kissing her lightly on the forehead.

"I'm sorry."

"You should be. I'm doing this for you."

"So I'm the only one who wants to have sex?" I tease. She cracks a smile.

"No, I definitely want to fuck. But a lot less right now than this morning."

"I like that. Say that again."

"Fuck," she says.

"You better stop before I forget your delicate condition. You're not ready to get back on your knees for me by any chance, are you?"

She giggles, rubbing her face against my chest. Since she came into my room last night, I've wondered several times if I'm dreaming. The tough exterior, the cruel disdain, is gone.

SENCHA SKEETE

She's turning into this soft, vulnerable woman. But how can I blame her for putting up that hard shell. I was the one who started off aggressive from the moment I walked into this house. What choice did she have but to give me back the same energy. She's not the kind of person to just roll over. Now, somehow, I've earned her trust, and as much as I love this version of her, I also feel guilty.

Deleting the video and pictures of her was a huge thing to her. It cleared the way for us to be like this. But, of course, I still have back-ups. It would blow our whole relationship up if she found out. I need to delete those as soon as I can. I have the real girl now, I don't need her pictures to get off. I'll miss looking at that *ahegao* face whenever I want, though.

Then there's the reason I'm in Devin's office. The reason I'm even in this house. What would she think if she knew the truth? She's vulnerable to me now, open and soft, and I'm still manipulative and a liar. I feel guilty, but not guilty enough to confess all.

"So, I never told you what the plan would have been for this afternoon," I say, dragging her over to sit on the leather loveseat across from the desk. It's brown full grain tobacco leather, buttery to the touch. I wonder how much of Anton's money Devin spent buying it.

"Weren't we going to come home?"

"I asked Rourke if we could come to his place."

She frowns. "Rourke van der Hoff? You're friends with that guy?"

"Why did you think I asked you to come over to his place before?"

"I don't know. You guys both play soccer? I didn't think you were on the kind of terms with him where you could just take a girl to his house for sex."

"He's not that bad."

"He's a drug addict!"

"He's not a drug addict. He's a recreational drug user, which by the way so are we."

"You?"

"I smoke weed." She looks like she's considering my argument.

"We're different, though. I use drugs occasionally, like on a night out or at a party, but I still get A's, I still make it to practice and games. Rourke is a mess. Did you know he got caught at school one time with a baggie of cocaine and the only reason he wasn't expelled is his dad donated an obscene amount of money to the school?"

"I didn't know that, but I want to point out that Rourke is one of the top three soccer players at Briarwood and our team is nationally ranked. He makes every practice and game just like you do."

"Okay," she says huffily, "but I still don't really want to go to his house."

"He's setting aside a room just for us to use whenever. His mansion is so big we can be in and out without ever seeing him. There's a maid to clean our room. It'll be like going to a fancy hotel. He even gave me a keycard to get inside any time I want, day or night."

"Did you tell him about us?" She seems alarmed.

"No. He figured it out a while ago and he hasn't said anything about it to anyone. We can trust him, with this secret, anyway."

She chews that over, worrying her bottom lip with her teeth. I swear she has no idea how beautiful she is. I could just stare at her face for hours, her high forehead, those dark, intelligent eyes, her soft lips.

"If we don't use his place, then we're doing it in the backseat of your car or an empty classroom after hours. That's even riskier than doing it here."

"Then why not just do it here?"

"Do you feel safe having sex in this house? Because I don't."

"Since when? We had sex last night."

"And it's a miracle we didn't get caught." She seems unconvinced, so I get behind Devin's desk and gesture for her to join me. She seems uncertain at first, but eventually comes to stand next to where I'm sitting. I log in and the screen resolves.

"What am I looking at?"

"Surveillance video." On the screen is a grid of eight squares showing different views of the house. I put the cursor over each one, naming the location as I do. "This is courtyard 1, courtyard 2, garage, front door, sliding door, kitchen door—"

"Isn't that the spot where I, I…" she stammers, embarrassed. The camera has a clear view of the spot where she got on her knees and gave me a blow job.

HE HATE ME

"Yeah," I say. "He keeps adding new cameras. There's been one outside the gate in the service alley for a while, but he just put this one up a few days ago. It's probably my fault for dropping a cigarette butt or something."

"That seems like overkill?"

"It does, and I haven't even shown you half. Here's three views of the back lawn, the exterior of the sunroom, inside the sunroom, inside the foyer, inside the family room, inside the kitchen—"

"I get the idea," she says, looking worried.

"You need to see two more of these." She nods hugging herself around the middle. This is really disturbing to her, as it should be. It's alarming to think someone might be spying on you without your knowledge, and it's worse when it's someone you trust.

I scroll down and show her a view of the hallway that runs from one side to the other of the second floor, and the interior of the downstairs powder room. Her mouth falls open.

"You think he just sits up here watching us? My friends use that powder room whenever they come over. There were probably eight cheerleaders peeing in there last weekend. People change their clothes in there. There has to be an explanation for this."

"I don't know, Deja," I say. I showed her the video feeds to convince her to come to Rourke's, but I also think she has a right to know this is going on. It's a huge invasion of privacy.

SENCHA SKEETE

"So when I came to your room last night, did the camera capture it? Does Devin know?"

I shake my head. "I don't think so. There are hundreds of hours of video if you tally everything up. There's no reason he would look at that specific 30 seconds. The hallway is pretty boring. I doubt he checks it unless an alarm goes off. The only alarms up here are on the windows."

She doesn't look entirely reassured, but I can't tell her that Anton hacked the system and deleted the few seconds of video. No matter how many cameras Devin puts up, he'll never see me where I'm not supposed to be. Anton is willing to cover Deja under that blanket, so I don't get kicked out; he still needs me here until I find the evidence Devin has against him. But Anton also had me plant extra cameras and bugs. I don't want Anton seeing intimate moments between me and my girl, and I don't want Deja wondering who I'm texting while we're together.

"We both have practice tomorrow, but why don't we go over to Rourke's Friday afternoon, hang out, and see if you feel comfortable. If you don't, we strike his place off the list."

She nods, her expression still tight. I don't share my backup plan, which is to rent a hotel room. She might jump at it, but we risk someone we know seeing us, plus she'll want to know where I got the money to afford it. I'll have to ask Rourke not to mention the dealing in front of her. And here I am again, lying to her by omission. There are so many already, though, what's one more. All of them are because of Anton, but my attitude about him sending me here is changing. If he hadn't asked me to spy on Devin, I'd never had gotten this

HE HATE ME

close to Deja. Imagine if I'd missed out on her, on the way she makes me feel? There's so much I still want to learn about her, so many things I want to do with her, it feels exciting, something to look forward to after Anton has what he needs. Until her, I only imagined a bleak future, waiting for my mother to die. Now things feel different. I have hope.

"I'm starving," she says, "but one last question."

"Shoot."

"How did you find out about this? I mean I knew they had cameras outside the front door and watching the pool, but the ones inside are hidden. And how did you get access to his computer?"

"Sit in the middle of the sofa," I tell her. "Okay. Now look at Devin's diploma." She moves her head an inch or two in either direction before her eyebrows shoot up.

"Wow! The whole screen's reflected."

"I was in here listening to him ramble on about responsibility and respect and I noticed I could see the family room. I'd watched him enter his password enough times I had a good idea what it was, so I logged in one afternoon before they got home to check if there was an angle that showed the kitchen door."

"Cause that's where you sneak out, right? To smoke."

"Selfish reasons, yeah. I snuck up here to see what the cameras could see, and I thought it was weird he had so many. And that's before I realized he was adding more."

"What is going on?" She shakes her head.

"I hope it doesn't have anything to do with our other mystery."

271

SENCHA SKEETE

"How could it?

"I don't understand any of this shit," I lie. It's only a partial lie. I know why Devin's obsessed with security—it's because of Anton. But why Deja's mother has been lying to her? No idea. God, I want this to be over so I can get the hell out of this house and stop lying to Deja. Maybe I'm overly optimistic to think she'll still want to be with me when she knows everything, but I have to try. I don't want to keep lying to her, but until my mission is complete, I have no choice.

Chapter 23

Deja

I THOUGHT I WAS ACCUSTOMED TO RICH PEOPLE SHIT. I MEAN places like the Asterburg mansion don't faze me anymore. After a few months at Briarwood and seeing some of my friends' houses, I decided my house was nice, but those bigger houses with movie screening rooms and fountains and statuary were what rich people lived in. Never mind they were all built in the last thirty years and the appointments weren't necessarily as grand as you'd expect from looking at the outside of the house, this was still it. I imagined celebrities like Oprah and Rihanna living in houses like that. And then I drive through the gate of Rourke van der Hoff's estate and I see how rich people really live.

SENCHA SKEETE

The driveway to Rourke's mansion winds through a thicket of trees. Maple and oak flank the road, their leaves a riot of orange, red and gold. I catch glimpses of manicured gardens through the trees. Symmetrical flowerbeds are dotted with the last blooms of annuals about to face their deaths at winter's hand. My mind supplies the soundtrack, something like Henry Purcell's Fairy Queen prelude.

The circular driveway is lined with boxwood hedges and stone benches. As we pull up, I see Rourke descend the stone steps from tall mirror-like glass doors, through which I see scrolling ironwork. The ironwork pattern is repeated in the fanlight and more subtly on the iron and frosted glass awning above the door.

I step out of the car and can't help but gawk at the size and grandeur of Rourke's home. The mansion is constructed of white brick and limestone, the latter giving the building a soft yellow hue. Rourke bounds down the steps wearing an ugly af sweatsuit that I'm sure costs hundreds of dollars. His hair is mussed, and his eyes red as a demon's.

"I'm going to scream like a girl," Rourke says, dapping Brandon. "Deja Marcus is at my house." He fans himself with his hands the way girls do when they're meeting a hot celebrity.

"I didn't come here to be mocked, van der Hoff," I say, with mock seriousness.

"Oh, I know why you came here." He chuckles knowingly. "Come on inside."

"Can I just leave my car there."

"Of course. Butler can move it for you if needed."

HE HATE ME

"You have a butler?"

"Oh, no," he says, shaking his head. "His name is Kyle Butler. I guess you could call him a household manager. He wears a lot of hats around here. We only have him and Selena—she's the housekeeper—as permanent staff.

"Welcome to my humble abode," he says, leading us through the door.

I have to wonder if Rourke van der Hoff owns a dictionary. Of all the words that could describe what I'm seeing, humble is not one of them. A gallery runs from one end of the house to the other, lined with eight-foot-tall windows. Each one is dressed with ivory and gold silk brocade drapes. The flooring is some kind of dark stone, polished to a sheen. There's an enormous marble-topped, gilt console table along the wall and above it a gigantic mirror with a fussy gilt frame. Oversize stone urns scattered at regular intervals serve as plant pots for small palm and citrus trees. Through the double doors nearest to me is a room with the same grayish-black stone floors and a light-colored Persian rug. Beyond it I can see another room with a polished wood spiral staircase and a dazzling chandelier.

I could go on like this for a long time describing the inside of Rourke's house, but my point is that Rourke lives in a house that could be a museum or hotel. It's that lavish, that perfectly styled. It even smells good, like someone sprayed orange blossom scent in every room.

"Did you get the package I had delivered here?" Brandon asks, speaking for the first time since our arrival.

"Yeah," Rourke says. "It's in your room."

"I'm going to go check on it," Brandon says.

"Can I give you a tour?" Rourke asks.

"Sure." As Rourke's guest I need to be polite and do whatever he asks within reason. He is doing us a favor, provided I get mentally comfortable enough to actually take my clothes off in a schoolmate's house.

The house has eight bedrooms and eleven bathrooms, plus a library, two dining rooms, conservatory, formal living room, kitchen and so on. It would take him all afternoon to show me the whole thing, so he just hits the most important ones—like the kitchen and the powder room. He tells me we can come join him on the third floor if we want to chat and takes me to the room Brandon uses.

The room is as large and lavish as everything else in this house. A king-size fourposter with brocade bed covers, a seating area, a walk-in closet, a marble-lined ensuite with separate tub and shower. I thought my bedroom was big; you could play soccer in here. Brandon doesn't look up when I come in, his attention focused on several red objects spread across the bed. When I get close enough to see what he's looking at, I freeze. I can recognize most of the objects: rope, a gag, two sets of leather cuffs, something that looks like a feather duster, a riding crop, a blindfold, and a tasseled whip-thing. There are a few other pieces I don't recognize. Everything is made of leather-like material except for a small piece of jewelry.

"Surprise," he says, smiling at me over his shoulder. I smile back nervously. He said he wouldn't go so easy on me

HE HATE ME

the next time we were together, but I wasn't prepared for a full on BDSM experience.

"Um, okay."

He cocks his head to the side looking disappointed by what he reads on my face. There's an angry energy around him, an intensity that I wish I knew the source of. It's not aimed at me, but I can still sense how strong it is. He was carefree and happy yesterday; today his smiles never reach his eyes. He wants something from me, I can tell. This is how he is before he starts one of those coercive episodes. I step back involuntarily. He shakes his head and starts putting the objects back into a cardboard box.

"Are we okay?" I ask, my voice wavering more than I would like.

"Us?" he says, "Yeah, we're fine. Me?" He sighs, sitting on the edge of the bed and staring at the floor. "I could be better."

"What's going on?"

He pats the bed next to him and I sit, letting him pull be closer to his side. His hand cups my hip possessively.

"Are you doing anything tomorrow afternoon?"

"Not really."

"Can you go somewhere with me?"

"Where?"

"I want you to meet my mom."

Contradictory emotions arise in me. I'm thrilled that he likes me enough to want me to know her, but also surprised. He barely ever talks about her, and she's never come to see him or pick him up from school or the house like I would have done in her shoes. As angry as Brandon is at Devin for what he sees as his betrayal of her, I'm not certain Brandon is close to his mother.

"Are you sure," I ask, trying to read his expression. It's dark, his eyes still on the floor.

"I'm sure," he says. "You'll understand me better, after."

I nod. I'm worried about him. I'm only just starting to understand this boy even though he's already dug his hooks into my heart. Man, I should say, though he seems to flip-flop from one to the other daily. So do I, for that matter. Being eighteen is interesting. I feel simultaneously like an adult and a child, chaffing under my parent's authority, but terrified when I have to navigate things on my own.

"Are you going to tell her I'm your…"

"Girlfriend? Yeah." Excitement surges through me. His girlfriend! Have I ever been thrilled to have someone call me that? The word seems to glow when he says it. Then a less happy thought occurs to me.

"Won't she tell Devin?"

"No," he says with a sadness that confuses me. "We don't have to worry about that. Do you want to go upstairs for a bit. Unless you feel comfortable enough already…?"

"This place is gorgeous and amazing," I say, "but I think I should get to know Rourke better. If this works out, we can always come back another time."

I don't miss the way his jaw tightens, but he doesn't argue. He pulls me to my feet and takes my hand.

"Let's go," he says.

HE HATE ME

* * *

We find Rourke in the bar on the third floor, which is well, a bar. It looks like someone took a whole ass pub with a huge oak bar, hundreds of mugs and glasses, upholstered bar stools, high top tables, a vintage jukebox, a dartboard and leather club chairs and slotted it into the house. There are more varieties of liquor than I think I've seen in my life. All the ones I recognize are expensive.

"You guys want a drink?" Rourke asks when we walk in. He's pouring a can of seltzer water into a glass. He slices a lemon while we watch and squeezes some of the juice into the glass. He cuts a thin slice as a garnish.

"I'll have a light beer," Brandon says. I ask for a diet soda and the juice for the rest of the lemon. I've already decided I want to come back here, but the last football game of the season is tonight, so I don't want to consume any alcohol.

Instead of taking one of the many empty seats, Rourke tells us about the history of the house as he walks around the corner into a large game room. There are vintage arcade games, though I can't tell if they work or are just for decoration. The centerpiece is a huge sectional sofa and the biggest flat screen I've ever seen. It's on mute playing the pause screen from a video game.

"Do you live here by yourself?" I ask Rourke.

"Pretty much. My dad's here a few days a month and the housekeeper lives in the carriage house. She has a kid. That's pretty much it."

"That sounds kinda lonely."

"Nah. I'm used to it, and I have people over on the weekends."

"So if we come over during the week…?"

"Yeah, you probably won't run into anybody. You don't even have to talk to me if you don't want to. I don't get why you don't want people to know you're together, though."

"It's because we live in the same house. My parents would freak out. They might ask Brandon to move out and…"

"I don't really have anywhere else to go," Brandon says. I look at him with surprise. He could still live with his mom, couldn't he, but it would be pretty hard to live in Old Town and go to Briarwood. Even Mello is staying with a family in Twin Oaks during the week.

"My lips are sealed."

"Thank you," I say.

"Don't worry about it. We're cool. Wanna get high?"

"Ah…"

"She doesn't smoke," Brandon says.

"I've got a vaporizer," Rourke says.

"Maybe another time. It's the last game of football season tonight and I have to cheer."

"Oh, no. That's so important."

"Ha ha. There's a thing after with the football team and, more importantly, our coaches. I can always get high tomorrow."

"I didn't say no," Brandon says, raising his hand. I shake my head while the two of them chatter about the strain they're about to consume and prepare the device. I'm kind of

HE HATE ME

annoyed with Brandon at first, but I can see some of the tension easing from his shoulders after a few deep inhalations. I take his hand and he squeezes my fingers, turning his head to smile dreamily at me. I scoot closer, momentarily forgetting where we are. He does the thing I love, holding me by the throat and crushing my mouth with a hard kiss. For a minute, I'm completely lost but then I remember where I am and pull away from him.

I turn to Rourke, ready to apologize, but he doesn't seem to be bothered. I'm relieved he's not being smirky either. Brandon stands up and pulls me to my feet.

"We're gonna head downstairs," he says, still holding my small hand in his much larger one. Our palms kiss, feeling more intimate than such simple touch has a right to.

Rourke nods in acknowledgment and picks up the game controller. He watches us go without comment and only when he can't see us anymore does he start playing. Formula 1 engines roar as we skip down the stairs to the second floor. Like kids, we race each other to the room, shoving and grabbing, hoping to get an advantage. I win, but guy six or seven inches taller than me who can spend up to 90 minutes running back and forth across a field.

He closes the door and sweeps his eye over me from my disheveled braids to the tips of my sneakers.

"Strip," he commands.

"No."

"Are you trying to earn a punishment?" There's a dangerous edge to his voice, one that would create both fear and excitement in me if I was in the mood. But this isn't what I want right now.

"Time out," I say, forming my hands into the letter T.

He sobers immediately, the malevolent air falling away to leave mild confusion behind it.

"I'm sorry," he says, "I misread the signals."

"That can easily happen when we haven't discussed what we're doing. I saw online you're supposed to have a safe word and we've never even talked about that."

"Okay," he says. "You're right. We do need to actually talk…sex."

I slip my shoes off and start removing my pants.

"What are you doing?" he asks.

"Just getting more comfortable. You should too."

He doesn't move, just watches me remove my sweatshirt and tee, leaving me in just bra and panties. He takes his pants and jacket off, but not his t-shirt.

"Are you hiding something?" I tease.

His blush surprises me. "It's nothing bad, just a little embarrassing."

Now I'm really curious. He rolls his eyes and pull the T-shirt over his head. Written over his heart in cursive is the name Lindsey. It wasn't there at the end of the summer, so that and the boldness of the ink tells me he got it recently. I couldn't see it in the dark when we made love, but in the afternoon sunlight it's bold against his pale skin.

"Oh, wow. You are such a momma's boy."

"And proud of it. Now can I get a kiss before we start our serious conversation."

"Okay, but it better be worth my while."

"Brat," he mouths.

He pushes me back onto the bed and follows me down, letting some of his weight rest on me. My legs hang off the bed awkwardly and I pull them up, hooking them over his thighs. He rubs his face in the hollow between my shoulder and neck, lightly sucking on the skin there.

"Is this the kiss," I ask, running my hands along his sides, learning the shape of him, what inch of skin is more sensitive than the rest. I count his ribs, shallow nubs up his torso, the broad muscles of his back, tight as he holds most of his weight up on his forearms.

"This is the prelude."

Chapter 24

Deja

This kiss was worth it. My midsection still feels warm from the glow of it. Brandon and I lie together under the covers of our bed in Rourke's house, our bodies touching, bare legs, stomach, arms. His skin is cool but warms as we cuddle together.

"How do you want to do this?"

"We can ask each other questions, I guess." I burrow my face into the curve where his neck meets his shoulder. "We answer each other honestly."

"Okay," he says, "you go first."

I feel nervous, but I can do this. It's necessary.

"Do you like me?" The long seconds before he answers are torture.

HE HATE ME

"Of course I like you," he says, as if it should be obvious. "I just told you I was going to introduce you to my mom as my girlfriend."

"What do you like about me?"

"It's my turn. Do you like me?"

It should be a simple question, but it isn't. I'm attracted to him, I find our interactions exciting, and he makes me feel alive. When he's not being an AH, he's funny and clever. But he's been cruel to me as well and tried to control me. But I'm overthinking it.

"Yes, I like you. Now."

"That's fair. I was awful to you. What do I like about you? You're beautiful and confident and caring."

"Caring?"

"You take care of your friends. Like the whole Gio thing. Do you have any idea the kind of things he was saying about you after Mello got hurt? And you still let him come to homecoming with you guys."

"Shelby likes him."

"That's my point. If you said he couldn't come, or she couldn't go with him nobody would have batted an eye and she would have listened to you. But you put her happiness first."

"I'll be honest. If it had been you, I would have banished her from my table for a month and stabbed you in the leg."

"Which leg?"

"Guess." I feel his shoulders shake as he hugs me more tightly.

"Did I ever tell you I love when you act possessive?" He'd hinted at it.

"This one's a little more intense. What do you like sexually. You've told me a few things, but I need a full list, so I know what I'm getting into."

He takes a deep breath and blows it out through his lips.

"I like to inflict pain. I like submission and sometimes humiliation—depends on the situation. I like bondage. I basically like a girl to be helpless and know that I can do anything I want to her."

"So if a girl was passed out...?"

"I'd let her sleep it off. I need her helpless but aware of what's happening. It's her reactions that get me off. Whether it's fear or pain or arousal. Ideally, I'm giving her what she needs and that's what gives me that high."

"You thought I needed the things you did to me?"

"You're jumping turns again."

"I can't help it. One question leads to the next. Answer."

"The spanking, but that wasn't primarily meant to be sexual. I guess I mean in a perfect scenario that's what I want to do. But I'm deeply flawed.'

"Alas!"

"Your turn."

I chew on my bottom lip, thinking about what I want to say.

"I don't know," I say, trying to be honest. "I'm still figuring it out. Until I met you, I thought I might be greysexual, maybe demi, but I hadn't met the right person yet."

"What about Jayden?"

"We fooled around, and I'd kissed guys before him, but it was just something I did because they wanted to do it and because I thought dating popular guys was a requirement if I wanted to be a popular girl. That sounds bad when I say it out loud."

He strokes my back, letting me know that it doesn't matter to him.

"But I don't think I'm demi because I still hated you the first time I felt attracted to you."

"When was that?"

"So when I saw you moving in, I thought you were hot, but it was like the way I think Jayden is hot. Like, I can see what makes him attractive, I just don't feel the attraction myself. So I guess the first time I sort of felt it was in the hot tub."

"When I got aggressive?"

"Isn't that fucked up?"

"I gotta say this because somebody very wise told me and it helped a lot. She said you can't judge yourself for your kinks. You like what you like. As long as you're not hurting yourself or anyone else who gives a fuck what society thinks?"

"But your kink is literally hurting people."

"No," he says. "My kink is to inflict pain, not do harm."

"Really?"

"So if I said I wanted you to cut me, you wouldn't do that?"

"Do you want that?" he asks, unable to hide his excitement.

"I don't know. But wouldn't that count as hurting me."

"I guess I mean it like, if you wanted me to give you small cuts that hurt and bleed a little, I'd like that, but I wouldn't do anything life-threatening."

"How did you figure out you were a sadist?"

"There was this woman who introduced me to it."

"How old were you?"

"Sixteen." He bites his lip, and I can tell he's a little uncomfortable."

"How old was she?"

He colors deeply, his cheeks looking almost bruised. "Forty-five, forty-six."

"Dude!"

"Age of consent is 16."

"I bet she reminded you of that a lot. Was she a teacher?"

"Her son was on my club team at the time."

"That's gross."

"It wasn't. She was really attractive, and I learned a lot from her."

"What if I told you a forty-five-year-old guy was sleeping with me when I was sixteen."

He looks away from me. This is obviously a sore subject, so I don't push it.

"Tell me what it was like."

"Um, she was a sadist, and I was just excited to be having sex. We never did penis in vagina, but oral was way more than I'd ever done before, and she was very good at it and she taught me how to be good at it. She was more of a psychological sadist. She liked to humiliate and verbally abuse her partners. She would edge me and then send me away without coming. One time she made me wear a chastity cage." He grimaces. "But she did cane me once. After the first couple times she would ask me questions about what I liked and what turned me on, and she told me what I was. She even let me play with her once and that confirmed my wiring. We stopped after that because we weren't sexually compatible. What about you? How did you figure out what you like?"

"You spanked me," I say.

"You had no idea before then?"

"None. And now I guess I know I like pain, but not how much or really what my limits are. I like when you're forceful, and when you hold my neck. I've started reading and there are a lot of things I'm curious about or I'd like to try."

"Like what?"

"Not right now, okay."

"Okay."

"I was thinking about the riding crop."

"You want me to spank you with it?"

I nod, swallowing.

"You want it on your ass, right? How about your thighs?" I nod. "Just the backs or can I get that really sensitive skin in between?" I imagine it and am immediately aroused. "You know the two places I'd really like to crop? Your pussy and your tits." I wave of heat rises up from my chest to my cheeks. It would hurt, but how much would depend on Brandon. Do I want it less or more intense? I think about the leather tip striking my nipples and my hips shift around, seeking relief.

"You like the sound of that, don't you," he says in a husky voice. "I'll focus on one nipple till it feels like it's on fire and then switch to the other one. There will be no mercy for that sexy little clit. And if you try to close your legs, I'll just tie them open and whip you harder."

"Fuck," I moan.

"Yeah?"

I nod vigorously, peeling my panties off. He cups my pussy, shoving two thick fingers roughly inside. He mashes my clit with the heel of his hand and captures my mouth in a ravenous kiss. I try to pull him closer, but he resists, easing away from me long enough to put on a condom. He pushes my legs apart and slides into me in one slow thrust.

"Let me in, baby," he gasps, "you're so tight."

"You feel so good," I tell him.

He unhooks my bra and clamps his mouth on my breast, sucking and biting. A gush of wetness floods my channel and cock glides more smoothly, in and out like a piston. I lock my legs around his waist and urge him on, begging him to go faster and deeper. He takes my lips, sucking on my tongue and lips, kissing me so fiercely that I can barely breathe. We are pressed tightly to each other, sweat slicking our skin, his cock hitting me just right at a steady pace that makes me want to scream. His teeth score my skin, peppering sharp bites over my neck and shoulder. He bites down hard and the pain mixes with my pleasure, taking me over the edge. My channel squeezes down hard on his stiff length, and he groans, holding still while I fall apart around him.

He flips me over like a rag doll, sliding a pillow under my hips so my ass is raised in the air. My arms lie limply at my side, I offer no resistance as he takes me from behind, his cock reaching deeper inside me than it did before. I'm full to the brim and too weak to do more than accept the hard fucking he's giving me. His hips slap against my ass, faster and faster. He's holding onto my hips with both hands, gripping my pelvis so tightly I'm sure there will be bruising later. He grunts and groans, I squeal and pant, like we're animals, stripped of everything but the base need to mate. He grips the back of my neck, and his other hand finds my clit. It only takes a few strokes for me to start coming again, and this time I feel him join me, the throbbing of his member and a guttural yell as he fills the condom with his come.

* * *

"Well, that didn't go quite as planned," I say some time later as I run a soapy washcloth across his back. There's a small scar next to his left shoulder blade from a fall when he was four and his ass is rounder than it looks when he has clothes on. I wash him everywhere, from scalp to feet, and I can tell he's a little uncomfortable at some points, but he's already done the same to me, finding the birthmark on the back of my left leg, sticking his soapy fingers into every crevice. His body is beautiful, muscled and strong with smooth, touchable skin that I could caress for hours. But what we're doing isn't really sexual. He's my man, and I'm learning his body the same way he's learning mine.

"Were we just supposed to talk?" he asks, kissing me lightly on the lips.

"Pretty much. We didn't even get to talk about limits and safe words."

"I'm sorry."

"It's not your fault. I was the one that got super turned on by the sex talk."

"And all we did was talk about it. I can't wait to actually do those things to you."

"And I can't wait for you to do them."

He caresses my cheek and gives me a brief but firm kiss on the lips. "You are so perfect for me." He smiles down at me, an expression I haven't seen that often. He's sneered and smirked and laughed, but this is just pure enjoyment, maybe even happiness. I smile back at him, knowing I'm reflecting the same emotions back at him. There's a little flip in my stomach, like the feeling when you're on a roller coaster, and I know that I don't just like Brandon. I left like behind some time ago. But I can't bring myself to say the words first. He makes me feel so vulnerable, I'm scared to reveal my feelings the way I've never been with other guys, because it's never mattered as much that they feel the same way about me.

"Why don't we text about rules later?" he suggests, "I won't be able to think about anything but you tonight, anyway."

HE HATE ME

We dry off and get dressed quickly, aware that we're expected home soon. We're standing in Rourke's foyer, hugging each other, when he finds us.

"Hey, guys," Rourke says, "wanna stay for dinner? Selena made beef roast with potatoes."

"We're expected home for dinner," I tell him.

"I think I'll hang back, actually," Brandon says.

"But—"

"Anyone who sees the two of you together will know instantly what you have been doing. Perhaps if you arrive home separately, they won't realize you were doing it with each other."

Rourke has a point. I haven't torn my eyes away from Brandon since we left the bedroom. It hurts knowing we'll be sleeping in separate beds tonight. Heaving a sigh, I give my boyfriend one last hug and go to my car, not looking back. As I'm pulling away, I pass Javi Garza driving towards the house with Camilla Alvarez in the passenger seat of his McLaren. What the heck is Afro-Latina Greta Thunberg doing with Rourke's South American soul twin? Speculating about that is enough to distract me so that I seem almost normal when I wave at my mother and run upstairs to my room.

Chapter 25

Deja

"I'M GOING TO THE SOCCER FIELD IN THE PARK," Brandon yells to no one in particular.

"You need a ride?" I ask, saccharine sweet.

"It's the weekend, Deja. Don't I have to deal with you enough during the week?"

"Suit yourself!" I say. "Mom, I'm going to the mall."

Not waiting for an answer, I exit through the front door and get in my car, taking my time to adjust my mirrors and pull up the directions to where I'm going. Brandon will be leaving through the back and wending his way along the forest track to a spot where I can pick him up. I don't know why we're going to all this trouble. I doubt the parents would see anything strange about us going somewhere together.

Twenty minutes later we're on the freeway headed out of town.

"Where are we going, exactly?" I ask. "I thought you and your mom lived in Old Town." Old Town is the most rundown part of town, where the brick is faded and crumbling, the sidewalks are cracked with dying grass poking through, and there are way more people standing on the corner or sitting on stoops than you ever see anywhere else. On the long slide down the socioeconomic ladder, Old Town is rock bottom. Man, does the knowledge that Brandon lived there for years feel different now that I care about him. It's a wonder Brandon didn't fall in with a bad crowd. Or maybe he was just lucky enough to make the right friends, like Mello.

"We're heading to the place where she's living right now. It's near the University."

"Oh. Did she get a new job?"

I guess things must be looking up for Lindsey. That area isn't super expensive, but it's a definite step up from Old Town.

"You'll see," he says. His tone is subdued, even the volume of his voice low.

He asks if he can turn on the radio and the car fills with dream pop. I wish it was something livelier because I like high energy music when I'm driving, but Brandon seems like he needs it.

As we pull into the parking lot, I look at Brandon in confusion. This isn't an apartment complex like I was expecting, but an annex of the university hospital. I look at the sign in confusion.

"What does that mean? Palliative care? Does your mom work here?"

Brandon shakes his head. He speaks softly. "No, she's a patient."

* * *

Brandon explains that he comes here once or twice a week, though the days he's able to come shift around. Years ago his mother suffered a brain injury and rather than regain function her brain has slowly degenerated.

I step inside and am immediately hit by the smell of disinfectant. At the front desk, a woman in lavender scrubs hands me a clipboard. She looks at Brandon and me with curiosity but asks only that I write my name in a black box and below it, his mother's name, Lindsey Bruce. I follow Brandon down a hallway lit by fluorescent lights. The building looks new and is brightly lit with many large windows. It would be a cheery space if I didn't know it is a place for patients to be "made comfortable" when there are no longer any treatments that can help them, or when they decide the treatment is worse than the disease. It's quiet, but we can hear the soft sounds of people talking and televisions playing as we walk down the hallway.

At the end, Brandon opens a door, gesturing for me to go in. The room is as bright as the rest of the building. There's not much in it—a hospital bed, a small sofa, miscellaneous medical equipment, and a few metal chairs with plastic seats.

There's another door that is ajar, and through it, I can see a shower and toilet. The walls are painted a cheery yellow, and there is a vase with fresh flowers on a side table.

Brandon's mother sits in a wheelchair, her black hair held back in a neat French braid. Her blue eyes, so much like Brandon's, stare off into the distance. She doesn't react to our entrance. She sits so still that a chill goes down my spine. If it wasn't for the tiny wrinkles around her eyes and her rounded figure, one might think she was a mannequin. She has a kind of raw beauty, but you can also see the signs of a hard life: wrinkles around her mouth, calloused hands, and coarse skin.

"Mom," Brandon says softly, "this is Deja."

No reaction at all. Brandon grimaces. He crouches next to her and whispers something I can't hear, but she still doesn't respond or even change her focus.

"I'm sorry," Brandon says, standing up. "She's been like this more and more lately. It's like she's not here." Like her body is an empty shell, I think, and the thought makes me shiver.

"She might come out of it before we leave," he continues.

"Don't worry about that." I walk over and hug him from behind, letting my actions speak for me. I'm not sure I could say anything to make him feel better anyway.

Brandon's body relaxes into my embrace, and we stay like that for a while, watching his mother in silence. I can tell he's grateful for the gesture, even if he doesn't say it. I take a deep breath and glance around the room, trying to distract myself from the sadness that hangs in the air. From the window, I can see the back garden. The leaves on the trees outside explode with autumn colors—red, yellow, and orange in different shades. There's a goldfinch standing on the edge of a bird feeder that sways with their slight movements, but the bird is unbothered by its unstable perch.

Brandon's mother suddenly stirs, her eyes flickering to life as if she's coming out of a deep sleep. She blinks a few times, and then focuses her gaze on her son.

"Brandon," she says, her voice raspy from disuse. "Why aren't you at school?"

"I just got home, Mom," Brandon says, pulling me to his side. "Are you feeling better?"

"Have I been sick?"

She looks at me for the first time, her eyes taking me in with curiosity and suspicion. "Who is that girl?"

"This is Deja," Brandon says. He doesn't explain who I am. But some spark of memory fires in his mother's brain.

"You look just like Jules," she says, cocking her head. "How is he?"

"I don't know who Jules is," I say, apologetically. Am I going to upset her by contradicting her? Brandon didn't correct her about the day of the week or where we are.

"Jules and Devin, like two peas in a pod," she says in a sing-song voice, "and then came Nia." She laughs, the sound jarring and too loud.

I feel Brandon stiffen. Have I done something wrong? My face heats.

"It's nice to meet you," I say, extending my hand to her. She takes it, her hand shaking and her grip weak. It's not just

HE HATE ME

her mind, then, that's affected, but her body, too. I don't know why I expected her to have old woman hands. Maybe it's hard for me to wrap my head around someone so young fading away like she is. Her nails are neatly trimmed and recently painted coral pink. I feel a spark of gratitude that someone here cares for her enough to do that and to fix her hair so beautifully.

"You're very pretty," she says, gesturing for me to sit next to her. "Tell me about yourself."

I tell her about school and cheerleading, being Brandon's math tutor, and my plans for college, though I can see as I go on that I'm losing her.

"Do you ever have dreams, dear?" she asks. I blink in confusion. "Do you ever have dreams that you're back in the basement of the house on Goshen. You're a passenger in your own body, and someone else is driving?"

I stare at her dumbfounded. What is she talking about? And what does she mean the house on Goshen. I lived on Goshen Ave until my dad died, stabbed in the service alley next to our house by a mugger. It had been such a shock to everyone that something like that could happen in Twin Oaks. How could she possibly know that I'd lived on Goshen unless she'd known my parents back then?

"It's time for your medication Ms. Lindsey," a broad woman with short brown hair and friendly eyes says, bustling into the room. She's holding a tray and smiles when she sees us. "Hello, Brandon. Is this your girlfriend?"

"Yes," he says, "this is Deja. Deja this is Glory. She's the nursing assistant that takes care of my mom. She's awesome."

SENCHA SKEETE

He says this last sentence abashedly, as if he's embarrassed to give the compliment but feels compelled to do so.

"It's nice to meet you," I say, still a bit shaken by Lindsey's comment. "Did you do Ms. Bruce's hair?"

"Yes," Glory says. "You don't like hair in your face, do you Ms. Lindsey."

Brandon's mom doesn't answer. She looks confused, searching our faces for something familiar, I think. Just as suddenly as she joined us, she is gone. She seems to recognize Glory, or at least find her familiar, as she takes her pills with minimal resistance.

Brandon squeezes his eyes shut and watches Glory tend to his mother, wheeling her to the bathroom to get ready for dinner.

"I'll see you next week," Brandon says.

His mother doesn't turn around. Glory smiles and waves goodbye.

I take his hand and lead him back down the hallway and out the front door.

"Oh, my God, Brandon. Have you been dealing with this the whole time? How long has she been like that?" I say once we're outside.

"A few months now. You never know what it'll be like," he says. "Sometimes we sit and talk for the whole hour; other times, she doesn't react to me being there, or even worse, she's scared of me and screams for help."

"That's awful."

"Yeah, well." He clears his throat. We walk back to the car in silence, each of us lost in our own thoughts. We sit in the car, watching traffic drive past on the busy road outside the hospital.

"I'm so sorry," I say. "Is there anything I can do?"

He shakes his head. "Just be with me. Just be you with me, that's all. There's no fix for what's wrong with her."

"What caused it?"

"Nobody knows for sure. Doctors say it looks like the kind of injury that happens when the supply of oxygen to the brain is cut off, but we're not aware of anything that could have caused that. I took her to specialists, but there's nothing you can do once brain cells start dying. Just keep her comfortable until time runs out."

"Are you sure you've done everything you can? There might be someone in a bigger city—"

"I took her as far away as New York. There's no-one else to see." He must see the surprise on my face because he goes on. "You don't want to know what I had to do to pay for it. For all of it." He gestures towards the hospital.

"I don't even know what to say."

"Let's go home, okay?"

I nod and start up the car.

* * *

Brandon

Deja's agitation is obvious by the time we get home. She stares out her window, trying to control her breathing. I hear it speed up and then the deep breaths as she tries to bring it under control.

"Do they know about your mom?" she asks.

"Tanisha and Devin? Of course they know. She's been sick since before she was fired."

"But my mom doesn't know her."

"Were you listening? They all knew each other. Your dad was Jules."

"I don't understand what that means. My dad's name was David."

"For years she told me these rambling stories about Devin and his best friend Jules and Jules's wife, Nia."

"I get how Nia can be short for Tanisha, but why Jules?"

"No idea. A private joke? The point is your parents lied big time. I don't know why, but it can't be good."

Her face droops. "I'm gonna ask. I have to know."

"Do you think they'll tell the truth?"

"I don't know, but I can't just let this go. I need to hear their side."

"You honestly think there's some version of this where they're the good guys."

"I'm not saying that," she says, "but maybe there are no bad guys either."

She wouldn't say that if she knew half the shit Devin has done. For years he's embezzled money from his company and based on what Anton told me, if it's ever discovered it will be Deja's mom who takes the fall. The man has everyone fooled. Only my mom has ever warned me to be cautious.

"All right," I say. "Let's talk to them after dinner."

* * *

HE HATE ME

"Sorry, guys," Deja's mom says, buttoning her coat. "I left some money on the counter for takeout. The Kiwanis dinner is tonight. Maybe we can talk tomorrow after church."

"There was nothing on the calendar," Deja says, which is totally in character for her.

Her mom shrugs. "I'm sorry; it slipped my mind."

I watch them walk to the garage, Devin's hand on the small of Tanisha's back.

Deja chews on her lower lip, wringing her hands. She swears and stomps into the kitchen, pulling out a small cucumber and biting the top off. She seems to take satisfaction in the loud crunch of the vegetable as she devours it. She opens a can of sparkling water and guzzles it down, banging the empty can on the counter when she's done.

"Let's go to the basement," she says, decisively.

"Why?"

"There's gotta be something down there to confirm once and for all if they knew each other. You found that stuff. There's got to be more. "

I should see this a spark of luck, the opportunity to search the basement without drawing suspicion, but I'm worried about Deja's state of mind. Her eyes appear almost feverish.

"Why don't we order something to eat and then we can go to the basement after dinner."

"I'm not hungry."

"You haven't eaten anything since lunch."

SENCHA SKEETE

"I just ate a cucumber and literally cannot choke anything else down right now. Go ahead, if you want, but I'm going down there."

"Fine," I say. "I'll grab a couple flashlights from the garage. It's not that well-lit down there."

* * *

I flip the switch on as we enter the unfinished part of the basement. Two naked bulbs turn on, one near the furnace and the other above the area where a random assortment of items are stacked together. I point Deja to the boxes I've already gone through, and I look through some plastic bins that turn out have nothing more interesting in them than Christmas decorations.

"I found something," Deja says, barely five minutes into our search. She shows me a photograph of Devin and her dad wearing fraternity sweatshirts. She keeps digging through the box and pulling out photos. She compresses her lips and shakes her head before speaking.

"Both of them were in this fraternity. Don't people usually keep their frat memorabilia? Paddles and whatnot?"

"I don't know," I say.

"All of these, Brandon," she says. "This is my mom and dad with Devin. They look really close, right?"

Both men were embracing Tanisha. David had his arm around her shoulders and Devin's looked like it was resting in the small of her back. Could the three of them have been more than just friends at some point? Could that be the motivation for hiding this from Deja?

"This one's weird," she says, handing me a photo of Devin and David dressed like characters from Pulp Fiction. They did bear a passing resemblance to John Travolta and Samuel L. Jackson.

"Do you have a phone?" I ask. "Can you look up the name of those two guys from Pulp Fiction? The characters, not the actors."

She opens a browser window and looks at me, impressed.

"Travolta played Vincent Vega and Samuel L. Jackson played Jules."

I point my fingers in triumph. "That's where Jules came from."

"You know I've heard my mom call Devin, Vinnie, before, but I thought it was a weird nickname De-Vin, you know. But if they kept calling my dad Jules, then it's probably short for Vincent."

"Those guys were murderers, though," I say. "Who would want to be like them?"

"They were cool, Brandon. They had all those badass lines. A lot of girls wanted to be the Bride from Kill Bill, but that didn't make them serial killers." Spree killers, technically, I think, but don't say out loud.

"I didn't say they were murderers, just that they seemed to identify with them."

I find an empty envelope on top of a stack of boxes and give it to Deja to put the photos in. I turn back to the boxes, my subconscious nudging me to look for something my conscious mind missed. There are two stacks of boxes. One, the one the envelope was on, has a thick layer of dust. The other is dusty, but not evenly or as thickly as the box next to it. I move the dirty box onto the slightly less dirty box and see a fuse box. I'm a little disappointed, but my brain is trying to help me again. Something feels not right, and it takes some careful observation to put it together. The handle of the fuse box looks shiny, the paint right under it rubbed off. Someone has opened this box often. I beam my flashlight across the room to double-check, but I'm remembering correctly. There is a much larger and newer fuse box over there, so what is this one for.

I pry it open easily to find a large metal lockbox jammed into a little alcove that's been carved out of the wall. My heart pounds with excitement. It's about a foot long, maybe one or two inches more on one side, and four inches high. It looks sturdy, but the padlock keeping it closed is flimsy. It will be so easy to open I wouldn't say it even qualifies as lock picking.

"What's that?" Deja asks, shining her flashlight towards me.

"It was hidden in the wall. I don't know what it is, but I'm really curious."

"It's probably a sex tape," she jokes.

"Yuck," I say, curling my lip in disgust.

"Why don't you go ahead and order dinner," I suggest. "I'll be up in a minute."

I rummage around until I find a small screwdriver and a paperclip. With minimal effort I open the lock and look inside the box to find DVDs. Each one is nestled in a jewel case and labeled with a letter and date. There are ten or fifteen that say

HE HATE ME

L and a date, all within a year of each other. One says L and D and a date and the last four, the most recent one dated six years ago, has just D and a date. I have no idea what these could be. I know people used to store data on these things.

Could this be evidence of some other scheme Devin was involved in? It's not likely to be relevant to his current activities, but I still want to know what's on them. My laptop doesn't have a disc reader. I don't know if they still make computers with those built in.

I text Anton requesting he intercept the surveillance cameras again even though he's getting more and more impatient with me, I think this may be worth the risk of annoying him. I pack the DVDs into an old kids backpack that might have been mine back in the day. I lock the box and put it back in the wall, putting everything back the way it was. On cursory inspection, everything looks untouched. You can see my footprints in the dust, so I scuff them a bit and move one of the cardboard boxes, so it looks like I was standing there to search through it. Once Deja confronts them about the pictures, they'll think nothing of it.

While I wait for an acknowledgment from Anton, I type up a summary of what's happened on my phone and send that to him as well. Fortunately, Anton doesn't keep me waiting long. Once I get his go message, I leave the basement to find Deja. She's in the kitchen, staring out the back window. I don't like the crease forming between her eyebrows.

"Are you all right?" I ask.

"Yeah," she says, but she looks sad and angry, the emotions seeming to battle each other on her face. I see it when she turns to look at me, a silent yearning for this to go back to making sense. I think she's bothered more by the lying than by the discovery of a shared history between Devin and her parents. For me it's the opposite. I never expected honesty from Devin and Tanisha, so the question that's plaguing me is whether this has something to do with Anton's quest. No obvious connection comes to mind, but people don't lie for no reason.

"Do you wanna go out?" I ask, tucking the backpack next to my leg where the cameras can't see it. Anton's guy could probably edit it out, but why chance it.

"Maybe. Where to?"

"Dinner. Did she leave enough cash for Olive Garden?"

She shrugs, scooping the money off the counter and jamming it into her pocket.

"I'm gonna change into a warmer coat and be right back."

"That's a great idea. I should do that too."

Chapter 26

Brandon

WE PARK NEAR THE CARRIAGE HOUSE AND TAKE THE BACK stairs up to our room at Rourke's mansion. There are at least a dozen cars parked in front, and once inside we can hear loud music coming from multiple rooms, incompatible styles warring with each other. We get into the house and up the stairs without anyone seeing us. As soon as I unlock the door Deja slips through, dropping her coat on the floor. It's so unlike her I freeze in place for a moment, staring at her. She unbuttons the demure flower print button down she wore to meet my mother, turning to look at me as she backs up towards the bed. My brain comes back online, and I lock the door, leaning my back against it to watch her. The shirt slides down her arms onto the floor. She unbuttons her jeans, never breaking eye contact, and lets them fall to her ankles. She kicks them off her feet, and they sail through the air, knocking over a trash can.

"You're making a mess."

"So what?" she asks, scowling. "If you don't like a mess, you can clean it up."

"Are you okay?" I pick up the coat and shirt, laying them on the foot of the bed. She flops onto the bed, face up, her eyes closed.

"No," she says tightly. "I've tried to think up a reasonable explanation for why they'd lie to me, and I've got nothing."

"We have a plan, though, right? We'll confront them in the morning."

She licks her lips and walks to the edge of the bed on her knees, motioning me to come over. Her eyes are stormy, the corners of her lips turned down. She unzips my jacket, pushing it off my shoulders. She takes the hem of my T-shirt and peels it over my head.

"Do you know what I need?" she asks. It's more a plea than a question.

"Is that what you want?"

She shakes her head. "You said you wanted to give me what I need, so here's the test. Can you?"

I stare into her eyes, seeing the storm of emotions swirling within. She's hurting, confused, angry. And she's looking to me for comfort, for escape.

HE HATE ME

Slowly, I reach out and caress her cheek. She closes her eyes and leans into my touch, some of the tension leaving her body. I lean in, brushing my lips against hers in a feather-light kiss. Then I grab her by the neck and throw her back on the bed. She scrambles, trying to escape over the other side. I'm on top of her before she can make it to the edge. I grab her wrists, holding them to her sides as she tries to buck me off.

"Remember your safe word?" I whisper in her ear.

"Fire." She stops moving for a minute and then begins thrashing again. I pull her wrists behind her, holding them with one hand and sit on her thighs.

"Your gesture?" I ask.

She taps her foot on the bed three times. "If my hands are free, I tap with my fingers."

"Great." I unhook her bra and pull it over her head and down her arms to tie her wrists.

"Let me go, Brandon!" she demands, but she knows what she needs to say if she really wants this to stop, and she's not saying it. The bra won't hold her for long, but while she tries to get out of it, I get the leather handcuffs from the cardboard box under the bed. I release her wrists from the bra just long enough to pull her arms over her head and fasten her wrists to the bedpost. These cuffs won't hurt her—they're lined with faux fur—but they're sturdy enough to hold unless she twists her wrists in just the right way.

I look at her below me, bare except for her panties. I get a few more items from the box and lay them on the bedside table. The ball gag, the flogger, the riding crop and the nipple clamps. These last are new to me. Ms. D found them too painful, so we never played with them. These are the simple kind that clip on, but I want to get the ones that screw tight if Deja tolerates these well. I have a feeling she will.

She already looks better, her previous tortured expression replaced by defiant anger. This is what I want, to give her an outlet for the intense emotions that have trapped her like a maze, circling from fear to disappointment to worry to betrayal and back again. Now she's focused on only one thing—me, and what I'm going to do to her.

I strip my clothes off and climb to the top of the bed, swinging my leg over her torso. One of these days I'll have the self-control to stay soft and make her suck me to erection, but that is not today. Just looking at her body has me hard, but what I have planned for us makes me throb. My hard cock nudges at her lips. She presses them together in defiance, trying to turn her head to keep me out. Mercilessly, I reach behind me and twist one of her nipples. She gasps, and my cock slides into heaven. She tries to push me out using her tongue and it feels so good. I push inside her mouth, till my tip hits her throat. I keep it there, not pushing so deep that she chokes, but holding it just a millimeter from that point. I see her eyes grow large, feel her chest heave as she begins to panic. I imagine my cock must feel heavy on her tongue. Her lips are stretched wide, a tear leaks from one of her eyes and a puff of air escapes her nostrils. The panic eases as she remembers that she can breathe through her nose, but now her expression is full of anger. I pull back a little and thrust back in, slowly fucking her mouth.

HE HATE ME

"You're such a good girl," I tell her, cupping the back of her head and pushing a little deeper. It's so hard to resist. Her mouth is hot and slick, her tongue slightly rough against the underside of my shaft. I push in, deeper than I should and feel her throat struggling to take me in or push me out. I pull out, loving the way her spit makes strings that wet her face. Her makeup is starting to melt, and she looks a nasty mess.

"Red, Yellow, Green?"

"Green," she says, hoarsely. The sound makes me want to jam my dick down her throat again, but I need to fuck her, take the edge off before we continue.

I cup her pussy and find her panties soaked. I grin at her.

"Little Thorn loves to be used, doesn't she?"

She shakes her head, her bottom lip outthrust. She's playing the defiant brat and I love seeing her expression fall apart as I push her panties to the side and ram my fingers into her.

I move between her legs, spreading them really wide the way I like them. I find her clit through the wet black fabric and rub it with my thumb. She pushes her hips up, swallowing my fingers and pressing more firmly against my thumb. She smells so heavenly, pure sex. I can't resist sucking her juices off my fingers. She tastes so good I almost decide to delay fucking her so I can eat her out. But I don't.

I grasp the waistband of her cotton panties and yank hard, ripping them at the seams. I pull it out of the way until it hangs off one leg and push the head of my cock against her opening. There's a moment of tension where her body resists the intrusion, and then her flesh parts, slowly yielding to me. I sink into her, inch by inch, her warm channel hugging my shaft tightly.

"You feel so good, baby," I tell her. "Can you squeeze me with that pussy? Oh yes, that's it."

Her face is tight, her bottom lip crushed between her teeth. She flinches, clearly in some pain and I still to let her adjust, and to savor her moue of displeasure. I lick her lips, coaxing her to release that bottom lip to me. When she does, I bite, sharply enough that she gasps. The involuntary movement of her body pulls her away from my cock and I instinctively follow her hips forward, driving my shaft deeper than before. She groans, the sound pained, then moans pained in an entirely different way. Her hips rock subtly, letting me know that she's ready for me to move.

I start with slow thrusts, pulling most of the way out, then driving back in. She's ready for me, tipping her hips up to accept my thrusts. Her eyes drift closed, and I watch emotions flow across her face: surprise, pleasure, need. I love watching her, seeing her react to every shift of my hips, how her vocalizations change based on whether I'm deep inside or circling my hips. I tell she's getting ready to come, but I don't want her to just yet. I change position so that I can still thrust deep without coming in direct contact with her clit. She's too inexperienced to realize what I'm doing as I pump into her channel faster and faster. Pleasure shoots up my spine like lightning. I pull out, holding onto my control by a thread, and jam my cock back into her mouth. I don't know if I was expecting disgust or reluctance, but she opens for me like she's wanted nothing more all night than to suck me dry.

HE HATE ME

Green, she said before, so I don't hold back. Her eyes bulge and I feel her throat closing around the head of my cock. I curl my hands around her skull and feel her throat give way as I force myself inside her. I shudder, shooting pulses of semen down her throat. I pull out while I'm still hard, flopping to the side while she gasps for air. My come bubbles out of her nose and she coughs, trying to clear her air passages.

"That was amazing, Deja," I whisper into her ear. "I love how your throat feels around my cock. You are such a good girl, aren't you?" She nods despite her obvious physical distress. She rolls my come around in her mouth, leaving it half open so I can see the disgusting mess. "You are such a dirty slut, aren't you? Swallow it." When she does comply quickly enough, I slap her tit, causing her body to jerk and twist. She opens her mouth to show me that it's all gone.

Now that I've come, it's time to really get started. I get a washcloth and clean up her face, then check in.

"Green, yellow, red?" I ask.

"Green," she says, her voice hoarse. Not that I'm trying to push her too far too fast, but I'm a little surprised she's still at green. Holy fuck are we going to have fun.

I scan her body, considering where I'd like to start. I realize I've forgotten something. I picked up a set of plastic clothespins at the dollar store on Friday. Like the wooden spoon I used to punish her, sometimes the best tools are improvised.

We texted back and forth last night, sharing ideas and figuring out what we might want to try, and what was definitely off the table. I'm learning as much as she is. I have my fantasies, some focused on domination, some on extracting pain. I've read and fantasized a lot since my relationship with Ms. D. After things ended with her, I had a really horny and uninhibited girlfriend for a while. She wasn't into pain, but she wasn't shy about telling me what she liked. Thanks to her I know way more about getting a girl off than most guys my age.

I unclip Deja's handcuffs from the bed and pull her across my lap. I rub her bare bottom, warming up the skin in preparation. She's tense and I know she's going to get hurt if she stays like this.

"Relax your muscles," I tell her. She quivers, trying to control her responses. She takes deep, slow breaths. Her ass tightens and relaxes a few times until she gets herself under control. She's pliant, but still nervous. Even though I just came, her fear and anticipation is starting to turn me on. I'm soft, but I don't know for how long.

I give her a few light swats on the rear, admiring the way her firm ass bounces more than it jiggles. She's quiet at first, but as my strikes get more firm, a soft whimper escapes her lips. I check her face, and she's not crying but her eyes are squeezed shut. I deliver four harsh blows, two to each cheek. I slip my hand between her legs, petting her swollen clit. Her lips are slightly engorged, but I plan to get her a lot more aroused than this. I spread her ass and press my thumb into the little black starfish. She stills, not knowing what to expect and I press my thumb firmly against her hole, dipping just the tip inside. Of course I like her ass—it's a fantastic ass—but I'm touching her like this because I know it makes her feel exposed and vulnerable. She needs to understand that no part of her is off limits to me. My thumb sinks into the tight ring of muscle. I love the resistance as her body tries to push me out. Her insides are incredibly soft and silky.

"How does that feel?"

"It hurts," she sobs.

"Poor Princess. How are you going to take my cock when you can barely take my finger?"

"No," she says. "Please don't fuck my ass. It's too small."

"Okay, I won't," I tell her, "but you have to do exactly what I say, or I don't care how tight that ass is you'll be giving it to me tonight."

"Please Sir," she begs, "don't."

"So you'll be good for me?"

"Yes, Sir."

"Do you know what I want you to do for me?"

"Yes, Sir."

"You do? What is it?"

"For me to suffer."

"You are such a good girl," I say popping my thumb out of her ass and replacing it with my finger. It's coated with her natural lubrication, but not so much that it's not uncomfortable. I know she doesn't want this, but also that a part of her does or she would have used her safe word or raised her color from green. I pump my finger slowly in and out and she wiggles in discomfort, but I can also feel her wetness leaking onto my thigh.

"Stand up."

SENCHA SKEETE

She gets to her feet, her limbs shaking. She looks at my face, her expression watchful and tinged with fear. Her pulse flutters rapidly in her neck and I can't resist licking and sucking at her pulse point. I bite down on her trapezius, not as hard as I would like because I don't want to leave a mark, but hard enough to hurt.

It's difficult to describe how good I feel right now. The things I'm doing I've fantasized about for the last two years, playing over in my mind what I would do if I found a girl who was into the same things I am. Part of the thrill is in inflicting pain, but another part is in her surrender to me. We are not just exchanging pleasure like most couples or power like many dominants and submissives. She has given me permission to hurt her and trusts me not to harm her and that's an intimacy beyond what most people ever get to experience. Of course I would enjoy inflicting pain on anyone, but the adoration I have for her makes it that much more fulfilling.

I position her at the foot of the bed with her hands clasping one of the posters. She faces it, bending slightly at the waist so that her butt sticks out. I pick up the flogger and trail it gently over her back and ass, down her thighs and back up, sensitizing her skin. She relaxes a bit, her face losing some of its tension. I let her have it, passing the soft leather strands over her breasts and stomach, across her shoulders and up her arms.

At first, I just tap her lightly with the flogger, producing barely a sting, but then I go harder and harder across her back and shoulders. Her sounds of distress grow stronger, and I'm glad I decided not to gag her. Her soft cries are pure joy.

"Green, yellow or red?"

"Green," she gasps.

I toss the flogger onto the bed and approach her from behind, bending my knees so that my hips are level with hers. I spread her butt cheeks and guide my dick between them, rubbing the head of my cock against her rear hole. The spearhead of my dick slides up and down her crack, the burn when I apply pressure foreshadowing the pain she'll feel when I take her back there. Or would feel if I didn't plan to take my time and do everything to make sure her first time is pain-free. What I'm doing now is fun because of the fear she can't hide, the slight wince when I push the tip a few millimeters into her asshole.

I pull back, my dick protesting at leaving the warmth between her curvy cheeks. I reach for the riding crop and test it, enjoying the whistling sound it makes as I wield it and the satisfying thwack it makes against my hand.

"Don't move or we add five more strikes with the riding crop." She glances over to look at the long, thick whip with a flap of leather at the end and a black silicone handle. "Every strike I want you to count, okay?"

"Yes, Sir."

I lay one hard strike across the middle of her buttocks, at right angles to her spine. She jolts and counts one. I lay the next few lines in a fanlike pattern across her ass, leaving welts, but not breaking the skin. Her response is outstanding. She wiggles like there are ants in her pants and squeaks out her number in a high-pitched gasp that turns into a grunt.

SENCHA SKEETE

When I'm done with the crop, I survey her ass, wondering if I'm being too ambitious. Her inner thighs glisten with moisture. I could probably make her come with ten seconds of direct clitoral stimulation. But I haven't come close to testing her limits and this is for me, too. I'm not satisfied yet.

I order her back on the bed and cuff her spreadeagled to the bed frame. She's completely helpless as I tease her nipples, suckling and tonguing them until they're swollen and erect. Her moans of pleasure turn to cries of pain when I fasten a clamp to each nipple and pull gently on the chain that runs between them.

"That really hurts," she says tearfully.

"You know how to make it stop," I remind her, but she just squeezes her eyes shut and shakes her head from side to side, apparently determined to endure it.

Smirking, because with her eyes closed, she can't see me, I open the bedside table and pull out the last two objects I plan to use tonight—a condom and a clothespin. I set the condom to the side for the moment and close my hot mouth over her clit, raising her arousal and sensitivity to an even higher level. Then I attach the clothespin to her clitoral hood, and she screams, writhing as much as her bonds will allow.

"Green—"

"Yellow," she gasps, her voice clogged with tears. I'm gratified to see that I finally have her weeping, hot tears flowing from the corners of her eyes like a natural spring. I caress her ribs and flat belly and kiss her face, licking away the salty tears. I give the chain another little tug and more delicious fluid leaks out of her eyes. I could drink her tears all day. I even love the way she looks with snot coming out of her nose.

I shift down between her legs and kiss her gently on the clit. She jerks, moving her hips in the small radius allowed by her bonds. Ignoring her clit for the moment, I lick her from top to bottom, probing her opening with my tongue. I nip at her labia, now so engorged they look like they were injected with fillers. I find it extremely erotic. Even my lightest touch draws a reaction from her, either of pain or of pleasure. I take a few minutes to luxuriate in the sweetest pussy I've ever tasted. I reach for the riding crop and push the handle inside her, coating with her slick essence. I pull it out and press the slightly rounded tip to her nether hole. It's about the thickness of my finger and I guide it in until the whole handle has disappeared between her butt cheeks. Her face is the picture of embarrassment.

"Is it humiliating having a whip handle in your ass, Deja?"

She nods.

"Use your words."

"Yes, Sir."

"Yes, Sir, what?"

"Yes, Sir. It's humiliating when you fuck my ass with a riding crop."

"You want me to exchange it for my cock?"

"No, Sir. Whatever makes you happy, Sir."

Oh, fuck. Gold star.

"You are such a good girl, Princess. I can't imagine a more perfect girl."

Amidst all the other emotions she's experiencing I can see the pleasure my words give her.

Leaving the crop in her ass, I don the condom and ram my cock inside her pussy with deliberate roughness. I hook a finger over the chain between her tits and give it a gentle tug every time I thrust inside her. She cries out in pain each time, then suddenly throws her head back, a choked scream erupting from deep inside her chest. Her body quivers and I feel her pussy fluttering around my cock. I pull off the clothespin and angle my body lower so that my pubic bone grinds against her sore clitoris with each thrust. Not two minutes later she comes again, this time spasming like she's having a seizure. I pull the nipple clips off and cup her breasts, gently soothing one with my tongue while cruelly pinch the other with my fingers. For the next few minutes I don't know if she's having one long orgasm, or her senses are just generally overwhelmed. When I can no longer resist the incredible pleasure of her tight cunt, I come with a cry.

I hold her tightly, trying to catch my breath. I don't want to fall asleep without taking care of her, even though that's all my body wants to do. Reluctantly, I ease away from her and dispose of the condom. I remove the crop and take it to the bathroom to sanitize later. I return to her and take off her handcuffs, then clean her up with a washcloth.

I pull the covers over us and she curls in my arms as trusting as a baby.

"That was amazing," she says, her voice hoarse. "I didn't know my body could feel like that or that I could come more than once in a row."

"You gave me just as much pleasure," I tell her. "I love watching your reactions to what I'm doing. It was so erotic. I…"

There's a lump in my throat. I don't think I can tell her how I feel. I don't even know where to find the words. Somewhere along the line I fell in love with her, but I'm scared to say the words because I don't know if she feels the same way I do. But I can take pleasure in seeing her complete relaxation. Her skin seems to glow with peaceful energy. She rests her head on my chest and drifts off to sleep.

Chapter 27

Deja

When we enter the house, Mom and Devin are in the family room. They're both wearing their church clothes, but obviously didn't go to church. I don't think we can talk our way out of this one. Though showered, we're both wearing the same clothes we had on last night.

"Where have you been?" my mother asks, stalking into the foyer. Devin is right behind her, his expression angry.

"I'm sorry," I say. "We fell asleep and overslept."

"You both fell asleep? Where?"

"Um, a friend's," I say.

"Rourke's," Brandon says, as if he's daring them to object.

"Isn't he the one who uses drugs?" my mom asks.

HE HATE ME

"We didn't do drugs," I say quickly, but Brandon undercuts me, shaking his head.

"We only smoked weed," he says.

"What is your problem?!" I snap at him.

"My problem is you're on the defensive when they're the ones who have a lot to answer for. We're both adults, Deja. We're not beholden to them."

"Young man," Devin says, wading into the conversation for the first time. "You live in our house. You want to be adults and stay out all night—get your own apartment. As long as you live here—"

"You'd better follow our rules," Brandon mocks.

All of us stare at him with our mouths agape. He is really pushing it.

"Deja," Brandon says, "give me the pictures."

"I'm not sure…" His look is withering, and I comply, not entirely happy with him but also curious to see what he's going to do. This is a lot more confrontational than what I had planned, but I understand that he's applying the "good offense" defense.

He shows a picture to them, holding up so both of them can see.

"Who is this man, Devin?"

I had always thought of Devin as a sweet, even slightly clueless guy with a tendency to tell lame dad jokes. But when he says, "I have no idea," so credibly that I almost believe him I get chills.

"That's my late husband," my mom chimes in. "Where did you get that picture?"

SENCHA SKEETE

"It was with my mom's photo albums," Brandon lied. "I found it in the basement."

Brandon holds up the next picture, this one showing Dad, Devin and my mom embracing.

Devin opens his mouth, ready to tell another lie (and can I say how disappointing his behavior is to me?) but my mom raises her palm in his direction and shakes her head.

"Let's go have a seat in the living room," my mother says.

The living room is formal, used only for special guests and important conversations. When they're about to dole out punishment, we go to Devin's office but for a "family discussion," it's the formal living room. It's a wood-paneled room with stiff backed sofas and an antique inlaid wood table. There's a glossy-leaved fiddle leaf fig tree in one corner and a vase of fresh flowers on the side table. I take a mint from the candy dish on the coffee table, twisting and twisting the plastic wrapper around.

"I want to apologize to you, Deja," my mother says, "and to you as well, Brandon. We haven't been completely honest with you. I didn't fool you with that story about St. Joseph's College, did I?"

"No," I say, shaking my head.

She sighs. "I should have known. You're so tenacious. When I met your father, he and Devin were roommates at McCrystal. All three of us became close friends, though obviously your father and I were more than friends." She smiles, as if recalling a fond memory.

HE HATE ME

"When you were about five, Deja, I got a call from Devin letting me know about a job in his department. Even though it wouldn't be reporting directly to him, Devin was on the hiring committee and technically shouldn't have had any input on my hiring."

"But he did," I cut in.

"Yes, I did," Devin says. "In light of that we felt that it would be smart not to mention our longtime friendship to anyone."

"We would both have been penalized," my mom says. "I might have lost my job, and we had moved here from out of state, David had just been accepted at his first practice. We couldn't risk it."

"But why keep lying for so many years. I'm sure you've proven yourself at this point. And why lie to me."

"First, we'd be outing ourselves as liars," Devin said. "Trust is a big part of being successful and once people see you as untrustworthy, it can cancel out all your good deeds."

But you are untrustworthy, I think.

"And as for you, that's even more embarrassing." My mother shifts in her seat, tugging down the hem of her skirt suit to cover her knees. "When Devin and I became romantically involved, I worried it might be confusing if you knew that we had been friends when I was married to your father. Just the appearance…"

"We're supposed to believe you lied for years," Brandon says, "because you didn't have an affair?"

"There was nothing romantic between us until after David's passing," Devin says earnestly. But I just saw him lie convincingly about not knowing my father when they had, in fact, been best friends. Devin was right. Once you knew someone was a liar, it really did make it hard to trust anything that came out of their mouth.

Brandon squeezes my hand, sensing my renewed agitation. Maybe my mom is telling the truth, but Devin is still lying about something, I can just feel it.

"Any other questions?" my mom asks.

"Did you guys ever hang out before my dad died? I have this weird memory of Devin being in the basement of our house on Goshen."

They both shake their heads, though I notice a slight brittleness to my mom's "reassuring" smile.

"We met for dinner a few times," Devin says, "but that was always at restaurants. I never came by before David…left us, did I?"

My mother shakes her head again, a small mouth of displease distorting her lips. "I think the wake was the first time. But I think it's your turn now, kids. What happened last night?"

"Just what we said," Brandon responds.

"I was asking Deja."

"It nothing exciting. We went to Olive Garden for dinner and then Brandon suggested we drop by Rourke's cause we still had a while till curfew."

"Why Rourke?"

"Most of my friends were at Christian Dubrov's party and I hate his guts."

"We got there, I peer pressured Deja into smoking weed and then she started falling asleep on her feet. I took her to an empty bedroom and left her on the bed. When it was time to go, I tried to wake her up, but she was dead to the world and I'd had some alcohol, so I lay down for a sec, just till I sobered up, and then I woke up this morning."

"The two of you slept together?"

"Not in the way you're implying," I say. "We were perpendicular to each other."

"More like an L shape," Brandon says. "You ended up at the foot of the bed."

"Such a gentleman, isn't he? Kicking a girl till she's squashed up against the footboard." We are cooking with gas here with this lying. I can't tell if they're buying it, but confusion has replaced anger, so I take that as a positive sign.

"We'll need to discuss this between us," my mom says, "but for right now, you're grounded. School home—that's it. No social media for a week."

"A week!"

"And whatever else Devin and I decide once we've talked about it."

"And since you got such a great night's sleep, why don't you get started on your chores. We'll expect you to make lunch and dinner as well."

"Both of us?"

"Both of you.

* * *

SENCHA SKEETE

We try to act as if we're suffering, but none of this is that bad. We warm up soup and make sandwiches for lunch and we both enjoy making dinner. I'm a little anxious about getting all my reading done, but it's not a big problem. As tense as our interactions are with my parents, we're vibing. It feels good to be near Brandon, and we work well together. I know we need to be careful, now more than ever, but I'm feeling so good after last night, my body just gravitates towards his.

"I'm curious about something," Devin says at dinner. "What were you doing in the basement? The area where we keep the storage boxes is locked."

Brandon freezes for a moment. It's quick but Devin doesn't miss it. His expression is now more intent.

"I'm working on a gift for my mom," Brandon says. "I thought the pictures might help her remember...before."

"I told him about the boxes and where the keys were kept."

"So you weren't snooping around the basement?"

"Is there buried treasure down there or something?" Brandon jokes.

"That area is off limits," Devin says.

"Fine. I already found her old albums. Unless those are a national treasure or something."

"Those may contain some of my memories, too."

"No offense," Brandon says, "but when you threw me and mom out, I think you lost the right to say stuff like that."

"Brandon," my mother says, her eyes pleading for him to chill.

"Go to your room!"

Brandon rolls his eyes, "Without any bread?"

"You can take your dinner with you."

"Do I have to stay in there? Deja's supposed to help me with my math homework later."

Devin's eyes narrow. What is he thinking?

"That's fine," he says. "You can go to her room after dinner."

I'm surprised he said my room. I would have thought they'd want to keep us apart, but then they don't seem to suspect Brandon and I are more than friends. Is that because we did such an excellent job convincing them we dislike each other?

I help my mom load the dishwasher when we're done eating, then go upstairs and rap on Brandon's door. It's ajar, so I poke my head in. He's lying on his bed, reading a book I recognize from an English class I took last year.

"You ready?" I ask.

"Give me a sec." He's changed into sweatpants and a white t-shirt and looks sexy as hell. I try not to stare at his dick print. Sleeping, that thing is still impressive. He gathers the items he needs and follows me back to my room. He closes the door and I purse my lips.

"Is that smart?" I ask, clearing a spot on my desk for him to set his books down.

"Only if you don't want us to be overheard every time one of them walks by."

"Okay."

SENCHA SKEETE

Brandon has a big test coming up, so we spend about an hour reviewing the material and talking.

"Did you buy their story?"

"I don't know. There's got to be more to it than breaking some company policy."

"I think so, too. That only explains why they'd lie to their coworkers, but why lie to you?"

"Not just me. They lied to everyone at church, all their mutual friends. It's weird. Hold on, you need to find the cosine."

"Do you think they were having an affair?"

"Maybe. I don't know. If that's what it is, I'm really disappointed in my mom. That would make her a complete hypocrite."

"And banning us from the basement. You think there's more stuff to find down there?"

"Like what? Evidence of a crime?" He says it in a spooky voice, and yet...No. They may be liars and phonies, but they're not criminals. That would be crazy.

There's a knock on the door and Devin sticks his head in.

"We're heading to bed," he says. "We have an early meeting in the morning. Don't stay up too late and try to be quiet; we need a good night's sleep."

We make vague sounds of agreement, and he closes the door.

"Was that weird?"

"Yeah, that was a little weird."

HE HATE ME

I poke my head into the hallway and see that the lights are off except for what's pouring from Brandon's open bedroom doorway at the other end of the hall.

"Last one."

"If I can solve this one without help, do I get a prize?"

I roll my eyes. "A feeling of accomplishment."

"A feeling of your tits," he says in a low voice.

"I thought we agreed not to risk it in the house. That was your whole argument for going to Rourke's."

"But that was before now," he says. "Plus, unlike any other time, I'm supposed to be in here and Devin shut the door himself. We'll be fine."

"As long as we don't go too far."

"Of course not," he says.

"Doubt you'll get the chance, though," I tease. "You'd have to do well at math."

"Ouch!" he says, with a cheeky grin. "I'll even give myself a handicap."

He takes my hand and lays it on top of his cock. It isn't hard yet, but it stiffens as I explore it with my fingers. I know he's working as I touch him, but I'm not paying attention to that. His dick swells in my hand and the feeling is so arousing. I'm getting wet already, my clit tingling. I squeeze my thighs together and fish him out. I immediately cover the head of his penis with my mouth, licking the opening. His dick stiffens further, swelling in my mouth and rewarding me with a bead of pre-come. As much as I don't like the taste of come, I love pre-come. I suck and lick him, my mouth watering with the increased flow. I want to take him deeper, but he pulls me off him.

"I'm done," he says. I straighten up and check his work, and it's correct.

"Pull your shirt up." I comply, enjoying the way my nipples tighten with his eyes on them. He presses his face into my sternum, breathing in the scent of my skin. I'm caught off guard when he picks me up and brings me down on his lap, straddling him. He pushes the crotch of my loose shorts to the side and smiles when he feels how wet I am.

He caresses my slit and tweaks my clit, then guides my hips over him, and fists his dick with his other hand.

"It's okay," he says, locking eyes with me. "Just let me notch it in and then…yes, there it is."

He fills me inch by inch, stretching me beyond belief. I don't know why he feels so much bigger from this position, but it's making my knees shake. I circle my hips experimentally, getting used to the sensation. My weight pushes him deeper inside me until it feels like I'm about to burst. He cups my butt, pulling me tightly against him. I press down and he pushes up, and it feels so good I want to scream.

It feels like every time we have sex it's better than the time before. For intensity you can't beat the way we played last night, but for pure carnality, this is better, rawer. No pain, no power play, just my body connecting with his, the smell of his skin, his hands, caressing my hips, his small sounds of pleasure and encouragement. I circle my hips slowly, bouncing gently on his lap. He seems to like it. He rests his hands on my hips and throws his head back, jaw slack.

"That's so good, baby," he moans. "Ride me like a cowgirl."

The request is so cheesy it makes me laugh, and a blush stains his high cheekbones. In an act of petty revenge, he pinches one of my nipples and I get him back by playfully slapping his cheek. He lowers his head to my breast but instead of the bite I'm expecting, what I receive is a warm kiss, his tongue teasing the sensitive bud. He suckles gently, his eyes closed, black lashes striking against his flushed cheeks. I bury my hands in his soft hair, holding him to me. He places a soft kiss between my breasts and switches to the other one, the soft pull both soothing and erotic. Yesterday he punished my breasts, today he coddles them. It feels affectionate, even adoring.

I touch his face, rocking my hips forward and back. The light stubble on his face tickles my fingers. He turns into my touch and looks at me, blue eyes nearly black with desire, lips red and I want him so much it hurts. I mean he's already inside me, but I want to be even closer, to know him like I know myself. I hold his face between my hands and bring my lips to his, tracing his lips with my tongue. He opens to me, and I moan, sucking on his tongue. He holds me tight against his chest, moving his hips in counterpoint to mine.

He moves inside me, the stretch and friction of his shaft sending ripples of pleasure through me, up my spine where his arm circles my waist, down my legs, hanging on either side of his chair. His free hand lands on my hip, guiding me up and down, while we kiss like we're each other's oxygen.

SENCHA SKEETE

Both his hands slip below the waistband of my shorts, cupping my ass. He gives my cheeks a squeeze, reawakening a shadow of the sting from last night's cropping. Is it fucked up that ratchets my arousal higher? He's being gentle, but my body remembers, not the pain, but the intensity of emotion and the calm feeling after. He could have done anything to me last night, but he did nothing that I didn't want.

Our bodies move faster now, the pressure building and building.

"You're so beautiful," he moans into my mouth. He buries his face in the crook of my neck, driving into me with such vigor the chair begins to creak. Over the sound of my own heartbeat, I hear my mother's angry raised voice.

"Brandon," I say, trying to alert him, but he's too far gone. He holds me tightly and his warm come spills into me in spurts. The door bangs against the wall, it's flung open so hard. My mother stands in the open doorway, her face distorted with anger. The last weak pulse of Brandon's come releases into me as I lock eyes with her.

"What are you doing!" my mother screams. She rushes towards me, her lightweight robe flying open to reveal her satin nightgown. I flinch back, but Devin grasps her arm and pulls her against his body. His pose is protective, his anger as obvious as hers, but colder.

"Can we get a minute?" Brandon asks, looking over his shoulder at them. You'd think by his tone they were in the wrong.

My mother opens her mouth to say something, but Devin rubs her arm soothingly and says, "Two minutes. We'll be outside the door."

My heart is in my throat. I knew we were dumb to do this. I don't know why I listened to Brandon's stupid head. Okay, I do know why. I wanted him. If I had my way, I'd spend every second of the day touching him. Having to spend the entire day pretending we can barely tolerate each other, built my need for him to an irresistible height. I accepted his weak arguments because I wanted the same thing he did.

He cups my cheek and kisses me, slow and sweet. We hug and I love the warmth of his chest pressed against mine, the strength of his arms tightening around me.

"I guess we'd better…" I say.

I stand up, feeling him slip out of me. We're a wet mess and our separation fills the room even more strongly with the smell of sex. Brandon hands me a stack of tissues from the desk and I dab at my crotch. I can feel the slow trickle of his essence leaking out of me. The crotch of my shorts and panties are soggy. Brandon wipes himself clean and pulls his sweatpants up, but they're equally stained.

"I think I need to change my shorts," I say.

"Yeah," he says, "probably a good idea." He reaches into the open leg of my shorts and pets my lips, wetting his fingers in our mingled spend. He gives my clit a light caress with the backs of his fingers before he helps me stand up all the way.

There's a loud rap on the door. It's been two minutes, I guess.

SENCHA SKEETE

"Just a little longer," I yell. I grab a change of underwear and clean pajama bottoms and go into the bathroom to change. I hear their voices muffled by the door as I give myself a quick wipe with a wet washcloth and put on fresh clothes.

When I go back out, the scene that meets me is unexpected. Brandon looks panicked. There's a toiletry bag on the bed and next to it baggies of weed and pills and what I'm guessing is cocaine. It's not a tiny amount either. I'm no expert, but there is more weed there than I've ever seen in my life. And there's a small digital scale. And empty bags.

"Shit!"

Brandon's head swivels towards me when I speak, his expression growing even more panicked.

"It's not what it looks like," he says only to me, as if he doesn't care what Devin and my mom think, but I'm more confused than upset. What the hell is going on?

"Where did that come from?" I ask, naively.

"From Brandon's room," my mother says, aggressively. "I can see you didn't know about it."

"Is this really yours, Brandon," I ask, hoping he'll tell me it's a mistake or a setup, but looks away, his face turning red.

"Of course it's his," Devin says. "Didn't he tell you he got sent to juvie for possession with intent while he was seducing you?"

"No! That's not true." But Brandon has never said anything to me about juvie, except to taunt me. I'm not even sure I really believed he'd been. Devin had said Brandon had gotten into some trouble and I'd told my friends he just got out of juvie because I was mad at him. I'd never honestly believed he'd committed a crime.

"Are you going to be a man and tell her?" Devin says.

Brandon runs his hands through his hair, pacing in a tight circle. He looks at me pleadingly.

"I haven't lied to you," he says. "This isn't…it's not…"

"Is this why Rourke is friends with you? Are you selling him drugs? Are you dealing drugs to his friends?"

Devin may be an amazing liar, but Brandon isn't. Or maybe, even though I haven't known him long, I know him better, because I can tell right away that I've hit on the truth. It puts "our room" at Rourke's mansion in a whole new light. Brandon's a perk for Rourke and his degenerate friends. How must he think of me, knowing I'm the drug dealer's girl.

"Brandon," Devin says, "when you asked to move in with us it was on the condition that you would stay out of trouble, and I was explicit that meant no drug dealing."

"You searched my room. That's an invasion of privacy."

"You came in here this morning reeking off marijuana. Deja has never touched drugs or even broken curfew and now she's staying out all night, smoking marijuana, having sex."

Brandon scoffs and I shoot him a warning look. I can see that he's tempted to out me to them, tell them about my previous drug use, but he just laughs bitterly. I get what he's not saying out loud, though, that I'm not the goody two shoes I've snookered them into thinking I am, but he can't be suggesting I'm no better than he is. I've never been arrested and the hardest drug I've ever used is E, and that was only once. There is coke on my bed. Brandon sells coke, probably uses it as well. What if it's worse than that? Meth? Heroin? I just let him come inside me.

I hug myself tightly, a feeling of betrayal rocking me. I'm sick to my stomach. I gave him my virginity, my trust, my submission, and he isn't worthy of any of it.

"Deja," he says, coming towards me and I flinch away from him, going to stand with my mom. He looks so hurt I almost think I'm misjudging him. He really cares about me.

"You can stay here tonight," Devin says, "but you need to find somewhere else to go tomorrow. We can no longer have you under our roof."

Devin moves to pack the drugs up, but Brandon shoves him out of the way, scooping items into the case as fast as he can.

"What are you doing?"

"This is my shit, Devin. Don't worry, I'll leave tonight, but I'm taking this with me."

"I cannot allow—"

"You cannot stop me, you mean," Brandon says. "I can bench two-seventy. Can you?"

They glare at each other. They're around the same height, but Brandon is visibly more muscular. And the sneer he's wearing right now, he looks like he'd be only too happy to deck his guardian. I feel like I'm looking at a stranger. I know he hates Devin, but to threaten to hurt him?

"Whatever," Devin says. He stands back while Brandon packs up the drugs and closes the case. He looks at me sheepishly as he retrieves his books and calculator. I'm a little surprised he's taking them, TBH. He tries to snag my hand one last time before he leaves, but I pull it back, avoiding meeting his eyes.

When he's gone, I collapse onto the bed, a hollow feeling in my chest. My mother's arm enfolds me, pulling me into her baby powder scented body. She strokes my back, soothingly.

"When I asked you about sex with Jayden, I guess I was looking in the wrong place, huh?" She's trying to lighten the mood and she is able to get a tiny smile out of me. "How long have the two of you been having sex."

"Just a few days," I say softly.

"Is that why you fell asleep at Rourke's last night?"

I nod.

"And the two of you couldn't wait more than a day to do it again?"

"I didn't expect sex to be so…addictive," I say. "I feel so stupid."

"Brandon's your first?" I nod. "I'm sorry, honey. It must hurt to realize you chose the wrong person to be with. You're eighteen, so I'm not going to talk to you as if you're a child. You screwed up, and I hope you learn from this. The right guy is out there, and he'll be worth the wait."

I think about last night, the wholeness I'd felt, the way Brandon looked at me with adoration. I can't imagine that with some other guy.

"Were you safe?"

I shrug. We were half the time. Tonight is borderline because the effectiveness of my birth control may or may not have kicked in yet.

I shake myself and stand up.

SENCHA SKEETE

"I need to finish my reading assignment."

"Deja?!"

"You know me, Mommy," I say. "Routine calms me. I'm going to read and focus on school and forget that boy ever existed."

She argues for a bit, but eventually I get her to leave. But I don't study—the hollow feeling inside won't let me focus. Too upset to study, I lie on my bed and let the tears fall to study, I lie on my bed and let the tears fall.

Chapter 28

Deja

I BLOCK BRANDON ON MY PHONE AND NOTIFY MY friends that he's been kicked out of my house and is to be avoided. They push for details, but I tell them nothing. I figure the truth will trickle through the grapevine eventually.

So I'm shocked when I get to school and find him waiting for me by my locker. He looks rested and based on what he's wearing, a black Balmain t-shirt under a soft and drapey sweat suit, he must have spent the night at Rourke's.

"Didn't you land on your feet," I quip, pushing past him to open my locker.

"Can we talk? I need to explain."

SENCHA SKEETE

"Let me guess? The drugs weren't yours, you were holding them for a friend."

He can't respond because we both know the drugs were his.

"We have something special, Deja. I've never felt this way about anyone. You can't just throw it away."

"Say that louder so everyone can hear."

"I don't really care anymore," he says. "I keep it a secret so I wouldn't get kicked out, but I'm already kicked out, so we cares. There is nothing wrong with us being together. You can't honestly tell me anyone else makes you feel the way I do."

"What is that? Used? Manipulated? Betrayed? You're right; no one else makes me feel that."

I slam my locker and make tracks for homeroom.

* * *

I have a free period before lunch, and I go outside to sit under an oak tree. It's cold, so I have the courtyard to myself. The leaves have just started to fall from the trees, a sparse layer of orange, red and gold littering the ground at my feet. I'm glad I wore a hoodie today, because I can look down at my feet and no one will see my tears. Some of you might say, oh, he didn't do anything to you, but after he shared his mom's illness and his sexual history, I figured if there was anything else big to tell me, he would have done it. It's not even that I have a problem with drugs per se, but it's this feeling like I've been taken for a fool. And the way he threatened Devin. That was scary. What else did he do in his

HE HATE ME

old life besides deal drugs? Was he in a gang? Has he beat down or even killed someone before?

Impulsively I get my phone out and text Mello.

ME: *Can I treat you to lunch? I need to ask you something.*
MELLO: *Sure. I love lunch.*
ME: *Meet me in the courtyard.*

* * *

I stay under the tree and try to pull myself together. By the time Mello finds me, the only sign of my tears is my red eyes and a slight sniffle. We don't have a lot of time for lunch, so we hurry to the parking lot, and I drive us to a nearby fast-food place. We find a seat and wait for our orders.

"How's your ankle?"

"As good as can be expected," he says. He's still wearing a walking boot and moves well, but I know ankles are tricky.

"Did they say when you'll be able to play again?"

He shrugs. "I can't speak to that. I try not to think about it too much. I just focus on healing. So what'd you want to talk about?"

I blow a noisy puff of air through my lips. Now that he's sitting across from me, his piercing amber eyes seeing too much, I feel awkward.

"You've known Brandon a long time, right?"

"Yeah," he says. "Since sixth grade, I think. Maybe seventh? I met him playing soccer."

"Yeah, Lisa told me."

"I'm not going to help you get back at him or whatever. Y'all need to work your shit out." His tone is friendly.

"That's not it. Keep it on the DL, but Brandon got kicked out last night. Devin found his stash."

"Oh. Okay."

"You knew?"

"That he was back doing that? No. But I saw him hanging out with RVH, so…"

"RVH?"

"Rourke. I did kinda wonder how he got in with that guy so fast. This makes it make sense."

"I was wondering what happened before. What did he do."

"He was just selling weed, nothing too hardcore. He mainly would go over to Merrill, hang out with the white kids over there and sell to them. You know about his mom, right?"

"Yeah," I say. "I met her."

"For real?" He looks at me like I'm a puzzle. "He doesn't really ever introduce people to his mom. But yeah, he was tryna help out."

A restaurant employee drops our tray on the table. I pick up my soda and take a sip. The smell of the greasy food isn't appealing, but I put a fry in my mouth and chew. I barely ate anything this morning and I have practice after school.

"But then he got in trouble, right?"

Mello nods, taking a bite of his sandwich. "He sold to some cop's kid and got popped.

"Did he go to jail."

"Did a few months in juvie far as I know, but that was like two years ago at least. I'd a thought living with y'all he wouldn't need money like that."

HE HATE ME

"You think maybe it's because his mom's in hospice?"

"I thought your stepdad was paying for that."

"Did Brandon tell you that? He told me the opposite."

"That's my bad then. I asked him and he said somebody was taking care of it. I figured it was your dad, but now that I think about it, if he was gonna do that, he would have done it years ago and Brandon wouldn't have gone to jail."

"Did he ever, I mean, was he using?"

"I mean everybody smokes some weed. Weren't you high the night I met you?"

"Yeah, weed, but he had pills and coke, too."

Mello shakes his head. "Like I said he's hanging with RVH. I mean, I get he'd want to make a buck off that coke head, but that shit is expensive. I hope he didn't get in with somebody dangerous."

I hadn't even thought of that.

If he was doing it to help his mom, that put a different complexion on it. It didn't really excuse the lying, but at least he wasn't just trying to make a quick buck.

"He and I…" I say, softly.

"I know," Mello says. His smile is compassionate. "You all don't hide it very well."

"Do you think everyone knows?"

Mello shrugs. "I don't think most of those kids can see past their own noses. I've never in my life met a group of people so self-absorbed. But I think a few people have noticed something."

"I don't know how to handle this. Last night I said I was done with him, you know. He lied to me and he's a criminal.

SENCHA SKEETE

But when I saw him earlier it was hard to look at him and think we weren't going to be together anymore. I'm in love with him, but I feel like I can't be with someone who's breaking the law like that."

"I understand," Mello says. "But those kids you're going to school with, the ones who are headed for Yale and NYU and Northwestern. How many of them do you think will be running stock funds that cheat people out of their life savings in ten years? Fifteen years from now, they'll be running companies that dump toxic waste into the ocean and lie about it or use slave labor and pretend not to see it. Would you feel like you had to give one of those guys up because he's less than honest, or is it only because Brandon's on the street and they'll be in a boardroom?"

"I'd have to—" I start to say, but then I get his point. It's all dirty. The entire system is dirty, we just pretend it's not. Rourke should have been expelled. Gio should have faced repercussions for hurting Mello. Ivy League schools shouldn't have legacy admissions and companies should have to pay for the environmental damage they do. But top to bottom, society is unfair, and the winners are those that figure out how to get away with it. Brandon selling a few thousand dollars' worth of drugs to the sons of the people ruining the world is not that bad in the grand scheme of things. Not bad enough for me to give up on the only guy I've ever loved.

* * *

Brandon

HE HATE ME

I pace the floor of my room, waiting for Anton to call me. Since I texted him last night that I was kicked out, and got an "okay," he hasn't responded to my texts until ten minutes ago when he finally said, "I'll call you." Now I'm watching the second hand of the clock, each sweep around the dial feeling like an hour. I've barely eaten today, and the soup I choked down half an hour ago is threatening to come back up. I don't even try to do homework; I know I wouldn't be able to concentrate and after all that studying I did last night, I'm almost certain I failed my math test. As if that shit even matters now.

"Hello," I say, as soon as the phone rings.

"I've got ten minutes. Tell me what happened—fast."

"Devin went into my room last night and found my stash. He kicked me out."

"Where'd you leave it that he found it?"

"In my room. He pretended they went to bed, but he was really searching my room. I was in Deja's room. I need your help."

"With what?"

"I tried to talk to her today and she wouldn't listen, and she blocked me. Can you get me into the house? I know if I could be alone with her, I could—'

"No."

"But—" I realize that I can't catch my breath. What the hell is wrong with me? If I could only get her understand how I feel about her, I know she'd take me back. It's not like I'm selling to drug addicts, just a bunch of spoiled rich kids. And it wasn't even my idea to do this, it was Anton's.

SENCHA SKEETE

"So now we've lost access to the house. That should be what you're worried about, not some little girl. If you had been guarding your shit instead of screwing her, Devin wouldn't have had the opportunity to find your stash."

"It was in the house the whole weekend. He could have found it any time."

"But he didn't get suspicious until you confronted him with those pictures. That girl is the root of all your problems. You need to let her go." I don't ask how he knows what happened when we got home on Sunday morning. He has access to all the security cameras plus the extra cameras and microphones he asked me to plant around the house.

"I won't," I tell him, and I mean it. If I'm not letting Deja separate us, I'm sure as hell not letting his asshole do it. If he won't help me get to her, I'll find another way. "She's my girl, Anton. That is not fucking changing. I don't even fucking want you to talk about her.

"If you think about it, though, he got freaked out because we were rummaging around in the basement. He must have been searching my room to see if I found something. You have control of the alarm system—you could disarm it tonight so I can go in and finish the search."

"That's not a good idea."

"Whatever you want is down there."

"Can you honestly tell me if you went there tonight you could stay away from her room?"

As much as I hate to admit it, he's right. I can close my eyes right now and smell her skin, imagine the warmth of it chasing away the cold that's taken over my chest since I saw that look of betrayal in her eyes. I can barely restrain myself now.

"Fine. I'll take a look at the DVDs tonight, then."

"What DVDs?"

"I thought I told you. I found a bunch of old DVDs hidden in the wall of the basement. The oldest ones are from ten years ago, give or take. I just got an external drive delivered today so I can see what's on them."

"They're not movies?"

"I don't know. They don't have any labels on them just a letter and a date written on the case in magic marker. It could be financial records. It's not nothing, though. You don't hide family pictures in a lockbox behind a fake breaker box."

"It's not what I'm looking for, but you never know what might be helpful. Let me know what you find, okay."

"Sure."

"Do you need me to replace your stash?"

"No, I brought it with me. Told him I'd beat the shit out of him if he tried to stop me."

Anton chuckles. "I wish I'd seen that."

"Be glad you didn't. You put a camera in my girl's room I'd have to kick your ass, too."

"Settle down, puppy. I'm glad you're finding your balls, but don't forget I'm the guy who'll slice them off and make you eat them."

"I will not forget that," I say. I must be losing my mind. We are searching for evidence of a murder Anton committed when he was around my age. He is not to be fucked with and the most violent thing I've ever done is knock out the teeth of some kid who tried to mess with me in juvie. "I need a gun."

"What'd you need a gun for?"

"You want me to keep dealing, I need a gun. Especially now I'm living in party house. Everybody's going to know I got this shit now, and a hundred people come through this house every weekend."

"You know you're not a juvenile anymore. You get jammed up with a gun and you're going away for a while."

"So if they steal from me, you'll just give me more, free of charge?"

"All right," he says. "Come by tomorrow. I'll have something for you."

After my nerves have settled, I go down to the front door and retrieve my package. When I get back to the second floor, I see a girl at the other end of the hallway slipping through the door of the servant's stairs that lead to the kitchen. I don't get a good look at her except I can see she's small and brown with a stubby ponytail sticking off the back of her head. She doesn't look like the type of girls that usually come over, and I didn't figure Monday at 4:00 pm was going to be hopping, but what do I know. Rourke is basically a wild card. She could be anybody.

I lock the door when I go in my room anyway. I'll need to add some security—a camera at least—and maybe a better lock. I wonder if Rourke would let me put a metal core door on here. I'm getting ahead of myself. I don't even know if his absentee dad will let me live here.

HE HATE ME

The DVD drive attaches to my laptop with a USB cable. I'm feeling so fucked up. I don't want to do this. I didn't even work out this morning and I'm feeling all keyed up. The disks are stacked on the coffee table, so I set up there, plugging my laptop in to the charger since I don't know how long this will take. The Wi-Fi signal is super weak because this place is so big, but I'm able to check my email. Nothing except the latest invoice from my mom's hospital and a bunch of spam.

When I open the first disk, there's only one file listed, and the name is just a date. I click on it and a video opens, showing what looks like a basement. The camera is pointed at a sofa with Devin and mom sitting on it. My mom has a dreamy expression on her face, like she's drunk. Her dark hair is cut in a bob, and she's wearing a going out to dinner dress. I hit play.

"Stand up for me, Lindsey," Devin says, and she does it, swaying a bit on her feet. She giggles.

"Now bark like a dog."

My mom goes, "Ruff, ruff, ruff." Devin laughs, slapping his knee and I can hear more laugher, though I can't see who's doing it. It sounds like a man and a woman.

"Bark like a chihuahua," Devin says, and my mom does that too, a high-pitched yapping noise.

"This fucking bitch will do anything I tell her," Devin says. My stomach twists. I remember her telling me that Devin was like family to her, yet here he is humiliating her. But why is she doing this? Could she be drunk? I've never seen anything quite like this. When he tells her to do something she does it, but otherwise she just stands there looking dazed.

Devin asks her to crawl on all fours and kiss his shoes and a bunch of other things like that, cackling the whole time. The video jumps and a number of items are added to the weathered coffee table between my mother and the camera. Peanut butter, a jar of pickles, a lighter, a cucumber. Devin takes his boot off and makes her lick the peanut butter from his toes. His face is alight with malevolence. What could she have possibly done to make him treat her this way? My mother is one of the most harmless people I've ever known. He makes her eat the entire jar of pickles, then drink the juice, which makes her throw up. A woman yells for someone to get a trash can and a black man, wait no, Deja's father, thrusts it under her mouth just in time. He looks at her with the same resentment as my father. I expect them to attack her with their fists at any moment. Once her stomach is empty, he takes her arm and leads her up the stairs with the trashcan in his other hand. The video jumps again, and she's back, the front of her dress soaked with water. Through all of this she still looks peaceful, her expression trusting and childlike. And then things get even worse.

"Show us your tits, Lindsey," Deja's father says, sitting next to her on the sofa. She's flanked on either side by David and Devin. I need to look away, but I can't, because I have to know if she'll really do it. But of course she does. She drops her dress to her waist, displaying her body for them with no self-consciousness whatsoever. I slam my laptop shut, my earlier nausea returning. I go over to the window and look

HE HATE ME

out, gripping the sill until my knuckles are white. The sound of my own heart is so loud I can't hear anything else. I knew Devin was a piece of shit, but I figured he was the regular kind—sleeping with his friend's wife, greedy, dishonest, a thief, and selfish. But torturing an innocent woman for the amusement of you and your friends? That's not normal. Doing what I'm pretty sure he is about to do? That's not close to normal either.

Except I won't know for sure unless I at least fast forward through the rest, and I need to know exactly what they did to her. I also now have the dilemma of deciding what, if anything to tell Deja about her parents' involvement in this. There's her father as plain as day, and I'd bet money the woman we never see on camera is her mom.

I feel queasy when I think about the first night I was with Deja. Is this what I look like to her, like a monster? But no, or she wouldn't be with me. I was honest with her about what happened, and she decided how to respond. I was shady, but as much as I thought I disliked Deja at the time, I never wanted to hurt or humiliate her. She wasn't like my mother is on that video. She was uninhibited, but still herself. She asked me to touch her, she insulted me, and she was even demanding. In the video my mother is a puppet with no will of her own. What Deja and I did together was mutual; what they had done to my mother was perverse. I know my behavior was shitty, but there's being shitty and then there's pure evil. Turning another human being into a mindless toy and treating them like an animal is evil.

SENCHA SKEETE

I run upstairs and find Rourke playing a military shooter with a headset on, yelling at someone in Italian. I try the door to the bar, but it's locked.

"You need a drink?" he yells, covering his mouthpiece with his hand.

"A fucking strong one, too," I say. He waves me over and unclips a carabiner from one of his belt loops.

"It's that orange one," he says, referring to a key with the FC Laurient symbol printed on it. "I'll get you a copy made."

"Why's it locked."

"Gets too crazy with people sometimes. Got some pricy stuff in there."

It's the first sign I've seen that Rourke's even aware that things cost money. I thank him and grab a couple of shot glasses and a bottle of vodka from the bar before locking back up. We do a shot together and then I go back downstairs to face the carnage.

***

I get through the rest of the video by fast forwarding. They sexually assault her and make her do something humiliating with the cucumber, but I'm relieved to get to the end without an actual rape occurring. On the next disk, I'm not so lucky. By the third one, I can't stomach it even when it's accelerated to breakneck speed. I copy the videos onto my hard drive, checking the first few shots to confirm that my mother and Devin are in them and then dropping them into a folder I'll zip and forward to Anton. It takes a while, and by

HE HATE ME

the time I get to the video that says L&D, I'm pretty drunk. The alcohol is not making this situation any more bearable.

I copy the first solo D disk and check the opening shot. My mother is not in it. Instead, a pint-sized Deja is sitting on the old sofa drinking juice from a glass with a straw. Devin is sitting next to her, a friendly smile on his face. I hit play and listen to him telling her about Disney World and asking what her favorite attractions are. He urges her to finish the juice and puts the glass aside, his expression affectionate. Only minutes later her eyes go hazy the way my mother's were. It's confirmation that my mom was drugged, and I want to stop the video here. Whatever is about to happen I don't need to know do I?

"Can you stand up for me?" he asks.

She does it, looking unsteady the way my mom did. He runs through the same sequence of weird actions he asked of my mom, barking, crawling, kissing his shoes. I realize now he'd doing it to make sure she's completely under the influence of whatever drug he gave her. Once he's satisfied, he tells her to strip. At that point I shut it off. I don't need to see this fucking shit. It's bad enough I have the knowledge in my brain, the actual image would just about destroy me. Even thinking about what he probably did to her makes my skin crawl.

My god. She's in that house, sleeping down the hall from that monster. I want to go over there and yank her out, but I'm too drunk. Why did I think it was a good idea to drink this much? I don't watch the last three videos, spaced months, and then two years after each preceding one. I copy all of them and zip the file. I text Anton.

ME: *This is some awful shit, man. Video of DT r-wording my mom and Deja ten years ago. Couldn't watch most of it. Not sure what you can do with it, but I feel sick. I'm uploading now.*

I log onto Anton's secure server and upload the files. A few minutes later I get a text "received." I wait, nerves driving me to take more shots until the whole world feels like it's spinning. One bad choice after another, but I haul myself up the stairs, to find Rourke in the same spot he was in earlier, fooling around on his laptop.

"Damn, dude, you look like shit."

"I need you to drive me to Devin's house?"

"What?"

"I gotta get her outta there."

"Dude, what are you talking about?"

"Deja." I sit next to him. The way he looks at me I know my expression is too intense, but I can't control it. "I found out Devin's a pervert, man. I've got to get her out of that house."

"I don't even know what that means," he says, "but you're drunk AF. You can't go over there. He kicked you out yesterday. They'd probably call the cops this time."

"Fuck!"

"Do you want to tell me what he did? Do you think he's going to hurt her?"

I shake my head and bury my face in my hands. Even as drunk as I am, I know that I can't tell him. If I do, then he'll know what was done to Deja and I can't do that to her. I

HE HATE ME

don't even think I should tell her. From what I can tell she doesn't remember it. I wondered at the time why my mom mentioned being in Deja's family's basement and how Deja had no idea what she was talking about. But my mom said it was a dream. Shit, I can't think straight right now.

"Hello," I say into the receiver. Rourke watches me warily over the top of his screen.

"I saw the first video," Anton says. "I recognize the other man."

"Can you help me now?" I ask, his words not really registering. "I need to get her away from him."

I hold my breath for several seconds as I wait for him to respond. "Are you drunk?" Anton asks.

"What would you do if you had to watch that shit with your own mother on it?" My words are slurred, I guess. I didn't notice till he pointed it out.

"Hang on," he says. "I'll send a driver to get you."

Chapter 29

Brandon

ANTON'S HOUSE OVERLOOKS A MANMADE LAKE WHERE Mallard ducks float gracefully across the water in tight groups. I take a sip from my coffee cup. My stomach is still a bit unsettled, but a pill took care of the pain from last night's alcohol binge. Still, my reflection looks pale in the floor to ceiling windows facing the water. Devin's wife is sitting perpendicular to me, her eyes locked on the screen where a video shows her husband's hand on her daughter's leg while he speaks soothingly to her. I don't look at it, and from the expression of horror on Tanisha's bloodless face, she wishes she didn't have to either. The video plays on for entirely too

HE HATE ME

long. I stand up halfway through, using the excuse of needing to pee to get out of there. I have only glanced at the screen throughout, but the sounds are disturbing enough, especially the ones announcing Devin's enjoyment. They make me want to scrub myself with bleach. I can't stand to see Deja's vacant little face, reduced by the drug to nothing more than a flesh doll for that monster's use.

I splash water on my face and remind myself why I'm here. It's for Deja. I only have to hear what was done to her. She had to live through it.

My surroundings are lavish. The powder room is large and brightly lit, the gray slate floor and marble counters creating a cool and spacious feel. I dry my face, trying to ignore the dark circles under my eyes. Yesterday I was dressed like a knock off Rourke; today I'm wearing a black long-sleeved button-down shirt with the sleeves rolled up and gray wool slacks. I look like one of Anton's "associates." All I'm missing is the shoulder holster, but that's fine because the gun he gave me is safely stowed in my duffle bag in the guest room. Getting in this deep was never my plan, but what do they say about best laid plans and good intentions?

When I hear the video stop, I return to the living room. Tanisha looks like she's been hit by a truck. She turns her head towards me as she hears me approach and flinches when she sees my face. She doesn't ask if this is real like she did when the video started. I guess there were details you can't fake. She moves her focus to Anton, who's sitting in the other armchair, lips pursed, an imposing sight in his impeccably tailored suit.

"No, I didn't know," Tanisha says, quietly. She squeezes her eyes shut. Maybe she's feeling the same skin crawling disgust I do finally knowing who she's connected to.

"But you knew about my mother," I accuse, the words bursting out of me before I can stop them.

She doesn't look at me, but she gives a slight nod.

"I knew they roofied her, obviously," she confesses, "but I never knew positively what they did with her after I left the room. That first night, when David took her upstairs to clean her up and she came back with the front of her dress wet, I got an inkling of where it was going so I left."

"You didn't try to stop them?"

"I disliked your mother, but that's not an excuse. I just tried not to think about it, and over time Devin convinced me that they didn't do anything too awful that night and they only drugged her one other time. He told me David never actually touched her. Devin told me he and your mother had been sleeping together, so when she came onto him, he didn't resist."

They hadn't, though. My mother had never viewed Devin as anything but her employer. I want to challenge Tanisha. I don't believe she really thinks that someone who acts the way my mom acted when Tanisha was in the room could turn around and become a seductress once she left. Or that they could have raped my mother in Tanisha's basement repeatedly without her knowing. But then, she was blind to what happened to her own daughter.

I want to ask her why they did those things to my mother, why she cackled like a witch while my mother was being tortured and humiliated, but that's not why we're here.

"Do you know why we're showing you this?" Anton asks.

"To make me hate him?"

"As rewarding as that outcome would be, my goals are much more concrete. Your husband has been holding onto an item that has great personal value to me and using it as leverage to make me finance his lifestyle."

Tanisha looks at Anton askance.

"Why would my husband need to do that? He makes a lot of money."

"You know I wondered that as well. I met your husband over ten years ago when I worked at a strip club my uncle owned."

"Devin doesn't go to strip clubs."

"Oh, he definitely does and back then…"

"I can confirm he used to come home all the time smelling of perfume with glitter on his suit," I tell her.

Tanisha still looks as if she doesn't believe us, but I remember the day when it all clicked, and I figured it out. I was eleven.

"He hired me to do a job and he paid me well. It was my first time doing something like that and I was a bit sloppy. Your husband helped me clean up, but in the process ended up in possession of something that could put me in prison for a long time.

SENCHA SKEETE

"For years I didn't think about it. I assumed he'd disposed of it. Then he contacted me about a year ago demanding money. Like you, I didn't understand why he needed the money. What I eventually learned is that your husband was one of the investors in Liberty Legacy."

"The Ponzi scheme?"

"Yes. He lost a half a million dollars of borrowed money, which he's been paying back by stealing from your mutual employer. Plus, I assume a little extra spending money here and there."

"How could you know this when I don't? I'm the controller of the company."

"My organization employs some very skilled hackers." Anton smiles, though the effect of it is like a shark baring its hundreds of teeth.

"I don't know what you want me to do," Tanisha says with an exhausted sigh. She rubs the top of her head, mussing her carefully styled straight hair. A single lock sticks up like a wood staple from her crown.

"Are you aware of any safety deposit boxes owned by your husband?"

"Yes," she says. "He has two, I think."

"Based on our investigation he has four. Do any of these look familiar?"

He hands her a piece of paper and she nods. "I recognize three of these as banks where we have accounts. The fourth, I'm not familiar with."

"Your name is on all four boxes. We'd like you to go to this fourth bank and retrieve the contents of the safety deposit box."

"And if I don't?" she asks.

"Of course you don't have to," Anton says. "We'll drop you off at home this evening and you can climb in bed with the man who drugged and raped your child. Also, you might want to know that the job Devin had me do was the murder of your first husband."

* * *

"I need to talk to you," Anton says after Tanisha leaves with two of his men. I'm tired and sick to my stomach. It's not his fault, but after watching the video of Deja's abuse, just being in this house makes my skin crawl. I need to get out of there. But I follow him into his home office. He offers me a chair and closes the door.

"I watched the tape labeled L&D and I want to give you a choice before I tell you what's on it."

"L&D is Lindsey and Deja, isn't it?"

"Does my mom…?" I can't bring myself to say the words poisoning my brain.

"Nothing like that," Anton says, "but it's very upsetting and knowing won't really change what we do. I'll still make sure Devin pays for what he's done."

"If you're even asking me this, it has to be bad." Is there any virtue in not knowing? I've decided not to tell Deja what Devin did to her. Sure, she has a right to know, but it won't help anything. I put myself in her shoes and the horror I'd feel if I knew that I had been raped without my knowledge is significant. As far as she knows it never happened, and so she's avoided the trauma for the most part. I'd be doing her a disservice if I told her about it.

Could this be similar? Something that it's better for me not to know? But it's not someone else deciding what's best for me. I already know this information exists, and I don't know if I could live with not knowing. It concerns the two people who are most important to me in the world. I have to know.

"Tell me."

Anton seems disappointed, but he doesn't drag it out or make excuses.

"The video has your mom on it with the usual happening. David's there as well, but he gets a call and leaves. Maybe ten minutes later Deja comes down the stairs. Devin tells your mother to sit in a chair and he gives Deja a drink. You understand what that means, right?"

"I do. So this is what happened the first time."

"Possibly he drugged her because she had seen him assaulting your mother, but I don't think she understood what she was seeing. Once she was drugged, well…"

"So that's it?" Anton shakes his head.

"While Devin is doing what he's doing, Lindsey seems to wake up or at least she becomes aware enough to tell him to stop what he's doing and curse at him, so he forces more of the drug on her until she becomes almost dazed. Then she stops breathing."

"What are you saying?"

"This is probably how your mother's brain injury occurred. He gives her a shot and then calls Deja's father. You see him dress Deja and carry her upstairs and the video keeps recording until the disk is full."

"A few weeks later, he calls me and says he needs me to clean something up for him. That something was David."

"So you think he had David killed because he knew about what happened to my mother?"

"Or possibly," Anton says, "because David noticed his daughter had been drugged. If he examined, her he would have been able to tell she'd been assaulted."

I don't even want to know what that means. Deja was eight years old. What the fuck?

"Based on the amount of time between the other four videos, my guess is he didn't have a lot of access to her."

"Why do think he stopped?" I ask, trying to hold onto my anger.

"Puberty? It would have been hard to explain away a pregnancy and they would have DNA tested every male she came in contact with."

"So it went beyond touching?"

"On the later videos, yes."

"I'm going to kill him," I say, feeling calm for the first time today. There's no more moral ambiguity, no more doubt. Devin needs to die. It doesn't matter that I've never killed anyone and never thought I would, there is no way I can continue to live in a world where that man is breathing. Those tapes would put him away for a long time, and an inmate would probably un-alive him for me, but that would mean revealing to the world what happened to Deja. I'm not doing that. She deserves to keep her peace.

"That's not a good idea, Brandon. You don't want that on your soul. Once the evidence is secured, I'll take care of him."

"You'll kill him?"

"You'll never have to worry about seeing him again."

"But will he be dead?"

"As good as."

I don't like this answer, but there's no point arguing with Anton anymore. I thank him for everything and tell him I'll be waiting at Rourke's for an update. I gather my things and he orders me a car to take me home. Instead, I tell the driver to take me to Briarwood. I need to make sure Deja doesn't go home. No matter what happens, she must never see Devin again.

* * *

Deja

I drag myself to my car after practice. I don't really have the energy to be social today. Mackenzie rubs my back soothingly before she heads for her car. She doesn't know why I'm upset, but she's trying to comfort me anyway. Shelby gave me her chocolate bar at lunch, and it's her favorite thing. This whole time I thought if I wasn't the perfect cheerleader my friends would abandon me, but here they are just trying to make me feel better. I wish I could tell them why I'm upset, but I can't.

HE HATE ME

I'm feeling kind of guilty as well after what Mello told me about Brandon's life. Did I judge him too harshly? I didn't see him at school today. I saw Rourke going to soccer practice when I was heading for cheerleading and felt a powerful urge to run over to him and ask if Brandon was okay. Of course, I didn't. What if Rourke kicked him out already? What if something happened to his mom?

He's by my car when I get out to the lot, dressed in dark clothes. He looks like a bartender or a waiter at a high-end restaurant. His face is pale, and his expression is hard. Is he angry with me now? Is he here to yell at me.

"Hey," he says.

"Hey."

He's standing in front of the driver's door, so I can't get into the car until he lets me.

"What do you want?"

"I need to talk to you," he says. "It's important and private."

"I don't think we work Brandon," I say, the words feeling like broken glass in my throat.

"We work. But that's not what I want to talk to you about. And it's not safe for you to go home."

"Get out of my way, Brandon. I'm not in the mood for this."

"Check your text messages."

I fish my phone out of my backpack and see the text message.

MOM: *Go with Brandon.*

"What the hell?" I unlock my phone and text her back.

ME: *Do you really want me to go with Brandon? Why?*

The reply comes back in under a minute.

MOM: *I'll explain later, but please go with him to Rourke's. Whatever you do, do not go home.*

"Did you hack my mom's phone or something?"

"I'm not even holding anything. How could I be the one texting you?"

"Right." I have no idea what's going on, but I figure I have no choice but to go with him. I unlock the car and he climbs into the driver's seat, holding his palm up for the keys. I ignore him and get in before handing it to him. He doesn't say much as he exits the parking lot. We pass Shelby and Mackenzie standing by Kenzie's car talking. Probably about me. Their eyes follow us as we pull away from campus.

"Did something happen to Devin?" I ask.

"I'll explain at Rourke's," he says, woodenly. "It's a long and complicated story."

"But he's involved?"

"Yes. And so am I."

"You did something?" I ask, alarmed. He shakes his head.

"There's so much you don't know, Deja, I barely know where to start. Let's go to Rourke's, have something to eat, and I'll tell you as much as I can."

He reaches over and turns on the radio, loudly enough to silence my questions.

HE HATE ME

* * *

Brandon opens his laptop, handing me a can of sparkling water. I take sip of the grapefruit flavored liquid and place the can on the coffee table, waiting to see what he'll do next. He's been extremely secretive since we got here, answering my questions with "soon" and "you'll see for yourself." But now it's finally time. I wonder if he's going to show me surveillance video from the house. But how would he even get that?

He double clicks on a video file, and it starts playing, filling the screen. I'm shocked to recognize the room, though I don't remember Devin ever coming to our house. The camera points at the old sofa I hid behind a time or two playing hide and go seek. Devin's sitting on it, and beside him is a much younger Lindsey. They start talking, and soon I'm feeling queasy and confused. What is going on? Why is she doing those things. I hear my mother's voice and then my father walks into the frame.

"When is this from?" I ask Brandon, more and more disturbed as the video progresses.

Brandon drags the cursor to the top of the screen, showing me the date in the filename. It's about ten years ago.

"Turn it off!" I tell him when the sexual assault starts. I stare down at my hands, not wanting to believe what I just saw my father and stepfather doing.

"Can you just tell me?" I say. "I don't want to ever look at something like that again."

"Are you sure," he asks, squeezing my fingers. "It's not the easiest stuff to hear."

SENCHA SKEETE

"You wanted me to know," I snap, an irrational burst of anger taking over for a moment. I'm not being fair, but I can't begin to process this.

"Those DVDs we found in the basement were exactly what you thought they were—sex tapes. The first one they mostly mess with her, but on the rest there's actual…r-word."

He's using a euphemism for something horrible, but I get it. The victim is his mother. I can't imagine watching someone do that to someone I love.

"Does she act like that on all the videos?"

"Pretty much. They roofied her first. A—the guy who supplied them the drugs told me what it was. He thought Devin was buying it for recreational use. I guess some people take it to get high. But it was really to drug victims. She has no idea he did it because the drug makes you forget."

"Wait a minute? You know the guy that sold them the drugs? Does he have something to do with the drugs you're selling?"

He sighs, looking very uncomfortable.

"His name is Anton. A few months ago he approached me and told me he'd arrange for me to go to Briarwood and pay my mother's medical bills if I'd spy on Devin and search his place."

"So you weren't really looking for pictures to cheer your mom up?"

"I wasn't not looking for them, but yeah, they weren't the main thing I was looking for. Ten years ago Devin paid Anton to kill someone for him. He's still holding on to evidence implicating Anton and he's now blackmailing him."

HE HATE ME

My head spins as he explains the murder for hire, the lost evidence, the reason for all the security at the house and all the crimes he suspects Devin of committing.

"Your mom is retrieving the evidence as we speak."

"My mom? How did you get her to do that. She worships Devin."

"I showed her the video. She claims she left the room before things got sexual and that Devin told her they only drugged my mom twice."

"Twice is more than enough! What kind of woman just stands by and lets that happen to another woman? She just accepted that my dad raped someone?"

"She says Devin told her your dad never touched Mom."

"And she believed that? What about Devin touching her then? Why was that okay?"

"He claimed it was consensual."

"And she marries this guy? She has him around me? Jesus Christ! Who are these people? How could I come from this crap? To think I thought you were a bad guy for selling weed when my own parents are so much worse. Good God! Devin is such a hypocrite. He kicks you out for dealing when he's ten times the criminal you are?"

I'm hyperventilating, and Brandon pulls me close, rubbing my back. I lower my head between my knees, fighting dizziness.

"Once we showed your mother everything, she agreed to help us."

"I don't get that," I say. "She had to already know deep down. Are you leaving something out?"

He grimaces. "The person Davin had killed was your father."

"And that's why she's turning on him. That's just fantastic. Is that everything?"

"Almost. Based on one of the videos it appears that Devin gave my mom too much of the drug and that's what caused her illness."

"So he's the root cause of everything bad in both our lives? This guy who sits in church every Sunday like butter wouldn't melt in his mouth?"

"For the most part, yes."

I take a moment to process everything I've heard. It's clear now why Brandon didn't want me to go home.

"Are you going to call the police?"

He shakes his head.

"I'm going to head over there. I have some questions I need to ask him."

"Don't do anything stupid, Brandon. He owns a gun, and he doesn't seem to have a lot of scruples."

"That's okay," he says, sticking both hands into the pockets of his jacket. I have a gun too."

"Where did you get a gun?"

"Don't worry about it." Don't worry about it? Is he crazy? He could get killed and if he kills Devin he'll spend years, maybe even the rest of his life, in prison.

He gives me a quick kiss on the lips and leaves. I have to figure something out. I can't call the cops, Brandon is as likely to get shot as Devin.

HE HATE ME

Pacing in front of the fireplace, I dial the only person I can think of calling right now. It rings four times before it's answered.

"Are you all right?" my mother asks, her voice sounding strangely choked.

"I'm fine," I tell her, "but Brandon just left to confront Devin. He has a gun. I don't know what to do. I'm scared Devin will shoot him."

"How long ago did he leave?"

"Five minutes, maybe. Do you think you can call Devin, maybe, get him to stay away from the house?"

"One sec."

I wait for what seems like an eternity for her to unmute the call.

"I was able to contact someone who can help. They're headed there now."

"It's not the police, is it?"

"No."

"Is it Anton?"

"How much did Brandon tell you?"

"He told me what's on the tape and what happened to Dad."

"How are you dealing with that?" she asks gently.

"The fact that Devin killed Dad? It's awful."

"It is awful," she says, "but I meant what happened to you."

"Can you be more specific?

"What did Brandon tell you was on the tapes?"

SENCHA SKEETE

"I—" My brain is moving at light speed. Brandon said the tapes documented Devin's sexual assault of his mother. So why was my mom asking about what happened to me?

"I'm on the tapes, aren't I?"

"He didn't tell you?"

I'm too overwhelmed to reply. My stomach falls and an ache spreads from my belly out through my whole body. I sit down, unable to stay on my feet. I think my mother is still speaking, but I'm trying to wrap my head around what I just learned. My memories of my life with Devin flash before my eyes. Every hug every touch, every time I sat on his lap looks different now.

"When?" I ask.

"Are you sure you want to know?"

"Did it happen after we moved in with him?"

"No," she says. "It was before…before he and I started dating."

"But you started dating when I was thirteen. What are you telling me?"

"I'm sorry I couldn't protect you."

For a few seconds, I sit there stunned. My mind reels as I try to process the revelation. Memories long buried begin to surface, hazy impressions of feeling disconnected from my own body and choking. I squeeze my eyes shut, willing the images away, but they persist, flickering like a horror film behind my eyelids.

"How old?"

HE HATE ME

My mother hesitates before answering, her voice filled with shame. "You were eight when it started. Not long before your father died."

"Those nightmares I used to have. I told you they started before Dad died, but you didn't believe me.

I remember meeting Devin at my father's funeral, how familiar he seemed, but also the strange squirmy feeling I used to get around him, like my subconscious was telling me to keep my distance from him. But my mother had assured me he was kind and for years I only saw him every few months at a party or when he dropped by to check on us. He listened to my rambling stories, he brought me gifts. He bought me off with cupcakes and the bare minimum of the fatherly attention I craved. The fatherly attention he had robbed me of when he had my father killed. Rage bubbles up inside me, feeling like heartburn. It's followed by a wave of nausea.

"Why didn't you stop him?" I demand. "How could you not know?"

"Deja, I'm so sorry, I never thought he'd hurt a child, and we were his closest friends. Whatever he did, he was never less than a gentleman with me."

"What do you mean, whatever he did? What did he do? I know you're not just talking about Lindsey."

"His fraternity had their charter revoked during their sophomore year. Devin said girls would get very drunk and do things with him and some of the frat brothers then claim later they didn't remember and hadn't consented. He said the allegations were false, but they got shut down anyway. I'm not sure, but I think it was one of the reasons David transferred out. Being black, people probably just assumed he was one of the perpetrators. I had no reason to think that they weren't telling the truth."

"Not even when they roofied Lindsey? You are so full of shit. I heard the way you laughed at Lindsey on that tape; you enjoyed seeing her humiliated. You knew they were probably rapists, but you married both of them. I can't even wrap my head around this, Mom. How could the two of you sit in church every week knowing what kind of people you are."

"I didn't—," she says, but I cut her off. I don't want to hear any more of this bullshit.

"You fucking did. If you had an iota of decency, I wouldn't have been…" I choke on the words. I can't say it out loud and I know I'll never watch the videos. I hate the horrible void where my memories of the abuse should be, but I think I'm also grateful for it. The shadowy memories I have are bad enough. I don't think I could handle more.

I hang up on her, and when she calls back, I ignore it.

Chapter 30

Brandon

THE RIDE SHARE DROPS ME OFF IN FRONT OF THE HOUSE. IT'S not yet 5:00, so I'm surprised to see Devin's car in the driveway. I thought I'd get here before him and be waiting when he got home. The house looms over me ominously, light glinting off the glass windows. I go through the open front door, my steps silent as I listen for movement. I hear a thud from upstairs and climb the stairs quietly. It takes only seconds to locate Devin. He's in his office, this door wide open as well.

"What's the rush?" I ask from the doorway. He looks up, irritation flickering across his expression. He's on his knees, frantically transferring cash from the safe into a duffle bag on the floor. His passport lies on the desk blotter. He continues to empty the safe, paying no attention to me.

I step inside the office and close the door behind me, pulling out my new gun and pointing it at him.

"Why are you being so rude, Devin?" He's still focused on his task and hasn't seen the gun yet.

"Didn't I kick you out?" Devin asks, not looking up. "What do you want?"

"Just looking to have some fun," I tell him, sitting on the leather loveseat across from his desk. This statement piques his curiosity enough for him to glance over at me and his jaw tightens when he sees the gun. He sizes me up, trying to gauge how dangerous I am. I think it's hard for him to fathom that I, still a child in his eyes, could present any real danger or actually derail his plans.

"Aren't you a little old to play with toys," he quips. He's cool as a cucumber. Like most people I'd be at the very least nervous if someone pointed a gun at me, but he appears perfectly at ease. He places the last few items from the safe into the bag and zips it closed.

He drops the bag on the floor behind his desk and sits in the task chair. He looks at the gun and shrugs his shoulders.

"I have to admit I didn't think you'd be this upset about being evicted."

"Oh, no," I say, laughing, "that's water under the bridge. I'm curious what all this is about, though." I gesture at the safe.

HE HATE ME

"Been a while since I traveled," he says. "Do you mind if I grab some things out of the desk?"

"I do, as a matter of fact. Hands on top would be much better."

He steeples his fingers. Even now, his face is affable, a smile implied by the slight curve of his lips.

"I'm sure you want an explanation," he says glancing at the door.

"No one's coming, Devin," I tell him. "Your wife is meeting with a lawyer so she can stay out of prison. Deja is never setting foot in this house again. And you, are never walking out."

"Brandon," he says, amused, "is that thing even loaded? Do you actually think you can shoot me."

"The man who gave my mother a drug overdose and then fired her? No, I don't think I'll have any trouble shooting you."

There's a flicker of surprise in his expression, but nothing more.

"I don't know what you think—"

"I watched the disks. I almost vomited a dozen times, but I watched what you did to them. An eight-year-old, Devin?"

He throws up his hands as if I just accused him of drinking milk directly from the carton.

"So you know." He shrugs.

"Why?" My heart races and I try to slow my breathing down. I need to stay in control. Based on his past actions Devin might not hesitate to use the gun against me if he gets his hands on it. I should just finish him now, but I need to understand.

"Why not?" he said. "Lindsey was so weak and easy to manipulate. It was pathetic. The more we saw her weakness, the more contempt we had for her. It was fun as hell to make her do every humiliating thing we could think of. Sex was just…we're men. Any man with control of a helpless woman is going to take the opportunity to stick his dick in her. The stupid bitch would wake up with her holes sore and never figure out that we'd fucked her."

Bile rises in my throat, and behind it a wave of anger like I've never experienced.

"Sweet little Deja just wandered in one night by pure chance," he went on. "I'd always been in love with Nisha, but she was Jules's girl. Deja was like having a little miniature version of her to play with. Until Jules found out."

"How'd he find out?"

"She had a tummy ache and he examined her. I was the first person he called; it never occurred to him I was the one who did it. Tanisha was out of town. I told him to wait till she got back before telling her or going to the cops. That gave me about twenty-four hours to set everything up. It didn't even cost that much money.

"Why are you dragging this out, anyway? Aren't you man enough to pull the trigger? Need me to work you up so you have the balls to do it. You know why your dad left you? I told him Lindsey and I were fucking, and the idiot believed me. Are you as much of a pussy as your sperm donor or did I rub off on you at all."

HE HATE ME

"I don't know how you fooled everyone into thinking you're a nice guy."

"Cause I don't give a fuck, Brandon. I'll say anything, because I don't give a shit about any of it or any of you. The only person who matters to me knows exactly what a piece of shit I am and loves me anyway."

"You think so? Is that why she retrieved the bloody clothes for us? Anton's already had them destroyed. There is nothing holding him back from crushing you like an insect."

He watches me, his eyes narrowed. I can see the wheels turning in his mind. His hand tightens into a fist, though he doesn't seem to be aware of it.

"So you took Tanisha to Anton. How long have you been working for him?"

"How'd you figure that?"

"My wife and I share our locations."

It's my turn to fill in the gaps. Devin was able to see where Tanisha was by looking at his phone. He must have been looking for her and seen that she was at Anton's home. He probably saw her go to the bank as well. That would explain why he's packing up to leave.

"I don't know how you forced her to help you," he says, "but you can tell your boss to watch his back. I'm not going to let some lowlife get away with threatening my wife."

"No one threatened her, Devin. All Anton had to do was show her the video of you with her daughter."

For the first time since I came into the room he looks truly upset. Is it possible that he really loves Deja's mom? It doesn't seem as if someone like him could love anyone.

383

SENCHA SKEETE

"I just need to talk to her," he says, almost as if trying to convince himself. "Nisha will be able to see that Deja wasn't harmed. She's perfectly fine—an overachiever, even. If she doesn't remember anything then it's like it never happened."

"You think the fact that your victims don't remember means what you did was, okay? What you did to my mother—"

"Was an accident. You're acting like I did it on purpose."

He laughs, as if the whole situation is no big deal. An almost serene feeling settles over me. I've heard enough. I'm not going to get satisfying answers from him because he's no more complex than an animal. A simple predator, he preys on others because he can, because unlike a normal person he has no empathy and no conscience.

But like an animal he has keen instincts. I start raising the gun, but he leaps over the desk with a gun in his hand and fires, almost before I can duck out of the way. The bullets drill into the loveseat, the acrid smell of gunpowder filling the room. I fire at him from the ground, a lucky shot catching him in the hip and another in the shoulder. He lists to one side, the gun no longer pointing at me. He hasn't made a sound, and his stoicism bothers me. I want to hear him scream.

I'm plowing into him before he can get another shot off. His gun goes flying and, in the collision, so does mine, but it doesn't matter. My fist connects with his face, the jolt going up my arm like I hit concrete. My hand explodes in pain, but it's worth it to see the blood flowing from his nose. The bones of his face are no match for the strength I've built up in the gym. He gasps, a beautiful, bloody gurgle coming from his

HE HATE ME

mouth. He starts to fight me, trying to throw me off, but I have the superior position and youth on my side.

"We actually have something in common," I tell him, kneeling on his uninjured right arm. He punches me with his left, but the angle doesn't allow for much leverage.

My hand shakes with adrenaline as I pull my knife from its sheath. His eyes widen, only now betraying fear despite already having been shot and beaten.

"I have a side of myself I keep hidden from other people as well." He tries to kick me, but I easily avoid his legs. Time seems to slow as I decide my next move. I feel a smile spread across my face as I drive the knife into his upper thigh. His scream covers the sucking sound of the knife exiting his flesh. A pool of blood spreads slowly under his body. Later I realized how lucky I was not to sever his femoral artery, but in the moment, I feel nothing but elation as his limb twitches feebly, the nerves he needs to control it sliced through by my knife.

"I really like that," I tell him, repeating the motion on his other leg, inches from the bullet wound. His scream is hoarse this time. "This is so much fun, and thank you for being such a piece of shit I can do this without feeling bad after."

I smile down at Devin's writhing body, my hands sticky with his blood. Until this moment I thought I would be horrified by the act of slicing through another's flesh, but I feel only satisfaction and the pleasurable hum that comes from inflicting pain. He was a dead man as soon as he touched Deja, and I like to think that I'm not only punishing him for hurting the women I love, but exacting the revenge

SENCHA SKEETE

David would have taken if he'd lived long enough to realize his friend was the one who raped his child. I press the knife deeper into his thigh, eliciting another raw scream.

"You're no better than me," he groans, sweat beading on his forehead. I ignore him, scratching my chin as I decide where to use the knife next. By the time I'm done he's screamed himself hoarse and I'm drenched in red. His breath comes in stuttered gasps, his muscles shivering as if he's cold, though I suspect he's in shock from the pain and blood loss. I've tried to avoid stabbing him in places that would cause rapid bleeding, but I've never done this before, and the sheer number of wounds made this outcome inevitable. I can see that he's fading, his breaths getting further apart and his eyes clouding. I don't have much time left to enact my last bit of revenge. With a cheerful whistle, I begin unbuckling his belt.

* * *

"Remind me not to piss you off," Anton says coming into the room just as I'm finishing up. I drop the recently excised meat on Devin's chest, satisfied that he saw me holding the bloody trophy before he died. "I told you to let me handle this. I'd at least have laid down a tarp."

"You watched the videos; you know why I couldn't."

He shakes his head, stepping over Devin's body and pressing two fingers to his neck. "I'll call a few of my guys to come deal with this mess. They're going to be pissed."

"Are we square?"

"Do I keep paying your mother's hospital bills?" Anton asks.

I look at the bag of money and valuables on the floor. It's hard to gauge how much is in there, and my mother's care is extremely expensive. "I don't know."

"You could keep working for me. Based on this," he says, motioning towards the body, "I think you would be an excellent fit for my organization. We can teach you a bit of finesse, I pay well, and cleanup is complimentary."

* * *

Deja's sitting on the bed when I enter our room at Rourke's.

I toss the duffel bag into the nearest chair, but she pays no attention to it. She runs to me and pulls me into her arms. I squeeze back, breathing deep of her sugar cookie smell.

"You showered," she says, pushing a lock of my damp hair behind my ear, "and changed. What happened?"

"Things got a little messy."

"Devin…?"

"Will never bother anyone again."

Her eyes widen as she processes my words, then she nods pressing her lips together.

"Did you…kill him?"

"It was mostly a side effect of using my knife to emasculate him."

She gazes up at me, a crease furrowing her brow. I'm worried that I might have upset her, but then she smiles brightly.

"Seems like the perfect way to handle a pedo."

It takes a moment for me to catch up but when I do, I scrutinize her face, trying to see if learning what was done to her has changed anything. I think I see new shadows behind her eyes despite her smile.

"Did you remember something?" I ask carefully.

"A couple flashes. What really happened is I called my mom to see if she could reach Anton. I was worried about you getting hurt. She thought I already knew. It turns out Devin and my dad were probably drugging and date raping girls in college and she knew about it but married them anyway. I don't think I ever want to see her again."

I kiss her cheek and hold her close. I know she means it now, but she and her mother have been relatively close most of her life. I'll wait and see. Even now I'm considering whether it might be time to reach out to my dad again and at least tell him what Devin told me about lying to him. The pain he's caused me is still there, but it's hard to give up on the hope that your parent loves you despite signs to the contrary.

She hugs me as tightly as her slim arms can manage, her face pressed into my chest. Then she smacks me in the same spot she just nuzzled.

"I hate how you turn me into a girl," she says, pouting.

"You are a girl," I say, tugging on one of her braids.

"I am a woman," she declares. She peels her dress over her head and tosses it on top of the duffel bag. I rush over and close the door, afraid someone might see her standing there in just her panties. I can't imagine what she's feeling, but I'm starving for her, my nervous system over stimulated by what I did to Devin, the pall of blood and death driving me to balance it with an expression of life.

HE HATE ME

I place my weapons in the bedside table and strip down to my shorts. We step out of our last garments together. She climbs onto the bed and lies on her back. I get on top. My cock rests between her legs. She's warm, her body soft, and she smells like heaven to me: coconut oil, vanilla, and woman. I kiss her mouth, her soft lips caressing mine, her tongue like a playful pup. I suck on her bottom lip, drawing a moan out of her, and take charge of the kiss, pouring everything I feel into her. Relief, gratitude for my good fortune, and most of all love. I don't deserve this woman, this happy ending, but I'm not looking a gift horse in the mouth.

She twines her arms around my neck, gently rocking her hips and her body gets ready for me. Her hard nipples poke my chest, feeling delightful as I rock my torso, applying subtle pressure to her breasts. She wraps her long legs around me, pressing me forward until I breach her core. We thrust gently against each other, my shaft thrusting shallowly into her tightness, each time going deeper until eventually I'm fully encased in her heat. Her legs tighten rhythmically, and I get the message, speeding up my movements.

I can't describe what it's like. We've had sex before, but this is something else. I feel so close to her like our breaths are one, our bodies so in touch with each other that we don't need any of the extra bells and whistles. This is just us, pure connection and it's exhilarating. I look into her deep brown eyes, black with arousal, her plush lips parted as she pants breathing more irregular as she gets closer to coming. I push her knees towards her shoulders and pummel her harder, already feeling my balls begin to tingle, but I don't want to come before she does. I lick her shoulder, her neck, then whisper in her ear.

"You feel so good, baby, so good. The way you squeeze me is exquisite. You want me to fuck you harder?"

"Yes!"

"Ask me, nicely."

"Please," she moans, "fuck me harder." Okay, maybe we don't need the bells and whistles, but a little dirty talk never hurt anyone.

"That's it, baby, take my dick. You going to come on my cock?"

"Yes," she whimpers. "It's so big."

I thrust all the way inside, stilling my thrusts to grind against her slowly. It's partly to stimulate her clit and partly to ease my body away from the brink of orgasm. It works. The pace of her breathing picks up, and she rocks her hips up and down, adding to our mutual bliss. I feel it build, the inexorable climb of passion, a feeling so eerie the hairs stand up on the back of my neck. She throws her head back, baring the line of her throat to me and I can't hold back from thrusting again, faster and faster, until she's writhing under me and moaning yes over and over. Her mouth opens in a silent scream as she reaches her peak. Her pussy clenches around me, her inner muscles squeezing me as she comes. I grab her hips, burying myself inside her and roaring as my orgasm decimates me.

We lay there for a moment, gasping for air. Intimately entwined, I lay on top of her, catching my breath, stroking her hair.

HE HATE ME

"I love you," she whispers, tracing my jawline with her soft fingers. I take her hand, kissing the tip of each one. I flip over, letting her lie on top of me. She feels so light, but warm and soft in my arms. I grasp a handful of her braids and drape them over her shoulder as I coax her to lay her head on my chest.

"I love you more, Little Thorn," I whisper back.

I don't know what's going to happen tomorrow. We essentially have no parents anymore, we're squatting at a friend's house, I have no idea how we'll pay tuition, or if Anton will really let me walk away. But we have each other. And it's enough.

Epilogue

Eighteen Months Later

Deja

BRANDON CROUCHES TO PICK UP A HANDFUL OF DIRT and toss it on top of the coffin. It's a beautiful, ornate white casket, its lacquered top gleaming in the sunlight. The day is bright and hot, and we're out in the open with no shade nearby. Sweat gleams on Rev. Billingsley's forehead. Brandon takes my hand, and I squeeze his fingers letting him know I'm with him. The pastor prays and Brandon's ten-year-old half-sister sniffles, trying to hold back her tears.

After Devin's crimes were revealed, it took us a while to put the pieces back together. The story Anton concocted was that Devin had run off with a portion of the stolen money. My mother had not been able to convince their company or the police she was unaware of Devin's crimes. She's serving the last few months of her sentence now. We know she wasn't involved with the embezzlement, but Brandon believes, and I agree, that it's the least she deserves for letting her men abuse Lindsey.

A few months after Devin's "disappearance," Brandon reached out to his biological father, Brad Keane. It was difficult and painful at first, but they've been steadily building a relationship. Brandon has two younger siblings—a teenage boy who look startlingly like Brandon, and the little redheaded girl currently sniffling while holding her father's hand. We learned that not only had Devin told Brad that Lindsey was unfaithful, but he'd also implied that Brandon's parentage was questionable. Seeing Brad and Brandon together it's patently obvious they are father and son, but I know just how convincing a liar Devin was. The best we can figure, he did it just to be spiteful and to make sure Lindsey's focus wasn't divided. Knowing why his father didn't support him and his mom made it easier for Brandon to forgive him and move on.

I thought I was okay with everything that happened, but a few months after Devin died it all hit me so hard it knocked me over. I didn't get out of bed for a week and I wouldn't let Brandon touch me. I had to confront the horror of what had been done to me and I wondered if my kinks were just me being me or a side-effect of the abuse. I've been in therapy ever since, and while I can't say I'm completely over it, I'm no longer haunted. It was Brandon who convinced me to go, but I'm still working on getting him to see a therapist.

Lindsey's finally at peace. Unfortunately, knowing what caused her brain damage didn't improve her prognosis. She

SENCHA SKEETE

stayed in some form of hospice through the end of her life. To pay for it, Brandon worked for Anton and when we moved to Chicago, he hooked him up with one of his associates. Brandon goes to the University of Illinois and I'm at the University of Chicago. I don't ask what work he does to pay his tuition and our expenses, but we both know his business degree is going to be used within Anton's organization.

It's not a bad life. We share a little apartment in the city, and we've made friends. Brandon has taken up martial arts and we regularly have his sweaty annoying friends in our apartment. We throw dinner parties with people we met at school, and we try to focus on what we have and the good things in our life and not all the awful stuff that's happened to us. Brandon's told me a couple of times that he wants us to get married once we graduate, but I'm in no rush. It will happen when the time is right. Until then, and for the rest of our lives, we have each other.

ABOUT THE AUTHOR

Sencha Skeete

Sencha Skeete is a California-based author who loves to write passionate romances featuring black women and the men who love them.

You can check out her available and upcoming titles on her website at: https://senchaskeete.com

Stay up to date with her latest releases by joining her newsletter:

Printed in Great Britain
by Amazon